# PETER THE GREAT

Roger Williams

Written for those who don't take themselves too seriously…
about those who do.

# Chapter One
## Cruise Control

*A*s Peter Grande trimmed the edges of his Van Dyke beard with an electric razor, he reflected on his image in the mirror and thought, *you are the most interesting man in the world.* Still, to any objective observer, it would have been a huge stretch to think of him as even the most interesting man in the School of Humanities, Arts and Culture at Grodin College, where he had taught for twenty-eight years. In truth, it could be argued that he was no more than the third most interesting man in his own Department of Literature, Drama and Language Arts, which sported a faculty of twenty-one, of whom nearly half were women.

In a wobbly first attempt to become '*interesting*,' Peter grew a beard during his junior year at Penn State after one of his occasional girlfriends had dumped him, telling him he was 'the most boring guy she'd ever dated.' But, as one who always looked at the bright side, it could have been worse—she could have told him he was 'the most boring guy she'd ever known.'

His next foray into the world of hirsuteness led him to sprout The Full Karl Marx. But, with his wild eyes and shabby undergraduate wardrobe, The Full Karl made him seem more like a homeless person than his hoped-for look of a dangerous revolutionary. More importantly, The Full Karl was a definite turn-off in the Girlfriend Department.

Later, while in graduate school at Indiana University, he went long with The Leon Trotsky. As an early Twentieth Century version of the Van Dyke, The Trotsky added some needed seasoning to his youthful grad-student appearance and imbued him with that subtle hint of *gravitas*. Over the years, Peter continued to refine and update The Trotsky until he came to believe that he had invented it, and he was non-too-pleased when Johnny Depp trotted out 'his look' in the first of the *Pirates of the Caribbean* flicks. However, Peter's attitude changed when the occasional coed, no doubt not-so-cleverly angling for a grade enhancement, asked if he 'uh, might be, like, uh…Johnny Depp's older brother?'

Near the end of his time in grad school, he began adding the letter 'e' to his last name. The Beard and the 'e' were the first steps in a long process that culminated in the calculated manufacture of the image of *A Person Worthy of Respect*, at least on paper, if not in the flesh.

It had worked.

Now at fifty-eight, he was Dr. Peter Grande, Associate Dean of the School of Humanities, Art and Culture and Chairman of the Department of Literature, Drama and Language Arts at Grodin College, a private four-year liberal arts school located smack dab in the buckle of western Massachusetts' college belt.

Not Ivy League, but hoping for a little rub-off by being geographically close, Grodin attracted students whose parents most fervent wish was that their offspring—though poorly-armed with a second-rate liberal arts degree—might mature enough in four years to develop some sort of real-world interest that eventually would lead to a career beyond that of a Starbucks barista. Yet the reality was that most Grodintes were destined for jobs which led nowhere—answering emails for Friends of the Earth or equivalent virtue-signaling NGO's, the 21st Century's version of stuffing envelopes—or they would end up taking the odd service job in the hospitality, restaurant or leisure industries while waiting for the Big Break they believed would surely come when the world finally got around to recognizing their greatness. These waitron-type jobs left plenty of time for clubbing, casual sex and Occupying-type protests in the streets of whichever major metropolitan center where they happened to land.

Except for a few nerds in the School of Science and Technology, Grodin's students gravitated towards the arts, environmentally-trendy subjects and courses related to issues of social justice. Anything requiring math or real science was to be avoided at all cost. And by simply taking up these 'more-refined' subject areas, the Grodinites saw themselves as morally-superior to those who had chosen the harder path of grinding it out in the STEM world.

The Geek-Squadders in Grodin's School of Science and Technology largely kept to themselves, sometimes living 24/7 in the Pei Wan Computer Science Building where they consumed mass quantities of pizza and non-diet Coke while arguing vociferously with each other over obscure coding techniques. The so-called hipper students largely ignored them but were willing to put up with their juvenile sarcasm and insults whenever they needed help with their computers. The Geeks wore T-Shirts proclaiming *We Make the S\*\*t You Play With*, and their sad motto was *For normals, math is hard, life is easy. For us, math is easy, life is hard.*

Most students went to Grodin because it was either that or live at home. The handful of students for whom Grodin was the first choice usually came from families of ex-hippies, parents with trust funds or from families of do-gooders who had instilled in their offspring the belief that the study of liberal arts was more humane, purer and more socially-beneficial than the hard sciences or, god-forbid, business or finance. The live-at-home option meant going to a junior college or a four-year state school while working part-time at places like PetSmart or Whole Foods to earn spending money for quinoa burgers and craft beers. It also meant that drugs, sex and rock-and-roll had to be finessed or negotiated. No such negotiation was necessary at Grodin, where the weekend fun unofficially started at the end of the day on Thursdays. By Friday mornings, both professors and students had begun to drift away, sometimes even skipping the last class or two...or even all of them. The non-faculty staff members were obliged to stick around until all the fancy people with no time cards to punch had disappeared into the weekend, whereafter they usually could safely depart post-lunch when no one was watching.

Grodin students considered themselves hip, cool and imbued with an almost-inborn ability to stay at the leading edge of the latest trends in the worlds of pop culture and politics. They were experts at using The Three I's—Phones, Pads and Pods—and looked down on those who weren't skilled at posting, texting, or tweeting despite the fact that they themselves lacked the actual knowledge needed to create the hardware and software which enabled them to post, text and tweet. Those of their generation who possessed those skills were either working in dorm rooms at Stanford, Harvard or MIT or had already dropped out and were writing code for real money in one of the software sweatshops which have taken over the grungy, but hip and happening hot-spots of our booming megacities.

Nevertheless, as associate dean and department chair, Peter no longer had to deal with actual students on a day-to-day basis. With those appointments, he had achieved the professorial nirvana of having maneuvered himself out of nearly all contact with the student body, aka, The Rabble. Oh, he still taught the occasional upper-division seminar, but only to 'keep his hand in' as he was wont to say. In his early years, he had enjoyed hanging out with *Da Yout*, but by the time he hit fifty, he had grown tired of answering the same questions over-and-over and listening to the same 'my paper's late because…' excuses. With the current crop of millennials, he also had grown especially tired of having to deal with their exalted and unearned sense of specialness and entitlement, which was further exacerbated by the fact that they viewed their professors as little more than well-paid servants.

At one time, he had coveted the deanship of the School of Humanities, Arts and Culture, but he came to realize that his career aspirations in administration had peaked with his associate deanship and the departmental chair. Politicking himself into the full deanship would have required a great deal more effort than he had been willing or able to put forth. Plus, he was comfortable in his current positions and could easily envision the future—several more years as Chair, a sabbatical, and then a few more years of teaching only those courses which interested him. Then he would be off to The Land of the Emeriti where even less would be required of him. Just hang out, pontificate and dispense sage advice, whether asked for or not. And, as always, bank the paycheck.

Recently, he had begun to think about where to take his next sabbatical, which was coming up in a couple of years. One of the sunny Mediterranean havens, Seville, Provence or Umbria would be preferable, but even clammy old England would do, provided he could land a non-teaching slot at a decent university where he could hang out and hold court by teaching a special honors seminar. All were possibilities, although he would have to negotiate this with his wife, Glynnyth, whose late-in-life real estate career had taken off and he knew she would have no desire whatsoever to give it up for the better part of a year—or any part of the year for that matter. Peter was also fairly certain she wouldn't care if he went on his own, but what would definitely be left unsaid was that he didn't want her to come with him. At this point in his life, the last thing he wanted to do was to spend the better part of a year in close, nearly total, proximity to his wife. After almost thirty-five years of marriage, their life together had become a daily routine of fairly-peaceful coexistence based on mutual indifference.

In general though, life was good...and predictable. What with war, famine, pestilence and poverty pretty much off the table, Peter's glide path to a comfortable retirement was one with no visible blips on the radar.

And although Peter knew in the grand scheme of things that life was not fair, he never expected it to be unfair to him.

## Chapter Two
### The Frenemy Next Door

*S*tanding in the dark in his garage, Peter fired up a home security app on his iPhone. As the opening notes of Beethoven's Fifth poured forth from his phone, the garage door slowly rolled up and a swath of bright sunlight spread across the concrete floor. Although it would have been much easier to open the door by simply hitting the switch on the wall, Peter got a kick out of even the slightest successful foray into the world of modern technology. He was a bit of a dunce when it came to anything high-tech, but he liked to fool around with it and he loved to show off, something he could only do when Glynnyth wasn't around, as she frowned at what she considered to be male silliness. A few years ago in a rare moment of *détente* between father and scion, Peter's son, Gary Glynn, had grudgingly set up the garage door app for him on his iPhone.

With the garage now open, Peter picked his backpack up off the hood of his black BMW, one-strapped it over his shoulder and walked his ten-speed bike down the driveway. He started to hop on and ride off when Harry Atwater, his next-door neighbor, called out to him from across the hedge.

"Morning, comrade. Off to the re-education camp?"

"Always, Harry, always. So many minds to indoctrinate, so little time. You back from Hawaii?"

"Costa Rica was great. Hawaii was over Christmas."

"You're gone so often it's a miracle your dog doesn't forget who you are and attack you when you come home."

Harry was Peter's age, a cheerful, energetic man who, while smoking a cigar, was vigorously pruning the shrubbery along the driveway with an electric trimmer. An American flag flew from a tall white flagpole that stood smack in the center of Harry's front lawn.

"The dog still loves me, but I'm not so sure about the cat. The little bastard has some sneaky ways of getting back at you."

"I wish I had time to take a vacation."

"Peter," said Harry, pausing for effect before delivering his punch line, "your whole life has been a vacation."

"Well, let the evidence suggest that I'm the one who's heading off to the salt mines and it doesn't look like you'll be working on the chain gang anytime soon."

"No, I thought I'd just putter around the yard this morning."

"And the golf course?"

"I might get in nine after Rotary."

"Humm...no work and all play seems very un-American to me. How does the auto-glass business survive without you popping new windshields into Beemers and Mercedes every day?"

"The kids are managing pretty well without me, though I do need to drop in now and then to make sure they're not stealing too much."

"God, I'd hate to be at the mercy of my children."

"If I were in your shoes, comrade, I wouldn't either."

"Early retirement is not exactly my cup of tea."

"I suppose they'll have to drag you kicking and screaming out of the classroom."

"Truth be told, Harry, I managed to drag myself out of the classroom years ago. And no kicking or screaming was involved. One of academia's dirty little secrets is that full professors don't teach, or at least don't teach that much—a fact that I'm sure you'll find quite amusing."

"It's amazing you're still alive. The stress of constant work avoidance would have killed most people," said Harry.

"My work is my life, Harry. I wouldn't trade it for anything." Peter straddled his bike and started to push off. "Enjoy your lunch at the Rotary."

"Oh, I will. I'll even recite the Pledge of Allegiance in your honor." Then leaning over the fence, he whispered conspiratorially, "no one has to know."

"Just don't hurt yourself saluting the flag."

Harry laughed. "I'd be proud to go out that way. See you around Quad."

Resigning himself to not getting the last word, Peter tightened the strap on his helmet and pushed off down the driveway and onto the street. And, to avoid even more ridicule, Peter purposefully didn't tell Harry about what was going down on campus that afternoon.

For the past decade, on the last day before finals, Grodin's faculty, staff and students celebrated the end of the school year with an intramural cooking competition. The Culinary Cook-Off, as it came to be called, featured teams of Food Network wannabes from each of the college's five schools who whipped up elaborate and exotic dishes which were then judged by a panel of local culinary celebs. It was exactly the sort of collegiate frivolity which Atwater would have scoffed at as symptomatic of the sad decline of academic standards.

Initially casual and friendly, the annual contest had come to possess all the intensity and joylessness of a late-season Yankees-Red Sox game with a pennant on the line.

## Chapter Three
### Let's Ride!

*E*ven though he was running late as usual, Peter pedaled leisurely towards campus through the village of West Beresford, making his way through leafy neighborhoods of well-maintained but tightly-packed two-story homes which possessed enough rough edges to let it be known that the real bourgeoisie, with vast, manicured lawns surrounding their McMansions, did not and dared not live in this neighborhood. Here in College Residential, front yards sported faded and tattered *Free Mumia* and other rebellious political signage as well as sculptures made from rusted automobile parts and deconstructed farm implements. The recent craze for decorative banners led some to indicate their political leanings with customized flags which sported stylized images of Che, Obama and other progressive heroes instead of the flower and animal pennants that graced the homes in the less-progressive 'burbs.

In this cradle of Radical Bohemianism, landscaping was scruffy and casual, but the garages and driveways were occupied by well-cared-for Priuses and Beemers, with the former reflecting their owners' deep concern for the environment and the latter demonstrating their appreciation of quality engineering while also displaying their refined taste. F-150s, Winnebagos and bloated powerboats on tow-trailers were neither visible nor welcome.

As Peter rolled on towards the campus, College Residential merged with College Commercial. Student-oriented establishments—pizza parlors, bike shops, coffee shops and tattoo emporiums made up a majority of the stores on the four-block stretch of West Beresford's Main Street. The basic service businesses which kept the town running—mom-and-pop groceries, gas stations, hardware stores and the like—were located down the side streets. Anyone needing to visit a Home Depot or a Whole Foods would have to cross the Naugahassett River to get to Great Beresford, the region's commercial center.

Peter slowed down as he glided past the Tipsy Spoon Cafe. When the weather was nice, he often stopped there for a morning coffee and sat outside with several other regulars to solve The Times' daily crossword. Today, the Usual Suspects were heads-down at their table out front, busily working on Friday's puzzle, the most difficult of the week. When Peter rang the tinkly bell on his handlebars and waved, one of his peeps lifted a coffee mug in mock-salute while another yelled out, "what's a seven-letter word for 'college professor?'" Because The Times had once inadvertently defined a member of Peter's profession as a 'slacker,' it became a standing joke amongst the crew. Peter had long since found their wisecracks tiresome, but knew there was no use complaining about it as it only would have led to even greater heaps of scorn and derision.

College Commercial's short run down Main Street ended abruptly at the entryway to Grodin College which was marked by a pair of granite columns. The left column tilted noticeably, causing someone seeing it for the first time to think it might topple over at any moment. However, photos from yearbooks past showed that, like the Leaning Tower of Pisa, the column had angled dangerously for decades, and barring a student prank gone awry, would continue to list for many years to come.

Beyond the columns, the main road leading into campus split in two with each fork circling behind matching rows of three-story Georgian houses which served as Grodin's academic core. These graceful Georgians looked out across an open expanse of closely-mown grass which was checker-boarded by an interlocking maze of cobblestone walkways. At its center was the Henri P. Squirrelle Memorial Plaza, a marbled cynosure known to the students as Squirrel Square. In actuality, Squirrelle was more oval than square, but the temptation to indulge in alliterative mockery proved too great, and even administrators had to work to remind themselves of its actual name whenever the still-wealthy descendants of the long-since deceased Henri P. Squirrelle visited Grodin.

Today on Squirrelle, swarms of Bobby Flay and Mario Batali wannabes were hard at work setting up elaborate outdoor kitchens for the afternoon's Culinary Cook-Off.

As often happened when riding his bike, Peter had mentally drifted off and realized nearly-too-late that he did not want to be shanghaied by his departmental cohorts into working at the Cook-Off, so he made a quick detour around the burgeoning encampment and took a back way to Jenkins Hall, home to his Department of Literature, Drama and Language Arts.

A once-elegant three-story brick Georgian, Jenkins Hall stood at the opposite end of campus from the college's main entrance and sat at the center of a cluster of a half-dozen older buildings which housed the various departments of Peter's School of Humanities, Arts and Culture.

With a sagging portico peeling paint and its many windows in need of cleaning, the old Hall looked much like a distinguished, but elderly gentleman whose once-stylish suit now hung loosely on his frail, bent body.

Jenkins' deteriorating state stood in stark contrast to its neighbor, the spanking-new Sarah and Jerome P. Wheeler Center for the Performing Arts. Built in 2006, Wheeler representing an architectural style best described as Nouveau Grotesque. An angular structure of glass and metal, it looked less like a building than the upthrusting front end of a '56 Buick whose shiny chrome grille grinned up at the midday sun.

The Wheeler Center was home to Grodin's School of Artistic Expression, which had been created several years earlier in the Great Schism of 2002, an academic rift that split apart Grodin's School of Humanities and led to the creation of Peter's School of Humanities, Arts and Culture and the new School of Artistic Expression.

Major internecine battles at the collegiate level usually revolved around empire-building. Everyday run-of-the-mill turf wars centered around perceived slights, trivial perks and assorted teapot-sized tempests. Feuds could simmer for years over who was gaining or losing a half-an-hour a week of shared secretarial time or about who was hogging space in or stealing from the departmental refrigerator. Such academic kerfuffles were tug-of-wars over minuscule changes in a zero-sum world—minor league scuffles that became irrelevant old news in 1998 with the arrival of J. Bliss Moynihan, a lowly assistant drama prof with high expectations.

Brash and charismatic, it quickly became apparent that Bliss had a penchant for bringing in money, a talent completely foreign to most of Grodin's faculty. Where others saw drudgery and boredom in fundraising events with the well-heeled alums and business-types, Bliss saw Opportunity with a capital O. He became a regular at the luncheons of the various community groups like the Elks, the Lions, and the Moose as well as the Rotary Club and Chamber of Commerce, all of which were totally-alien venues to most of the faculty. As a fund-raiser, he started an annual golf tournament which was first known as *Duffers for Drama Queens* until Grodin's LGBTQ community pressured him to drop the '*Queens*' sobriquet. He hosted his own cable show, shamelessly ripping-off *Inside The Actors Studio* by bringing in local theater stars, lesser-lights from Broadway and the occasional big show-biz name with a second or third home nearby. He schmoozed and flattered the Board of Trustees, most of whom the faculty considered to be complete boobs and rubes.

He also had a penchant for rubbing his colleagues the wrong way, but the worst of his sins was that the students loved him. While most of Peter's colleagues were still toiling under the impression that their dry scholarly work might someday lead them out of the intellectual wasteland of Western Massachusetts and on to an academic institution more suited to their imagined talents, i.e., one with more research dollars, higher pay and fewer teaching responsibilities, Bliss was one of the first to realize that there was gold to be mined in the hills of student self-discovery and self-expression. Although the bar of academic achievement at Grodin had been set so low that any student with the faintest glimmer of intellectual vigor could have stepped over it with eyes closed, Bliss found ways to lower that particular bar even further. Despite the faculty's plea for rigor and scholarship, the students voted with their feet. They flocked to his classes and the waitlists to get in were always full. In short, 'expressing oneself' was fun.

None of this sat well with the established faculty—a lowly prof intent on self-aggrandizement and empire-building. To them, Bliss was both a threat to the established order and a royal pain in the butt. Students be damned, the overwhelming majority of the School of Humanities' faculty desired nothing more than to be rid of him. And, after a few years it was clear that despite his popularity, he would not be granted tenure and would have to move on—having been cast out into the wilderness along with other lone-wolf intellectual vagabonds and forced to scramble for sustenance wherever he could find it. Of course, Bliss was no fool and was aware of his untenured untenability.

It was at this juncture that he did The Unthinkable.

The Impossible.

He landed a whale.

This particular whale came in the form of a check for thirty-five million dollars from the Sarah and Jerome P. Wheeler Foundation, along with the promise of a ten-year commitment to support ongoing operational expenses. In total, the Wheeler's donation was more than ten times the size of any previous single gift to Grodin. To say that this sent seismic shock waves through the Grodin community does a disservice to seismologists. This particular earthquake sent shock waves through the campus that even woke the emeriti dozing in the faculty lounge.

There was harrumphing: about not following established procedures and protocols, going outside normal channels, soliciting without permission, etc., etc. And there were questions: how could a lowly professor have made such an end-run around the Grodin administrators and scored such a coup without anyone knowing? How would the money be spent? Who would be in control?

But the most important question was how could a lowly, unpopular-with-the-faculty assistant professor who was about to be denied tenure now be given a collective thumbs-down? He couldn't be, of course. Not when he was holding a check for thirty-five million simoleons.

So despite their misgivings, the Powers That Were granted Bliss tenure and allowed him to establish and run a center devoted to creative expression under the umbrella of the School of Humanities. This proved to be a brief and futile attempt to fold both him and his dollars into the existing organizational structure because Bliss was not really into sharing. He'd landed the whale, and he, and he alone, would decide how the beast would be carved up.

It turned out that Bliss had a long sleeve full of tricks.

Over the objections of then-President Feldspar and every able-brained member of the faculty, he persuaded the Board of Trustees to establish a new School at Grodin, The School of Artistic Expression. Run by Bliss himself, of course.

The professoriat and the administration fought back, but in the end, a compromise was worked out with most of the faculty remaining in the renamed School of Humanities, Arts and Culture, while a few renegades/traitors jumped ship to join Bliss in the new School of Artistic Expression. Peter's group, which was made up of the great majority of the tenured faculty, retained control over the core curriculum, guaranteeing that much like a union shop, students would have to take enough of their courses in the so-called areas of 'rigorous academic studies' to keep the faculty fully, if not gainfully, employed.

Bliss's new School employed only a half-dozen tenured professors, the minimum number required to maintain accreditation for a college of Grodin's size. Most of the new School's classes were taught by outside lecturers and adjuncts, none of whom had any say in how the school was run and were completely dependent on the moods and whims, of which there were many, of the new Dean, J. Bliss Moynihan. Of course, some of these part-timers hoped to become full-timers sometime, somewhere, but most were realists who were using this temporary gig as a résumé-enhancer. Others were visiting scholars from similarly-situated colleges and universities who could trot out tired, old course material which could seem fresh in a new theatre of operations. Bliss also became an expert at luring second-tier celebrities and artists to Grodin to teach a class or two, essentially offering them a temporary refuge from career train wrecks, substance abuse issues and/or angry ex-wives or husbands.

With students flocking to popular classes in art, drama, film, multi-media, J. Bliss Moynihan swirled all of this into an attractive academic concoction which he, and he alone, controlled. And the first big *entrée* on his menu was the design and construction of the Sarah and Jerome P. Wheeler Center for the Performing Arts, which soon became known in the students' vernacular as 'Wheeler-Dealer Hall.'

For several years after its construction, Peter and nearly every other faculty member entertained fantasies about myriad ways and means of engineering its destruction. But now, a decade after the Schism, Peter had finally come to an uneasy acceptance of the state of play regarding Bliss and his baby, the School of Artistic Expression. Oh, there was the occasional brush-fire skirmish between the opposing forces, but by and large, the greater war was over, especially since there was no clear path to possible victory from Peter's side and although the faculty still nursed its grudge against Bliss, it was unclear as to whether he even gave them a moment's thought.

## Chapter Four
### The Hallowed Halls

*A*fter arriving near the front door of Jenkins, Peter slid his not-worthy-of-being-stolen ten-speed into the bike rack and locked it to the frame with a heavy, plastic-sheathed chain which he kept there. On the brick wall behind the rack hung a sign that read 'Reserved for the Department Chair.'

Only in academia would such a minor perk be deemed worthy of a brass plaque, and the faculty's cluelessness about setting aside a reserved parking space for a bike was lost on them as they grumbled about the quasi-official sanctioning of unequal treatment according to status. The Grumblers pointed out that there was no dearth of slots in the rack where, in the spirit of egalitarianism, anyone could conveniently hitch their bikes.

It was also lost on them that as a matter of standard operating procedure, they failed to practice what they preached every day. As members of their profession's officer class, they strictly enforced distinctions among full, associate and assistant professors and were acutely-aware of status differences in the enlisted ranks among the lecturers, instructors, fellows and adjuncts who served as the shock troops on the front lines of academic battlefields.

Peter had once thought about removing the plaque himself, but it had been securely-bolted to Jenkins' brick wall to keep it from ending up in some random student's dorm room. He was also certain that any official attempt to remove it was sure to bring about endless and unwanted discussion at the next faculty meeting regarding the pros and cons of such a policy change.

With helmet tucked under elbow and backpack slung over his shoulder, Peter crossed the creaky floor of the foyer and stopped at the doorway of Harlan Moore's office. As the department's most junior faculty member, Harlan's space was quite properly the least desirable in Jenkins. Its wide, glass-paneled French doors exposed him to the main entryway, creating a situation that forced him to occasionally act as the department's unofficial receptionist. To discourage this, Harlan had turned his desk to face the window and always wore a pair of noise-canceling headphones while working at his computer.

"Morning, Harlan," said Peter loudly.

Startled, Harlan swung around quickly and snapped off his headphones.

"Do you think you might pull yourself away from your computer and head on down to the Cook-Off this afternoon?"

"I've never been one to pass up a free meal, Dr. Grande," said Harlan, regaining his poise.

"Hard to leave those grad school habits behind, I suppose," said Peter. "Make sure you bring your lovely wife."

"I'm sure she'd love to come, but I'm afraid she wouldn't be able to get off work."

"Ah, yes, I forgot," said Peter. "Insurance, isn't it?"

Harlan nodded.

"Well, please thank her for the delicious artichoke dip she sent over for the faculty lunch last week. If I were judging, it would be a sure winner this afternoon."

"Hard to beat artichokes, mayonnaise, cheese…and bacon," said Harlan.

"Ah, yes…bacon, the miracle ingredient," said Peter. "No wonder it was so tasty."

"She is from Alabama, so artery-cloggers come with the territory."

"I won't let the food Nazis know if you won't," Peter said as he started back down the hallway.

"Mum's the word, Dr. G.," said Harlan, who sat down and went back to work on his article.

With a Ph.D. from East Tennessee State, Harlan specialized in Appalachian Literature which focussed on the lives of hillbilly-rednecks, or redneck-hillbillies, if such narrow parsings were possible. Unfortunately for Harlan, the plight of poor whites living in the hollers was not one which attracted much, if any, attention from academics, as hillbillies were not high in the hierarchy of victimhood. Only those officially-recognized oppressed groups, gays, women, the transgendered, people of color, people of hue, etc., etc., were of interest to academics who maintained a rigid pecking order of faves in the complex world of Marginalized People's Literature. Harlan had yet to realize that he'd entered a career-stunting blind alley and sadly, no one had told him.

Early in his career, Peter had spent some time up his own blind alley. As an undergrad, he had majored in American Literature and his Ph.D. was titled *When Fools Rush In: The Quest for the Great American Novel from Melville to Mailer—And More!*

After a few years of teaching at Grodin, he realized that the Era of The Great American Novel and its authors had passed. Not only were writers like Hemingway, Faulkner and Fitzgerald no longer read, they were also openly-scorned as being representatives of…well, you know the drill, and anyone promoting them would soon find him or herself, although it was usually a 'himself,' boarding *The Heteronormative White Male Express Train To Nowhere.*

Realizing that the trend was not his friend, Peter shifted into the hipper and more *au courant* world of Comparative Literature, a field where anything went as long as 'anything' was viewed through the intersectionality lenses of patriarchy, race, gender or class—whichever one would most definitively prove that Western Civilization was responsible for all the ills of the world.

When an assistant professorship had opened up two years ago, Harlan had not been Peter's top choice, but he was overruled by the hiring committee. Simply put, Harlan lacked *gravitas*. Short and sporting a scraggly beard, he was too eager to please and his constant nervousness made other people nervous. However, the presence of his beautiful wife, Jennifer, more than made up for Peter's assessment of Harlan's physical and academic short-comings. A sweet, non-cynical woman who mailed hand-written thank-you notes after even the most casual social occasion, Jennifer was way out of her depth with the other faculty wives, but she was definitely at the top of the male faculty's list of those whom they would most like to be stranded with on a desert island.

## Chapter Five
### The Admins Are All Right

*D*espite being the last official day of the school year, Jenkins Hall was practically empty. With almost all of spring quarter's classes having been completed, Peter's footsteps echoed in the long, wide hallway as he headed for the faculty-staff lounge at the far end of the building. A jack-of-all-trades room for printers, copiers and supplies, the lounge also housed some downtrodden chairs, a sofa and a small, built-in kitchen consisting of an ancient refrigerator, a coffee machine and a beaten-up microwave. The only ones there were two senior admins, Betsy and Meg, who now were more than a few years beyond that 'women of a certain age,' thing and were carefully counting down the days until retirement.

Peter stuck his head in and said, "Morning, ladies, how's it going?"

Meg looked up from the copy machine and said, "It…went. And hopefully, we'll be following 'it' soon."

"I hear you," said Peter. "So you're not helping out down at the Cook-Off?"

"Oh, what do we know?" said Betsy. "Meatloaf, mashed potatoes and gravy doesn't really cut it with that crowd."

"Chef Margaret and Chef Brian have everything under control and have let it be known that they are not in need of our assistance, thank you very much," said Meg.

"Maybe that's why we've lost five years in a row," said Peter. "Or is it six? Do you want me to…"

"Oh no…no," emphasized Betsy. "That would not go down well at all, believe me."

"We don't mind," said Meg. "We'll still go down and enjoy ourselves this afternoon. I understand that for dessert they're making a saffron arborio rice cake with lemon verbena gelato, whatever 'lemon verbena' is."

"It might be two different things," said Betsy.

"I think it's one, but I'm no expert," said Peter.

"We can always Google it," said the ever-practical Betsy.

"Whatever it is, I'm sure it will be '*absolutely fabulous*,'" added Meg sarcastically.

Even though he agreed with their sentiments, Peter didn't want to get too deep into intra-departmental badmouthing and decided to get to the point of his stopping by. "So, when are you two taking off for vacation this summer?"

"Betsy's going in July and I'll be visiting my son and his wife in Seattle in August," Meg answered.

"Early August," added Betsy, knowing they would both be needed by the end of that month to get ready for fall quarter.

"Ah, Seattle. Lovely city," Peter said.

"If you say so," replied Meg.

"It can be in the summer…if you're lucky," said Betsy.

"Wasn't that *Fifty Shades of Grey* book about winters in Seattle?" said Meg.

"Humm…" said Peter. "I may have to reconsider not going to a Comp Lit conference there next year," Betsy laughed courteously at his little joke, but Meg frowned a bit, not out of disapproval, but because it wasn't particularly clever. Or funny.

"We'll both be back a couple of weeks before fall quarter starts," said Betsy.

"I don't know what we'd do without you,' said Peter.

"And if we can help it, you'll never find out," said Meg.

"I assume you've got an intern or two lined up to help out while you're gone," said Peter.

"Nicole Molinari's daughter, Tessa," said Betsy with a sigh. "Again."

"Again?" said Peter.

"Nicole was very persistent about our hiring her, shall we say," said Meg.

"Well, at least we'll all be brought up-to-date on the latest in the world of pop culture," said Peter.

"We'll make sure she re-learns how to operate the copy machine," said Meg. "Just don't expect her to show up at nine and stay 'til five."

"Oh, I'm aware of her proclivities," said Peter.

"And make sure you don't use words like proclivities around her," said Meg. "That will just confuse her and she might think, 'like, uh, you know, you're, um….like, coming on to her.'"

'I'll see to it that everyone is on his or her's best behavior," said Peter.

"It's not the 'her's' in the 'his or her's' that you should be worried about," said Meg.

Peter was quite aware of the accuracy of Meg's opinion and thought it best to change the subject. "Is Pierce in?" he asked.

"He texted me a little while ago that he'd be in around noon," said Betsy.

"Thanks," said Peter. "I'll be my office."

Peter left and headed up the stairs to his third-floor office. Despite his tepid response to Meg and Betsy, he secretly looked forward to having Tessa around the department again. He had thought about putting a word in with Meg to see if she could get her back again this summer, but he was afraid that such a direct request would have been too obvious. Of course, Tessa was worthless as a worker, but she was cute and flirty. She also had piercings which were reasonably tasteful and last summer she'd hinted that she had some interesting tattoos in places where, with the proper encouragement, she just might be inclined to show off. Still, nothing had happened nor was anything ever likely to. Although everything about Tessa flashed Trouble and Danger with capitals T and D, Peter knew where the lines were and how to set limits. Still, there was no harm in thinking about what it might be like should certain lines be crossed.

# Chapter Six
## The T.T.B.

*A*fter leaving the lounge, Peter trudged up the tiled stairs to his third-floor office. Each of the two upper floors was precisely bisected by a dimly-lit hallway with a stairwell at each end. The height of the office doors lining the hallway suggested that Jenkins' early occupants might have been warriors from the Masai tribe, but a quick glance at any of the old photos in the faculty lounge would have dispelled that notion instantly.

With Jenkins' interior matching the faded elegance of its exterior, the Hall's Glory Days clearly lay well back in the early Twentieth Century. Now a hundred-plus years later, it was a gloomy, old-fashioned relic that seemed even gloomier when compared with the modernity of its next-door neighbor, the new Wheeler Center for the Performing Arts.

Given Jenkins' many inconveniences, it was small wonder that many on the faculty preferred to 'work at home' on the days when they had no classes. With most of the faculty already down at the Cook-Off, only a few were around, mainly because they had foolishly scheduled appointments with students who, were they to even show up, would likely want to turn in papers at the very last minute or beg for an extension. The old 'the dog ate my homework' type of excuse had morphed into more elaborate technological explanations dealing with a take-you-pick of computer/printer/internet failures, which often were described in terms which so confused the faculty, especially those in the humanities, that they often worked. But the truth was, as long as the delay didn't cut into the faculty's summer vacation time, reprieves were usually granted after the obligatory lecture on the virtues of timeliness and personal responsibility.

But for today, Peter was upbeat. The last day of classes for the year was almost over and after next week's exams, the students would depart, leaving the faculty with three months of summer to recuperate from their onerous teaching responsibilities. His only obligation for the day was to show up at the Culinary Cook-Off, sample the offerings and make appropriate appreciative noises and gestures about the amazing quality of his team's culinary creations.

However, to get to his office, Peter first had to pass through that of Henrietta Rhys-Peters. A stout, commanding black woman in her mid-forties, Henrietta had been the department's secretary for more than ten years. Before being hired on, she had been a 'floater,' working temporarily here and there around campus, but when the secretarial position opened up, she saw an opportunity for permanence and grabbed onto it with both hands. While interviewing, she saw a faculty so ridden with liberal guilt and so desirous of making a Person of Color happy, she knew immediately that she could do with them whatever she wanted. Within a few months, she had the faculty trained to stay, sit and roll over. Their obedience came not out of a desire to please, but from abject fear. It became obvious very quickly that Henrietta possessed a full deck of race cards which she made known that she was ready to play at a moment's notice. Of course, she rarely had to—she just made sure that everyone believed that whatever card they were holding would be trumped by one of hers.

Henrietta understood every policy nuance regarding coffee breaks, lunch breaks, breast-feeding breaks, maternity/paternity leave, parental leave, bereavement leave, holidays, birthdays, sick days, vacation days, personal days and good old-fashioned 'I don't feel much like comin' in' days. She held this arsenal of knowledge in reserve, ready to be deployed whenever she perceived even the slightest breach of any rule of conduct cited in the *Grodin College Manual of Employee Rights.* And although those involved in administration feared her deep knowledge of the college's rules and regs, she rarely had to wheel out the heavy artillery, because the 'fancy people,' as she called the faculty, rarely noticed anything about what the little people were doing unless the Xerox machine wasn't working.

Once, in a failed attempt to build solidarity with the staff, Richard Marsden, the department's former Chair, quickly found himself in deep trouble when, at a staff meeting, he called Henrietta 'The Queen of Jenkins Hall,' assuming that she would take it as a compliment. He was immediately and publicly informed that calling a black woman 'the Queen of Anything' was 'racial stereotyping.' As she put it, 'when you call a black woman a Queen, no one be thinking 'bout no Queen of Egypt. They be thinking Welfare Queen and that be racial stereotyping.'

Although Henrietta spoke perfect English, she would default to Ebonics whenever someone needed remindin' of her minority status. When she was in a good mood, she used Ebonics-lite, and when slightly-peeved, she turned to extremely-formal standard English. But a fully pissed-off Henrietta became a flame-thrower whom no one wanted to be near when she unleashed her 'mother-f***ing' this and 'mother-f***ing' that full ghetto-blaster arsenal of abuse.

When Marsden foolishly followed up and asked how his remarks were 'racial,' he was told, 'because I say so.' Marsden wisely decided to never to 'diss,' 'mess with' or in any way 'disrespect' Henrietta again, as he had already been written up in her book as insensitive on numerous counts and any additional infraction would have initiated a series of public kerfuffles and grievance hearings which would have ended in no way other than badly for him.

Peter had a few friends on the faculty with whom he could privately refer to Henrietta as the 'T.T.B.,' or 'Ticking Time-Bomb,' which one day would either explode and take out everyone within a hundred yards or would be so deeply aggrieved by an only-visible-to-her slight or offense that she would mercilessly destroy the perpetrator in a take-no-prisoners campaign worthy of Attila the Hun. The faculty's problem was that no one could know precisely which incident would provide the spark that would ignite the T.T.B.'s incredibly short fuse.

Peter's strategy for resolving the T.T.B. Issue, which thus far had failed, was to move Henrietta up the pay scale as quickly as possible until she topped out in her pay grade. He then hoped that with the offer of a pay increase elsewhere, she could be enticed to move up and out to another department. The salary boosts did buy Peter some short-term good-will—an obvious benefit—but Henrietta knew that there was no weaker, less attentive and more malleable faculty than that of the Comparative Literature Department, unless it was that of the Marxist progressives in the School of Critical Social Theory whose vast reservoirs of liberal guilt oozed out of their pores.

Peter stopped near Henrietta's desk and checked his inbox for mail. There was rarely anything important, but he leafed through the stack anyway.

"Any calls?" he asked.

"They be on your desk. Nothing urgent. Or important, for that matter."

"It is the end of the term so there's not much going on," said Peter. "Is the coffee hot?"

"It is, and you know where to find it."

Peter almost said something about 'the good old days,' when secretaries made coffee, but quickly remembered with whom he was dealing.

"I'll get some later," he said. "Could you hold my calls? I'll be working on my book until I head down to the Cook-Off."

"Yes, sir, Dr. Grand-day," said Henrietta, intentionally mispronouncing his name. She curled up the corners of her mouth in a slight smirk, knowing exactly how hard 'Dr. Grand-day' would be working on his book.

"Thanks," said Peter, ignoring her sarcasm as he went into his office.

Peter knew Henrietta wouldn't be going to the Cook-Off, as she referred to the competition's cuisine as 'White Folks' food.' At one time she'd considered filing a bias grievance, but decided that an unofficial half-day off with pay at no cost to her accrued vacation days was a decent trade-off and not worth the playing of even the lowest deuce from her deck of race cards. Staff members who didn't participate in the Cook-Off were expected to stay on campus, but at Grodin, there was no one foolish enough to challenge Henrietta on her decision to 'beat the (non-existent) traffic' and head home shortly after noon.

## Chapter Seven
### Inside the Sanctum Sanctorum

*H*enrietta's skepticism about Peter's claim that he would be 'working on his book' was a truism which even Peter had to acknowledge. Despite his consummate ability to self-deceive, he realized he was no longer even slightly interested in doing what he needed to do to finish his book. Many months ago, his publisher had informed him that his company would no longer market textbooks which hadn't been revised within the past eight years, and Peter's opus, *A Field Guide to Comparative Literature: A 21st Century Primer for the Beginner,"* had just passed the seven-year mark. His last revision had been easy, thanks to the century's rollover. He'd simply thrown in a lot of mumbo-jumbo about the transition from the 20th Century to the 21st, 'blah-blah-blah,' and left it at that.

This time, however, he needed a new hook. As more and more scholars left tradition fields of study for those they saw as more wide-open, the competition for staking out claims in the new territories with definitive texts had become fierce, or as fierce as competition could be among people who sat in front of computers and wrote for a living. Peter's *Field Guide* sold only a thousand or so copies a year and with a royalty of five dollars per, it was hardly worth the effort from a financial point of view. Still, Peter felt he needed to keep his tome circulating for a few more years, lest his forgetful peers begin to think that both he and his time had passed. After much back and forth, his publisher agreed that a major rewrite wasn't necessary; a revised introduction and a new chapter at the end would suffice.

Twenty years ago, he could have knocked out both over a long weekend, but recently his ability to concentrate had begun to fail and thus far he had spent far too much time in his office either staring blankly at his computer or distracting himself by checking his emails and surfing the web. His writer's block had gotten so bad that he had almost begun to sympathize with his students, but whenever he drifted too far in that direction, he quickly came to his senses, as such thinking was a direct violation of his profession's unofficial code of conduct. He occasionally thought that for a couple of hundred bucks and an acknowledgment, he might even get one of the lecturers or adjuncts to do the majority of the work for him. Still, his lack of progress on the book was only a minor annoyance. He knew that eventually he would find a way to get it done.

This was not Peter's first encounter with writer's block. He'd gone to Penn State with the idea of becoming a doctor, but that was before he ran into the buzzsaw of organic chemistry. Then, after graduating with a degree in American Literature and thinking he wanted to become a writer, he worked for a few months to build up his bank account, then headed to rural France for the winter where he sat in front of a pot-bellied stove and fed sticks into it, hoping its glowing embers might spark him into writing his *opus*. He was lonely, he never fit in and the locals looked at him with suspicion. He loved literature, but discovered that he didn't like to write, not to mention that he wasn't very good at it.

Still, he'd always liked the laid-back casualness of college life (as an undergrad, he tried to never take a class that started before ten in the morning), so he headed back to grad school, got a Ph.D. in literature and became an academic.

After grad school, he landed a two-year contract to teach American Literature at Boston University where he met Glynnyth while she was getting a masters in social work. They married and in his second year, he sent out résumés and received several tenure-track offers, one in Abilene, another in North Dakota, and the third from Grodin. With a baby on the way, both Texas and North Dakota seemed to be cultural deserts best left explored by others. He knew next to nothing about Grodin, but at least western Massachusetts was familiar territory, so he accepted its offer.

Like most of the younger profs of that era, Peter viewed the Grodin posting as a mere way station on the path to greater glory. By keeping his head down and his aspirations up, he had hoped to climb up a rung or two on the academic ladder at Grodin before moving on to a more prestigious school.

But by the late-1980's, life in the academy had changed. With the number of better opportunities in the world of the liberal arts having shrunk rapidly, Peter made all the standard inquiries, but the Harvards, Yales and Stanfords had not come calling. So he had stuck it out at Grodin, a half-dozen years as an assistant prof, three as an associate, then nearly fifteen as a full professor.

But several years ago, when Mr. Opportunity knocked in the form of a heart attack which took out the former Chair, Richard Marsden, Peter was there to answer the call. First as the Acting Chair, then as the Interim, and finally, after several months intense politicking, the training-wheel modifiers came off and he became 'The Chair.'

He found 'The Chair' to be very comfortable indeed.

After dropping his backpack and helmet onto the floor near the door, he sat down at his desk and woke his computer from its slumber. His desk faced two ceiling-height corner windows and Peter had angled it slightly to afford him a view of the woods beyond Grodin's core campus. It also kept him from having to look out at the annoying presence of the Wheeler Center next door.

His office read Befuddled Academic. Tall oak-veneered bookcases lined the walls and books of all shapes and sizes filled the shelves, punctuated by a few framed photographs and an occasional vase. Beneath the windows and in the corners of the room, towers of books stood against the wall like city skyscrapers, In turn, they which were surrounded by a suburban sprawl of newspapers, journals and manuscripts that had spread out across the floor. Despite the chaos, the room had a casual charm, mostly supplied by autographed author's photos, theatrical masks, and framed playbills from old Broadway productions. A large vase of dried flowers which sat on a pedestal table served as the room's only homage to the traditional norms of interior design.

Employing one of the many delaying tactics that kept him from working on his manuscript, Peter began skimming through his emails. Unfortunately, none was pressing enough to keep him from getting on with his rewrite. So, after finally realizing he could dither no longer, he opened Word to where he'd left off and stared at the screen. He tried to force himself to concentrate and get back into it, but, he had...nothing.

Nada.

Zip.

Zero.

*Rien du tout.*

He was going nowhere.

After a while, he sighed, closed his eyes, leaned back and felt the need to 'rest his eyes' for a few minutes before getting back to the business at hand.

An hour later, a knock on the door woke Peter from his slumber. "You won't believe this..." said a slyly-grinning Pierce Harrington III as he leaned in through the open doorway, "... but 'Little Jimmy' is freaking out over his graduation speech." Pausing for dramatic effect, Pierce raised an eyebrow and continued, "Writer's Block."

Pierce was Peter's best friend on the faculty. Having arrived at Grodin at roughly the same time, they shared a common history and more importantly, held similar world views. Known around campus as 'The Two P's,' Pierce and Peter were charter members of a small and steadily-shrinking group of mostly male profs who could yak away with each other without fear of having their covers blown and careers shattered by the public disclosure of their sometimes politically-incorrect humor.

"Oh, God, that should teach him to stop sucking up to his students," said Peter, momentarily forgetting his own struggle with the same beast.

"The curse of popularity," said Pierce.

They both chuckled. James 'Call Me Jimmy' Terman was a recent addition to the faculty of the School of Artistic Expression. Operating as an unctuous butt-kisser and a smarmy ingratiator, Terman had zealously worked his way up from part-time lecturer to full-time assistant prof in just four short years. Jimmy's most popular course was *An Introduction to Media Mania: Or How I Learned to Stop Worrying and Love Pop Culture,* one which no one failed and everyone enjoyed, which was the contemporary recipe for academic success.

His classes were a *mélange* of film & TV clips, improv exercises, whacky stunts and performance art. He once had several students wrapped up like mummies in rolls of white hospital gauze, whereupon they were carried around Squirelle on Egyptian litters in a mock funeral exercise. That stunt ended abruptly when one of the gauze-wrapped students, feeling claustrophobic, melted down with an anxiety attack so severe that it required hospitalization and massive doses of sedatives. Fortunately for Grodin and 'Call Me Jimmy,' the mummy stunt did not result in a lawsuit, but it was definitely a close encounter of the tort kind.

This year's seniors had overwhelmingly selected him to deliver the faculty's 'Charge to the Class' at commencement. There was no doubt that Terman's popularity with the students topped the charts, but he would also be delivering his speech to a much more critical audience, the hundred and forty-odd members of the Grodin faculty who would be sitting on the stage behind him—in judgment.

Although overt striving was frowned upon in the academic community, slack might have been cut for a young, ambitious faculty member were his footprints on their collective backs not so fresh. Should James 'Call Me Jimmy' Terman experience a failure to launch moment at Commencement, there was near-unanimous hope among the faculty that said failure would be spectacular, and the fact that they would have front row seats at the debacle... well, that would be seen as a nice bonus.

"I heard he's begging for jokes from that kid who writes for *Saturday Night Live*," said Pierce.

"I hope the kid charges him at least a year's worth of tuition," said Peter. "That way he'll at least get something back for wasting his parents' money."

"I predict he won't bomb, but I wouldn't mind seeing the so-called 'coolest guy on the planet' sweat a bit."

"And I predict that he'll never get tenure," said Peter. "Little 'Call Me Jimmy' has gotten a little too big for his big-boy pants. Bliss will end up having to take him down a notch or two."

"And if anyone knows how to take someone down, it's Bliss," said Pierce.

They both paused at the thought of their mutual nemesis, J. Bliss Moynihan, who, in a few brief years, had managed to turn Grodin's sleepy academic culture upside-down.

But like his best bud, Peter, Pierce was never one to dwell too long on the negatives. "You ready to take on the Iron Chef wannabes?"

"Is it that time?" said Peter, whose 'resting his eyes' moment had managed to kill what was left of the morning.

"It's High Noon at the High-Cholesterol Corral, baby."

"Then let's roll," said Peter.

## Chapter Eight
Food Fights

*L*inked together like strands of DNA, streams of multicolored pop-up tents dotted the grassy lawns of Squirrelle Plaza. Protected from the noonday sun by fluttering canopies, teams of Grodinites from full professors to lowly freshmen, chopped, stirred, marinated and mashed a variety of proteins, fats, starches and sugars which they hoped to transform into gourmet *tours de force*.

Outside the tents, frisbee-tossers played their version of football while clumps of students in varying states of undress sat on blankets, drank beer and listened to a pair of appropriately-scraggly folk singers strum guitars and warble about suffering.

At the center of the Plaza, a student rock band tuned up on the stage which would later serve as the judging platform. Rising up behind it, a sturdy metal scaffold supported a huge flat screen that displayed a shaky video that was being streamed from one of the kitchens. At their control center behind the stage, uniformed guys from Grodin's AV unit were working hard to tweak the video signal into some semblance of stability.

By early afternoon, a thick bluish haze began to hover over the plaza. Even an untrained nose could detect in the smoke not only the traces of applewood, hickory and oak emanating from the charcoal-fired grills, but also more than a hint of burnt *cannabis sativa* coming from those areas on the Plaza occupied by members of the student body.

The Culinary Cook-Off had begun a decade ago as a spontaneous competition between the School of Critical Social Theory (The Crits) and the School of Humanities, Art and Culture (The HACs) to determine which School could grill the better burger. Following that opening skirmish, the Cook-Off quickly escalated into an intense, full-scale internecine war among Grodin's five Schools.

The basics of the Cook-Off were simple: each team was to prepare a selection of dishes based on a theme chosen by—what else?—a committee. Of course, the Cook-Off Committee needed the advice of a second committee to decide how best to create a committee that would accurately reflect the full diversity of the Grodin community. As with most things in the academy, that which was initially simple quickly grew to become something nearly as complex as the Federal Income Tax Code. Once the competition became an annual Rite of Spring, a thick compendium of rules, regulations and restrictions emerged from a long series of kerfuffles that were thrashed out through the usual means of information exchange: letters of outrage to the student newspaper, petitions, protests, lists of demands (both negotiable and non-negotiable), blogs, Facebook posts, Twitter tweets, etc. etc., until

President Brooks Manchester finally appointed a permanent Task Force to oversee the Cook-Off. "One of my greatest accomplishments," he later confided to a young scribbler who was writing a puff piece for the alumni magazine and who was not in a position to argue.

In subsequent years, the lead chefs from each school would spend weeks creating menus, recruiting talent and planning the logistics for getting the stoves, ovens and grills into operational readiness for the next Battle of Squirrel Square. Early on in Peter's term as department chair, various Pooh-Bahs from the five schools spent many hours debating whether the head chefs from each School should be given a *de minimus* teaching load during spring term so they could strategize and prepare a game plan the coming campaign. Even Peter, who usually was favorably disposed towards any proposal that leaned towards less work and more time off, felt this was a bridge too far in the battle for culinary supremacy.

Once, when reporting back to his school's faculty on this issue, after he offhandedly mentioned that prepping for the Cook-Off was not like planning the Invasion of Normandy, he had to explain to some of the younger faculty members exactly what the Normandy Invasion was, whereupon he was denounced by some for comparing the life-affirming celebration that was the Culinary Cook-Off to a military campaign. In his defense, Peter first trotted out his life-long anti-war *bona fides* and then reminded those easily-offended junior faculty members that he, as Chair and Associate Dean, had a very strong say about who would be granted tenure and who would not. With that, the nascent brush fire fizzled out, although its embers would undoubtedly smolder for years, and the fact that Peter had to fall back on his hierarchal authority as his defense, would also be stored away in each junior professor's personal Vault of Grievances, ready to be hauled out at a time when a *coup d'état* might be more successfully launched.

Not all of the Schools stayed the course. After finishing dead last several years in a row, the Geeks from Science & Technology realized they were being badly outgunned in the culinary battles and withdrew from the formal competition, especially since their tastes and inclinations did not rise above pizza and Doritos. Despite their School's formal withdrawal, a rump group of students and junior faculty kept up an ongoing guerrilla campaign that featured sneak attacks and wild stunts. Their goal wasn't winning but making a splash was, and if they crashed and burned in spectacular fashion, so be it.

Their first big attention-getter took place in the *Year of the Sandwich* when Cook-Off featured a last-minute surprise ingredient, 'pulled pork.' After a hasty huddle, the Nerds mobilized. They commandeered a paper-mâché chariot from the theatre department, stole a pig from the School of Natural Science's farm and strapped it into the chariot. They then hitched themselves to the wagon and 'pulled the pork' through Squirrelle Square.

During the following week, Grodin's sizable PETA group squealed loudly, claiming that the stunt was 'an egregious act of unacceptable cruelty towards animals.' The Geek Squad responded logically by saying, 'at least our pig is still alive,' and then added, somewhat contradictorily, that 'we're saving our bacon for another day!'

This year's contest was called *A Taste of Italy*. Initially, the Task Force had decided on the punnish theme of *Pick Your Poisson*, but when someone pointed out that because the Cook-Off was to be held on a Friday and because the choice of *poisson* could be interpreted as implying a subtle endorsement of Catholicism, the fish theme was quickly jettisoned. Instead, the Task Force's Sub-Committee on Comestibles determined that *poisson* would be downgraded from the primary to a secondary ingredient, although each team was still given the option of choosing the species of fish it would prepare. To the Task Force's dismay, the Geeks from S & T came off the sidelines and jumped into the competition by making it known that their *poisson* of choice would be cod, and immediately began creating numerous variations on the combinations of cod and piece. When news of the Geeks' plan leaked out, Plan B quickly morphed into Plan C. The committee determined they needed a new common ingredient and, at that point, the decision not to pick zucchini was a no-brainer, even for a gaggle of academicians. After much haggling, the Task Force finally settled on eggplant. Though not anyone's favorite vegetable, it was thought that no one could come up with a way in which eggplant could be turned into a suggestive joke.

The first few years of the competition saw the winning School take home as a symbol of victory, the coveted Blackened Tongs, a three-foot-long pair of industrial-grade burger-flippers which the winning HAC's team asserted to have been a crucial factor in its victory in the initial Better Burger competition. Inevitably, however, it was determined that the term 'Blackened Tongs' contained multiple negative racial subtexts, so the Task Force's Competiton Committee substituted a more racially-neutral prize, the Silver Spatula. But even that decision ran into trouble when the Silver Spatula was deemed to represent a commodity long-associated with colonialism, imperialism, elitism, along with several of the other lesser 'isms.' It was also noted that the Silver Spatula itself represented a gross misallocation of a precious natural resource. The Competition Committee finally came up with what they felt was a suitable trophy, the Eco-Bowl—a large, bland, nondescript biodegradable piece of dishware made from organic potatoes.

One wag opined that Grodin should end the Cook-Off altogether and present the last winning school with the *Stick-A-Fork-In-It Award* and get back to teaching. But, as one might have suspected, his suggestion was ignored completely.

When Pierce and Peter arrived at the Square, the race for the Eco-Bowl was entering the home stretch. Under the canopies and atop long tables, heaps of vegetables and whole fish chilled on piles of ice while they awaited their inevitable rendezvous with the long knives. Decked out in kitchen whites and toques bearing each School's crest, gangs of students, faculty and staff worked feverishly through the early afternoon. With no established home base, the

Geek Squadders wandered through the encampment, easily-identifiable by their oversized black toques which, wobbling like a drunk on a balance beam, seemed to be in danger of falling off at any moment. The last-minute elimination of the cod theme had left the Geeks without a plan to make, in true *Animal House* fashion, 'a really futile and stupid gesture,' as they refused to settle for anything less than a truly spectacular piece of tasteless performance art. Two years ago, when the theme was *Where's the Beef?*, the Geeks decided to build a solar cooker which could roast a whole steer on a slowly-rotating spit. Despite their superb engineering, they unfortunately failed to inform the sun of its 'responsibility,' so to speak, to rise and shine on the appointed day. In the dim light of a mid-day drizzle, the steer not only failed to brown, but failed to heat up above room temperature, and even those who liked their steaks rare might not have been able to muster up much enthusiasm for a thousand pounds of *carpaccio*. Undaunted by the failure of their solar cooker, the Nerds quickly broke out acetylene torches to provide the finishing touches to their *boeuf brûlée*. Sadly, all this firepower proved to be a bit too effective as their effort to flash-cook the steer sent waves of smoke bearing the smell of searing flesh rolling through Squirelle. It was rumored that several bystanders ended up in the emergency room not to be treated for smoke inhalation, but for extreme nausea. Some also credited the Geeks' spectacular failure for an increased interest on campus in vegetarianism.

Snaking their way through the makeshift outdoor kitchen, Pierce and Peter finally arrived at the HAC's tent where their peeps were furiously prepping a variety of ingredients at different stations. Two wine-barrel-sized pots of water were held near full boil, waiting for the chefs' pasta of choice to be dropped in and cooked to *al dente*. Restaurant-sized mixers blended cream, egg yolks and sugar into a frothy base for the dessert.

Coming from consumption rather than production side of the culinary world, Peter and Pierce turned to a large whiteboard to attempt to decipher what was being prepared, but the board offered little in the way of explanation, covered as it was with a confusing array of multicolored arrows, boxes and timelines which indicated who was responsible for what in the prepping, cooking and plating of each dish. Nearly as much thought had gone into planning this culinary battle as had gone into organizing the Manhattan Project.

Fortunately, Pierce found a stack of printed menus which 'splained things and handed one to Peter. It announced that the School of Humanities, Arts and Culture would proudly put before the judges:

- Parmesan-battered zucchini blossoms stuffed with goat cheese, shallots and chives

- Grilled endive salad with roasted hazelnuts, watercress purée, fresh caper berries in a blood orange sauce

- Eggplant rollatini stuffed with fresh ricotta and spinach over a Sicilian tomato-raisin purée
- Cappellini with saffron-shallot cream sauce topped with Tellicherry pepper and Hawaiian black lava salt
- Grilled branzino over caramelized leek and carrot mirepoix with mustard-tangerine sauce
- Saffron arborio rice cake with lemon-verbena gelato.

After a lengthy stare at the menu, Peter asked, "what the hell is 'branzino?'"

"I think it's a European sea-bass," said Pierce, "but I wouldn't stake my Ph.D. on it."

"I know this is a stupid question but why can't they just call it 'European sea-bass'?"

"You're not really asking, are you?"

"It's more of a rhetorical whine," said Peter.

"I'm afraid we're not the target demographic for this sad affair."

"Ah, but think of all the camaraderie and excellent team-building that's going on."

"I prefer to think of it as a day-off…with pay," said Pierce.

As they worked their way through the kitchen, peeking over shoulders and saying their hellos, Pierce was vigorously elbowed aside by Margaret Dreighton, a slight, but fierce-looking woman in her early forties. She appeared to be carrying a large and permanent chip on each of her slender shoulders, which, under her kitchen whites, were supported by linebacker-sized shoulder-pads.

"Peter, I…am…hot," she said, emphasizing each word separately.

Peter stopped himself from making a joke about how sorry he was for not being the stallion he used to be and instead, took the safer route, "well, it is sweltering in here, but I doubt that's the kind of 'heat' you had in mind."

"Don't toy with me, Peter," she said. "Did you see *The Times* this morning?"

Peter glanced at Pierce and smiled slightly. "That wouldn't be the *New York Times*, by any chance?"

"Of course it's the *New York Times*," she said, with a glare on her face which silently added the words, 'you idiot,' to her comment.

"Sorry, but I'm afraid I didn't get any further than the crossword puzzle," said Peter.

Margaret tossed her hair back in preparation for a major diatribe launch. "An article in the lifestyle section compared salaries at all the colleges and universities across the country and did you know that we are only in the seventy-sixth percentile?" She crossed her arms defiantly as though her statement was game, set and match.

"Not only did I know that, though perhaps not down to the precise percentile, I am, if not eternally-grateful, at least extremely so when, on the twenty-second of every month, a fairly substantial sum of money is automatically-deposited into my bank account."

"Well, you may be satisfied with what you're getting, but I can tell you I am not happy and I demand that you, as department chair, do something about it."

"And what is the 'something' you have in mind?" asked Peter.

"Do I have to spell it out for you? Okay, Peter, read...my...lips. 'Show... me...the money.' Is that clear enough for you?"

"If you like, Margaret, I'll bring it up with Brooks."

Margaret scoffed. "Great. Wonderful. Now I have an absolute guarantee that nothing will happen. That old coot has one foot in the grave and the other on a banana peel. He's officially O.T.L."

Peter and Pierce looked at her quizzically.

"Out...To...Lunch," Margaret explained. "They ought to just get rid of him."

"They are 'getting rid of him,' as you put it," said Peter. "He's retiring, in case you didn't know."

"Yes, but he'll be here for what? Six more months? Nine months? A year? Standing, or should I say stumbling and bumbling around in the way of progress?"

"Patience, Margaret, patience," said Peter. "We'll have a new president waiting in the wings by next winter. Then you can work your wiles on him."

"How can you talk to me about 'patience?' As the single parent of a gifted child in a private's school, I don't see how anyone can expect me to live on a hundred and twelve thousand dollars a year. It's not fair! It's just...not...fair!"

"I thought your ex was paying half the tuition?"

"That rotten bastard. With the money he makes, he should be paying all of it," said Margaret.

"It's not as though you're about to find yourself out on the street," said Peter.

"No, but after the divorce, I had to move to a neighborhood where they park plumbing trucks in the street. And overnight, for God's sake. Not to mention their gigantic boats in the driveways. And the Yahoos who live there, all they do is play softball and drink beer."

"The horror," said Peter, mostly to himself but with a nod towards Pierce.

"I swear, Peter, I am not going to put up with this. I know what I'm worth in the open market and I want...no...I demand to be paid accordingly."

Peter looked at Pierce who shook his head and mouthed the word 'no,' indicating he would advise Peter against commenting on that one.

"Margaret, do you know what it means to be in the seventy-sixth percentile?"

"I understand numbers, Peter," Margaret said. "Before I got my degree in Renaissance Art, I double-majored in math and physics."

Pierce and Peter managed to suppress wry smiles at this obvious confabulation. Despite having been married to a computer scientist, Margaret was one of the least-likely candidates for a STEM degree anyone could have imagined.

"I'll take it to the Board of Trustees if I have to."

"Sometimes it's best to just take it to the bank."

"You are such a whiney little coward. No wonder you never went anywhere."

"Then why are you the one asking me for help?"

"You know, for once, you are right. I should never have even bothered talking to you."

Margaret stormed back into the kitchen, peered into a large sauté pan and shouted, "who's in charge of the Béarnaise? It's breaking! It's breaking!"

No one dared step forward and take responsibility.

Margaret seized a stiff wire whisk, quickly added some ice water and began thrashing the Béarnaise mercilessly. "Do I have to do everything around here?" she exclaimed.

Peter glanced at Pierce and said, "shall we?"

"Get out of Dodge?" said Pierce.

"While we're young," said Peter.

"And still alive," said Pierce. "Here there's nothing but crazy people wearing funny hats and wielding knives."

"Could be a lethal combination," said Peter.

## Chapter Nine
*El Presidente*

*O*fficially, only beer and wine were allowed at the Cook-Off on the well-founded grounds that the sight of students passed out on the lawn at high noon did not constitute appropriate landscape design. Beer and wine, after all, took some time to kick in, even for the novice drinker.

Peter and Pierce stepped out of the tent and into the sunshine, whereupon Pierce declared he was going to find something a little more potent than vino or Sam Adams.

"I think I'll stay and circulate for a while, but see if you can't bring back a cup with a little Jack Daniels in it," said Peter. "No ice."

"Will do," said Pierce as he walked off.

Peter sighed and hoped the headache he felt coming one would dissipate. Margaret was a double-dose of trouble; not only was she a weak faculty member, but she also was a continual pain in the butt. She had come to the department eight years ago as the 'trailing spouse' of her husband, Stan Dreighton, a computer science superstar.

Colleges and universities always hyped a husband and wife hire as an equally-beneficial Twofer, but in most instances, one spouse was the planet and the other was the moon. At Grodin, the 'moon' was usually hired as a lecturer/adjunct or at the most as an assistant professor, so if something went awry, the school would not be on the hook for the less valuable member of the pair. But in this case, Grodin was so unused to landing a 'planet' the size of a Stan Dreighton that the administrator-in-charge of writing up the terms of the contract failed to take into account what, in the end, became a highly-salient contingency—Margaret's tenure.

The Dean of the School of Science and Technology was thrilled to have landed Dreighton, who could have gone anywhere, but after a stay of only two years, he moved onward and upward to Stanford, leaving both Grodin and Margaret behind. Peter later suspected that this had been Dreighton's plan all along, with Grodin being both a convenient and necessary pit-stop in his Dump-The-Wife strategy. No sense in having an ex-wife, especially a brazen and hardened schemer like Margaret, skulking about and making trouble in his newer, more prestigious, neighborhood. At one time early on in Bliss's reign at the School of Artistic Expression, Peter had hoped that by incessantly talking her up he could albatross her around Bliss's neck, but Bliss was not one to be taken in so easily. With tenure at Grodin and no prospect of another college ever taking her on, it was likely that Margaret would never leave and that she would be the School of Humanities, Arts and Culture's problem for another third of a century.

After leaving the HAC tent, Peter caught sight of Grodin's President,

Franklin Brooks 'Brooksie' Manchester, hobbling slowly towards the judging platform, struggling upstream against a swift-moving stream of students. Recently, a mild stroke had impaired his balance, but his wife, Helene, kept him steady with a firm grip on his arm. With a push here and a not-so-gentle tug there, Helene kept him on track as though she were taking a wandering puppy on a walk in the park.

Now in his early seventies and though slightly-stooped by age, Brooks Manchester was still an imposing figure. A shock of silver hair, purposely left a bit unruly, topped his angular frame and with his tanned, waxlike face fixed with a permanent, slightly open-mouthed smile, Brooks' countenance epitomized that of the generic Distinguished Elder Statesman. With his milky, pale-blue eyes seemingly focussed just beyond what was directly in front of him and with his right hand outstretched in an open and locked position, Brooks moved forward through the crowd like a slow-moving statue of a politician in permanent meet-and-greet mode, ready to either shake a hand or turn a doorknob.

Brooks' greatest talent had been to marry for money, which he had done twice. His first wife had died unexpectedly at thirty-six, leaving him unencumbered with children, but encumbered with a fortune large enough to enable him to parlay a modest career in the state legislature into an appointment as lieutenant governor, which was then followed by an expensive, but ultimately unsuccessful run at the governorship. The brighter lights of statewide politics exposed his chief failing, which was that although he looked the part of The Great Man, he wasn't really very smart. But then, while dead-heading in the office of Lieutenant Governor, at age fifty-two he married Helene Bennett Lowell, age thirty-eight, who was, for his next career, conveniently a Grodin graduate. Her substantial family fortune combined with his geniality and stately appearance paved the way for a post-political career in the non-profit world of well-heeled foundations dedicated to environmental and social change. But the world-improvers who ran these organizations would never have taken him on for even the ceremonial positions he held without the hope that someday he and his wife would leave behind a good portion of the spousal inheritance which traveled with them.

It was a variation on the moneybags factor and Helene's connection that led Grodin's Board of Trustees to hire him on as president. A non-academic, Brooks's job was to raise money, discretely, of course, and look good while doing it. The actual job of running the College was left to the Provost, Anne-Marie McAdams, who had openly lusted after the presidency, but because she was such an overt striver and unscrupulous as well, she lacked the board and faculty support necessary to mount a successful campaign. Nor did it help that personally, no one could stand her.

But the hoped-for big money never arrived, at least not in the amounts the Board thought the Manchesters' substantial contacts might garner. The truth was that other than marrying well, Brooks had never been much good at anything. Now, with his contract expiring at the end of the year and with his health impaired by the stroke, Brooks was the hobbling definition of a lame-duck. Before his stroke, the Trustees had been looking for a graceful way to ease Brooks out which would not offend Helene and cause her to withdraw her pledge of a substantial gift to Grodin upon her passing. But with his health now a legitimate reason to gracefully dump him, the search for a successor had begun, and upon its successful conclusion, it was understood that Brooks would leave "to spend more time with his family," even though the actual number of family members was but one.

"How are you, Peter?" said Helene as Peter approached.

"I'm fine, but the more important question is 'how are you?' Not to mention the Man, the Myth himself," said Peter, nodding towards Brooks.

"We're fine, though some days are better than others."

As if on a seven-second tape delay, Brooks' face brightened upon seeing Peter and he asked, "Peter, so good to see you. I hope you'll be joining me on the judges' stand."

"My tastes are way too plebeian for that," said Peter. "Besides, I think they're looking for impartiality."

"I've always found the judging difficult. I hate to disappoint anyone, you know," said Brooks. "And having to make comments like, 'I thought the sauce was too heavy and it over-powered the delicacy of the squib.'"

"It's 'squab,' dear," corrected Helene.

"Yes, 'squab.' Of course," said Brooks.

"Whatever happened to 'I liked it,' or 'Ummm, that was delicious,'" asked Peter.

"We are in the business of drawing distinctions," said Helene, "and grading efforts of all kinds."

"Yes, but hopefully only on subjects we know something about," said Peter.

Helene arched an eyebrow but withheld comment.

"Well, this will be my last rodeo," said Brooks.

"You will be sorely, sorely missed," said Peter. "Any word about your successor?"

"I appreciate it, Peter, but that might have been one-too-many 'sorely's.' And they don't keep me in the loop on that, though I have heard that it's likely to be someone from the outside."

"That would be a relief to some and a bitter, bitter disappointment to a many."

"That's true, and that's just the right number of 'bitters,'" said Brooks.

"Have you given any thought as to where you might go?"

"We'll certainly be spending the winters in Boca," said Helene. "Beyond that, it's too soon to say. We still have plenty of time. As you know, they clearly don't want to appoint an interim."

Again, Brooks chimed in late, as if on tape delay, "before they boot us out of Haverford House?"

"How we'll miss those frozen water pipes in January," said Helene. She turned away and looked out over the horizon as if peering into the future. "Someone else's problem now."

As they moved on, Helene whispered to Peter, "he's not judging this year."

Peter watched them slowly inch through the crowd. Personally, he had always liked Brooks, but was aware of his many shortcomings. Almost anyone else would be an improvement, but Peter was comfortable with the status quo and knew that with a new president, anything could happen. He would adapt, of course, but he hoped that whoever came in, he or she would be his last Dear Leader and that he could ride out whatever changes the new guy or gal brought in until he finally rode off into the sunset of retirement.

Despite being drummed out by Margaret's rant, Peter felt he should make a return visit to the home kitchen and spend a bit more face time with his peeps. This time he would make sure his internal GPS was set to the 'Avoid Margaret' mode.

## Chapter Ten
Sliced and Diced

*W*hile Peter was schmoozing once again inside the HAC's tent, J. Bliss Moynihan, Dean of the School of Artistic Expression, arrived at the edge of the Plaza and moved through the crowd like a heavyweight champ on his way to the ring. Charisma didn't just ooze out his pores, it shot out of his hair follicles like bolts of lightning. A swarm of sycophants swirled around him, along with a scraggly crew of video undergrads from the Communications Department, led by a dressed-all-in-black female student producer who exuded self-importance. Despite their clearly-amateur status, the all-male members of the video crew showed that in some areas they had risen to the professional level, having already mastered the art of dressing badly and displaying butt cleavage whenever they bent over to pull cable. At the fringe of the swarm, several groupie-wannabes hoped to catch the eye of the Great Man and be received, even if only temporarily, into his entourage.

Tall, lean and handsome, Bliss Moynihan had the easy grace of one accustomed to the spotlight. His greying hair, carefully-sculpted into perfect casualness, served as a comfortable nest for a pair of sleek Italian sunglasses which he dropped down now-and-then to keep the bright sun out of his ice-blue eyes. For today's Cook-Off, he had chosen to wear a bright-green tropical shirt and white linen pants. His Ralph Lauren style set him apart from the drab uniformity of the faded blue shirts and cotton khakis favored by most of the faculty.

As he moved from tent to tent, Bliss conducted man-on-the-street interviews which were broadcast live to the Squirrelle crowd on the huge Jumbotron at the back of the stage. He wielded his microphone like a fencing foil, occasionally thrusting it at a surprised interviewee, then holding the pose while his victim recoiled in mock horror. Then, with a flick of his thumb, he would turn on the mike for the interviews, which he wisely kept short and to the point.

When Bliss and his posse entered the HAC's kitchen, they headed straight for Peter, who, with his back turned, failed to notice the approaching horde as it rolled towards him.

"Dr. Grande, I presume," boomed Bliss.

Surprised, Peter turned and realized he was trapped by the camera crew and the microphone which Bliss had aimed at him. He was going live on the big screen with no prep, and he knew immediately that Bliss's objective was to make him look as bad as possible.

Desperate, he smiled weakly and muttered, "Been following yourself much, Bliss?"

"Hummm, I don't believe I've ever heard that one before," said Bliss sarcastically. "Very clever, Peter."

Bliss then switched on the microphone and turned to the camera. "We're here with Dr. Peter Grande and that's Grande with an 'e,' for those of you keeping score at home. Peter is Chairman of the Literature Department. Peter, what's cooking in the Humanities, Arts and Culture's kitchen today?"

"I hope it's something with meatballs," said Peter, "although I seriously doubt it."

"I doubt it, too. Food for Joe Sixpack is not what I'm seeing out here today. So, Peter, what's been your contribution to today's Culinary Challenge?"

"Like our colleagues in the medical profession, my goal is to 'first, do no harm,' and thus far I've succeeded in that respect by staying out of the way. And, just for the record, I've been asked, and not very politely, 'to stay out of the way.' In fact, the exact words were 'stay the bleep out of the way.'" He nodded towards the huge Jumbotron hovering over the stage. "I see we're live, so I've edited the actual statement for family viewing."

"Thank you for that, but since we're not even on cable, we do have some latitude in that department. No verbal wardrobe malfunctions for us, though that might be interesting." Bliss got back on topic with a second round of culinary questioning. "Would be fair to say that whatever culinary expertise you have leans more towards the consumption side?"

"Not only fair, but accurate," said Peter. "Everyone should do what he or she does best, Bliss, and those who can't, should stay out of the kitchen."

"Dr. Grande, could you take us through the menu that your team is preparing?"

"Bliss, I have no idea what's going on," Peter said. "It's...."

Given that opening, Bliss pulled the microphone away from him. "That sounds like something you could admit to nearly every day. Thank you, Dr. Grande, for your unique insights. Most illuminating."

Bliss turned the mike off and addressed Peter as if nothing had happened, "so, Peter, I'm sure you have a very busy summer ahead of you."

"You know, no one likes being blind-sided."

"You're a full professor. Speaking extemporaneously for any length of time should come easily to someone who's been teaching since...?"

"1984."

"Really? That long in one place? No wonder your student evaluations have slipped."

"Bliss...the mike is on," said Peter.

Startled, Bliss checked the mike and saw that it was off. "Nice."

He then pointed the muted mike at Peter, posed dramatically and said, "here's looking at you, kid." He and his posse then turned away and moved on to hunt down their next victim.

Pierce, who had returned and had been standing off to the side during the interview, handed Peter a paper cup of whiskey and nodded towards the screen. "Good job. Second City stuff."

"Ambush journalism," said Peter. "The bastard."

"But this round clearly went to you, Dr. Grande with an 'e.'" Pierce raised his cup and said, "here's really looking at you, kid."

Peter smiled as they touched their cups full of Jack Daniels in a mutual toast.

## Chapter Eleven
Judgement Day


*B*y mid-afternoon, the exhausted teams of culinary artistes had readied their masterpieces for the judges who had assembled on the stage. This year's panel included Granville Sparks, the rumpled, grumpy restaurant reviewer for the local PennySaver who supplemented his small journalist's pension by writing a once-a-week *Stepping Out With Sparky* column in which he shamelessly plugged the restaurants, diners and taco stands which advertised in the Great Beresford Almanac. If you didn't advertise, you didn't exist, at least in *The World According to Granville Sparks*, but if you popped for even a two-inch ad, your restaurant could miraculously spring to life as a gourmet's paradise, at least in the eyes of the Almanac's resident food guru. Granville didn't make much on his column, but he never had to rustle up his own dinner at home.

He was joined by Eileen Northrup, the mayor of West Beresford. She was a 'twofer,' filling both the political and the feminist/lesbian slots on the panel. Representing the local eateries was restauranteur Terry Melville, who, with his partner, Tommy Henderson, had founded the Double T-Bone Steakhouse. Because they were running a steakhouse, Melville and Henderson always made it clear, subtly, of course, that they were business partners only, not that there would have been anything wrong with that, mind you, had they been..well, you know…more than that. And finally, representing the academic community, there was Max Sweeney, a bearded, dressed-in-black Marxist from neighboring Mount Hoakum College. As a non-Grodinite, Sweeney was neutral as to which School won the Cook-Off competition, but he was ready and eager, at the drop of a lamb chop, to deconstruct Western society's obsession with *haute cuisine* as just one more symbolic representation of a culture in decline. Still, despite his personal and professional disdain for the whole affair, he was, after all, an academic, and the offer of a free meal and an audience to whom he could pontificate was enough to suppress any ethical or philosophical qualms he might have had about appearing at such a decadent, self-indulgent event.

At one time, the panel had expanded to nearly a dozen judges to ensure that it represented 'the full diversity of the Grodin community,' but because all the panelists were expected to offer up witty comments, that number made for some interminable judging sessions which caused the food to get cold and the hungry audience to become sullen and restive as they were forced to wait for their turn at the trough.

The camel-back-breaking straw over the diversity issue occurred one year when the Judges' Committee picked Joe, 'The Homeless Guy,' to serve on the panel. Having established a near-permanent residency at the main entrance to Grodin, Joe was notorious for his clever signs. His favorite shtick was to flash a *Will Work For Food* sign at passersby, and if that failed to score some cash, he would grin wickedly and flip it over to reveal *You're in College Now. Don't Believe Everything You Read!*

Joe's judging career was short-lived. He had a digestive condition that caused him to belched loudly after swallowing only a few bites. Egged on by some male students who found this hilarious, he discovered within himself the ability to emit lengthy, rolling, operatic belches that echoed around Squirrelle Square like summer thunder in the Rockies. Of course, as an official V.O.S. (Victim of Society), no one dared attempt an immediate intervention, but prospective future judges were subsequently vetted more carefully and their total number mercifully reduced.

As Master of Ceremonies, Bliss roamed the stage with his wireless Talking Stick, introducing each of the judges with embellished anecdotes about their backgrounds and culinary idiosyncrasies. He went into detail about Sparky's alleged love of glazed donuts topped with whipped cream and maraschino cherries. Sparky was not amused, but he was an expert at hiding his contempt, especially since it barely registered as something different from his normal expression of sullen dourness.

As Bliss continued with the introductions, a rolling crescendo of high-pitched shrieks and squeals began to emanate from the coeds in the crowd that surrounded the stage. Feigning surprise, Bliss proclaimed, "Did I forget something? Did I forget to mention that we have a very special guest joining us today? Did I?" He looked around in mock-surprise and then continued, "I think you can tell we have a very special someone joining us on the panel today. Someone who's a valued member of the Grodin community, was one of the first graduates from the School of Artistic Expression and is someone who has become a tremendous supporter of our Advanced Acting Program. Ladies and gentlemen, straight from the studios of Hollywood, California, I give you Grodin's own...." Bliss paused dramatically before pointing with his Talking Stick to the edge of the stage where the shrieking was building. "...Joey D'Allesandro!"

The crowd rose, whooped and whistled its welcome to Grodin's most famous recent graduate, 'Joey D,' as he was known to the under-thirty set. A member of Hollywood's young hipster elite, Joey D fancied himself to be a true Renaissance Man—actor, entrepreneur, philosopher, auteur—although it was doubtful that he could come within a couple of centuries of guessing when the actual Renaissance took place. However, he was knowledgable about social media, was hip to the latest high-tech fads and thus far had managed to keep his name out of the worst of the tabloids.

Joey D occasionally came back to Grodin to burnish his self-imagined image as a generational Thought-Leader. He regularly visited other colleges and universities and sat on panels which discussed innovation, technology and politics at such lofty theoretical levels that no actual subject matter expertise was required. He had yet to land a leading role in a blockbuster movie which would have established him as a major star, but thus far he had carved out a solid career playing The Sensitive Guy in chick flicks. His intellectual preening mattered not at all to the young women of Grodin, all they cared about was that he was good-looking and A Movie Star. And, because many in the current crop of Grodin students harbored similar ambitions, he was in-the-flesh proof of their own possibilities.

Had anyone asked, even Peter would have had to admit that Joey D was a 'good get,' as they say in show biz.

After engaging in several minutes of celebrity banter about how great it had been to work with Scarlett on his last movie and how cool it was to be back at Grodin 'hangin' with his homies' where he could 'get down and get real,' the panel itself finally got down to its business at hand—munching and judging. But for the female members of the audience, the most important thought running through their minds was 'how can I get up close and personal with Joey D?' And they weren't thinking of just taking a Selfie.

With the judging finally underway, Peter stood at the back of the crowd and thought about leaving. After his brief and somewhat-successful *mano-a-mano* with Bliss, he felt too wiped out to stay for the rest of the Cook-Off. He had already made his obligatory appearance and didn't need to spend another hour or two listening to amateur judges banter with each other and critique amateur chefs with their clumsy attempts at meaningful criticism. He had heard too many variations of how 'the kumquat and raisin sauce atop the grilled fennel truly brought out the sweetness of the squid,' to want to waste the rest of the afternoon listening to such tripe (pun intended).

But just as he was about to take his leave, he was on the receiving end of a poke in the ribs by a very sharp elbow. The poke was hard enough to cause pain, but discreet enough to not attract attention. Fellow faculty member Janet Baker crossed her arms across her chest, leaned over and whispered fiercely in Peter's ear, "you were supposed to call."

Peter recovered quickly and lied, "sorry, but I got caught up in a meeting with Meg and Betsy about vacations."

"That wasn't the plan."

Peter then remembered he was supposed to have called to arrange a possible get-together over the weekend. That he had forgotten was a sad reflection on the state of a relationship that had once consumed him.

"We could still..."

"Too late. I've made other plans," snapped Janet.

"Sorry, my bad," said Peter.

But Janet didn't leave and Peter wasn't sure what to make of that.

Peter hadn't hired Janet when she'd started seven years ago, but as Chair, he had been trying, in an under-the-radar kind of way, to get her on board as a permanent lecturer. For several years she had been teaching a course on *The History of American Film and TV* and the students loved it. Of course, nothing appealed more to the modern student than watching movies and TV for credit.

She had a Master of Fine Arts degree in film, but her only publications were a slew of movie and TV reviews for smallish local newspapers. As a consequence of not having a formal academic track record, she had no real chance of being hired for a tenure-track position, especially since she had often publicly expressed her contempt for such 'phony scholarship.' Although privately some of Grodin's tenured faculty members might have agreed with her, they were united in the belief that there should be no public airing of professional dirty laundry and could be counted upon to defend the status quo whenever necessary, which was whenever a civilian deigned to question the established academic order.

Peter made a mental note to send Janet a box of candy or some flowers.

On stage, the Tree-Huggers from the School of Human and Natural Sciences were the last ones up in the appetizer round and offered the judges a Wheatgrass cocktail topped with turnip foam, chia seeds and edible swizzle sticks made from dehydrated seaweed. The Tree-Huggers always fared poorly in the competition, dominated as they were by organic and natural food purists who believed that if it didn't taste like alfalfa, they weren't trying hard enough.

In his critique, Joey D rambled on about how much he appreciated the 'organic-ness' of organic food, and because it was, "like, well…you know, so…'organic,' and we all, like, know what that means for the Earth." He leaned back and smiled, expectantly waiting for applause, of which he got a smattering.

"My first year in teaching he made a pass at me," said Janet.

"Was it a completed pass?" asked Peter.

Janet gave him a look that could have vaporized a galaxy.

Peter back-tracked, "I'm kidding."

"He may be good-looking, but he's a complete moron."

"Most of them are," said Peter.

"Why are we even in this business?" asked Janet.

This was the kind of trap question women asked, to which Peter knew enough not to answer directly. Any aspirational response, such as striving to better humanity, promoting the common good, etc., etc., would be belittled as hopelessly naive, and any self-centered response such as 'we do it because we can' or 'what's better than getting paid to miseducate the youth' would immediately be interpreted as being the mindset of a hopeless cynic. So, when backed into a corner, Peter took a path he had learned from his many years of teaching—he answered a question with a question.

"You know," he said, pausing as though he was giving it deep consideration. "I haven't thought about that in a long time. What do you think we do it?"

Tone was important and it put Janet back on track, especially since she didn't have an answer either. After a long pause, she said, "we need to talk," the four dreaded words which no man wants to hear and from which nothing good can come. Janet then added, "give me a call…if you can remember."

With that, she left.

Peter had been romantically-involved with Janet for several years, but their interest in each other had begun to wane, primarily because on the career front, he had over-promised and under-delivered, and Janet was definitely not a member of the long-suffering and infinitely-patient Old School of Femininity. In the back of his mind, Peter had sometimes wondered if her career self-interest might overcome her hatred of Bliss, since his School of Artistic Expression was better suited to her talents than was Peter's. However, Janet was definitely a charter member of the 'Always Remember, Never Forget' Modern School of Femininity, as she could hold a grudge like nobody's business. Peter never knew what the cause of her hatred was. When he occasionally brought it up, Janet always answered with a look or a stare that said, 'you ought to know.'

Meanwhile onstage, Granville Sparks was doing a slow-burn at the rank amateur critiques offered by the stage-hogging antics of Joey D. After Joey had finally finished his critique of the cocktail appetizer by saying 'he'd have to have his personal chef learn how to make it,' Granville stated that in his 'professional opinion,' a wheatgrass cocktail with seaweed swizzles was barely fit for farm animals.

Bliss quickly stepped in and riffed about how wonderful it was that they were all at a place that tolerated a diversity of opinions on matters great and small. He then asked the other judges to opine on the wheatgrass cocktail while making a mental note to disinvite Granville Sparks for next year and for all the years thereafter.

After Janet left, Peter decided that he, too, had enough. Upon returning to his office, his first priority was to figure out how to patch up the mess with Janet. He ordered some flowers online and added a limerick:

*Roses are red,*
*Violets are blue,*
*Your absent-minded prof*
*Is thinking of you.*

It was corny, but he knew it would be the thought that would count—at least that was his hope. He then decided he'd better add a few sprinkles to the top of the figurative cupcake and ordered a box of See's Candies, all dark chocolate truffles, of course. Janet's faves.

When finally his thoughts reluctantly turned back to his unfinished book, he also heard the couch calling, and his ten-minute power nap turned into a serious two-hour snooze. When he finally woke up, it was time to head home for dinner.

Chalk up another day of hard labor in the salt mines of academia.

## Chapter Twelve
A Night at the Movies

$P$eter arrived home to find a note on the fridge saying that Glynnyth was having drinks and dinner with some friends and that he should go ahead and order a pizza on his own. For years, Friday nights at the Grande household had meant pizza, popcorn and a movie. Because Peter had yet to master Netflix streaming and Glynnyth believed that all technical issues fell under Peter's bailiwick, they had only recently graduated from videotapes to DVDs. Increasingly, Glynnyth had begged off from their Friday night togetherness, claiming either new-found digestive issues which precluded pizza and popcorn or citing a lack of interest in the evening's movie fare because Peter liked action flicks while she leaned towards English costume dramas and contemporary romances. Recently, she also claimed she needed to prep for weekend open houses because Springtime was Primetime in the real estate world.

When their two kids were in high school, Glynnyth took a job in Great Beresford's Social Services Department. She quickly discovered that she hated both bureaucracies and poor people, although she couldn't publicly cop to the latter. She then struck out into the world of real estate, first as a stereotypical Susie Short-skirt, buying and selling homes for her personal circle of friends, but it didn't take her long to figure out what it took to become a real estate pro and she soon became one of her company's top salespersons.

Peter had mixed feelings about her success. He liked the fact that she was more than helping out by making some serious dough, but when she started bringing in way more than he, it grated. Still, her success was not something he could complain about publicly and most definitely not to her. His main problem with her success was that she enjoyed making money, and a lot of it —a trait which was frowned upon in his circles, though not in hers. Their once-overlapping areas of common interest were now definitely separate and distinct.

Peter's pepperoni, olive and onion pizza was delivered by a former student in his department. In his opinion, a too-significant number of Grodin grads hung around West Beresford long after graduating, doing odd jobs or perhaps working for a non-profit until, as their friends moved on, they, too, eventually drifted away. It was always slightly embarrassing to see them not doing anything with their lives and Peter sometimes felt sorry for having sent them out into the world without any readily-marketable skills, equipped only with a degree in some form of Grievance Studies. However, that feeling usually passed after the second glass of wine, and it was definitely 'out of sight, out of mind' after the third.

After microwaving some popcorn and opening a bottle of Chianti, Peter settled in on the couch and channel-hopped until he found an old Bruce Willis action flick. He was soon joined by Bark, the dog, and Meow, the cat. Peter got a kick out of watching people's reactions when he told them the pets' names. Introducing them, he would say 'the dog's Bark and the cat's Meow,' so quickly that it would sound like 'dogs bark and cats meow.' If they still didn't get it, he would say, 'Bark, come here...good boy, Bark' until they did.

Glynnyth had grown tired of Peter's insistence in trotting out this old chestnut, partially because he enjoyed it so much, but also because they had never agreed on the names. To her, the dog was 'Smokey' and the cat was 'Custard.'

For the record, Bark responded to either name while the cat had yet to acknowledge it had even one.

Peter watched a young Bruce Willis dispatch half the population of Moscow and end up with only a smudge on his forehead. Eventually, Peter's inner critic emerged: Where do they get the ammunition for all that shooting? Why do we never see anyone loading a magazine? Popping a full clip into the gun, yes, but bullets into a clip? Never. Or going to the bathroom? Bathroom scenes in movies usually occurred only when something bad was about to happen, generally involving toilets and submerged heads.

He ended up falling asleep on the couch and woke up to find all the popcorn had disappeared and a shredded microwave bag on the floor. The situation had all the paw-prints of a Bark caper.

# Chapter Thirteen
## Breakfast With Cybelle


*W*hen Peter woke the next morning Glynnyth had already gotten up. Wearing his bathrobe and still slightly hung-over from the deadly pizza, popcorn and vino combination, he staggered down the stairs and dragged himself into the kitchen where he was surprised to see his daughter, Cybelle, standing at the stove stir-frying vegetables in a wok. Sitting on a barstool at the kitchen island, Glynnyth sipped her morning coffee and chatted with Cybelle, who was dressed in cut-off jeans and a plaid blouse which she had tied up above her waist to display her trim midriff. She had her hair pulled up into a tight bun, although some rebellious strands seemed to be attempting a jailbreak, as she looked as though she had been living in the jungle for months.

Her equally-bedraggled boyfriend, Toor, sat at the other end of the kitchen island where was deeply-immersed in his iPhone while simultaneously ploughing through a plate of scrambled eggs and hash-browns.

"Hi, Daddy," said Cybelle.

"Cybelle, honey," said Peter as he gave her a hug. "It's wonderful to see you." He gave her a second big hug which she barely tolerated. "When did you get here?"

"About an hour ago. We were on our way to Toor's parents' place in the Adirondacks, so we decided to stop by."

Then, as if seeing him for the first time, Peter noticed Toor, who, with his Apple earbuds firmly implanted, chuckled and bounced back and forth on his chair while he scrolled through his Twitter feed. He looked like they young Richard Dreyfuss in *Jaws*—all hair, granny-glasses and a scraggly beard. Peter couldn't remember whether or not he'd met this particularly boyfriend before.

Cybelle sensed his discomfort and said, "Daddy, this is Toor. I emailed you about him?"

Peter looked at Glynnyth. "Did we get that email? I don't think I got it."

"We talked about it," she said. "Remember?"

"Oh, yeah, of course." But, of course, he had forgotten. Peter held out his hand to Toor. "And how was Nepal?"

Toor took it, shook it and mumbled a "pleased to meet you,' before he resumed his multi-tasking, with one hand thumbing his iPhone while shoveling hash-browns and eggs into his mouth with the other.

"Oh, Daddy. It was Nicaragua, not Nepal." She returned to her veggie-stirring and muttered to herself, "you never listen."

"Oops, sorry. My bad. Of course it was 'Nic-a-raugh-gua.' I knew that, but how many times have I said there ought to be a rule that no one should be held accountable for anything they say before noon."

"It's not the 'before noon' time-frame that you should worry about," said Glynnyth as she sipped her coffee.

"What do you think, Todd?"

"It's 'Toor,' Daddy,"

"Toor…right…sorry. See what I mean?" He glanced at Toor and cocked his head sideways apologetically, but Toor didn't look up as he continued mainlining his internet fix.

"Is 'Toor' Scandinavian?" asked Peter.

"It could be, but he was named after the dal," said Cybelle.

"The dal? Interesting," said Peter.

"He's Scotch-Irish, actually," said Cybelle, "but his parents were sort-of hippies."

"They must be proud," said Peter.

"Daddy!"

"I mean that sincerely," said Peter.

"He's brilliant, actually," said Cybelle. "He almost dropped out of school to write apps, but decided what he really wanted to do was to help people built waste management systems."

"You're talking about 'sewers,' right?" said Peter.

"Oh, Daddy, that is so paternalistically first-world. There are a lot more creative solutions to problems like that that let people leapfrog the entire hard infrastructure thing."

"I think we can agree that working toilets, however constructed, are a societal good," said Peter, hoping to end a discussion which had taken several undesirable turns.

As it was with Glynnyth, conversation with his daughter was filled with hidden potholes and land mines, but he didn't like to be too critical of Cybelle and her current choices in either men or careers. She had drifted as an undergrad but finally settled into majoring in Race and Gender Studies at Worcester State. This was followed by a couple of years of partying and waitressing in Boston while she tried her hand at a folk-singing, but only a constant stream of parental financing kept even this hand-to-mouth existence at a life-support level.

When the folk-singing fantasy finally played itself out, she decided what she really wanted to do was to travel the world and live in yurts. Peter made many calls to help her get this latest obsession onto a potential career path by finagling her into a Cultural Anthropology graduate program at a university in Boston, which shall remain unnamed to protect the guilty. Whether she could eventually translate this into regular employment in academia or in the non-profit world was still at best an even money bet. But, even though she was a bit of a 'loose thinker,' Peter appreciated that she wasn't a namby-pamby and wasn't mind-numbed by technology as most of her generation seemed to be, including her current and hopefully not-to-be permanent boyfriend. Plus, she seemed to have things under control in the ankle-biting, rug-rat department, a fact for which Peter was extremely grateful, as being a grandfather in no way comported with his self-image.

Needless to say, Glynnyth held a different opinion.

Peter didn't have to worry about grandchildren with the older of his two offspring, son Gary Glynn, who, were he to become a father, would have to take the adoption route, having exited the closet when he was a junior at Oberlin.

Three years older than Cybelle and now thirty-one, he sported a Ph.D. from Dartmouth in 18th Century English History. With an assist from his doctoral advisor, he had landed a prestigious, but temporary two-year fellowship at Oxford, only to discover that upon leaving, his only job offer was that of an assistant professorship in Stillwater, Oklahoma, a place which was not exactly at the epicenter of LGBT life, or of anything else for that matter. Glynn, as he preferred to be called, felt that after his stint at Oxford, he deserved something more prestigious, but Stillwater was the only college that had come calling.

Despite their shared professional interests, Gary Glynn and Peter were not close. They rarely spoke, mainly because Glynn was a quiet loner who viewed his father as a loud blowhard, one whom anyone who was truly-cultured would avoid if possible.

Professionally, Glynn struggled with lectures and in seminars. He spoke so slowly and softly that people had to strain to hear him, but had he even noticed, it wouldn't have mattered to him. He believed his thoughts and ideas were so superior to those held by ordinary people that whatever inconvenience they experienced shouldn't matter. He viewed scholarly research as humanity's highest calling and held in disdain anything he saw as common and unrefined. He would have been perfectly happy had he inherited a seat in the House of Lords.

In short, to paraphrase Sir Winston Churchill, Glynn was a snob with nothing to be snobby about.

Later that morning, after a hasty bustle of refrigerator-raiding and pantry-rifling, the two young adults left for Toor's parents' Adirondack cabin. As he sat at the granite-topped kitchen island and sipped a cup of coffee, Peter settled in for a Saturday morning of emailing and web-surfing on his IPad.

Now dressed like the real estate pro she was, Glynnyth passed through the kitchen and headed towards the garage on her way to host an open house. Without looking up, Peter asked, "did you know they were coming?"

Glynnyth stopped and answered, "do we ever? They just 'dropped by,' as they say. Still, it was good to see her."

"I'm not sure about 'Toor.' Here he is eating our food and he can't even take those things out of his ears to say hello. He seems to have left his manners back in junior high."

By not responding, Glynnyth made her 'no-comment' comment on the situation. Again, she started for the garage. "I should be back around five."

"What is it?" said Peter.

"It's a four-bedroom, three-bath colonial in the Murchison sub-division. Two stories. Nice neighborhood. Well-landscaped."

As she described the house, Peter's attention had drifted back to his IPad. Seeing that he wasn't paying attention, Glynnyth paused, then continued, "it has a wrap-around deck and features a fully-functioning whorehouse out back."

When Peter didn't react, Glynnyth stopped speaking and stared at him until Peter looked up. "You know that part about the whorehouse? It's not true."

Suddenly jarred into alertness, Peter asked, "What whorehouse?"

"If you ask a question, at least have the courtesy to listen to the answer," said Glynnyth, who huffed out and slammed the door behind her.

At one time, Peter would have committed to putting in several hours of serious *mea-culping* to extract himself from this conversational blunder, but at this point, their relationship had so deteriorated that Glynnyth probably would not even bother to bring it up. However, Peter was certain it would be filed away in that vast Vault of Slights and Grievances which Glynnyth—and it should be said—most women kept, the contents of which could be readily retrieved at a moment's notice and submitted into evidence whenever the need arose.

## Chapter Fourteen
Pomposity and Circumstance


*G*raduation Weekend. Time to tie that final ribbon onto the end-of-the-year package. Students loved Graduation. For decades it had meant 'no more pencils, no more books…no more teacher's dirty looks,' but with pencils and most books now consigned to the dustbin of academic history, only the 'dirty looks' remained. Graduation meant adulthood was just around the corner. It also meant escape from the four-year prison of *in loco parentis,* but for many Grodin grads, the tunnel to freedom under the jailhouse yard led straight to a room in their parents' basement.

Most of the professoriat hated Graduation. Even though it meant the end of teaching and the start of summer vacation, it also meant glad-handing the parents and lying to them about their sons and daughters' talents and abilities.

At Grodin, graduation weekend began on Thursday with the arrival of the parental units who showed up in fits and starts throughout the day. Their offsprings' primary duty was to escort them around campus, introduce them to friends, and generally kill time until the evening's awards dinners, the first of the official graduation events. Dinner started early, at six, so the graduates could eat, get their parents settled in for the night and then rev up their party engines.

Only a few professors turned out for the awards dinners, but for appearances' sake, it was necessary that at least a few of the elder statesmen to show up, and to Peter's credit, he was one. Dean Barry Cromlich didn't much care for making speeches, mainly because he wasn't very good at it, so it fell to Peter, as Associate Dean, to act as the Master of Ceremonies and deliver a short speech in which he poked fun at the clichés about the 'making a difference,' 'following your dreams' and, well…'blah-blah-blah.' Of course by this time, framing a post-modernist critique of traditional graduation clichés had, itself, become a cliché.

Still, Peter enjoyed the dinners. He told jokes and stories about the students, a few of whom he actually knew and for the others, he relied on notes from fellow faculty and staff. He handed out awards for most fun, most industrious, most helpful, most 'woke', bravest, kindest, nicest, to name just a few. By the time it was over, everyone got something, as the modern tradition of giving out participation awards for just showing up established in grade school continued unabated in higher education.

Commencement, Grodin's formal graduation ceremony was held on a Friday, which was inconvenient for some parents. With travel on the day before, it could mean losing two days of work. But because the more prestigious sister schools nearby had already staked their claim to the prime-time weekends, the weaker sisters had to adjust, as there were only so many hotels, motels and B-and-B's to go around.

Faculty attendance at commencement was now mandatory. A few years back, so many professors had gotten into the habit of taking off early for summer vacation that their noticeable absence became a public relations problem. One year there were so few profs on-campus that then-President Geoffrey Feldspar had to round up stray staff members and stuff them into graduation robes so the parents might feel they had gotten some semblance of their money's worth after four years of shelling out the big bucks.

Of course, this mandatory attendance policy led to much grumbling in the ranks, but then nearly everything led to grumbling in the ranks. But with the emergence of iPads and smartphones, the professoriat quickly figured out that they could sit in the back rows, surf the internet and appear to be listening to the clichés and platitudes dished out in traditional graduation oratory.

This year, when the big moment finally arrived, luck was on the side of the graduates as it was a Goldilocks kind of a day, neither too hot nor too cold, and since it was early June, cold was an out-of-the-money option, but at least it wasn't raining. By mid-morning, it was time for the participants to strap it on and bring it.

Having partied all night, the drink-til-dawn students donned their robes in their dorm rooms while the faculty reluctantly gathered to 'gown up' at Bliss's place, the Wheeler Center for the Performing Arts. When Peter arrived, he headed straight for the pastry table. Even with a full continental breakfast laid out for them on the morning of, the faculty saw that as a much too small a recompense for the misery and suffering they were certain they were about to endure. There was more *pro forma* grumbling, and the grumbling continued while they donned their robes and continued to down the free coffee and pastries.

After loading up his plate a second time with a chocolate croissant and a cherry danish, Peter joined Pierce in the queue to pick up their gowns.

"Did you hear that Matt Damon was at Bliss's awards dinner last night?" said Pierce.

"No way," said Peter.

"Well, technically speaking, it was 'way.' He was on a live video feed and he did answer questions."

"The guy never quits, does he?"

"Apparently not," said Pierce.

While Peter and Pierce were slipping into their black robes, Associate Dean of Students, Kathleen Glazier, who was charged with getting the faculty ready for the procession, stepped onto a small riser and addressed her troops like Patton preparing his to cross the Rhine. Resembled a burkha-wearing fireplug in a cap and gown, she delivered her marching orders. Had the Third Army listened as disinterestedly to Patton, the French would now be speaking German. Her most important piece of advice was to warn them that the ceremony would last for well over two hours, so they should plan their bathroom stops accordingly, as in 'take care of your business now.'

After the gaggle had finished robing, she began to organize them into a line, sometimes by grabbing and physically jockeying them into position. A few of the faculty members were so involved in their conversations that they scarcely noticed they were being moved around like tackling dummies at a football practice. Eventually, everyone ended up in the proper position: standard-bearers at the front, deans and other pooh-bahs next, followed by those who would be speaking and finally with the ragtag army of regular faculty bringing up the rear.

Normally, Grodin's president would be the first one down the aisle after the flag-bearers, but President Manchester didn't join the march, lest the parade drag on interminably. Instead, he waited at the edge of the stage with Helene and, like Rosie Ruiz at the New York City marathon, stood ready to step into the front of the procession when it reached the stairs.

At last, it was time.

With the professoriat assembled at the back of the Square, the AV department fired up the *Earle of Oxford's Marche* and the faculty, one-hundred-forty strong, proceeded down the aisle towards the stage. Even without Brooks, it was a slow march, as no army moves more faster than its slowest member. Wily veterans that they were, Peter and Pierce gradually drifted to the back of the pack until they encountered resistance from other like-minded back-benchers who stood ready to hold their position against the interlopers.

When they finally assembled on the stage, the faculty stood in front of their chairs and applauded the audience of parents and relatives, fully-aware and grudgingly-thankful that those in the audience were the ones who had forked over the thousands of dollars that paid their salaries. The least they could do was pretend to appreciate them.

When the *Earle* music faded and the opening chords of *Pomp And Circumstance* filled the square, the audience stood and applauded. Led by a single standard-bearer displaying the Grodin flag, the graduating seniors straggled up the aisle. With some half-drunk and all sleep-deprived, the ragged and unserious bunch of graduates waved and posed for photos as they slowly made their way to their seats. After what could have passed for at least a couple of eternities, the actual ceremony finally began.

Commencement exercises have nothing to with fitness but everything to do with endurance. Learning to sit without squirming or falling asleep is one of the keys to surviving many of life's most over-rated rituals, and the Grodin graduation ceremony was no exception to the 'seen one, seen 'em all' bromide.

That this year's ceremony would be a struggle became apparent early when President Brooks set an agonizingly-slow pace with his opening remarks. With this being his last hurrah, his only task was to deliver some brief 'Welcome to Grodin' remarks, but even that proved to be too much as he fumbled through his notes, misplaced his glasses and lost his place several times. Sitting behind him, the faculty nervously shifted in their seats, concerned that Brooks's stumbling presentation was not presenting an image of even minimal competency to the assembled relatives of the graduating seniors. Seizing the opportunity presented by what seemed to be an ending point in Manchester's talk, Associate Dean Kathleen Glazier stood up and began to applaud vigorously. One by one, others caught on and joined in, clapping loudly as she stepped to the podium, edged a puzzled Brooks aside, thanked him profusely and then led him back to his seat in the front row.

The applause continued until everyone had stood up in a massive virtue-signaling gesture which demonstrated their compassion and tolerance in putting up with a past-his-prime Old Guy who was on his way out the door. They were also hopeful that Manchester would not speak again and that he could get through the next few hours without requiring the services of an EMT team, at least until the ceremony was over.

Dean Glazier then assumed the role of Mistress of Ceremonies and efficiently kept the ball rolling by handing out a series of awards to students for 'Most Considerate,' 'Most Inspirational,' and assorted other 'Mosts.' Each award required the recipient to climb the stairs to the stage, deliver a short 'thank you' speech and depart to enthusiastic applause, shouts, huzzahs and hoots from his or her friends in the audience. Mercifully, the appetizer round was finally over and it was finally on to the *entrée*, or in today's case, *entrées*, as in the Italian tradition of offering both *primi* and *secondi* courses.

The honor of presenting the *secondi* would go to J. Ward Kiesel, a local writer of historical fiction whose biography of Grodin's founder, Prentiss Hancock Grodin, was the reason for his appearance. By any standard, Kiesel was far down on the list of desirables, but, to be fair, so was Grodin, which had no chance of snagging a U.S. Senator, a Fortune 500 CEO or an A-list celebrity. To be sure, a state senator or the head of the West Beresford Chamber of Commerce could easily have been persuaded into delivering a commencement speech, but the cultural values of third-tier politicians and local business types were hardly aligned with those of Grodin's faculty and students.

But before Kiesel was up, the honor of presenting the *primi* was given to the recipient of the Hermoine Gillette Sanderson Award for Outstanding Teaching. Voted on by the senior class, this year's honoree was James 'Call Me Jimmy' Terman. It was common in most circles for someone to introduce the speaker, after which the speaker would speak, but in academia, there seemed to be a need for someone to introduce the introducer; consequently, Dean Glazier introduced the president of the senior class who rambled through a long list of exemplars as to why Terman was deserving of the Sanderson Award. When the student finally finished her introduction, it was James, 'Call Me Jimmy,' Time.

Sitting in the front row, 'Call Me Jimmy' twirled a finger in the air as a signal to the AV team to fire up a CD of wall-banging, tub-thumping rap music which caused the older members of the audience to cover their ears and wonder what the hell was going on. After bouncing and jiving in his chair for a few bars, Jimmy stood up, popped on a pair of oversized sunglasses and slowly be-bopped his way over to the podium where, with his hands gripping the sides of the lectern, he rocked back and forth, his shoulders shakin' and gettin' down 'wid da beat.

With riffs full of 'yo's,' 'bros,' 'disses' and 'dats,' Jimmy rapped ghetto-style on the graduating seniors' 'achievements.' Droppin' his g's, he pointed to his 'homies' in the audience and called on them to stand up and "be phat, be blow, don't let da busta crackle yo flow.'" He tossed in phrases like "let no razz be jackin' your jazz," "yo' mamas be fly" and "don't tizzy with da boss of the shady Lizzie." His poetry jam on steroids may have made sense to those in his personal posse, but it was totally-indecipherable to normal people.

A trio of dancing coeds emerged from the audience and shook and jived their way onto the stage where they boogied down with the music, but clothed as they were in heavy graduation gowns, they looked like three nuns trying to ward off a swarm of angry bees.

As Jimmy continued to riff on their achievements over their four years at Grodin, his groupies in the audience excitedly bopped and rocked in their seats; however, were one able to read the collective minds the parental units, they would uniformly be filled with 'we paid good money for this?' and variations of 'WTF? although not the acronym, but the actual words.

'Call Me Jimmy' rapped on until the music on his CD began to skip. Then it sputtered...then splattered...then restarted and skipped and sputtered again before finally coming to a screeching stop, whereupon the PA system emitted a feedback buzz that rose in volume until it threatened to shatter every window on campus. Eardrums instantly became an endangered species. The panicked AV squad scrambled into action and twisted knobs, unplugged cords and yelled and screamed at each other before finally ending everyone's collective misery by pulling the power to the entire sound system.

Without the mind-numbing beat of the 'music' behind him, 'Call Me Jimmy' lost his nerve. Voice cracking, he faltered, fumbled and finally stopped rapping and began reading. Without the pounding beat of the music, 'Call Me Jimmy's' words sounded even more ridiculous when read than when rapped. By this time, even his most ardent student supporters recognized that he'd lost his mojo; they fell silent and sank down into their seats in embarrassment. Now finding the whole thing quite hilarious, the Geeks in the audience began to snicker. When he finally struggled to the finish line and stopped, there was scattered, light applause, although most of the audience sat on their hands in stony silence. Jimmy slouched back to his seat, slumped into his chair and hung his head, but, realizing that acknowledging defeat was a bad look, he lifted his head defiantly. However, the sunglasses stayed on to hide his tears... and his shame.

Pierce leaned over and whispered to Peter, "looks like 'Lil Jimmy' done 'effed hisself." The Two P's then exchanged a discreet, congratulatory fist bump.

There had not been such a spectacular public flame-out since Geraldo Rivera opened Al Capone's vault on national TV.

Following the 'Call Me Jimmy' debacle, it was a relief to everyone that J. Ward Kiesel's speech represented a regression to the mean. No one had vetted him and he was terrible, but he was terrible in a traditional sort of way. He dipped liberally into the *Speakers' Handbook of Graduation Clichés* and droned on about how "the graduates were the future.; He exhorted them to "aim high, "make a difference," and "don't be afraid of failure."
"Never stop learning."
"Seize the day...seize the week...seize the year."
Blah-blah-blah.
Nothing to note.
Nothing worth remembering.
And as soon as he sat down, nothing was.

After the four-hundred and twenty-nine graduates had accepted their diplomas and shook President Manchester's crusty hand, the faculty left the stage, marched back up the aisle to Wheeler and got out of their heavy gowns as quickly as possible.

For the faculty, the annual commencement ceremony represented one more notch on the old academic bedpost. But for the students, college was a singular event, and graduation was a huge milestone on their path to adulthood. But, important as it was, they could look forward to a lifetime after Grodin. Oh, a few would hang around campus for a couple of years doing odd jobs here and there until they, too, would finally drift away. In the distant out-years, some grads would hold tight to their old-school ties, but most would come to recognize that their time at Grodin was but a singular phase in their lives and one which would recede in significance. At this point in their time on earth, they were hardly aware that they were part of a continuous cycle of 'rinse and repeat.'

In the fall, the faculty would welcome a batch of new students who would arrive, get miseducated, and after four years, they, too, would leave. But the faculty would remain and continue, or if you please, be condemned like the Groundhog, to rinse, repeat, and rinse again.

## Chapter Fifteen
Boogie Nights

*I*n Peter's world, the final Rite of Spring was the annual faculty party which he and Glynnyth hosted before his flock flew away for their summer R & R.

As the deep-blue darkness of an early summer's Saturday night took over the sky, Peter's house glowed from the light spilling out of every window. With drinks in hand and hanky-panky in their hearts, professors and their civilians—wives, husbands, boyfriends, girlfriends, and significant others of various persuasions—filled Peter and Glynnyth's two-story Victorian to overflowing. A jazz trio thumped away on the patio, but it was too early for wild dancing. That would come later, after the alcohol had kicked in and the party reached full-tilt boogie overdrive.

A hyperactive host, Peter moved through the room at high speed, a hug here, a quick handshake there, followed by a getaway pat on the back, yet always with an eye out for a pretty face. One in particular was that of Jennifer Moore, Assistant Professor Harlan Moore's young wife, who was sitting next to her husband amidst a klatch of younger people. After seeing Jennifer leave for the upstairs ladies' room, Peter approached the young student who was tending bar.

"Ted, you look like you could use a break," said Peter. "I'll have someone relieve you for a few minutes. A ll right?"

"Gee, that's okay, Dr. Grande. I'm kind of having a good time here."

Peter raised an eyebrow and nodded towards an attractive young woman who was arranging plates of appetizers on a table. "I think Abby could use a little help with the *hors d'ouveres*."

For a Grodin undergrad, Ted caught on fairly quickly, smiled and said, "sure enough, Dr. Grande. Thanks!"

"I'll send someone right over," said Peter.

Peter moved back through the crowd towards the group Jennifer had just left. He leaned in and whispered, "Harlan, could you do me a favor?"

As if receiving a jolt of electricity, Harlan snapped to attention, seemingly willing to kill himself and others should Peter so desire. "I'd be delighted to, Dr. Grande. What do you need?"

"Our second bartender hasn't shown up. I was hoping you could spell Ted for fifteen minutes or so. And don't start in with 'T-E-D,' okay?"

Harlan laughed a little too loudly at his boss's ancient joke. "So that's how it's spelled. I've wondered about that."

"The department's paying for the booze…so let your conscience be your guide."

"I'll do my best. I may not know how to make 'em right, but I know how to make 'em strong."

Peter laughed and gave him an encouraging thump on the back which sent Harlan off in the direction of the bar. Peter immediately headed for the upstairs, but a commotion at the front door sidetracked him.

The Manchesters had arrived, which necessitated a certain amount of obligatory cooing and clucking on his part. Peter then led them over to a group of older guests and the Manchesters sat down on the couch next to the hard-of-hearing Professor Emeritus Gordon Hapgood-Smith.

"Wonderful speech yesterday, Franklin," said Peter. "It certainly ranks up there with your best."

"No need to put a gloss on it, Peter. It wasn't my finest hour."

"I just hope that the young audience appreciated what you had to say."

"I think they were all too hung-over to notice," said Manchester.

"Oh, Franklin, please. Give them some credit," said Helene.

"Now, don't you patronize me, Helene." Franklin turned to Peter, "I bet you nodded off there for a while?"

Peter chuckled, "When you were handing out diplomas, I may have given my eyes a rest. The heat was killing, especially under those robes."

Peter occasionally glanced over towards the second-floor landing as he tried to determine where Jennifer was, yet not neglect the Manchesters.

"Well, next year you won't have to put up with me. The curtain is coming down on this old warhorse."

"And we all appreciate what you've done for Grodin. I know I do," said Peter.

"Thank you, Peter," said Helene, smiling politely.

"I'm off, duty calls."

"Do tell Glynnyth we're here."

Peter tried to get away. "I shall. I shall."

"Where is she?" Franklin asked.

"The kitchen. Where else? Apparently we have a caterer who requires constant supervision."

"Ah, yes, of course…in the kitchen," answered Helene. "Believe me, I'm well-aware of what's involved in putting on these little get-togethers."

Peter scurried off, then called back to Helene. "I won't forget to tell Glynnyth."

Franklin whispered to Helene, "I bet he does."

"Franklin!" said Helene, though not entirely scandalized.

Once again Peter tried to scale the stairs, which now served as the hangout of choice for the party's avant-guard contingent of younger guests who were so involved in their conversations that they scarcely noticed it was their host who was trying to maneuver his way past them.

About halfway up, Peter squeezed by Janet Baker. Making sure their bodies did not touch, they made eye contact only.

"Dr. Grande, I presume," said Janet, insouciantly. She had been drinking, as had everyone else except for the Petersons, who were from Utah.

"And a very good evening to you, too, Professor Baker," said Peter.

Janet lifted an eyebrow, tilted the tip of her Heineken at him and took a suggestive sip.

"Thank you for the chocolate. And the flowers."

Peter acknowledged her thank-you by raising his own eyebrow before continuing on up the stairs.

Once on the landing, he glanced down the hallway and saw that the bathroom door was closed, presumably with Jennifer Moore behind it.

Leaning over the balcony railing, Gunther Hass, a professor of $20^{th}$ Century European Literature, and Peter's buddy, Pierce, looked down at the party below them like two cattlemen assessing their herds at an auction.

Gunther waylaid Peter by saying, "great party, Peter. Great little wing-ding, as per usual."

"Excuse me, Gunther, but are you tenured?" asked Pierce.

"I most certainly am," said Gunther.

"Then there's no need for you to suck up to The Chair, is there?" said Pierce.

"That's also why I can say nice things now and then. Kind of a reverse truth to power. Academic freedom and all that rubbish, you know," said Gunther.

"Ah, yes, we have the freedom to pontificate on all matters, great and small," said Pierce. "Mostly small, of course."  Pierce paused, then asked Peter, "isn't there some nasty committee you could put Gunther on, just to let him know that 'The Chair' is still in charge?"

Peter looked at the ceiling as if in deep thought. He then said, "We could probably use more faculty input on the New Student Orientation Committee."

"Oh, god," said Gunther. "This is what happens when those in power have too much time on their hands."

"But thinking up stuff like that is half the fun of being Chair," said Peter, "knowing that you can make someone's life completely miserable."

"Ah, the sweet privilege of rank," said Pierce.

"What is power for if it can't be abused?" said Peter.

"You know though, that if you put either of us on that committee, we'd just screw it up," said Gunther. "The admins do a fine job of making the trains run on time. Don't over-think this, Peter."

"Yes, we're idea-people, not detail-people," said Pierce.

"But isn't "over-thinking things" what we do for a living?" said Peter.

"I wouldn't go there if I were you," said Pierce. "*Canes dormiens non movere*. Sleeping dogs and all that."

"No worries, Gunther.  If I were to stick someone on a committee like that, it would be someone like, well, um...no need to name names." Peter trailed off, content to let the conversation on this topic die.

"Great party, Peter," said Gunther, taking the heat off by reverting to the original subject.

They all chuckled and sipped their drinks while turning their attention to the scene below. Seeing that Harlan had replaced Ted behind the bar, Peter maneuvered around Gunther and Pierce so he could keep an eye on the bathroom door, which was still closed.

"Any hot rumors about who'll be the next president?" asked Gunther.

"All I know is that he—or she, of course—must be a person of great intellect, a superb scholar and an inspiring leader, but I've already let them know I'm not available," said Peter.

They all laughed.

"It's a good thing Franklin isn't reapplying. He wouldn't make the first cut," said Pierce.

"I heard from one of the board members that they're looking for a business type. Someone from outside 'the community,'" added Gunther.

"Oh, God save us from the bean-counters," said Pierce.

"If the worst happens, we'll just have to school him...or her...on what academia is all about," said Peter. "Have to let him...or her...know that a college is not a popsicle stand."

"You mean it isn't?" exclaimed Pierce. "The things we learn in the winter of our discontent." He paused, then added, "um, make that 'content.'"

They all laughed again. When Peter saw Jennifer leave the bathroom, he broke away to intercept her at the top of the stairs.

"Jennifer, hello," said Peter. "I'm sorry I haven't had a chance to talk with you yet. I've been a perfectly rotten host. I hope you're having a good time."

"Oh, I am," she said.

"I know that these faculty get-togethers can be a bit much when you don't know everyone."

"Oh, no, everyone's been just great, Dr. Grande."

"Peter."

"Peter," she said. "Real nice."

"So, I imagine you have some exciting plans for the summer?"

"Oh, no, not really. I mean, Harlan's going to be busy with his book, and I...well, I have my job at the insurance office," she said.

Peter looked at her with a seriousness that was completely feigned. "You seem....concerned about something."

Jennifer looked puzzled. "Concerned? No, I'm okay. Really."

Peter looked around then moved closer to her. "Jennifer, many speak with you for a moment?"

Jennifer looked puzzled. To her mind, they were already speaking with each other. "Sure, I guess."

Peter took her arm. "Come with me. Just for a minute." He guided her into his upstairs office and turned on a tiny desk light.

"Jennifer, in the short time you've been at Grodin, I've seen how you've been Harlan's source of strength, his rock, so to speak, and I know you must be worried about his tenure situation because that's the kind of person you are." He sighed heavily, hoping to give the appearance of deep sympathy. " I hope you realize I'm very fond of Harlan, too, and that I hold him in the highest regard."

"Oh, you do?" Jennifer said.

"Of course, but…" he paused, "…I'm afraid I see a bit of a problem. A small bump in the road."

"Oh, no!"

"You must realize that this is very difficult for me to say, and I must ask that what I tell you be held in the strictest confidence." Peter looked up at the ceiling and sighed, as though he were about to reveal a state secret upon which the fate of the world rested. "I think Graham is giving Harlan some rather poor advice on his book, and if his book were to come out right now in its present state, it could seriously damage his tenure possibilities. Of course, officially we shouldn't even be having this conversation, but I felt I should let you know the seriousness of the situation."

"Dr. Grande, that's just terrible."

"Peter," he said, hoping to correct her. "Yes, potentially tragic. It would be a terrible loss for the school. And to you."

Now in agony, Jennifer asked, "isn't there something you…we…can do?"

Glad that, at long last, she had asked, Peter answered, "Because he's working with Graham, there's nothing that I can do directly, but I do have a plan. I think…that you should advise him."

"Me? But I don't know a thing about 19$^{th}$ Century Amish Literature."

"I know, my dear, I know. But fortunately for our side, I do."

Peter knew that he knew nothing about Amish Literature regardless of the century, but he also knew that if he spent five minutes on the internet he would know enough to assure Jennifer that he did. After all, speaking convincingly on any subject was, indeed, what he and his fellow professors did for a living.

"But, if you can't even talk to him about it?" said Jennifer, her voice trailing off with the question.

"Here's what I'd suggest. I know that you work with him concerning grammar, style and that sort of thing, so, over the course of the summer, I'd like you to bring me the work in progress, but not to the department…nor by email, " he added quickly. "We'll go over it and I'll make a few suggestions about things you can bring up with Harlan."

Peter put his hands behind his back and took a few steps away from her.

"I hope you realize the delicacy of the situation. Because of Graham, I can't advise Harlan directly, and he mustn't suspect that you and I have been working together. He also has to believe that the suggestions are coming from you."

Having blurted this out, Peter took a deep breath and tried to assess its effect. "Jennifer, if your husband had to leave, it would be a terrible loss for Grodin…and the profession."

"Oh, Dr. Grande." Near tears, Jennifer gave him a big hug.

Rolling his eyes heavenward, Peter hugged her back. He gently grasped her arms and looked directly at her, his face just inches from hers. "We'll make a great team." Peter quickly kissed her on the forehead and, with his hand barely touching the small of her back, he gently guided her back to the door to the hallway.

"Duty calls."

He sent her off and peeked out from the doorway as she walked down the hallway to rejoin the party. Although she was either hopelessly naive, dumber than he thought, or both, Peter knew that this was potentially a very dangerous, not to mention a totally-stupid move on his part, but she was oh-so good-looking that he felt compelled to give it a shot. If it didn't work out, he could step back gracefully and act as though there had been nothing untoward in his actions. No Weinsteinian crudities would be involved; this would be a traditional, conventional seduction with Jennifer showing a willingness to come to him.

Downstairs, those guests who felt obliged to pay homage to the Manchesters had formed a ragged, impromptu queue in front of them. In turn, each approached, smiled, shook hands, chatted a bit and then moved on.

While Franklin was talking with one of the guests, Margaret Dreighton barged her way to the front of the line and stood over Helene, who was sitting next to Professor Emeritus Gordon Hapgood-Smith, who seemed to have fallen asleep. She was loosely-trailed by Paolo Antonelli, a good-looking young Italian who was dressed in South Florida casual. He appeared to be bored by the party and was indifferent to everything and everyone except when he noticed an attractive woman, a detail which did not go unnoticed by Margaret, who forged ahead nonetheless, knowing she would correct that particular bit of bad behavior at a time and place of her choosing. Her immediate objective was to pay homage to the Manchesters.

"Helene, I'd like you to meet Paolo Antonelli, a brilliant young poet from Dante's homeland. We met at a conference in Firenze this spring," said Margaret, drawing out the 'Fir-en-zay' in her best attempt at the Italian pronunciation.

Helene offered her hand. "I'm delighted to meet you, Paolo."

A bored Paolo bent over, barely touched her hand and flashed a tight smile before lapsing back into what seemed to be his normal state of sullen indifference.

On the couch next to Helene, Hapgood-Smith had slowly tilted forward with his head hanging down. It was still unclear as to whether or not he was awake, but now it was also unclear as to whether he might not tip forward and fall face-first to the floor.

Margaret continued, "the poor boy, there he was at the Literature conference, standing alone and looking around forlornly for a sympathetic shoulder to cry on, hoping, waiting for someone, anyone, who could understand both his poetry and his sensitive nature. Helene, I'd love to send you some of his verse, it will move you as deeply as anything you've ever read."

"I'm sure it would, my dear," said Helene.

Hapgood-Smith suddenly lurched backwards and whispered, "Helene, the boy's not wearing any socks."

"I'm sure he knows he's not wearing any socks, Gordon. He just doesn't want to. It's a fashion statement," said Helene quietly.

"Oh," said Hapgood-Smith, who then lapsed back into his normal state of somnolence.

Helene patted him on the thigh and smiled up at Margaret, giving her the entirety of her consummate professional attention.

"Paolo is incredibly, incredibly talented. I'm trying to find him a fellowship, but you wouldn't believe how difficult it is these days to get support for a young poet. Now if he were a computer programmer writing some stupid app, I'm sure the money would be pouring in, but when you're a poet...you suffer."

Hapgood-Smith lurched back to life and addressed Paolo, "Sonny, you forgot your socks."

Affronted, Paolo stared at him as though, through his remark, Hapgood-Smith had questioned the legitimacy of several generations of Antonellis. He then looked away scornfully.

"It's all right, Gordon," said Helene. "He hasn't forgotten his socks. He just doesn't like wearing them."

Margaret stared across the room at Peter, who was coming down the stairs, conveying with a glare her opinion that the guest list would have been improved significantly had it been shortened by one Dr. Gordon Hapgood-Smith.

"Obviously Paolo prefers natural spontaneity to boring conformity," countered Margaret. "I just wish the world could celebrate his specialness."

Trying again, Helene addressed Paolo, "what do you think of the United States, Paolo?"

"It sucks," said Paolo.

"Don't you just love his honesty? So direct," said Margaret.

"What is it about America that 'sucks,' as you put it, Mr. Antonelli?" asked Helene.

Paolo clearly had neither a coherent opinion nor an inclination to answer, so, undaunted, Margaret answered for him.

"Paolo is used to a much more sophisticated and refined life than what he finds here where we have completely forgotten...no, intentionally-disregarded...the life of the mind and the heart. Paolo is dedicated to the absolute pursuit of truth and beauty...beauty and truth. The pursuit of money, the almighty fucking dollar, totally disgusts him." Margaret stopped and crossed her arms in a defiant huff, as if waiting for a rebuttal which she would tear to bits.

"Do send me some of his work, Margaret," said Helene.

"I shall, Helene. I certainly shall."

Mission accomplished, Margaret turned and beamed at those waiting in line to talk with the Manchesters. Then, after scanning the room for another victim, she grabbed her boy-toy by the elbow and escorted him away.

Hapgood-Smith leaned towards Helene and repeated, "the boy wasn't wearing any socks."

"It's all right, Gordon," said Helene, patting his hand. "It's not his lack of socks that matters."

Surrounding the granite island in the kitchen, Glynnyth, Betsy, Meg and several young women from the caterer were busily assembling plates of *hors d'ouvres*. As reluctant partiers, Betsy and Meg used the kitchen as a refuge, preferring to help out there, thus minimize the mingling which might have been expected of them. Their husbands had long-since made it clear that they did not care to attend an event where the other participants cared not a whit whether they were there or not. Henrietta was a perennial no-show, arguing that unless she was being paid, there was no requirement in her job description that demanded she 'fraternize with the enemy' on her own time. No one dared to counter her argument.

Following his Mission-Accomplished with Jennifer, an energized Peter burst through the doorway with a force that would have sent small animals scurrying for cover, had there been any present.

"And how are the beautiful and lovely young scullery maids doing this evening?" The young women in question smiled awkwardly and quickly turned back to their work with renewed effort and focus.

"Would that description be including us?" questioned Meg.

"Always, Meg, always."

Meg scoffed, but Peter didn't notice.

He circled the island and gave Glynnth a peck on the cheek before realizing he still might be carrying the scent of Jennifer's perfume. He quickly backed away and stated boldly, "and how are you, my dear?"

"Try to keep in mind that I am holding in my hand a ten-inch chef's knife," said Glynnyth.

Peter picked up a deviled egg and popped it in his mouth. "Delicious. Why don't you come out and mingle? I'm sure these young ladies can carry on without you for a while, can't you, ladies?"

The ladies nodded that they indeed could, hoping that Peter would just go away.

"People out there are asking for you," said Peter.

Glynnyth lowered her voice and glared at him, "did it ever occur to you that I'd much rather be in here? And no one is actually asking *for* me, they're politely asking *about* me. They aren't really interested in civilians, especially those in 'the trades.'"

"The Manchesters are here," said Peter.

"Good," said Glynnyth curtly. "And soon they shall depart." She picked up a platter of *hors d'ouvres* and carried it to the door just as a young girl came in with an empty. In one swift move, Glynnyth swapped the empty tray for the full one. The girl spun around and headed back to the living room with the full platter held triumphantly out in front of her. Glynnyth took the empty tray over to the sink and washed it off.

Peter came up behind her and whispered, "Glynnie, please. Couldn't you just make an appearance for a couple of minutes?"

Glynnyth did not reply and Peter tried again. "Okay, thirty seconds. Say a couple of 'hellos,' a couple of 'how are you's' and you're out of there."

"Need I remind you that I gave up being an official faculty wife long ago."

"Glennie, it's the Manchesters. You actually like them."

"It's still a 'no,' Peter." She rinsed the tray and picked up a towel to dry it. "Besides, I'm sure you can find someone to stand in for me. You always have."

Peter grimaced, then tried another approach. "They'll probably be selling their house next year."

Glynnyth gave him a disdainful look. "And if they want me to list it, they'll call."

"I have to tell them something," said Peter.

"They'll understand. Or she'll understand. And they'll be too busy to notice anyway."

"No, but everyone else has noticed. But I don't care about them. All I care about is the Manchesters. Just them. I won't bother you for the rest of the night if you just go out and spend two minutes with them."

This offer hit home.

"One...one minute." Glynnyth took off her apron and dried her hands. With a sigh of relief, Peter escorted her to the door, lagging behind just long enough to pick up a second deviled egg and pop it in his mouth.

Later, under the darkened skies, after all the guests with small children, canes and hearing aids had said their goodbyes and left, the hard-core partiers carried on. To the neighbors' dismay, the retainers had gathered outside on the backyard patio where the hired-hand jazz trio had long since given way to an ad-hoc band of faculty members who tootled away on a hodgepodge of instruments. Playing his saxophone, Peter managed to struggle through a somewhat-recognizable version of *Let's Twist Again*.

Using her long scarf as a lasso, Margaret towed a reluctant Paolo to the center of the impromptu dance floor where she led him in an incongruous tango to the beat of Chubby Checker's greatest hit. By alternately holding him in a close embrace and then striking dramatic poses worthy of Isadora Duncan, her performance was, if not artistic, was highly-entertaining.

In the shadows at the edge of the crowd, members of the younger set coolly smoked some weed and snickered at the goings-on of the so-called adults in the room.

By midnight, the caterers had packed up, leaving Peter and Glynnyth to survey the damage. Together, they silently worked their way through the detritus in the living room, straightening lamps and chairs, picking up the odd glass and stuffing napkins and paper plates into black plastic trash bags.

"Thanks, Glynnyth…for putting up with all this," said Peter.

Glynnyth silently continued to clean, then said, "the entire office is coming over next weekend. I imagine you'll be free to cook, clean up, smile at everyone and have a good time."

"Aren't we going to the Bradfords on Saturday?"

Glynnyth stopped cleaning and stared at him, letting him know that she being sarcastic. "Make sure the cups are empty before you toss them in."

"We could have had the party somewhere else. The department would have paid."

"Then, I would have had to mingle. I'd rather have this than that," said Glynnyth.

She paused and lit a cigarette.

"I didn't know you'd started smoking again," said Peter.

"Only when I feel the need to reward myself," said Glynnyth. "Besides, it helps mask the smell of all the academic bullshit."

"You used to enjoy our parties."

"When we had over only people we both liked."

"Who don't you like?"

"Don't push it, Peter. I'm not in the mood."

They continued to clean up in silence until Peter broke it, "still, I think it all went pretty well."

"Next time keep your saxophone in the closet."

## Chapter Sixteen
### Summertime—And The Living Is Easy


With school out, it was time for *Summers Off*—three months of indolence accompanied by a side-helping of sloth. Or perhaps it was *vice-versa*—three months of sloth with a side-helping of indolence.

For the faculty, the official stated purpose of *Summers Off* was to prep for the coming year by recharging the old intellectual batteries. It was an article of faith in academic circles that this activity was best realized at lakeside cabins, English B & B's and Italian villas, or while trekking the Himalayas or by lending one's expertise to an educational cruise where one might deliver one stimulating lecture per day and then lead an expedition ashore to explore a pile of ancient rubble—all capped off by cocktails and a five-course meal. The unstated reality was that all these modes of rest and relaxation were essentially value-signifiers and thus were carefully-planned to cover the important bases of personal growth, social good and résumé-enhancement.

Unless one had young children, visits to Disney World, Disneyland or any theme park with 'Adventure' or 'Wild' in its name were out of the question. Exploring nature was acceptable if the destination was exotic. Camping and road trips were looked down upon unless they were part of a world-improving mission to Third-World hot spots like BotswanaLand or some other fourth-tier hellhole which had recently experienced an unfortunate natural or man-made disaster. And, if installing a septic tank in Gambia was to be followed by a stopover in London to take in a play or two…well, that was a factor in 'Doing Good' that simply could not be helped.

Vacationing in a high-end European villa was acceptable if it was accompanied by rigorous cultural excursions to cathedrals, museums and galleries followed by up-close and personal analysis and evaluations of local cuisines and vinicultures. And if one were to get stuck having lunch in a two-star Michelin, such was the burden of overseas travel.

Social media posts had replaced postcards as the means of communication, although it was essential that they be artistic, humorous and insightful, yet appear to have been little more than casually tossed-off afterthoughts. One could earn extra credit if one returned from traveling with harrowing anecdotes of lost luggage, missed connections or examples of extraordinary rudeness dished out by surly locals, as long as said locals were not members of an officially-recognized oppressed or victimized group. However, should the anecdote be one of extremely-high conversational value, that rule could be ignored and the rude or surly behavior on the part of an oppressee would be excused if accompanied by appropriately-sorrowful descriptions of said unfortunate's suffering and misery.

No one could admit to visiting Fly-Over Country unless it was a mandatory event such as a relative's wedding, family reunion or funeral. If compelled to attend such occasions, upon their return, they could regale colleagues with amusing tales of culture clashes experienced while visiting Rube City, Hicksville or Boondocks' Landing. The subtext of these accounts would invariably confirm their conviction regarding the superiority of their own intelligence, judgment and manners—those qualities of character which lifted them into that rarified air high above the Land of the Great Unwashed. Of course, every member of the faculty would have died and gone to a non-secular heaven had they been able to secure a weekend invitation to the Hamptons or Martha's Vineyard, after which they could 'tsk-tsk' and be horrified by the excessive lifestyles of investment bankers, hedge-fund managers and movie stars—all while scarfing down their hosts' caviar and quaffing their Cristal champagnes.

Simple lounging-around was acceptable if done at a heritage cabin, cottage or summer house which had been in the family for generations, places where one was obliged to visit out of family loyalty.

For his part, Peter had come to prefer to stay close to home. He hated the details involved in planning his own trips and recently, with the assent of his sister, Mary, had begun to rent out the summer cottage in New Hampshire which they had inherited. With the kids long gone, it was now a relief not to have to spend time and he would be the first to acknowledge the dirty little secret about the various Lake Woebegones scattered throughout the Northeastern woods—the viciousness of the local mosquitoes in August was well 'above average.'

For Peter, with school now officially out for three months and with the arrival of the first lazy days of summer, everything felt different: plants were blooming, the days were heating up and the women had begun to show a little more skin.

His personal wearables changed with the season as well. Tweed jackets and khaki pants went into the closet and out came the Bermuda shorts and polo shirts. Unless there was a special event, every day was now a Casual Friday. With their shaggy Bohemian appearance and summer attire, the faculty as a group signaled to the world why they would never consider or be considered for corporate employment—except for the women, of course, who didn't go in for that sort of thing.

Today, Peter wore his favorite pair of experienced tennis shoes, plaid Bermudas and a faded Che Guevara T-shirt. Planning a leisurely ride to campus, he pushed his bike down the driveway. Across the hedge, Harry Atwater was busy pruning his roses.

"Morning, Peter," he said.

"Morning, Harry. I hope last weekend's party didn't keep you up too late."

"You had a party?"

"Yeah, about fifty-sixty people. For the department."

"Did the cops come?"

"No. No cops."

"Then it wasn't a party. The cops come…it's a party."

"Ah, these little differences of opinion are what makes America great."

"America is great, Peter, despite what all you lefties think."

"Yep, America is great, but we can always do better," said Peter.

"Yes, let's strive for greatness. We can agree on that," said Harry. "Looks like you're off to put in a hard day's work at the office."

Peter failed to notice the irony. "It's summer quarter. I'll just pop in for a few for appearance's sake and then hole up in my office and work on my book."

"Ah, yes, your book. How's the old best-seller coming?"

"Ha-ha," said Peter. "It's coming, Harry. Slowly, but it's coming."

"By the way, we're heading off to Europe for a couple of weeks later this month. Would you mind keeping an eye on the place? Of course, we have someone coming in to take care of the critters, but, you know, late at night…" Harry raised his eyebrows.

"I know, Harry. We live in a veritable crime zone," said Peter.

"You never know when a gang of Young Socialists might decide that my wine cellar needed liberating."

"Knowing you have that half-case of Margaux sitting down there, I might join them."

"Once a redistributionist, always a redistributionist."

"Share the wealth, baby. That's what we teach."

Peter pulled on his helmet and swung his leg over the bike. "I'll look after the old castle, Harry. Just let me know when you're going."

"Thanks, Peter. See you around Quad."

"Toodle-oo," said Peter as he pedaled off.

## Chapter Seventeen
### Crosswords At The Cafe

*I*n the summer, Peter biked to campus nearly every day when the weather was nice. Not only was the exercise good for him, the ride gave him time to think and organize his day without distractions, but for today, there was nothing on the agenda except for his weekly meeting with Betsy and Meg. As far as he knew, nothing important was happening, so he would sit down with them, chat up what few colleagues who were around and then spend what was left of the day working on his book.

Peter's ride to campus sometimes included a pit stop at the Tipsy Spoon Cafe, where he and some of his cronies had staked a claim to their own table out front on the sidewalk. For more than a decade Peter had been stopping several times a week at the Spoon for 'crosswords and coffee,' spending an hour or so 'exercising his intellectual muscles' while he and the gang worked at solving the Times' crossword puzzle.

When he arrived, most of the regulars were already there. The day's lineup included Jason, a routinely out-of-work computer-nerd who printed out copies of the puzzle and distributed them to whomever showed up; Harold, a semi-retired freelance copy editor who periodically paced off the mandatory twenty-five feet from The Spoon's front door to a spot where he could legally smoke a cigarette; Amanda, a sharp-tongued lesbian who co-owned *Les Deux Femmes Libre*, a feminist-oriented bookstore located just down the street; and Theodore Millet-Smith, an emeritus prof from the Human and Natural Sciences School, who enjoyed the company, occasionally contributed to the puzzle-solving, but usually dozed off, despite having just downed a couple of double expresso mochas. Except for Millet-Smith, all were work-averse coffee addicts who enjoyed nothing more than solving crosswords and commenting acerbically on the world scene from their seats in the nose-bleed section of the bleachers.

Peter pulled an extra-large coffee mug from his backpack and went inside to have it filled with his 'usual,' which was whatever was the Daily Special. By bringing his own mug and for a buck-fifty, 'the usual' came with free refills, to which he always added a generous teaspoon of sugar and a dollop of half-and-half.

Kendra, The Spoon's owner, loved making up names for her coffee blends. Today's Special was *Kenyan North Slope Killermanjaro Gorilla-In-The-Mist* extra-dark roast, and the fact that it differed in name only from yesterday's *Bill and Ted's Most Excellent Expresso Adventure* didn't bother her at all.

Peter picked up an almond bear claw and joined his fellow puzzle addicts at their table. He sat down next to Jason, looked over his shoulder and began filling in the partially completed puzzle onto his copy.

"What's the time so far?" asked Peter.

"Almost twenty minutes," answered Harold, without looking up.

"Jeez, what are we? A bunch of college students?"

"It's Thursday, remember? It gets tougher later in the week," said Jason.

"I lose track of the days in the summer, but. I'm here and am ready to rumble," said Peter."

"Thank God the crossword guru has arrived," said Amanda. "We can all relax now."

"Anyone have an eight-letter word for 'reliever'? Forty-five across. Blank, A-X, and ends in E?" asked Harold.

They study the puzzle intently.

"What do you think? Baseball?" said Peter, guessing at the puzzle's theme.

"No," said Jason, "it's medicine. Or health."

A tall man about Peter's age stopped and said hello. "Hey, Peter. Hard at work, as usual, I see."

"Hey, John. All work and no play, you know, dulls the…whatever," said Peter.

"From what I can tell it's more like 'no work and all play,'" said John, "but I'm just an outside observer."

"Life is hard," said Peter. "I could use a vacation, though not now. No sense in wasting those hard-earned vacation days during the summer."

"Like during the school year?" said Harold.

"You're a quick study, something I can't say about most of my students," said Peter.

"Some might say you've been on vacation your whole life," said John. "Try working in the private sector sometime."

"But I am in the private sector. I'm sure you're aware of the fact that Grodin is a private college. We proudly manage our own affairs, and if we happen to determine that for the overall good of the institution that the faculty needs a bit of time to rekindle the old intellectual fires, so to speak, well… that's why we have summers off."

"Seems pretty inefficient to me. Couldn't you just take a long weekend now and then?" said John. "Looks like the inmates are running the asylum."

"Now there's an original phrase," said Peter.

"I believe we did have an English Department at MIT, although they were kind of hush-hush about it," said John.

"Ah, the fear of the humanities strikes again."

"Yeah, the sight of a bunch of scruffy guys in leather-patched sports coats usually sends me running the other way as fast as I can, but that's mainly because I'm tired of being lectured to death about what a bad person I am," said John.

"That's what we do, John, speak truth to power," said Peter, "it sounds like it's 'Mission Accomplished,' as your guy once said."

"No politics, guys," said Jason.

"Everything's political," said Amanda. "Especially these days."

"With that, I think I'll 'move on,' before a class war breaks out," said John as he started walking away. "Have a great day, everyone. Be productive and keep the old economy humming."

"Oh, we will," said Peter.

John went off down the street and The Gang watched him until he was safely out of hearing range.

"Fascist asshole. "I don't know how you stand him," said Amanda.

"Our wives are friends," said Peter. "For a right-wing knuckle-dragger, he's not so bad," said Peter.

"He just needs to be educated," said Jason.

"Too late for that," said Harold. "Some people just need to be ignored." He paused, then added, "or shot."

"*Viva la revolution*," said Amanda as she took another sip of her five-dollar free-trade double-latte mocha.

"Doesn't he have a Ph.D. in Bioengineering or some other science thing like that?" said Jason.

No one responded until Peter finally added, "it's BioMolecular Genetics. He's got a company that's worth a couple of hundred million dollars."

"What do they make?" said Harold. "Germs?"

They all chuckled and then lapsed into silence while each contemplated what even a single one of those millions would mean to them.

The silence was broken when Jason said, "forty-five across. Laxative."

Everyone penciled it in on their copies.

"So that's how you spell 'relief?'" said Harold.

"I don't think that's a Times-worthy definition," said Peter.

"There's definitely been slippage," said Amanda.

They continued to work on the puzzle as Janet Baker, jogging down the street, held her hand up to her ear and mouthed 'call me' to Peter as she ran by.

## Chapter Eighteen
Side Hustle


*A*fter the gang completed the crossword at The Spoon, Peter left and headed on to campus. As he pedaled past the Wheeler Center for the Performing Arts, he was surprised to see a horde of black-clad waiters and waitresses hustling trays of food from several catering trucks up the stairs to the front veranda where they set them down onto cloth-covered buffet tables.

When he got to his office, he looked down at this beehive of activity and wondered what the hell was going on. It was summertime and such a hubbub was unusual. He called Meg, who came in and they stood at the window and looked down at the teeming swarm of workers.

"I've heard that Bliss is renting out Wheeler to outside groups this summer and I'm sure it's totally in line with Grodin's educational policy guidelines," she added sarcastically.

"One thing's for sure is that someone's spending a boatload of money. Look at that spread," said Peter. "Maybe we should think about it."

"For Jenkins?" said Meg skeptically.

"Just a thought," said Peter. "It wouldn't hurt to bring in a little extra money."

"I'll put it on the agenda for the fall faculty meeting," said Meg as she headed for the door, knowing full well that Jenkins would be at the bottom of anyone's list as a desirable rental venue and come the fall, Peter most likely would have forgotten he'd ever thought about it.

Meg left just as Pierce came in. He came over and stood at the window with Peter.

By now a large crowd of well-dressed adults had emerged from Wheeler and were attacking the elaborate buffet. The feeding frenzy was watched over by uniformed waiters and waitresses, who stood by attentively, ready to refill and replenish the tables' bounty as needed.

"Want to crash it?" said Pierce.

"I think someone might know who we were," said Peter.

"I knew a guy in grad school who kept a bunch of different name tags in his desk and when he saw a spread like this he would put on a sports coat, stick on the right tag and mingle. Never got caught and enjoyed loads of free food," said Pierce.

"So there is such a thing as a free lunch."

"If you play the name tag game right," said Pierce, "but unfortunately, we'll most likely be paying our own way today."

"And getting a lot less for it," said Peter.

With that, Pierce and Peter headed to lunch at the faculty club.

## Chapter Nineteen
The Faculty Club


$O$n Thursdays, Pierce and Peter regularly dropped in for lunch at the Markham Faculty Club, mainly to catch up on the latest gossip because no one went there for the food.

With a professoriat numbering only around a hundred and forty, Grodin could not support a faculty-only club for such a relatively small number of potential diners, so the profs shared a kitchen with the students. However, each group had its own dining room with the primary differences between them being that the faculty side had tablecloths, better china, and silverware that wasn't plastic.

In the summer, the clientele on the student side consisted of the captive members of whatever outside groups the administration could rope in and bring to campus to pay for tuition, room and board—anything that might bring in a few extra bucks to help pay for the fixed costs of running the college. These special week-long summer conferences and workshops ranged from *Quantum Mechanics for Dummies* to *Animal Husbandry*, which was not a colloquium for or about lonely sheepherders. Because these groups usually consisted of adults, there was not the usual general din generated from the student side as there was when school was in session. The one exception occurred in late June when Grodin hosted a camp for cheerleaders called Spirit Week. At breakfast, lunch and dinner, gung-ho teams of high school girls practiced their chants between bites, much to the consternation of the professors dining on the other side.

Once, facing the third day in a row of a lunch which featured unappetizing slabs of meatloaf smothered in congealed gravy, the girls (and two boys) began chanting "hey, hey, ho, ho…mystery meat has got to go," alternating that chant with shouts of "what do we want?"

"Pizza!

"When do we want it?"

"Now!"

At the insistence of the faculty dining on the other side, the administration arranged for Domino's to deliver for the rest of the week.

Lunch at Markham was always served buffet-style, so The Two P's picked up their plastic trays and pushed them along the chrome rails which ran in front of the deli case that displayed the day's offerings. After passing on the kale and quinoa salad, Peter loaded up on the day's special—pork chops, mashed potatoes with gravy and a couple of gummy Parker House rolls. His flyover of the kale and quinoa salad induced in him a momentary tinge of guilt, but he mentally offset that by also passing on the tantalizing tuna melt. Then, in a token oblation to the food gods, he added a cluster of red grapes to his plate, but then, demonstrating his usual lack of will power, he picked up a thick slab of chocolate mousse cake.

With Pierce right behind him, Peter slid his fully-loaded tray to a stop in front of the cashier's station, which was deserted. Irritated that there was no one at the register to check them out, he finally caught the eye of the Club's head chef, Oscar Gravelitis, who scowled back at him through the narrow window that separated the buffet line from the kitchen. Peter made a 'what are we to do' gesture to Oscar, who deepened his scowl, but finally came out from the kitchen, wiped his hands on a towel and, without a word, grumpily punched their lunch cards.

As a side gig, Oscar was the main union rep for Grodin's service workers —the janitors, groundskeepers, maids, hospitality workers, etc. He was terrible at his day job as head chef, but as a union rep, he was superb. Tough and unreasonable, he had battled the administration for over twenty years. Known to be a no-holds-barred street-fighter, he had once, during a negotiation, uttered the phrase, "I spit on your grave," and then, after a pause, added the syllable, 'ey.' This led those on the management team to worry whether this was his way of hinting he might have been seasoning the kitchen's otherwise undistinguished offerings with his own personal 'special sauce.'

With sartorial preferences that leaned towards Marlon Brando T-Shirts that showed off his hairy armpits and ample chest hair, Oscar's scowling presence dominated the faculty club's kitchen and had frightened and intimidated a generation of students and faculty. All that was lacking to complete the Full Brando Look was a cigarette that dangled dangerously from his lips over a hot sauté pan, but Oscar Gravelitis, for all his vices and shortcomings, didn't smoke.

As the two of them made their way to their usual table, Peter noticed Margaret sitting with her coven of female friends in the corner—a space described by some of the male faculty members as Harpy Central. Margaret first instinctively glared at him, but then broke character, waved and gave both of them an uncharacteristic wide smile. Peter knew something had to be up and figured he would find out about what it was soon enough.

With the student side now empty after graduation and faculty attendance decimated by summer vacations, the Faculty Club was usually quiet, almost funereal. Today, however, Jack Harwood from Environmental Studies was in the middle of one of his famous rants—this one about saving the world by using compressed alfalfa pellets as a peat and coal substitute. Apparently, some fellow environmentalists in Ireland were pressuring peat excavators to curtail their activities because not only were they altering the state of the natural landscape, they were also contributing to the dreaded global warming climate change.

Harwood was famous for the extreme lack of concern he had for his personal appearance. His everyday 'uniform' of heavy denim pants, steel-toed work-boots and long-sleeved wool shirts worn even in summer, in itself was well outside the norm, but it was his personal hygiene that brought him campus-wide notoriety. It was suspected that he bathed only once a quarter and his hair was always at least one standard deviation beyond what would normally be considered as unruly.

The students had nicknamed Harwood 'The Fang,' because occasionally a long, thick shoot of nose hair would sprout from his nasal foliage's heavy undergrowth and curve out menacingly from one of his nostrils. It was a recurrent matter of speculation as to whether, with a sudden turn of his head, 'The Fang's' fang could impale an unwary fly that had unwisely buzzed into the killing zone.

"Economics be damned!" Harwood shouted to Donald Duong, who was the only person actively paying attention to him. Peter knew Duong only by reputation; he was a militant environmentalist whose 'Save The Planet' views included advocating for the extreme culling of the human herd. Naturally, he believed that he and his fellow like-minded 'evolved thinkers' should be the ones in charge of the herd-thinning process. He was also the kind of guy whose neighbors would describe as extremely quiet and polite after having learned he had 'Gone Postal' in a faculty meeting, which, should a confidential survey be taken, would show that 'Going Postal' was not an uncommon fantasy amongst members of the faculty.

Long experience had taught the Grodin professoriat that it was best to simply let Harwood's rants run their course. Interruptions or attempts at diversion were futile as they inevitably led him down new paths of thought which also had to be fully explored. It was best to let him go until his argument, like the river that flows to the ocean where it dissipates, is absorbed and finally disappears.

After finishing his rant, Harwood abruptly picked up his tray and departed, thus allowing normal conversations to resume, whereupon Peter and Pierce continued their discussion of Bliss's expanding empire. Peter was less sanguine about it than Pierce, who always looked on the brighter side.

"Look, old chum, it's not worth being bothered about. Let it go. We're coming to the end of the line. Just put the old jalopy on cruise-control."

"Isn't that what we've been doing for years?"

"Now, now," said Pierce. "Save the truth-telling for later. After we've retired."

As they were on their way out after finishing their lunches, Margaret quickly stood up from Harpies' table and rushed over to them.

"I need you to sign this," she ordered, shoving a clipboard at them. It held a petition that called for the administration to improve the faculty club's cuisine.

"We should not have to put up with this," she said. "The food is terrible and everyone knows it. We should have paninis with buffalo mozzarella. Plates of antipasti. Wagyu beef. Kale salads, and ..."

"We already have kale salads," said Pierce.

"Yes, but they're terrible. They use that crappy curly kind instead of Tuscan Black Lacinato." She continued on, "what do we have? Mac and cheese that's the consistency of rubber. And Meatloaf! Meatloaf's diner food, for god's sake. We're prisoners here. We have no alternatives. The nearest so-called restaurant is that ridiculous Taco Bell down on Main."

"I'm glad to see that you're working hard to improve life on campus. I'm behind you all the way, Margaret," said Peter said as he signed the petition.

"Pierce?" Peter asked as he handed him the clipboard.

"Oh, I'm on board as well," said Pierce. "The food here is definitely swell...um...I mean, 'swill.'"

"Finally, Margaret, something we can agree on," said Peter.

"Thank you so much," said Margaret, uttering the words 'thank you' as though she had never used them before.

After she was out of earshot, Peter said, "running into her is a good way to spoil your lunch."

"And a spoiled lunch here is a very low bar," said Pierce.

"Anything that gets her out of what's left of my hair is fine with me," said Peter.

"How about sending her on a permanent sabbatical?"

"If I thought I could get it through, I would," said Peter.

"Speaking of meatloaf, The Times once had an article on Meatloaf, the rock and roll guy?"

"I know who he is. Or was," said Peter. "Is he still....?"

"Good question. I have no idea," said Pierce. "After the first paragraph intro they kept referring to him, in Times-speak, as 'Mr. Loaf.'"

Peter laughed. "At least it wasn't 'Mr. Meat.'"

Peter stopped and started off in another direction, prompting Pierce to ask, "going back to the department?"

"Um, no, I have to see someone."

"Going to see a man about a dog?"

"Maybe," said Peter

"Do I know that particular dog?"

"You might,"

A bitch?

"Sometimes more than I would like, but..." said Peter, smiling.

# Chapter Twenty
## The Ultimatum

"*D*on't hurt yourself," said Janet.

Groaning feverishly, Peter huffed and puffed and twisted the edge of the bed-sheet with one hand while supporting himself with the other. Beneath him, Janet Baker sighed in boredom and stared at the ceiling. Peter continued gyrating wildly, his excitement mounted. After he groaned and finished, Janet kissed him gently on the forehead.

"Good boy," said Janet, who, with her Long Island accent, pronounced 'boy' as 'buoy.'"

Exhausted, Peter flopped back against a pillow as Janet leaned over, plucked an apple from a bowl on the bedside table which she bit into with considerably more enthusiasm than she had shown at Peter's exertions in their tussle between the sheets.

She sat up, pulled the sheet up over her and said, "I'm thinking of taking that job in Albuquerque."

"Seriously?"

"Yeah, seriously."

"You can't," said Peter. "You absolutely cannot."

"And why not?"

"It's a nothingburger. It's not tenure track so there's no future in it," said Peter, still trying to catch his breath.

"Unlike here," said Janet sarcastically.

"Stay here and you'll have a full-time position in a couple of years. I guarantee it."

"Is someone going to retire that I don't know about?" She then turned over to face him. "Or have a heart attack while fucking his mistress?"

"Can't we could talk about this later?"

Janet shrugged, "you never want to talk about anything."

"Anything?" said Peter. "Isn't 'anything' a bit of an exaggeration?"

"Okay, you're right. Turn this into a discussion about semantics."

"You know I'd hire you in a New York minute if it were up to me."

"Yeah, well, I'm thinking about New Mexico," said Janet, "but I repeat myself."

Peter sighed and got up. He put on one of Janet's robes, went over to the refrigerator and looked in. "You never have anything to eat."

"We could go out," said Janet.

Peter glanced over at her with a look that said 'going out' wasn't possible and she knew it.

"Then try bringing something besides yourself to the party." Janet propped herself up on the pillows, lit a cigarette and languidly exhaled.

"Maybe I should just murder someone like they do on those English TV mystery shows. Oxford and Cambridge seem to be real hotbeds of crime."

"Yeah, but the murderers always get caught."

"Depending on who gets murdered, it could be worth it."

We're going to Rhode Island for the Fourth," said Peter. "I'll see what I can do when I get back."

Janet looked at him skeptically.

"I will," said Peter. "Seriously."

"The ball is in your court," said Janet, as she blew out a puff of smoke.

## Chapter Twenty-One
### Road Trip

$P$eter always liked the Fourth of July. With the student body off for the summer and the faculty playing hooky in far-flung vacation spots, by early July West Beresford had almost become an academician-free zone. Regular citizens were able to hold a traditional parade and celebration without the usual *pro forma* grumblings from the Grodinites about such overt displays of patriotism, overlooking the fact that patriotism was the *raison d'etre* for the holiday. But because West Beresford was a municipality still located in the modern, progressive state of Massachusetts and was now over two centuries removed from the freedom-loving Colonial mindset which led to the armed rebellion against the Crown, open displays of patriotism were counter-balanced by acts of whimsy and general goofiness.

High school bands marched, veterans' groups in moth-eaten uniforms waved to the sidewalk crowd and kids walked with their pets on leashes, or *vice-versa*, depending upon the size of the dog and the size of the kid. Local businesses sponsored commercial floats and auto dealerships provided rides for the local politicians who could pay their obligatory homage to the holiday without having to endure the discomfort of actually pounding the pavement. Wearing flat-top straw hats, members of the Elks, Moose, Lions, Oddfellows, and other civic clubs rode by in vintage convertibles. Buffed-out, hunky firemen, promoting their annual beefcake calendar, stood on firetrucks as they drove past the Dunkin' Donuts store on Main where several unbuffed local cops looked on enviously as they bit into their favorite hunk of fried dough. And bringing up the rear, just ahead of the city's street-sweeper, a band of self-proclaimed artists and ne'er-do-wells played kazoos and pranced around, signaling the parade's end and the beginning of holiday picnics and barbecues —all leading up to the evening's fireworks finale.

Unfortunately for Peter, this year he would have to forego his secret pleasure as Glynnyth had made other plans—for the both of them. An old college friend from Rhode Island had invited her down for the Fourth and, for reasons left unclear, she wanted Peter to go with her.

The drive down on the Third was uneventful, except for their usual spat about 'direct' versus 'scenic,' with Glynnyth opting for the latter and Peter arguing that there was nothing 'scenic' about any route between Great Beresford and Newport. Also as usual, Peter lost. The only virtue in losing was that he could ignore all of the so-called scenery, because as was the case on all of their road trips, Glynnyth drove while he read. In a continuous display of displeasure, he assiduously studied his IPad and looked out the window only when he needed to keep from getting carsick.

Needless to say, conversation was minimal.

By being forced to come, Peter figured he was being punished for some unknown transgression which had been long stored away in Glynnyth's personal Grievance Vault. Through extensive experience, he knew it was best not to make inquiries into the particulars of his *peccadillo*.

Glynnyth's friend, Denise, was her college roommate for a couple of years at Georgetown.   Several years ago, she and her husband, Ralph, purchased an old shingle-style beach house on the western shore of Narragansett Bay. After retiring from his Manhattan law practice several years ago, Ralph immediately plunged into remodeling the three-story building which sat above the shore of a small inlet. However, while they were away two winters ago, a freaky, fierce nor'easter froze the pipes on the windward side of the house, after which a neighbor noticed what looked like a gigantic pimple forming on the lawn and called Ralph just as it burst and completely flooded their new basement. After much haggling, lawyer Ralph got the insurance company to pay for most of the damage and the once-restored house was then re-restored.

Glynnyth and Peter arrived in the late afternoon and Ralph, Denise and Glynnyth immediately embarked on long discussions about contractors, repairs, renovation and real estate values—all of which were talked about in excruciating detail over drinks, dinner and dessert, after which Ralph broke out his fancy tequilas and poured everyone a series of tasting flights.

The next morning, Peter woke up with his head throbbing. He had forgotten how easily tequila went down and the nasty kick it could deliver. To feel better, Peter felt he needed more than the hair of the dog, he needed a whole dog, but unfortunately, it was the Fourth of July and the pound was closed.

Glynnyth and Denise had gone for an early morning walk down the beach, so Peter was left to recuperate on his own. He managed to dodge Ralph for most of the morning, citing the always-handy excuse of needing to work on his book.

The group plan for the Fourth was to drive around the Bay to Bristol and catch the local parade, which, compared to West Beresford's amateur hour, was a huge deal. Ralph was excited because Tom Brady was to be the parade's Grand Marshall. Despite being New Yorkers, Ralph and Denise were hardcore Patriots' fans, which was a major factor in their decision to buy a second home in Rhode Island. They were thus able to attend every home game in Foxborough and yet easily head back to Manhattan for get-togethers with their kids and grandkids. The women, naturally, didn't mind checking out Tom Brady, although not sharing Ralph's man-crush on TB, Peter wouldn't have minded a Gisele-sighting, were there to be one.

The parade route was jammed with people, but Ralph knew a local attorney, so they were able to sit out on a second-floor office balcony above the rabble that packed the sidewalks and spilled out into the street. Denise had brought a picnic basket, so Peter was able to work on his hangover with an occasional sip of white wine from a styrofoam cup.

The distant sound of *Stars and Stripes Forever* signaled the parade's approach, and after several renditions of a couple of other Sousa classics, the Bristol high school band finally swung into view, led by a trio of spangly-clad twirlers who expertly tossed their batons into the air. The crowd cheered as Tom Brady waved at them from the back seat of a 1934 Cadillac Phaeton convertible, which had been freshly-painted in Patriot Blue.

Unfortunately for Peter, there was no Gisele-sighting, but there was one of his arch-nemesis, J. Bliss Moynihan. Sporting a fedora and Pince-nez glasses, a smiling Bliss looked very much like FDR gracing the masses with his presence as he entertained a laughing Tom Brady in the back seat of the Phaeton. All that was missing was the long cigarette holder clenched between his teeth.

Peter suddenly felt sick to his stomach and it wasn't from the previous night's tequila-tasting.

After the Brady/Bliss Phaeton passed out of sight, Glynnyth eagerly enumerated the degrees of separation which existed between themselves and The Brady and determined there were way fewer than six. Summarized succinctly, husband Peter knew the guy sitting next to The Guy. Peter didn't know, nor did he want to know, how Bliss had finagled his way into the Brady entourage—it was dispiriting enough just to know that he'd been able to. If golf was a good walk spoiled, then being forced to watch the success of one's arch enemy was at least a good day ruined. Maybe even a month or a year.

As the rest of the parade passed by, Peter consoled himself with a mimosa that Ralph had whipped up. Now able to truthfully claim a continuing headache and citing the inherent difficulties of completing such a mission, he resisted his companions' efforts to find and congratulate Bliss with their mutually-unspoken hope of upgrading their brush with fame from economy to first-class. For Peter, the last thing he wanted was to run into Bliss in a moment of triumph.

Back at Denise and Ralph's, Peter woke from his late afternoon nap and came downstairs to find Ralph at his computer assiduously searching the internet, trying to determine where to best view the evening's fireworks. Ralph was all-too-willing to share his thoughts as he scanned and reviewed videos of past performances and strategized about where the primo spots would be. He iterated his thoughts about the details in a stream of consciousness fashion which was simultaneously annoying and amusing. It was hard to comprehend that such a matter would command the intensity of attention that Ralph was bringing to it.

Peter eventually figured out that the plan was to take Ralph's fifty-foot boat out and, depending on how much wind there was, either sail or motor over to the location and weigh anchor directly under the fireworks. This whole undertaking did not appeal to Peter as he hated boating and had a life-long predisposition towards motion sickness, but he doubted that he could beg off.

Ralph finally decided that Newport offered the best opportunity, both for viewing and for the quality of the fireworks extravaganza.

Meanwhile, Glynnyth and Denise had been joined in the house by another couple, the Brinkmans, who were from D.C., but had a summer place nearby. They had been classmates of Glynnyth and Denise at Georgetown.

The Brinkmans, both short people with high-pitched nasal voices, were attorneys who had spent their adult lives working for non-profits and think tanks in D.C. With the male Brinkmann topping out at five-two and his wife at four-ten, they occasionally joked about being 'ten feet of trouble,' since they viewed their mission in life to be that of defending the 'little people,' both figuratively and literally, from 'The Bigs,' whether the behemoths were giant corporations or governmental entities. At one time, they had considered changing their name to Brink(wo)man, but quickly abandoned that fleeting notion, correctly thinking that such an idealistic move was perhaps not career-enhancing should they ever, god forbid and heaven forfend, be forced to labor in the private sector. With the three wives and the male Brinkman having gone to college together, there was plenty of reminiscing about the good old days at Georgetown and when the conversation diverged from that topic, it turned to D.C. insider politics and legal discussions. All this left Peter on the outside listening in, and although the foursome made an occasional small move to include him, in truth, he didn't mind being ignored.

As the sun was setting behind the house, Ralph asked Peter to help him haul up dinner from the dock. Ralph had spent a good part of the days prior to the Fourth buying up sacks of oysters from various spots around Narraganset Bay, hauling them home and submerging them off his dock to keep them fresh. With the grill now fired up, Ralph planned to serve some on the half-shell and roast the rest for a major-league oyster-tasting. Peter dutifully helped him haul the oyster-filled canvas bags up to the deck where some of the mollusks would meet their end over hot coals. Peter was glad that lobsters were not on the menu, not that he had any compunctions about eating them, he just preferred not to be present when they were dispatched.

With dinner in the offing, Ralph had put on a chef's jacket and a yachting cap and set out bowls of marinades, flavored butters and hot sauces. Uncorked bottles of Chablis and champagne lay in wait nearby in a large ice-filled tub. Alongside each plate, Ralph had placed a pre-printed scorepad for the serious business of grading the quality of the various *huitres* which he had collected.

After the guests assembled on the deck, the feast began.

Peter quickly discovered he was especially partial to the Oysters Rockefeller—*huitres* grilled and topped with a complicated sauce of butter, shallots, garlic, spinach, herbs, Romano cheese and, ummmm…wait for it… bacon. If you've ever watched cooking shows on TV, you soon realized that the universal go-to ingredient was bacon, the one component guaranteed to send any dish into gastronomic overdrive, including even cookies and ice cream. Like the tequila tasting the night before, Peter discovered that taken together, oysters and Chablis went down easily and well.

Perhaps too easily and too well.

On the way over to Newport and the fireworks, Peter spent most of the trip staring at the horizon while hanging on to the stern rail in an ultimately unsuccessful effort to avoid throwing up. The fireworks which eventually burst overhead against the velvet sky were the perfect metaphor for the rumblings going on down below in his digestive tract. By the end of the evening, Peter felt that taken together or separately, fireworks and boating were vastly over-rated.

Another morning, another hangover.

Peter's head was throbbing as they said their goodbyes and began the drive home. As on the drive down, Glynnyth was behind the wheel. After a few miles, she said, "I knew you wouldn't have a good time."

Recognizing a marital minefield when he saw one, Peter weighed his response carefully. To say he had 'had a good time' would be to deny the obvious, yet to admit that he hadn't would open himself up for criticism about his lack of effort, commitment, etc., etc., any of which was likely to lead to an unwelcome discussion about the state of 'The Relationship,' something he always wished to avoid, but particularly now, while trapped in a car, inconvenienced and partially-disabled by his hangover.

He decided his best alternative was to minimally admit to his own failings without a complete grovel. He certainly knew that Glynnyth was looking for a fight and he wasn't up for one.

So…yes, he said that he tried to have a good time, but confessed that he could have tried harder. He argued that it was not entirely his fault as these were not his friends and even though they were nice, interesting people, he didn't have a lot in common with them. He ended by saying that despite all that, he was glad that he'd come and hoped that Glynnyth had had a good time.

He knew this was not a complete mollification, but was just enough to prompt Glynnyth to get on the phone with clients and set up appointments for the coming week. Peter took advantage of this and slept for the rest of the drive home, where Bark, as usual, was glad to see him. Meow…not so much…also as usual.

## Chapter Twenty-Two
Summertime—And The Living's Still Easy

*B*y mid-month, the horror of the Fourth of July weekend was well in Peter's rear-view mirror and Summers-Off was on cruise-control—at least until after Labor Day when fall classes would start-up.

In Peter's neighborhood, the sounds of leaf blowers and Taco-truck music filled the air. Plump robins stalked worms on the ground while sprinklers lazily sprayed their haloed mists over lush-green lawns. Under leafy maples, a gaggle of kids had left their cellphones and computers inside and had dared to venture outside to bounce a rubber ball off the wooden front steps of an old Victorian. A delivery man hoisted a plastic bottle of spring water onto his shoulder and lopsidedly trundled it up to a front porch. Nearby, a postwoman in Bermuda shorts slowly pushed her three-wheel cart down the sidewalk and distributed to each house its daily allotment of junk mail.

In his upstairs office, Peter's computer displayed a page from his *21$^{st}$ Century Field Guide,* but, as usual, he wasn't working on it. Instead, he was peering intently into a tripod-mounted telescope that was aimed at his neighbor's backyard pool, which was being cleaned by a nubile young woman wearing only the southern half of a bikini. She moved the vacuum languidly up and down the sides of the pool wall, apparently content, if necessary, to spend the rest of the summer cleaning it.

Peter's iPhone rang. Seeing that the call was from Glynnyth, he let it go to voice mail. When she'd finished and hung up, he expertly thumbed through the phone menu and listened to her message without taking his eye from the telescope.

"I'm going to have to pass on tennis with the Duchins. Would you let them know I'm sorry I had to cancel? I'm having dinner with a client and will be home around nine-thirty. See you then."

With a practiced move, Peter ended the message and punched in a number from his list of Favorites.

Janet answered. "Hello, Peter. What's up?"

The pool-cleaning nymph had turned toward the telescope, displaying the full extent of her talents.

"Hi, Janet. I was thinking about you when I got a call from the Duchins about doubles at the Club. Would you be free around four?"

After a long pause, she answered, "I suppose."

"It would be helpful if you stayed in his good graces," said Peter.

Janet sighed.

"Your enthusiasm is overwhelming."

"It's the Duchins, Peter. I mean, she's okay, but God, Chet is the most boring guy imaginable. And who goes by 'Chet' these days anyway?

Especially when you're seventy-goddamn-something years old."

Peter thought about saying, 'Chet does,' but stopped himself. "So he's a little old-fashioned, but he is on the hiring committee."

Janet said nothing, thinking it over.

"You wanted me to do something, I'm doing something," said Peter.

Janet sighed again. "I'll be there."

## Chapter Twenty-Three
Drama Drama


*W*ith late afternoon tennis in the offing, Peter drove to campus in his Beemer instead of riding his bike. It was one of those rare summer days in Massachusetts when he regretted that he hadn't popped for a convertible when he bought the BMW. He figured he'd put in a token appearance at the department, work on his book for an hour or so, then hit the tennis court with Janet and the Duchins. Stopping by Meg's office, he asked her if there was anything going on.

"Figg-Thornton just called. He won't be able to teach the afternoon session today," said Meg.

Peter looked at her quizzically.

"The Summer Institute. Cummings had the morning session."

Ah, the High School Drama Teachers' Summer Institute. Peter had forgotten all about it. For nearly forty years the Summer Institute had brought in fifty-or-so high school drama teachers for a two-week-long 'immersion' program in the art and craft of teaching drama. (Pierce called it 'Drama for Dummies,' but he refused to say whether the 'Dummies' in question were the high school students or their teachers.). Now down to only a week due to cutbacks in high school drama programs, the teachers, Dummies or not, still filled one residence hall from Sunday night to Saturday morning, which, after deducting the cost of room, board and other expenses, brought in roughly two hundred dollars per Dummy to the department. After paying the participating profs five hundred bucks per half-day session, whatever was left over went into a slush fund which allowed Peter to upgrade the annual faculty-staff retreat, if not to first-class, at least move it up from to business from coach.

"I hope Figgie isn't ill," said Peter.

"He's not, but he has to take his dog to the vet," said Meg.

"You're kidding."

"No, definitely not kidding," said Meg.

"Now I've heard everything, 'my dog ate someone's homework and got sick,' so now I can't teach?" said Peter angrily. "Tell him to get in here."

"I already tried," said Meg. "You know how he feels about Marlowe. He won't be budged."

Peter stewed for a moment, then asked, "who do we have who can fill in?"

"You mean 'whom do we have?'" said Meg, who was a stickler for grammatical correctness.

"Of course 'whom,'" said Peter with exasperation. "Do we have anyone?"

"The pickings are slim," said Meg. Then, eyeing Peter, she added, "you might be our last option."

"No way. I have a tennis match at four...with the Dean," he added, implying that it was 'business-related.'

Walking by and hearing Peter's retort, Henrietta scoffed, then headed straight for the coffee machine.

"Henrietta," asked Peter, "do you know if anyone's around who could fill in for Figg-Thornton? He has to take old Marlowe to the vet, if you can believe it."

"Good morning to you and no, I don't," said Henrietta.

"Sorry. Good morning," said Peter apologetically. "There's got to be someone who could take over?"

"Good Lord, Dr. Grande. It's the middle of July. You don't seriously expect to find an extra professor hanging around, do you?" said Henrietta.

"Great," said Peter.

"You could always cancel," said Henrietta.

"No, no, that wouldn't be good. They're only here for a week so they're no way to make it up. I'll teach it if you can't find anyone," said Peter, responding to his conscience's faint call of duty.

How about Boykins?" said Meg as she looked over the names on the faculty mailbox. "I think he's still around and working at home."

Henrietta poured herself some coffee and smirked at the notion of 'working at home.'

"Good idea," said Peter.

"But you should call him. He'll just lie and brush me off," said Meg.

"He'll lie, regardless," said Henrietta. "Is there any cream around here?"

"Just the fake stuff in the little plastic containers," said Meg.

Glumly, Peter headed for his office. "What's the topic for this afternoon?"

Meg leafed through a syllabus then read, "$20^{th}$ Century Drama: The Struggle for Meaning from Ibsen to Ionesco." Meg looked at Peter. "Do you think Boykins can handle it?"

"He'll damn well have to," said Peter.

"There's been some grumbling in the ranks," said Meg.

Wondering what she meant, Peter looked at her questioningly.

"Next week Artistic Expression is starting a new program called Broadway in the Berkshires. Dean Moynihan is bringing in some Broadway actress and her Off-Broadway director-husband and for a week of afternoon workshops, then dinner before taking in some summer stock at night. Our students found out about it." She paused, then added, "hence the 'grumbling.'"

"Sounds like it has all the academic merit of recess," said Peter.

"They said it sounded like 'fun,'" said Meg.

"So I suppose the 'grumbling,' as you call it, is because we're not wining and dining them and offering them field trips?"

"I believe 'boring,' was the word they used most often."

"So they talk to you?"

"I hear things."

"Good Lord, you'd think they'd act like professional educators instead of spoiled brats," said Peter.

"Just be sitting down when you read the course evaluations."

"You'll have to call Boykins," said Peter. If I called, I might bark at him."

"He'll probably try to beg off," said Meg.

"Then tell him to get in here or I most certainly will bark at him," said Peter.

Peter stomped off to his office, recognizing once again Bliss had gone on the offensive, although in his single-mindedness he doubtlessly was unaware that he had invaded another School's provenance.

At one time, the Summer Institute had been a strong magnet for the local players in high school drama circles, but Peter was well aware that its popularity had slipped. In its heyday, it had drawn a younger crowd, many of whom were as much interested in 'play' as they were in plays, and spending two weeks in a college dorm rekindled old memories of all-night bull sessions, pot parties and summer romances. In the early years, Peter and other faculty members had occasionally dipped their toes in the same waters, so to speak, and a good time was had by all. But now, with the aging of the teaching population, after-hours fun and games had given way to talk of pension plans and retirement communities. Also, other colleges had started similar programs and there was now no faculty member at Grodin who was sufficiently interested in giving up a significant chunk of his or her *Summers' Off* to try to pump new life into the Institute. So, on the verge of cancellation, it shuffled along, barely breathing.

Peter made a mental note to ask Meg to check on how registration for Bliss's new program was going—discreetly, of course. He hoped it would flop, but feared it wouldn't. As he was ruminating about how Bliss always seemed to be ten steps ahead in promoting his programs and himself, Meg knocked and stuck her head in the door.

"I called and Boykins doesn't seem to be around or he's not picking up his phone…" She paused, knowing that Peter would be unhappy with the thought that he'd have to fill in, then continued, "…but Harlan said he'd do it, though he warned me that he knew 'darn little about Twentieth-Century Drama.' His words, not mine."

"Well, at least I'll give him credit for stepping up and taking one for the team," said Peter.

"He also said his wife was pregnant and that the extra money would help," added Meg.

Peter hadn't given Harlan's wife much thought since the party, mainly because he hadn't been able to think of an approach which wouldn't have seemed like an obvious ruse, even to someone as dim as Jennifer. So he'd let it go, thinking that he'd take a chance on a serendipitous meeting. If it happened, it happened. Now that even that was out, he felt some relief, knowing he'd avoided a potentially-huge pothole. Better to have let some sleeping dogs lie, although there was nothing at all dog-like about Jennifer Moore.

# Chapter Twenty-Four
Tennis Anyone?

$A$ goodly number of the Grodin faculty belonged to the Witch Hill Country Club, which, though lacking both witches and a golf course, was a reasonably-priced option which allowed the professoriat and their families to retreat from the hubbub of town/gown life and get a taste of the lifestyle of the semi-rich *bourgeoisie*, a fact which they kept very much on the QT. Located on a wooded ridge high above West Beresford, the Witch Hill clubhouse looked down on one side at an Olympic-sized pool and a string of tennis courts, while to the east, it commanded a view of Great Beresford and the Naugahassett Valley.

The Duchins, Lois and Chet, were more delighted to play with Janet than she with them. Playing doubles, Peter lobbed up an easy shot for Lois to return, but she barely-managed to dink it back over the net, setting up Janet for a smash. Janet was happy to oblige and whistled the ball back at Lois who was barely able to dodge the incoming Scud.

As Peter walked back to serve, he whispered to Janet, "try and go a little easy on her."

"So we should just let them win?"

"No, they'd know we were tanking. Just don't rub their noses in it."

Peter bounced a ball at the serving line, as he waited for Janet to take her position across the net from a still-game, but now Scud-shy Lois Duchin. Peter served and volleyed with Chet until the ball came to Janet, who thought briefly about lobbing up a dying quail to Lois, but instead blasted another rocket past her for a winner. Once again, Peter whispered to Janet on his way back to the baseline.

"Are you sure you really want to get hired?"

"I'm not sure I want to make 'tennis' a part of some deep departmental political strategy," said Janet sarcastically.

"Everything is political, my dear," said Peter.

"Thank you, Chairman Mao," said Janet.

"Just make an effort," said Peter

After tennis, the foursome shared cool drinks on the club's veranda where they could watch other players thwack balls back and forth on the courts below. Occasional shouts of 'good shot,' and 'thirty-love' were the only sounds that penetrated the languidness of the humid late afternoon air.

It was summer and life was good.

"So, Peter, how's the new book coming along?" asked Chet.

"Pretty well. I've been busy hacking away at it every day this summer."

Chet leaned back, looked up into the hazy sky and launched a monologue, "God, how I envy you. Having the time to write...think...create...to contribute to…to…..." He paused, having lost his train of thought. "I swear I'm going brain-dead in the Dean's Office. Nothing but meetings, paperwork, putting out fires all day, every day. Believe me, it wears you down." Chet paused again, then leaned forward to deliver an obviously well-practiced and oft-delivered line, "the only thing I don't miss about teaching…is the teaching."

"Ah, yes," said Peter. "The teaching."

Chet continued to pontificate, "if we could only set up a college without students, life would be perfect."

"You seem to forget that I was one of those lowly students not that long ago," said Janet.

"So, how does it feel to be a traitor to your class?" said Peter, stepping in and hoping to ward off an argument, something which Janet was particularly adept at starting, especially with people she didn't like.

"I'm afraid I wouldn't know. I'll let you know when I get a real job," said Janet.

Chet chimed back in, delivering every line with an air of absolute certainty. "Oh, you'll love teaching, at least for the first ten years or so. But stay out of administration. It'll destroy your soul." Of course, Janet believed that Chet had no soul to destroy and that it had not taken much to destroy what was left of his rather feeble brain, but she managed to stop herself from uttering a sarcastic comeback.

Chet stopped a waiter who was walking by and asked, "could I get another one of these?" He looked around to the others. "Anyone?"

In assent, Janet cocked her empty glass towards the waiter.

"I'll have one, too," said Peter.

"And bring us the ticket," said Chet.

Lois Duchin shifted in her chair and leaned in, having decided the conversation had stayed on 'office talk' long enough,

"How is Glynnyth these days, Peter. We haven't seen much of her lately, I'm afraid."

"Ever since she got serious about selling real estate, I haven't either. Despite the economy, her business seems to have taken off and apparently so has she," he said.

Janet sank back into her chair. Any talk about Glynnyth was a sore point with her.

"How she stands it is beyond me," Peter continued. "The world of real estate is unbelievably mundane. Now, I don't like to use absolutist terminology, but I see no intellectual challenge in it whatsoever. And the people she deals with…I swear, some of them had to have been born wearing polyester."

"It does seem like such a waste of talent," said Lois.

"I've tried to talk her out of it, but…" Peter waved his hand and shook his head resignedly.

"Why does she do it, then?" asked Lois.

"She says she likes it," offered Peter.

Janet decided it was a good time to toss her opinion into the conversation, "I can't imagine anyone not liking twenty-five thousand dollars a month."

While the Duchins sat in stunned silence, nearby chickadees filled the void by Tweeting bird data back and forth to each other.

"A month?" asked Lois.

"In dollars?" added Chet.

"That's what I hear," said Janet, nodding towards Peter to get his assent. "On average."

Peter shrugged, indicating that the figure was fairly accurate.

The waiter returned with a tray of drinks and as he distributed them, Chet whispered to Lois, "Good God, for selling real estate? Talk about being overpaid."

Finishing up to 'thank you's' from the assemblage, the waiter tucked the check into a leather folder and set it down in the demilitarized zone in the middle of the table. Peter and Chet both eyed it as a potential source of The Plague.

Breaking the stalemate, Chet served first, "I was going to pick up the check, but now that I know you have a female Donald Trump in the family, I think I'll let you take care of it."

Peter returned Chet's serve by saying, "don't think that I've seen any of that money. She may have made that once or twice, but we're not quite ready to retire to the south of France. I still have to make do on my professor's salary, which, I'm sure you'll agree, should be going up soon."

Chet volleyed back with a winner, "not much chance of that, old chum. Thanks to our Dear Leader's financial wizardry, or lack thereof, the kitty's pretty much empty right about now."

Whereupon Peter reluctantly picked up the check and signed it.

After the couples said their goodbyes in the parking lot, Peter and Janet drove off in separate cars. As they were getting in, Lois looked across the top of their Camry at Chet and said, "I bet they end up at her apartment."

"Peter? Good god, Lois, the man is a rock. Not in a million years," said Chet as he settled into the driver's seat.

Before getting in, Lois rolled her eyes heavenwards.

## Chapter Twenty-Five
Trouble in Paradise

*W*earing a fluffy white terrycloth robe, Peter stood at the window of Janet's studio and stared out across the complex's swimming pool at the apartments on the other side, all now shuttered to protect the inhabitants from the late afternoon heat. Wrapped in a towel with her wet hair shimmering, Janet stepped out of her bathroom and stood in front of a mirror. Peter came up behind her, took her in his arms and nuzzled her neck. Janet pushed him away.

"Peter, I just took a shower."

"And you smell wonderful when you're clean."

"Good God, such a wonderful way with words you have," said Janet sarcastically, "and for a literature professor, no less."

Peter tried to nuzzle her again, but Janet was having none of it.

"No, Peter, fuck off. I have to be at the theatre by six-thirty. I'm still working, you know."

"Janet, please. I'll be in Toronto next week. For the Comp Lit planning meeting."

"Oh, right. The big Comp Lit conference. When is it? Next spring? It would have been nice to be able to tag along and maybe get a lead on a real job somewhere instead of another year of this lecturer crap."

She broke away and opened her closet to pick out something to wear. "I'm still seriously thinking of Albuquerque, by the way."

"You know I'd take you if I could."

"Is Glennyth going?"

"Are you kidding? That's the last thing she'd want to do. I'll be there alone. Thinking of you."

Janet scoffed. "Thinking of me? You'll just be one more aging tomcat on the prowl."

"Janet, please. I want you."

"Forget it, Peter. You're just horny."

"Horny? I haven't heard anyone use that word in thirty years."

"Just because you haven't heard it doesn't mean it doesn't apply. After you stick it in and wiggle it around for thirty seconds, you'll be thinking of how fast you can get out of here and I'll have to take another shower. No thank you."

Deflated, Peter turned away and looked out the window. "You're such a romantic."

"I live in the real world, Peter, and I'm running late."

"I should go," said Peter.

"Yeah, you should. There are things in life other than getting laid."

Janet went back into the bathroom while Peter got dressed, knowing that now was not the time to question the truth of the matter just asserted.

# Chapter Twenty-Six
## Together at Last

*P*ropped up on a bank of pillows, Peter was reading by the light of a single bed lamp when he heard a Glynnyth's car in the driveway and the sound of the garage door going up. He continued to read until he heard her footsteps on the stairs, at which point he put on a sleep mask, turned off the light and pretended to be asleep.

Glynnyth left the bedroom door open and turned on the light in the closet where she undressed and slipped into her nightgown. After crawling into bed, she then turned on the lamp next to her.

"Do you mind if I read for a while?"

Peter gave her a muffled grunt.

"You can't be asleep yet. I saw the light on when I drove up."

Peter lifted the eyeshades. "I was resting my eyes and must have just dozed off."

Glynnyth smirked. "How was your day?"

"Not bad. Made some progress on the book."

"Good."

"How was dinner?"

"Good. We went to Rudolpho's."

"Oh. What did you have?"

"Lobster ravioli with a lemon-asiago sauce."

"How was it?"

"Good," said Glynnyth.

"Good," replied Peter.

After a long pause, Peter pulled himself up on the pillows, turned on the light and reached for his reading glasses.

"I'm feeling a little less tired. I think I might read for a while."

"You don't need my permission," said Glynnyth.

"I'm delighted to hear that," said Peter

"Let's not spat."

Peter said nothing, but put on his glasses and opened the book he'd just put down.

## Chapter Twenty-Seven
### The End of the Beginning or the Beginning of the End?

*T*he late July heat wave that had brought all of western Massachusetts to a standstill was so bad it had some residents dreaming of January. Although the sun was out, its rays barely penetrated the haze that enveloped the townships in a sweltering bath of humid air. Below ground, even the earthworms had slowed their crawls.

Instead of working at home, Peter had gone in to Jenkins where the air conditioning was better. As usual, he was 'working on his book,' which meant that his computer was on, his Word program was open and was quietly waiting for attention to be paid. Also as usual, Peter had dozed off when Pierce opened the door and leaned in.

"Have you heard?" Pierce asked.

Peter hadn't and looked at him quizzically, waiting to be filled in on the latest gossip.

"The Board of Trustees just sent out an email. There's a faculty senate meeting at eleven o'clock." Pierce paused dramatically, "this morning."

"Why would they even bother? We couldn't possibly get a quorum together at this time of the year."

"Maybe we have a new Supreme Leader," said Pierce, hoping to spark speculation about the intent of the Board's email.

"But why call us in? Business as usual is 'they ignore us, we ignore them,'" said Peter. "Who were the faculty reps on the search committee?"

Pierce thought for a moment, then answered, "Hendrickson in Biosciences and Mastricht from Critical Soch."

"Surely one of them would have let the cat out of the bag were there either a cat or a bag," said Peter.

"Care to stroll over and find out?" said Pierce.

Peter thought for a second, then replied, "Downstairs at a quarter-'til?"

"Jolly good, cheers and right-o, old chap," said Pierce. "See you then."

With that, shortly before eleven, the two of them strolled over to the Goeffrey Manning Holt Administration Building, unaware that their futures were about to undergo a monumental change.

## Chapter Twenty-Eight
Food in the Foyer


$M$rs. Agnes Sturdivant, President Manchester's elderly assistant, scurried around the foyer to the president's conference room, hastily setting up Starbucks coffee urns, pitchers containing half-and-half, low-fat milk, non-fat milk, soy milk, almond milk and good old regular milk-milk, along with bowls of various sweeteners. Assisted by a young admin, they'd already set out biodegradable coffee cups and made-from-potatoes knives, forks and spoons which would break down quickly when they eventually would come in contact with the hungry micro-organisms that inhabited Grodin's ecologically-correct landfill. A second admin emerged from the kitchen with a tray of bananas, apples and oranges which she set down next to several trays of pastries, thus establishing the outer extremes of the healthy vs. unhealthy food spectrum.

The twenty or so faculty senate members who had arrived swooped in on the banquet table like hungry hyenas at a zebra kill. Most were dressed in the two main variants of professorial summer fashion—athletic-wear vs. Polos and Bermuda shorts. Only a few of the men appeared to have shaved recently and their hair was in various stages of rebelliousness. Even the least self-respecting rock band would have been appalled by the slovenly and disheveled looks displayed by Grodin's *crème de la crème*. The one exception on the men's side was Professor Guillaume Fowlkes-Bowles, a Race & Gender prof from the School of Critical Social Theory. He never appeared in public without his trademark look—a dark black suit, a too-tight-in-the-collar white shirt and a neon-colored bow tie. His bushy, henna-treated dreadlocks splashed down to the middle of his ample back like Niagara Falls after a flood. The half-dozen faculty women in the crowd stood out, not because of their gender, but because they dressed like normal people.

Peter had changed into his tennis whites. Although there was no tennis on his schedule, he figured he could use it as an excuse to duck out early in case the meeting ran long. After all, everyone agreed that in Western Massachusetts, even a sweltering summer afternoon should not be wasted by having to sit through a faculty meeting.

Anticipating a potentially-lengthy conclave inside, Peter and Pierce vigorously attacked the food display. Peter loaded up his plate with a large cheese Danish, a couple of mini-croissants and a poppy-seed bagel with a smoked salmon schmear, all of which he surrounded by a jumble of cubed pineapple and strawberries—his token nod to healthy eating. He set his plate aside and prepared a decaf Americano in a large cardboard cup which he sleeved in an insulated gripper. While he was adding cream and sugar, Chaz Henderson, a black prof from the HAC's Sociology Department, joined them.

"I can see the headline now: *Grodin Faculty Meets And Eats While Children Go Hungry In Harlem*," said Chaz.

"I'd say, 'let them eat cake,' but I like cake," said Peter.

"Then let them eat kale," said Chaz, chuckling.

"I think we can all agree on that," said Pierce.

"It can't be good if it's good for you," said Peter.

"Amen to that," said Chaz. "Do you have any idea why they've called us in? We're well short of a quorum, so they can't expect us to decide anything."

"My guess is that they've decided on a new president." Peter chuckled, then said, "or maybe they've narrowed it down and they want our input."

"Who knows, maybe they want some cover," said Chaz. "After all, they picked Manchester with minimal faculty input. At the very least, I hope it's someone who understands liberal arts *and* can raise money. Poor old Brooksie couldn't do either."

Ted Campanaris from Statistics joined them and eyed Peter's heaping plate of carbohydrates. "Peter, why don't we do lunch after the meeting? My treat," he smirked.

"Can't make it today, but I'll take a rain-check," said Peter.

"Sorry, but the offer's good for today only," said Campanaris, who then nodded at Peter's plate and snickered, "enjoy the heartburn." Campanaris turned away and joined another group across the room.

"Leave it to Campanaris to make you an offer you have to refuse," muttered Pierce.

"Cheap bastard," said Peter.

"A well-known and total asshole," said Chaz, as the three of them continued to munch away on the free food.

Standing near the door to the conference room, Mrs. Sturdivant picked up a small bell and shook it gently. "Ladies…gentlemen…the Faculty Senate will convene in five minutes. And remember, no food in the Governor's Room. Liquids only."

Realizing they were now on the clock, Pierce, Peter and the rest of the faculty sped through what was left on their plates like Pac-Men chomping through lines of helpless dots.

## Chapter Twenty-Nine
### Surprise!


$T$he dark, oak-paneled Governors' Room contained an oval table so large it was possible to consider that the room had been built around it. As was their wont, Peter and Pierce took their seats at the back of the room, far from what could be considered to be the head of the table. They sipped their coffee while the other senators came in and sat down. The boisterous cheeriness they'd all felt in the foyer slowly dissipated in the ornate gloominess of the Governors' Room where, contrary to conventional wisdom, form had firmly imposed its will on function.

After everyone had settled in, J. Bliss Moynihan strode in, followed by Miles Plummer, a tall man who wore a close-cropped salt and pepper beard with hair to match. Clearly not an academic, he wore his elegant steel-grey Italian suit with the grace of a continental movie star enjoying a night out on the Via Veneto. Bliss sat down near the head of the table, removed his sunglasses from their usual resting place atop his head and casually slid them into the pocket of his off-white linen jacket. He smiled expansively at his peers, but said nothing. Miles carefully placing his thin attaché onto a credenza behind the main table and sat down next to it. Resting an elbow on the credenza, he slowly scanned the room as though he were taking a mental photograph of each person there. The faculty eyed him warily, as he appeared to them every inch the type of man who, should he ever run for public office, they would unanimously and enthusiastically vote against.

After an uncomfortable wait with no one apparently in charge, Mrs. Sturdivant quietly opened the door and two men and a woman filed in and sat down. Unlike the faculty, they were dressed in business suits and, by their collective demeanors, appeared to have just left a convention of undertakers. Mrs. Sturdivant sat down in a chair off to the side, opened a spiral notebook and uncapped a pen, which she hovered over the notebook, ready to record every utterance for posterity.

The trio in business suits whispered among themselves, shuffled some papers and then came to attention by folding their hands together and adjusting their postures. After a couple of nods, Harold P. Graves, a balding sixtyish man, stood up and nervously looked around the room.

"Good morning. For those of you who don't know me, I'm Hal Graves, President of the Board of Trustees. We also have with us this morning Loretta Lopez-Mouton and Frank Jamison, who are also long-serving members of the Board."

Both Jamison and Lopez-Mouton looked around the table and nodded to the faculty, but their tight smiles clearly signaled that they would rather have been anywhere else but here.

"I recognize that we don't have a quorum, but we're not here to conduct business. We have some extremely important information to convey about the future at Grodin and we thought it best to get it out to you, the leaders of the faculty, as soon as possible."

"And the winner is," came a call from one of the senators.

Graves forced a smile and waited for the chuckling at this *non sequitur* to subside. He continued, "we're not here today to discuss the appointment of a new president, in fact, I can inform you that Franklin Manchester has resigned from the presidency, effective today. Also, Provost Anne-Marie McAdams and Chief Investment Officer, Frank Mangiani, have been...ah...let go...um... resigned, and her assistant and two others in the President's Office have been placed on leave, pending an investigation."

Experiencing an unexpected 'Uh-Oh' moment, the faculty senators began to squirm apprehensively, realizing that there was way more on the agenda than what they had expected.

Graves unfolded a sheet of paper, put on a pair of reading glasses and glanced at his notes before continuing, "my...our...primary purpose in calling you together today is to inform you that it has come to our attention that Grodin College has experienced a sudden and precipitous shortfall in capital."

Graves now had everyone's full attention.

"As you know, at Grodin, we have never fully-funded our expenses through tuition, grants and gifts, although we have always assiduously worked towards that goal and have been, or thought we had been, making significant progress towards it. Over the years, we have made up the difference through bridge loans and an occasional, but minor drawdown from our endowment, which, as you know, has been dedicated primarily to long-term capital improvements and to the creation of endowed chairs."

Graves paused and nervously opened a bottle of spring water, downed a quick swallow and continued, "however...it appears that over the past several years, in an effort to improve the return on our endowment, our investment team invested heavily in..." he paused for a moment to consider what he'd said, "...that's two 'investments' in a sentence, so strike that. Our endowment team invested in a Cayman Islands hedge fund which..." He paused again and looked over at the other two trustees, "it is the Caymans? Right?"

They nodded affirmatively and he said, almost to himself, "it's always the Caymans, isn't it? Why? I have no idea."

He took another gulp from the water bottle and continued, "unfortunately, the fund performed very, very poorly and, to make a long story short, the endowment fund lost a significant percentage of its...uh...endowment."

He paused, looked around the room and continued, " when this came to our attention two weeks ago, the Board asked Miles Plummer of Dewey, Plummer and Howe, to conduct an extensive forensic audit which revealed, in essence, that the drawdown of the endowment fund was practically one hundred percent. And, due to subsequent accounting manipulations by the investment team to cover their losses, there also exists a considerable shortfall in current income relative to expenses. As a result, we are going to have to institute dramatic structural changes in the way we manage our affairs in order to continue even the most basic operations." He paused and took another swig from his water bottle.

By this time, the room had become very quiet. "What kind of numbers are we talking about?" asked one of the Econ profs. Though spoken at almost a whisper, he was heard by everyone.

Graves glanced back at Miles Plummer as if to ask permission to deliver the *coup de grace*. Miles looked at him impassively, then nodded for him to go ahead. "At this point in time, we don't know. Any guess would be premature, but we can say that there will have to be significant changes." He paused, then continued nervously, "there are many variables to consider."

Irritated by the waffling, Miles interjected. "I think we can say with absolute certainty that budgetary cuts in the range of thirty-five to forty percent will be necessary. Just to keep the doors open."

As the reality of the magnitude of the problem set in, the assemblage sat in stunned silence until the tableau was broken by Marcos Santos-Zimbrano, the Chair of the Critical Studies faculty, who stood up, shook his finger at the ceiling and thundered, "This...Will...Not...Stand!" He looked around the room, then gathered himself and began a diatribe against the evils of capitalism, corporatism, anti-intellectualism and a multitude of other "isms" which he considered to be responsible for the degradation and misery experienced by the powerless unfortunates of the world which, according to the general theme of his ramble, included the underpaid, indentured servants who made up the tenured faculty of Grodin College of which one Marcos Santos-Zimbrano was one of its longest-standing, and soon-to-be longest-suffering, members.

No one listened to him, of course, as they were too busy showing their own unhappiness with the situation. Following his lead, everyone spoke and shouted at once, spewing forth in a volcanic eruption of questions, threats, demands and 'woe-is-me'-isms—all variations on the themes of:

"What the fuck happened?"

"Whose fault was it?"

"What the fuck are we going to do?"

The three board members sat quivering at the head of the table, unsure about what to do and wondering if they might have to make a run for it.

The bellowing continued until Peter finally shouted, "Quiet!"

"Please!"

"Let them talk!"

The shouting faded and those standing sat down, allowing Peter to begin a practical discussion by quietly asking, "can't we just borrow some money to tide us over?"

"Or raise tuition?" asked another.

Grateful at having regained somewhat limited control, Graves looked down at his notes and ran the palm of his hand quickly over his bald head. He took a deep breath and plunged in. "We will be looking into borrowing, but we've already been told by banks and private individuals that without serious restructuring, borrowing is impossible. The numbers just aren't there and there's nothing to borrow against, unless we want to sell off a building or two, which is…um…obviously impossible. As for raising tuition, both the Board and Mr. Plummer's associates believe it's imperative that we maintain a tuition structure which will ensure the stability of our current student population."

"You mean come up with a number that won't give the parents a heart attack," said Pierce.

"Or send them running off to Bootstrap J. C.," said another.

Graves nodded and added, "it's important that this be seen as a bump in the road rather than a brick wall." Graves paused for a moment to measure the effect of his clearly-practiced metaphor on the group. Seeing that it had none, he continued, "it's not that we're trying to hide anything, we just don't want to cause a panic. The situation is very difficult, but not dire," said Graves. "Not yet, anyway."

"Not dire for you!" yelled out one of the profs. "You're not going to be laid off or have your salary cut."

Frank Jamison piped up for the first time, "board members aren't compensated for their time. We work *pro bono*."

"Compensated or not, you've made a fine mess of things," said another, politely refraining from saying 'you've really fucked things up,' in mixed company.

With the faculty on the verge of another outrage breakout, Graves pleaded for calm. "Let's try to move forward, please," he said. "We're working with the appropriate authorities to try to sort out what happened and what, if anything, can be done about it. But for now, we all need to recognize that we're in a difficult financial situation and that we have a difficult path ahead of us."

Graves checked his notes again and plunged ahead. "In order to deal with the financial aspects of our situation, the Board has authorized Mr. Plummer and his company to develop new budgets for each of the five Schools."

Graves paused and looked around the room in an attempt to measure the effect of his words. Sullen, overt hostility was still the prevailing mood of his audience. He continued, "and to ensure that we continue our commitment to maintain Grodin's academic standards and its tradition of educational excellence, the Board has asked Bliss Moynihan to assume the role of Acting President. Bliss has generously agreed to take a leave of absence from his Deanship while the search committee seeks a replacement for Brooks Manchester."

Upon hearing the words 'Bliss Moynihan' and 'Acting President' spoken in close proximity to each other, Peter was nearly overcome by a severe bout of nausea. Had he not already been sitting down, he would have had to.

While Graves droned on about the greatness of Bliss and the copious talents, gifts and qualities he brought to the table, a feeling of doom spread through the room. Everyone knew that as the new president, Bliss would have the power to make or end careers, dispense or withhold favors, and, unlike the bumbling, incompetent but affable Brooks Manchester, he would wield his new power efficiently and ruthlessly. In short, the comfortable and predictable life they had known at Grodin had—in an instant—come to an end.

When he finally ended his tribute, Graves stood aside as Bliss rose to speak. But before he could say a word, first one, then several members of the faculty put their hands together and clapped—slowly at first, but then with increasing fervor, lest none be thought to be less enthusiastic than anyone else. All in all, a more sickening display of excessive groveling and figurative ass-kissing could hardly be imagined.

Peter was one of the few who clapped politely. He exchanged a quick glance with Pierce who was applauding with somewhat more enthusiasm, but who arched an eyebrow knowingly, indicating that he was doing only the minimum amount of sucking up required by the circumstances.

Bliss let the applause wash over him and waited for it to die down before he proceeded, "we all know each other here, so I won't sugar-coat this with some B.S. about how if we all pull together we can make this work. We have a tough, daunting task ahead of us and there will be pain." He paused and tilted his head and allowed a slight wan smile to cross his face as though he deeply regretted the very real pain he was about to inflict on Grodin's faculty and staff. Whether one believed Bliss's bromide or not was a matter of opinion, one which was influenced heavily by one's opinion of Bliss.

He continued, "it's going to be tough. Damned tough. And if Grodin is to survive, we are going to have to make major changes in the way we do business. In the coming days, I'll be meeting with members of the Board and Miles Plummer's staff to come up with an operational plan that will keep Grodin afloat."

Bliss paused again and looked around the table. "Yes, 'afloat.' Head above water. It's that serious."

Bliss went on to explain that there would be layoffs, cuts in services, and changes to the curriculum, but even though it was a genuine crisis, he did not want to cause a panic, especially among the students. It was essential to keep them from jumping ship, so to speak, as Grodin's finances now, more than ever, depended on the steady cash flow from parental pockets into Grodin's bank account. He also assured the senators that whatever pain was to be dished out, the tenured faculty would be the last to feel it.

Peter had known for years that Grodin, like most liberal arts colleges, was in danger. The forces of history and finance were conspiring against it, but he had held out hope that the leaky old rust-bucket would be able to pump enough bilges to get him to retirement with a comfortable pension. No need for the old tanker to embark on any foolhardy voyages. In fact, there was no need to even try to get out of the harbor. Just staying afloat was good enough. But now, with this news, even that was in jeopardy.

With the bad news delivered, Bliss then opined about the opportunity *The Situation* presented for Grodin, and although he never invoked the 'lemons into lemonade' metaphor, he sipped at its edges. He went on about how he wanted Grodin to become the 'Stanford of the East,' a veritable Startup U. where techies and artists could meet, share visions and create synergies for change and innovation.

The usual bullshit.

But few listened as Bliss droned on about his plans for transforming Grodin. Every person at the table began to rummage through memories of past encounters with Bliss and began the creative remixing of events, downplaying the negatives and polishing up the positives with the hope that by bringing the shiny reimagined object to Bliss's attention at the opportune moment, each might improve his or her's relative position in the New Pecking Order.

However, Peter, for one, didn't engage in the group fabulation. He had no doubt as to his position in the New World Order: he would be looking up— way up—at the very bottom rung of the ladder.

# Chapter Thirty
*Après Le Deluge*

$A$fter the meeting, the members of the senate went outside, got on their phones and immediately began calling, texting and tweeting. The fact that they were about to deliver news which was guaranteed to ruin a fellow professor's vacation was the only positive they could derive from *The Situation*.

As was his wont, Pierce decided he was in need of liquid fortification, so he headed off to the golf club where he would take his place atop his favorite barstool at the Penobscot Country Club's Bar and Grille.

As he walked back to Jenkins Hall alone, Peter felt an unfamiliar knot of dread start to tighten up in his stomach. During his career, he had lived through academic tiffs and kerfuffles galore, but they had all been of the type which ended up as amusing anecdotes to be recounted at faculty dinner parties. This one felt different. With the ultimate outcome unknown, *The Situation* threatened the basic gentlemen's agreement of guaranteed professorial leisure and lifetime security.

This time, the only certainty was that the ride ahead would be rough.

When he arrived back at Jenkins, word of the impending catastrophe had preceded him. As he made his way to his office, concerned and frightened staff members came up to him one by one asking in hushed tones what to expect, but all he could do was promise that he would do his best to protect the department and save their jobs from the wrecking ball. Of course he meant it, but at this early stage, he had exactly zero knowledge of what was about to be done by Bliss, Miles and their minions.

One who appeared unfazed was Henrietta, who sat ramrod-straight at her desk and was busy working for a change. It was no doubt her way of acknowledging the new reality. And, in a rare set-aside of her usual *Henrietta Against The World* attitude, she asked, "you okay, Dr. G?"

Peter sighed deeply, "it was a bloodbath."

Henrietta paused to think for a moment, then answered, "it seems to me it was a whatchamacallit...a 'prelude' to a bloodbath. We ain't seen no actual blood shed yet."

Well, it's coming," said Peter. "We need to stick together and figure out a way to fight this."

Then *Henrietta Against The World* re-appeared and scoffed, "when has anyone around here ever stuck together? Pretty soon we going to be playing musical chairs to see who stays and who goes. No time to be nice."

As much as he hated to think it, Henrietta was probably right, but he was too worn out to put forth even a token counter-argument.

He spent the rest of the afternoon contacting all vacationing staff and faculty via email or phone alerting them as to what had happened. He developed a short spiel that quickly got out the facts about *The Situation*. There were questions, there was anger and there were tears, but Peter let it be known that at this point, he had not even the faintest glimmer of an idea as to exactly what was going to happen.

He tried calling Glynnyth, then Janet, but had to leave a message for each. Recently, Glynnyth had been increasingly hard to reach and, in Peter's opinion, had been over-screening her calls. Clients and contractors got through, but the husband did not. Peter left a 'just call me when you get a chance' message in a tone that implied he had something of import to tell her. He wasn't concerned about setting off alarm bells because Glynnyth's recent attitude had been one of indifference, if not contempt, towards anything related to Grodin. And towards Peter, for that matter.

By the end of the day, nearly everyone had checked in and had been updated.

As was his custom, Peter decided he needed some time to calm down and think and there was no better place to accomplish that than atop his office sofa. After setting his phone to airplane mode, he cleared the couch of the detritus which had mysteriously washed up onto it, climbed aboard and settled in for a good think. After a few deep breaths, he closed his eyes and promptly fell asleep.

When he woke an hour later, he felt extremely refreshed until he remembered *The Situation*, whereupon the feelings of uncertainty quickly settled in again. Constitutionally, Peter was unprepared to deal with long-term adversity, as his normal *modus operandi* was that of a sunny, but sarcastic, wisecracking optimist. In the long run, he was not sure either how, or if, he was going to handle this.

He checked his iPhone, but Glynnyth hadn't called. Nor had Janet.

He called Janet again and this time she picked up. He asked if he could come over as he had 'some bad news.'

"You don't have to," she said. "I heard."

"Then you know it doesn't look good," he said.

"You are such a Master of the Obvious," said Janet.

"We'll fight this. We'll figure something out," said Peter.

"Sure you will," said Janet. "What are you going to do? Print money? Con some dying alum on his or her deathbed into forking over their fortune to good ol' Grodin ?" Peter almost corrected Janet on her incorrect use of a plural possessive pronoun, but fortunately managed to stop himself, thus preventing the world's first telephonic murder.

"You sound a little bitter," said Peter.

"And why shouldn't I be? I've spent years waiting, and now it's over. Not…agonna…happen."

"You can't just give up on your academic career."

"Give it up? I haven't had one yet."

"We're all in this together," said Peter. "We're all going to be sacrificing."

"Sacrificing? By your having to teach an extra class or two? You've got tenure…a pension…a working wife. Cry me a river," said Janet. "I'm heading to New Mexico, the fucking Land of Enchantment. Goodbye, Peter."

She clicked off.

Peter sighed, leaned back in his chair and closed his eyes.

But nothing went away.

## Chapter Thirty-One
### The Home Front

*E*ventually, Peter made his way home. He was hopeful that Glynnyth might offer some support, if not answers, but she was an unwilling sympathizer. When she finally got off the phone after a lengthy discussion with one of her clients, their conversation could be summarized thusly:

Compared to a Kennedy, your life is hard, but compared to that of the average person, you are sitting on top of the world with your feet hanging over the edge.

Though others will, you're not going to get laid off. So what if you actually have to work like most people?

Nose…meet Grindstone.

Welcome to the Real World.

Peter was a bit shocked as to how both Glynnyth and Janet's analyses of *The Situation* had taken the same course.

## Chapter Thirty-Two
### Crying Towels

*C*haos ruled the next few days. Vacations were cancelled. People who hadn't paid attention to budgets for years suddenly grew green eyeshades. Employment contracts were parsed for nuance like the Dead Sea Scrolls and the comings and goings of Bliss and Miles Plummer were tracked like incoming missiles.

As word of Grodin's problems spread to their home offices outside the comfortable confines of the academe, the adjuncts, lecturers and part-timers phoned in. Peter fielded their anxious calls as they asked about their status for the fall term. He had no real information to give them, but anyone able to do simple math understood that this kind of major hack to the budget could not be made up just by cutting back on printer cartridges and paper clips. What was becoming clear to even the densest among them was that all staff members were at risk and all untenured profs were likely gone as well.

Now it was every man, woman and self-identified other for himself, herself or...well, you get the idea.

It would be *Game of Thrones* without the swordplay.

After arriving at his office around ten, as usual, Peter spent another fretful morning doing more of what he had done for several days—field phone calls, listen to complaints and commiserate with the complainers. By noon he felt like he was beings slowly dragged downstream towards a figurative Niagara Falls.

Feeling he needed a break, he called Pierce to ask him to lunch at the Faculty Club. Pierce, however, was on the fourteenth tee with a chance to break eighty, so he said he would try to catch up with Peter later. Peter decided to head over to the Club on his own.

At Grodin, there was no other single place on campus for the faculty to gather informally and today there was only one topic—*The Situation*. But other than knowing that massive cuts were coming, it was unclear as to exactly what the nature of *The Situation* was, so it was also very much up in the air about what could be done about it. Nevertheless, speculating without facts was something members of the faculty were supremely qualified to do.

At lunch, diners normally walked in, picked up a tray and headed straight for the buffet, but today, Peter was surprised to be greeted by a young man who was spiffily-dressed in a crisp white shirt and tie. The young man pointed to a large menu board propped up on an easel and recited the day's 'specials,' even though the totality of the day's offerings was readily apparent to anyone who pushed a tray down the line. After polishing up a plastic tray with a flourish, the young man handed it to Peter who proceeded to load it up as he pushed it down the chrome rails.

At the cashier's station, head chef Oscar Gravelitis greeted Peter with a broad smile which displayed a glittering gold front tooth. Peter couldn't recall ever having seen Oscar smile before, let alone notice the gold tooth. Now freshly-shaven and wearing a white chef's smock, Oscar had transformed himself into the sparkling image of a Culinary School graduate, having no doubt realized that with everyone's head now on the chopping block, future employment elsewhere was unlikely for one who would barely-qualify as a short-order cook at IHOP, especially for one so distinctly-deficient in the personal charm department.

After paying Oscar, who thanked him so profusely for coming that it became embarrassing, Peter finally escaped Gravelitis' uncharacteristic obsequiousness and looked around for a place to sit and someone to sit with.

Usually, the professoriat stuck to their own kind at lunch or dined alone, happy to peck away solipsistically on their iPhones or IPads, but today, the electronic gadgets had been set aside and people who hadn't spoken to each other for years clustered together and yakked away. The din was overwhelming. It was like a 1950's ladies' bridge club where everyone talked at once and no one paid any attention to the cards.

Peter sat down next to Hank Robanser, a computer science prof from the School of Science and Technology. He had served on several committees with Robanser and knew him to be an outspoken straight-shooter, as were a few on the faculty of that rationally-oriented school. He was a garrulous sort who didn't mind sharing the occasional politically-incorrect remark, which, were any to become public, would likely get both of them reprimanded, if not canned in Peter's School or in the extremely politically-correct School of Critical Social Theory. Robanser had warned Grodin about hiring Stan Dreighton, saying he was not in it for the long-term, but since he and Dreighton taught in similar subject areas, his warnings were taken as grapes soured by jealousy. When he was proven to be right, few remembered that fact, but unlike most members of the faculty who would have seethed for decades after having been thusly dissed, Robanser was constitutionally incapable of holding such a grudge. He simply let it go and moved on.

Peter hoped to get Robanser's take on what those from the Geek and Tree-Hugging side of campus thought about *The Situation*, but before they could talk, they were joined by the table-hopping husband-and-wife team of Harold K. and Penny Loeb from the School of Critical Social Theory. After arriving together years ago, Pierce had joked that their individual scholarly research and teaching abilities were so poor that it was impossible to tell which one was the 'trailing spouse.' The Spritzers were full of bubbly enthusiasm and bursting with ideas about what to do.

They squeezed into a spot between Peter and Robanser and took over the conversation without a hint of an apology for interrupting. They wanted to organize a sit-in of the president's office and picket the homes of Grodin's trustees. They had already selected themselves as the ones to head up the Santa Barbara wing of the Occupy Movement and stake out the home of one of the wealthier board members who was rumored to be a neighbor of Oprah's in Montecito. They also were demanding there be an investigation of the investigation of the hedge fund fiasco, which, after three days, had thus far had turned little more than evidence that a fiasco had indeed taken place.

The Spritzers were also excited about exploring the possibility of getting federal bailout money, their rationale being that since federal student loan money had been lost in the debacle, the government obviously ought to reimburse Grodin, which, through no fault of its own, was now woefully short of funds. "They bailed out the fucking banks, why not us?" The fact that it might have been the fiduciary duty of Grodin's administration to supervise the handling of said funds was a point which thus far had not factored into the Spritzers' thinking on the matter. To them, the only issue was why was it taking so long to find the money and return it *tout suite* to Grodin's bursar for proper distribution, first to the faculty and then, should anything be left over, to other, lesser, needs.

For professors like the Spritzers, the crisis was, if not career-enhancing, at least career-enlivening, as it offered the armchair community organizers and social justice warriors an opportunity to put theory into practice.

The Spritzer Invasion seemed to go on as long as the Hundred Year War and despite his efforts to find a place in the conversation for himself and Robanser, neither of them could get a word in. Like many an academic seminar, the conversation had gone wildly off-topic. Midway through their collective harangue, Robanser excused himself, leaving Peter as the lone recipient of the Spritzer offensive.

Peter's salvation came from an unlikely source when Margaret Dreighton made a dramatic *Hello, Dolly*-style entrance that shouted 'I'm here!' to the assemblage. She spotted the Spritzers and immediately headed over to their table. Ignoring Peter, she stood and directed her remarks at Penny, who was one of her fellow Harpies. Catching her breath dramatically, she exclaimed, "I was in Venice and came back as soon as I could. I couldn't get a flight out of there so Lars drove me to Milan."

"Lars?" asked Peter. "What happened to Pablo?"

"Paolo," corrected Margaret, adding her patented glare. "Obviously he wasn't ready for me." She turned back to the Spritzers. "Lars is a Swedish shipping billionaire. We were cruising the Adriatic on his yacht when I heard."

She wiggled her way into the spot vacated by Robanser.

"So fill me in," she said to the Spritzers. "What are we going to do about this…this debacle?"

The Spritzers both excitedly began talking at once and Peter took that as his opportunity to make his escape.

After Peter left, the faculty club continued to buzz with rumor, speculation and…well, more rumor and speculation. Wild schemes and ideas were bandied about, but without knowing Bliss's plan, there was nothing specific to react to, other than the total and complete unfairness of *The Situation*. Peter had gone hoping to find some reason for optimism, but this brief lunchtime encounter with other faculty members left him with the growing sense that unless there was an unforeseeable intervention of some sort, in the end, the outcome was most likely going to be bad.

Peter was adept at living an untidy life. Chaos and disorder didn't bother him as long as the disorganization involved such trivial misdemeanors as misplaced papers, late-arriving students and forgotten instructions from Glynnyth about what to pick up from the grocery store. He had come to believe, and past experience had confirmed, that if ignored long enough, most of life's problems went away on their own. For years, his had been a life of predictable routine with only a few bumps in the road. And yes, he had hit some of those bumps, but no problem had turned into a sinkhole into which large and or even small cars could disappear. So, believing that the turmoil involved in going through life-altering events was long past, Peter was psychologically unprepared to cope with *The Situation*, which he now felt was going to be a long-term ulcer-inducting nightmare.

An impartial observer might note that living with *The Situation* was hardly comparable to landing on Omaha Beach in 1944. But, in fairness, it should also be noted that thresholds of individual discomfort vary.

# Chapter Thirty-Three
## Reality Strikes


$B$ack at his office, Peter woke from a brief post-lunch nap and had a minute or two of feel-good time until he remembered *The You-Know-What*. His stomach was the first organ to react and it did so by tightening up. His brain reacted by recognizing that the stomach was right.

He was shaken out of this unpleasant self-assessment when Pierce knocked gently on Peter's door and came in without being asked. Pierce took a flask out of his jacket and pour an amber liquid into two paper cups he'd brought with him.

"I thought you might be ready for something a little stronger than iced tea."

"Are we celebrating you breaking eighty?" Peter asked.

"Nope. Blew up on the last three holes. Still, even a bad day at golf is better than a good day at work, as they say," said Pierce. "How was lunch?"

"It wasn't even a bad day at golf, not even close," said Peter. "Margaret's back."

"So now we're drinking to bad news," said Pierce. He tipped his cup to Peter then added, "but you know me, I'll drink to anything."

"A fine example we're setting here, Ollie," said Peter.

"If anyone asks," said Pierce, "we're drinking sherry. It looks like sherry anyway."

"God, do I hate sherry," said Peter. "My money says Bliss is a sherry drinker."

"I heard he may have had a problem once," said Pierce.

Peter chuckled. "He's pretty loose for a someone who's on the wagon. His only redeeming virtue, as far as I can see, is that he's not a prude. A prick, to be sure, but not a straight arrow."

"You did hear the rumor that he was a Navy Seal?" said Pierce.

"No way!" said Peter.

"Just a rumor. Probably started by The Blisster himself," said Pierce.

I'd believe it about that guy, Miles. He looks like the kind of guy who would go to the gym at four in the morning and then run a half-marathon before breakfast…on a Saturday.

"He's a killer, all right," said Pierce.

"But Bliss a Seal? That, I seriously doubt," said Peter.

They sipped again from the cups.

"Funny how we know so little about him and how he now has so much power over us. How did that happen?" said Peter.

Early on, the Two P's code name for Bliss was *Gatsby*, due to his murky past. In the first years following his arrival at Grodin, rampant rumor-mongering abounded about his sexual orientation, his personal relationships and his entrepreneurial nature, which was far different from that of the standard-issue academic. Because Bliss didn't mingle, he offered little to dispel the speculation. As far as he was concerned, the more mystery the better.

"One of life's great mysteries is how the totally-undeserving end up with so much," said Pierce.

"So, you're not a believer in karma?" said Peter.

"Oh, I believe in it. You just have to live long enough to see it work out, because karma can definitely be a lagging indicator."

"Hopefully we'll still be around for *le denouement*," said Peter, " but right now I'd settle for just being left alone."

"Given our present circumstances, I'd say there's not much chance of that, old chum."

## Chapter Thirty-Four
### The Other Shoe

$O$n the evening of Day Six *Après Le Catastrophe*, Bliss tweeted, texted and emailed the faculty, informing them of an All-Hands meeting to be held at eight o'clock the next morning.

That night, many a cellphone battery died as the faculty discussed what to do. But since they didn't know what they were supposed to do something about, they did what they did best, speculate wildly about what they didn't know.

What they did know was that it was Bliss's Plan. *Ergo*, it couldn't be good.

Peter rose early and groggily, drove to campus and walked over to the Wheeler Center where Bliss had scheduled the meeting. No doubt Bliss had planned the eight o'clock start because 'grogginess' was precisely the state of mind he was looking for in his faculty. And since so many profs were unaccustomed to doing anything at eight o'clock in the morning, there was also no doubt that some would oversleep.

After stepping into the lobby, he was annoyed by the loud squeaking sounds his sneakers made on the smooth marble floor which clearly announced his arrival to the several dozen faculty members who were milling about the utilitarian metal tables which had been set up for coffee. Unlike the spread at the faculty senate meeting, there were no Danish pastries, bagels or bowls of fresh fruit. Just two large aluminum coffee urns, some powdered Coffee-Mate, sugar, cardboard cups and plastic spoons.

Austerity On Parade.

There was also none of the usual 'good ol' boy' jocularity which preceded most faculty get-togethers, instead, just a few nods of acknowledgment and muted conversations. No one was in the mood for small talk. Peter fixed himself a cup of coffee and tried to take it with him into the auditorium, but a security guard politely stopped him. "Sorry, sir, no food or drink are allowed inside the auditorium."

Peter grumbled and thought about contesting the order, but decided it wasn't worth making an issue out of it.

At precisely eight o'clock, a loud buzzer went off.

"What is this…junior high?" stage-whispered one prof.

"Looks like recess is over," muttered another.

The faculty filed in and randomly took their seats in the auditorium.

The stage was bare, but for two leather chairs and a modernistic glass lectern. After everyone had settled into their seats, Bliss and Miles Plummer walked out onto the stage. Acting as though the world was their oyster, Miles eased into one of the chairs and Bliss took command of the lectern.

Peter had to admit that Bliss cut an imposing figure. With his posture ramrod straight and wearing a sleek, cool-gray suit and a bright-green silk tie, his bearing contrasted sharply with that of the faculty, who, looking more like their students, was dressed in workout gear and scruffy sneakers. A few even sat with their legs casually splayed out over the backs of the seats in front of them.

Bliss took out his notes, set them down in front of him and slipped on a pair of half-frame reading glasses. He then stood silently at the lectern and allowed his gaze to slowly pass over the crowd. Even at eight in the morning, the faculty was ready to rumble at the first sign of executive overreach, although in the professorial world, a 'rumble' would consist mainly of impassioned rhetoric and name-calling.

Indicating that he was ready to begin, Bliss nodded and the auditorium lights dimmed. He clicked a remote and a Powerpoint slide, *Seven Steps to a Greater Grodin,* appeared on the screen. Only after he had everyone's full attention did he begin to speak.

"Thank you all for coming this morning. With the assistance of Miles Plummer and his capable team, we have come up with a long-term plan to save our school. Yesterday afternoon, the Board of Trustees approved the plan's general structure and in the next few weeks we will move forward with all possible speed to work out the details and begin to implement it."

"We have copies in the back which we will distribute after the meeting, but first and foremost, I wanted to inform all of you of the plan's two key components, without which Grodin cannot continue as a financially-viable institution."

"Bad news comin'," thought practically everyone in the room, except for Professor Emeritus Jacques Henderson, who had already dozed off.

Bliss clicked the PowerPoint device and a new slide appeared on the screen: *The Road Ahead.*

"We will immediately return to the traditional college structure of two Schools instead of five—the School of Humanities and the School of Science and Technology. This step alone will allow us to significantly reduce administrative overhead."

'I'm out of a job,' thought Peter.

Bliss continued, "of course, we will fulfill our commitment to our students by ensuring that they can take all the courses they'd signed up for this fall. And in keeping with Grodin's dedication to excellence in innovative instruction, we have decided, and the Board has agreed, that starting this fall, our students will have the benefit of learning directly from the very best."

Bliss paused again and looked around the room. He needn't have, as at this point he definitely had everyone's full attention.

"To that end, we will be eliminating all of our temporary adjunct and lecturer hires so that our tenured faculty can return to the classroom to teach, full-time, those courses which were previously taught by outside instructors."

Bliss paused to let the weight of his decision to sink in.

Were Bliss charged with notifying the faculty that the world was about to end, that event would have been less dispiriting than this—the fact that they would now have to teach courses they had previously sloughed off onto adjuncts and lecturers.

But Bliss had more.

"Unfortunately, there will also necessarily be some cuts to the support staff and all budgets will be closely monitored by Mr. Plummer and his team. But, with these additional cuts in staffing, we believe we can reduce our overall operational expenses to a manageable level and thus honor all of our contractual obligations to tenured faculty."

But this audience of tenured professors was not interested in what might happen to others. One stood up and interrupted, "Excuse me! Excuse me! What, exactly, do you mean by 'full-time?'"

Bliss answered without checking his notes, "full time means teaching three courses per quarter with at least one at the freshman-sophomore level." He paused a moment to let that sink in, then added, "three quarters a year."

"But that's nine hours a week in the classroom—at a minimum!" shouted another. And then, demonstrating the mathematical acuity possessed by most of the non-technical members of the professoriat, quickly added, "or twelve, if they're four-unit courses!"

"You can't make us do that!" yelled another.

"We have checked the basic employment contract and, yes, we can 'make you do that,' as you put it, but we'd prefer not to use the threat of termination to force anyone to do anything. However, I imagine there might be some who will find this new arrangement not to their liking, and in anticipation of that, Mr. Plummer has drafted resignation and buy-out agreements which he will be happy to go over with you."

Miles smiled and, as if tinkling a small bell, held up a sheaf of papers and gently waved them in the air.

Peter sank back in his seat, thinking that his life as he had known it, was over.

The mood in the auditorium had gone from somber gloom to now one of riotous outrage. Several profs stood up, shook their fists at the stage and shouted out their full-throated displeasure.

Trying to maintain control, Bliss continued, "Miles and his staff will be setting up meetings with individual departments to go over the budgetary adjustments that will have to be made. We will also be issuing the new teaching assignments in the next few days."

But the mob was unassuaged and Bliss's voice was barely heard of the rising din. The faculty now stood *en masse,* shouting cries of "you won't get away with this!" "No way!" along with a few "bullshits" and "motherfuckers" thrown in for good measure.

Attempting to be heard over the rising roar, Bliss leaned over and shouted into the microphone, "copies of the plan are available at the back of the auditorium." He motioned to the rear of the hall where several grim-faced admins, now worried that they might become collateral damage, had set out spiral-bound copies of the plan.

As the mob raged on in the pit of the auditorium, Bliss could scarcely be heard and, when he realized that fearing for his personal safety might be a reasonable assessment of the situation, he shouted with a final flourish, "this meeting is adjourned!" He and Miles then quickly exited stage left, mustering up as much dignity as they could under the circumstances.

The faculty continued their hubbub until they collectively realized that there was no one left to rail against. They stormed out, vociferously shouting at each other the buzzwords and talking points which they would refine for the many verbal battles that were sure to come. And, in a move he would later attribute to revolutionary fervor instead of a personal loss of control, one Race and Gender prof upend the table that supported several stacks of the *Seven Steps*, sending them flying into the air as the admins scurried to safety.

Never had the faculty been so much of one mind about a single issue since the election of George W. Bush. (That unanimity might have exceeded one hundred percent in 2016, as that election probably emboldened several profs to vote more than once.)

For the senior faculty, tenure was the moat that surrounded their castle, ensuring that theirs would be lives of comfort devoid of all but the most minor of irritants. With tenure, they were destined to live in a stress-free cocoon where they were at liberty to think great thoughts—insulated from many of the worries and hassles of everyday life. Never mind as to whether their 'great thoughts' had any impact on the world outside the academy, that was for Time and future Nobel Prize committees to determine.

Although they were not immune to dramatic changes in their private lives, once tenured, their most difficult professional decisions were where to vacation and how to avoid the dreaded eight o'clock class. They had grown accustomed to dropping in at the office in the mid-to-late morning to chat up their co-workers, check their emails, surf the web, maybe write something, have lunch, surf the web some more, and somewhere along the way perhaps meet with a student or two, then grab their briefcases or backpacks and head for the gym or home around four. And, every now and then, actually teach a class for an hour or two.

Now, all that was gone.

Over.

Finito.

The faculty was now faced with the reality of having to teach basic courses to freshmen and sophomores. They not only felt betrayed and humiliated, they most of all were terrified by the prospect of actually having to work for two, or three or four hours a day, every day—and at teaching, no less.

To quote the great Joseph Conrad, "The horror! The horror!"

## Chapter Thirty-Five
Rage Against The Machine

*O*utside, after the meeting, the professoriat raged against the injustice. There had to be a way around this. Endless talk of group action came naturally to those permanently 'down with the struggle.' They vowed to fight to the end and deploy the full arsenal of tactics traditionally trotted out to confront The Man: Bullhorns. Barricades. Occupy. Non-negotiable demands. They would mobilize the troops (although they would exhaustively discuss how to avoid 'the troops' trope, as that designation was obviously excessively militaristic.)

In the coming days, they would Text. They would Tweet. They would Instant Message. They would pen erudite letters to the New York Times in which they raged at the injustice, the inhumanity, the inconvenience of...of... of...actually having to teach.

In the classroom.

To students.

Sadly, they would soon learn that those students, other than the 'what do I have to do to get an 'A' suckups,' were largely indifferent to their plight. They would hardly be disappointed to learn that senior faculty members were being forced to spend more time with them.

When a light drizzle began to fall and thus temporarily dampened the fires of their revolutionary fervor, the gaggle slowly dispersed, but not before affirming again to each other and to the world that, united in their solidarity, they would fight to the last man and woman against this latest outrage.

But, when a boat capsizes in deep waters far from the shore, the potential drownee's first thought is not about the well-being and safety of his fellow passengers, but rather, 'where the fuck is my life preserver!'

So, while silently humming *We Shall Overcome* and firmly believing in truth, justice and, if not in The American Way, at least in the righteousness of their cause, most would eventually begin to think about how to minimize his or her own particular burdens, sacrifices and inconveniences.

And if, in the end, others were to suffer 'disproportionate adverse impacts,' well, so be it.

Cookies crumble.

That night Peter had a nightmare of the first order—he dreamt he was teaching *Beowulf* to freshmen and sophomores, most of whom thought they had signed up for a class about werewolves and vampires. In the real world, of course, he wouldn't be teaching *Beowulf* because no one taught *Beowulf* anymore. Or Chaucer. Even a course featuring old Will-The-Thrill was a less than an even-money bet to make the cut in the world of post-modern literature.

There had to be a way out. But no grand solution appeared to him in a burst of insight. No comic book light bulb went off above his head. There was no Eureka moment…at least for now.

## Chapter Thirty-Six
The Hired Guns of August


*I*f the professoriat was primarily concerned about their jobs, Bliss was not. As he saw it, his first order of business was to prevent wholesale defections from the student body. Despite attempts to keep things on the QT, word of Grodin's financial problems leaked out with the speed of a National Enquirer story on Bill Clinton's latest bimbo eruption. It was imperative that the enrollment numbers hold the line as that now represented the only source of funding which could keep the old Grodin sausage factory in the business of churning out product.

Even though it was too late for most students to go elsewhere, it was imperative to discourage the natural inclination of some students to take some time off to 'find themselves.' Usually, those who were interested in 'finding themselves' found themselves smoking pot in Amsterdam or studying wave dynamics in the South Pacific from atop a boogie-board.

So, General Bliss Moynihan launched his 'Blisskrieg,' with Field Marshall Miles Plummer leading the troops.

A few days *Après le Catastrophe*, a small platoon of twenty-something consultants descended on Grodin and set up a command center in the President's Office where they hunkered down and worked feverishly late into the night, every night. Like an occupying army, they were aberrations within Grodin's academic culture, where anything that approached even a nine-to-fiveish workday was considered to represent near-sweatshop conditions. In terms of focus and single-mindedness, Miles' Minions only peers at Grodin were the nerds in computer science who rarely strayed from their computer screens, with the primary difference between the groups being that the Minions wore business suits while the nerds rarely bothered to change clothes.

Under Plummer's direction, the Minions revamped and ramped up Grodin's presence on Facebook, Instagram, WhatsApp, Snapchat, Twitter and other social media platforms where they wooed students like LeBron James would have been had he ever considered hooping at Chattahoochie State.

As the official adult in the room, Bliss sent out a more formal letter and DVD to the parents and older alums. He promised accountability to the point of offering a money-back guarantee, but, like a good politician, should the guarantee ever have to be paid, that remittance would take place well after his time in office was over. (Message: read the fine print.)

The overall word coming from Grodin was 'We Care. Everything's great, but we're making it even better.' He might as well have stamped 'New!' and 'Improved!' on the forehead of every faculty member. The pitch couldn't have been clearer: the 'New Grodin' would be nurturing, sensitive and ready to adjust to the needs of the students and their parents—especially the parents—

who could now expect to get more bang for their buck, and, after graduation, possibly get a competent young adult who was unlikely to move back into the family basement.

Behind the scenes, Miles and his fellow number crunchers moved swiftly to revamp Grodin's organizational structure in an attempt to balance inflow versus outflow. But, of course, that rebalancing would have to come on the backs of 'The Expendables.' Whatever happened to the little people was sad and unfortunate, but in hard times, one had to expect collateral damage.

## Chapter Thirty-Seven
Fighting Back


*W*hat was to be done to stop this onslaught on their way of life? With the Huns now not just at the gate, but inside and firmly established in the President's Office, the faculty needed to respond, and fast, to the Barbarians in Charge.

A quick and expensive consultation with a labor lawyer confirmed that as long as the tenured members of the professoriat were paid, Bliss was within his rights to ~~adjust the terms of their employment agreement~~ screw them over.

For the faculty, the thought of having to deal with even the slightest increase in their teaching load was abhorrent and was seen as a direct threat to their way of life, one to which they felt entitled by dint of first suffering through the drudgery of graduate school and then by enduring the groveling and ass-kissing humiliation needed to get to tenure. Then, having captured the 'Holy Grail of Lifetime Job Security,' they naturally believed that a life of graceful living—steeped in the contemplative arts—was their just due for all they had been through, and the fact that they had then arrived at the Promised Land was *a priori* evidence of their inherent superiority and deservedness.

But now, faced with the fact that their way of life was under assault, they were forced to think about it.

Hard.

And fast.

Oh, they could try to find another job elsewhere, but most were too old for that, and frankly, many of the senior faculty had already taken their shot at the majors and had struck out. Landing a tenured position at Grodin had saved them from being forced to ply their trade at a junior college or, heaven forfend, at a public high school. And unless they had inherited a trust fund, either by marriage or by virtue of having picked the right parents while in the womb, their only option was to take a job outside academia in the Real World of commerce and business—a world which the faculty suspected to be a veritable hell-hole inhabited by hicks, rubes and yahoos whose idea of a great night out was dinner at Appleby's.

The very thought of working a regular nine-to-five job was depressing, to say the least. In times past, a few had entertained fantasies about becoming an entrepreneur, but in order to succeed at that, one had to have an idea which could be transformed into a product people were likely to buy. There were cautionary tales aplenty from the artists on the faculty who, when younger and hoping to become the' Next Big Thing,' had stepped into the world of commerce by offering their creations to galleries and collectors. The fact that they had ended up in academia proved the point that success was difficult and involved serious risk-taking—a disquieting and completely-foreign concept to those who had become accustomed to living the secure 'Life of the Mind in the Land of the Big-Brains.'

Opting for Bliss's buyout was a possibility, but most had never planned on leaving the profession before a time of their choosing, not to mention that the terms of the buyout were not stacked in their favor. Since the onset of *The Situation*, many had looked at their pension plans and realized there was a significant gap between their hopes and dreams on one side of the ledger and the harsh reality of the skimpy numbers on the other.

The truth was that there was not much of a market for over-forty academics with few practical skills who possessed only the self-ascribed title of 'Official Smart Person.'

So, Real Life was happening.

To them.

And it wasn't fair.

They had to do something. But what?

Their usual method of handling problems was to form a committee, meet sporadically and, like Marx's imagined ideal, let the problem wither away or hand it off to an admin under their customary *modus operandi* of 'let someone else deal with it.'

But this time there was no one else.

So, despite the massive institutional predisposition which favored inaction and inertia, the faculty began to organize against the injustice. After the giant bombshell that Bliss had dropped at the All-Hands meeting and after several days and nights of on-line haggling, the professoriat finally managed to come together for their own version of an All-Hands meeting, though it was not quite 'All-Hands,' limited as it was to only tenured faculty. The jayvee team of assistant professors was not asked to attend and invitations to the town teams of adjuncts, lecturers and visiting profs were never even considered.

The first order of business was location. The organizers decided to meet in the Laurence and Maryanne Pratt Keebler Auditorium in the School of Science and Technology. With its long oval shape and a shallow well in the center, meeting in Keebler would allow the members of the audience to face each other, thus engendering a hoped-for sense of equality and fraternity rather than the typical teacher-on-stage, students-in-audience arrangement of most classrooms.

Though still not at full strength, a majority of the faculty had returned early from vacations because of *The Situation*. Upon seeing many of their colleagues for the first time since graduation, they greeted each other as though they were coming together at a funeral. The older male faculty members began their greeting ritual with solidarity handshakes and grim, 'we're-all-in-this-together' shoulder-clutches. The younger men engaged in hand-clenching *jujitsu* moves and elaborate fist-bumping maneuvers while the female faculty first greeted each other with happy-face smiles, muffled shrieks of joy and polite hugs, but then, remembering the seriousness of their circumstances, quickly donned sad and somber faces that showed they were down, way down, with the struggle.

Sitting across the well, Margaret shot Peter a steely glare before resuming her animated conversation with one of her fellow Harpies. Peter sat down next to Pierce, who, with an eyebrow raised, acknowledged that he'd witnessed Margaret's 'friendly-fire' greeting.

With an eye on assuming a leadership position in 'The Resistance,' several professors worked the room, leaning over and whispering into the ears of their peers, then with a deft pat on the shoulder, they moved on to their next prospect.

Because they had been unable to settle on a single leader or even a strategy, the informal faculty group who had called the meeting decided to select an Interim Chair through a random drawing from the pool of junior faculty, hoping to select someone who would not use his or her temporary power for personal advantage. That unfortunate's task would be to lead the discussion at the first meeting. The figurative 'short straw' had been drawn by Associate Professor Renée Framboise from the School of Critical Social Theory, who, by her own admission, had no designs on running anything—ever.

With gavel in hand, Ms. Framboise stepped to the lectern and hammered away at it until she got everyone's attention. This took nearly a minute because members of the faculty were accustomed to yakking away until they were finished and, by and large, they weren't.

After finally getting everyone to sit down and shut up, she thanked them all, introduced herself and laid out the ground rules. She clearly had thought things through overnight and had come up with a plan. The morning session would be devoted to a discussion of possible courses of action with each speaker allowed only one minute to get his or her idea out. She assigned another junior prof, Ted Quackenbush, to white-board the suggestions. At the end of the brainstorming session, the group would narrow down the proposals and after lunch, discuss the main options in detail and vote on what to do next.

So, the suggestions piled in one after the other until Quackenbush had to call for a second portable white-board to be wheeled in. Naturally, with a room full of accomplished filibusterers, limiting each speaker to a single minute proved to be nearly impossible, but Framboise held her ground and fiercely gaveled those who went overtime into submission—an act which, in years to come, might scuttle her promotion to full professorship as faculty memories of minor or imagined slights were infinitely long. As the suggestions came in, Professor Framboise summarized each with a short phrase that Quackenbush quickly wrote on the white-board while the next person was speaking. Barely able to keep up, he had to stop occasionally and flap his hand in the air to shake off the numbness.

Peter marveled at her command of the professoriat and wondered how Grodin had been able to attract and hire her. He had seen her around campus, but didn't know her and had never seen her in action. Of course, as was his wont, he began to wonder what her personal life was like and thought about Googling her on his iPhone, but didn't, as he feared he might be seen doing it by someone sitting nearby. So he put that idea on hold and made a mental note to wait until he was back at the office.

After nearly two hours of brainstorming, Framboise called for a fifteen-minute break, after which the group would narrow down which suggestions to bring forward for further discussion.

Overall, Peter was impressed. Perhaps the professoriat could come together after all and figure a way out of the mess.

After the break, the morning session dragged on until well after noon. Hunger had set in and restlessness soon followed. Fortunately, a text message on her phone alerted Professor Framboise that the box lunches had arrived.

Everyone had been asked to fork over ten bucks for the privilege of eating tuna, chicken or grilled veggie sandwiches, a bag of potato chips, an apple and an oatmeal cookie. There were complaints, of course, about the lack of gluten-free, sugar-free, organic and sustainable locavore options, which forced several profs to leave Keebler and forage on their own for a suitable meal.

Pierce and Peter picked up their box lunches and repaired to the outside patio where they sat on stone benches to eat. They were joined by the former Dean of Students, Charles 'Chet' Duchin, who sat down uninvited and immediately launched into a bitter soliloquy about the unfairness of his demotion from the high calling of the Deanship back into the ranks of those lowly mortals who merely taught for a living. It was clear that he hoped to enlist Peter, who had suffered a somewhat similar fate, into his personal grievance-mongering society. But now that Janet had departed for the Land of Enchantment and because the former Dean was no longer a factor in faculty hires since there weren't going to be any, Peter declined to join Chet in his indignant acrimony.

The trio became a quartet when Chet's diatribe was interrupted by the arrival of Mark Kohl, a prof from the Chemistry Department. Kohl glanced around furtively as if to make sure no one had noticed that he was associating with a group of obvious kooks, anarchists and ne'er-do-wells. A burly man with a stiff brush of a mustache, Kohl always wore a suit and shirt that were too small for him, causing his neck to swell out over his collar like an inner tube. To complete the look of an FBI agent wannabe, he sported serious jet-black aviator shades.

"Some of us have gotten together to run a little background check on our boy, Bliss," Kohl said in a voice so low that the Three Amigos were forced to lean forward to hear him.

They stared at him quizzically and he lowered his voice even more.

"We're looking into hiring a P. I."

He leaned back, seeming to believe that this explained everything, but as an experienced prof, he quickly interpreting the look on Chet's face as one of total incomprehension, so he added the explanatory words, "private investigator."

Pierce, who had understood all along, said mockingly, "Oh! A gumshoe!"

Kohl continued with a tone of mild irritation, "no, no, we're not going to follow him around...not yet anyway. We don't want to tip him off. We'll just be conducting a little O.R...opposition research."

"Well, good luck with that," said Pierce.

Kohl hoped for a more positive response, but getting none he added, "we've found a guy over in Milton who comes highly recommended."

"Great. As Pierce said, 'good luck with that,'" said Peter.

"We need about five large," said Kohl.

"So, is this like Pledge Night on PBS?" asked Pierce.

"Everything will be strictly confidential. You'll get updates."

"Visa or Mastercard?" said Pierce, clearly enjoying himself.

Getting exasperated, Kohl looked at Pierce sternly. "Cash only. We don't want anything that's traceable. Just in case."

"Will you take it small bills?" said Pierce.

"I see I've come to the wrong place," said Kohl, standing up to leave.

Pierce leaned to the side and pulled his wallet out of his back pocket. "No, no, I'm in," he said as he handed Kohl some money. "Anything for the cause."

Peter sighed and said, "okay, put me down for a C-Note, but I don't have it on me."

Kohl then nodded towards Chet, "Chet?"

"Okay, put me down for a couple of G-Notes," said Chet.

Kohl's eyes bugged out as he wondered if Chet knew what he was saying.

"I think you mean 'C-Notes,' Chet," whispered Pierce. "A 'G-Note' is a thousand bucks."

"Oh, right. Make that a couple of C-notes then...C-notes," added Chet quickly.

"Thanks," said Kohl as he turned to leave. "I'll be in touch."

"Do I get a receipt?" asked Pierce, but all he got was a glare and a shake of the head.

After Kohl left, Pierce said, "Ah, Liddy lives."

(So that those of you under forty, or maybe fifty, don't have to look it up, G. Gordon Liddy was the only Watergate figure who went to prison without having ratted out his fellow co-conspirators.)

With restroom visits, phone calls, general dithering and in keeping with the long-standing academic tradition of never staying on schedule, the thirty-minute lunch break stretched out to nearly an hour, at which time the group finally straggled back into the auditorium and reconvened.

Now, with multiple white-boards full of suggestions, the meeting was ready for lift-off, but the afternoon session soon began to devolve into a not-so-subtle struggle for the power of leadership, as there were many in the crowd for whom wresting control of the process was the prize and they would try their best to drum-major their way to the front of the parade. While it was difficult to foresee whether overall success or failure was in the cards, it was clear that the turmoil around the financial crisis would generate a significant amount of *sturm und drang*—so much that it might behoove those individuals with a bent towards self-promotion to maneuver themselves into a position where the public spotlight might shine more brightly on certain aspiring pundits and wannabe spokespersons than on others.

So, as they discussed action items, strategies and agendas, the underlying subtext was about who would lead and who would follow, with the central problem being that there were far more self-described Chiefs than Indians, although there was no one in this group who would dare use those words, as collectively they were mostly an assemblage of privileged white males.

Among the presumptive 'Chiefs' angling for the top dog spot, one of the first to nudge himself forward was Phil Bittman from the School of Critical Social Theory. Bittman saw in this crisis a way to relive his long-past but fondly-remembered glories of 'Sticking It to The Man in the Sixties.' As befitting one from that era, he wore a fringed, beaded leather vest over a sleeveless tank top which appeared not to have been washed since the Trial of the Chicago Seven. Now balding, he pulled what was left of his greying hair back into a thick braid which hung halfway down his back, a personal trademark that led the students to snicker-name him 'Ponytail Phil.' He viewed himself as a Lenin-like figure, one who would never directly lead the charge to the barricades, but who, behind the scenes, would direct others in the creation of a New World Order. Phil's problem was that no one either liked him or liked listening to him. Still, this did not prevent him from trying to guide the discussion with long-winded Marxist deconstructions of *The Situation.*

Rich Van Zandt was another who inserted himself into the mix by standing and harrumphing 'point-of-order,' whenever the discussion violated one of Robert's Rules, which happened so often that he seemed to be doing jumping-jack exercises in gym class.

Van Zandt's normal look was a tie, white shirt and no jacket with slacks pulled up well above his waist and cinched tight with a thick belt. The result was that his plump belly spilled out in all directions, making him look more like Winnie the Pooh than Winston Churchill. A social technocrat, Van Zandt had complete faith in the ability of academic experts to run huge governmental bureaucracies, failing to understand that they were the same people who could figure out a way to lose money running the booze and hooker concessions at the Democratic National Convention. No one with a modicum of common sense would put either him or his cohorts in charge of a lemonade stand. Pierce had already dubbed him 'No Chance Van Zandt.'

One with even less of a prospect than 'No Chance' was Jay 'Mad Dog' Cramer, whose bombastic personality caused fellow profs to avoid him by ducking behind the nearest available shrubbery as he charged around campus.

A stout tug-boat of a man, Cramer had opinions on everything which he expressed frequently and at top volume, showering those unfortunates who were on the receiving end of his diatribes with an unwelcome spray of spittle. 'Often Wrong, But Never In Doubt' could have been his personal motto had he the self-awareness or insight into how others saw him, but of course, he didn't. He believed he was a natural-born leader and could only sadly shake his head at the way the world continually failed to recognize his greatness. Fortunately for those at the meeting, whenever he stood up to launch one of his filibusters, Ms. LaFramboise fiercely gaveled him into temporary silence the second his time expired. He then sat down and glowered at those around him, arms folded in defiance, as he waited for the next opportunity to launch into full bloviation mode.

There were several candidates of the standard-issue variety and the favorite in this group was Carol(e) Mobutu-Swann, a recently-tenured forty-somethingish woman of intentionally-indeterminate sexual orientation and ethnicity. With her smooth, deep-olive skin, she could have been black, Hispanic, Asian, Southern European or any combination of them. And, given the new craze for multi-cross-genderization, even the basic man-woman distinction was in question. She dressed conservatively, usually in a trim jacket with matching pants and with her clipped, precise persona, she gave off hints of lesbianity without overtness. She was also efficient, organized and direct—qualities which would be considered positive in most circles, but at Grodin were viewed with deep and barely-disguised distrust because they aroused the suspicion that she might be angling for a position in administration—a career move anathema to most right-thinking academics. By dint of earnest politicking, she was the leader at the clubhouse turn, but admittedly, there was a long way to go and her support was thin as the veneer on a K-Mart cabinet. The pack would not hesitate to desert her should a more attractive candidate step forward—i.e., one who perhaps could more clearly check off the requisite political, gender and ethno-identity boxes.

So...after several more hours of soul-destroying harangues, screeds and impassioned diatribes by the Founding Members of The Society Of The Perpetually-Outraged, some of the profs who were less-obsessed with grabbing hold of the controls began to drift away. Pierce had already slipped out early, suggesting his destination to Peter with a pantomime of Johnny Carson's golf swing.

Peter could see where all this was headed—it was high school student council all over again. The faculty would hash, re-hash and hash over again about what was to be done until the resulting concoction resembled nothing more than a thick pablum, and unless one was willing to wade in until one was way more than knee-deep in the muck, it would be a complete waste of time.

Peter realized that this was not for him. Though he wished them well, he did so silently as he left and headed for his personal *sanctum sanctorum* where he could ponder his future. All he wanted was to have his life back, but the odds on that fell into that very narrow zone between slim and none.

Soon he was asleep on the familiar and well-worn couch in his office.

If one ever wondered how we get the politicians we get, observing the dynamics of group meetings would explain a lot, where success often comes to whoever is the last man, woman, or differently gender-identified person standing. They are the ones who are willing to listen, haggle, bargain, and blunderbuss their way to the finish line, long after more sensible people had found more enjoyable ways to waste their time, rather than engage in the endless migraine-inducing quibbling, the soul-destroying charades of self-promotion, the scheming subterfuges, the manipulation and the outright lying essential for political success.

# Chapter Thirty-Eight
Plan B


*N*ow nearly three weeks *Après Le Catastrophe* and several days after their own All-Hands meeting, the faculty received a voluminous directive by email entitled *Twelve Steps Towards a Greater Grodin*. By sending it out as a PDF, it was clear that Bliss was unwilling to risk a second All-Hands meeting, at which the faculty might drop their unanimous opposition to the Second Amendment and arrive packing heat.

If the cash shortfall announcement hit Grodin like a ton of bricks, the *Twelve Steps* missive hit the campus like the asteroid that wiped out the dinosaurs. It outlined a new organizational structure, a new curriculum and, most importantly, laid out precisely who would be teaching what, when, where, and to whom.

And, most importantly to the faculty, how often.

Sitting in front of his computer screen, Peter stared with foreboding at the unopened *Twelve Steps* icon. It took him back to his senior year in high school when he held a letter from Harvard Admissions and, by weighing its heft in his hand, tried to divine whether the news was good or bad. Harvard had been his one long-shot roll of the dice to make it to the bigs in the college admission crapshoot. Unfortunately, his roll came up snake eyes and he ended up at Penn State.

With the PDF icon insolently hovering on the computer screen and refusing to even hint at its contents, Peter finally clicked on it to open it up. The document was nearly two-hundred pages long and in small print. Peter spent the better part of an hour scanning through it in an attempt to understand the new organizational structure that Bliss, Miles and their minions had created.

As advertised, there were now only two Schools with the traditional division between Humanities and Sciences, but beyond that, everything had changed. Out of what had once been nearly twenty deans on the academic side, only two remained, one for each school. Associate deans, assistant deans, assistants to the assistant deans—all were gone. Department chairs, also gone. At the bottom of the academic totem pole, all lecturers and adjuncts were let go and all of the untenured assistant profs would not have their contracts renewed. The administration offices had also been chopped, but not as severely, as it was clear that Bliss's plan was to control all of Grodin's administrative issues from his command post.

In one fell swoop, practically the entire administrative hierarchy had been eliminated.

Equality had finally come to the faculty lounge and Peter knew that no one would be happy about it. Now, with no release time for chairing the department, Peter was heading back to the classroom—a place he had spent years trying to escape. Needless to say, his mood was not good.

He skimmed through the PDF until he found his Fall quarter teaching assignments. He had a three-unit lecture course, *"Foundations of Modern American Literature.* No problem there, he thought. He could wing that one with minimal research and prep.

He discovered he would also be teaching a section of the Writing Skills Workshop for incoming freshmen, known amongst the faculty as 'Riting for Retards. Previously, adjuncts, lecturers and part-timers had taught the Writing Skills Workshops because it was considered to be a waste of time and talent for a full professor to teach basic composition to incoming students. Fortunately, this was easily doable, but he'd have to reacquaint himself with the limitations and idiocies of the freshman mind.

He then found his third course, *Entering the Labyrinth: The Flowering of Third Wave Feminist Literatur*e, an upper-class seminar which was extremely popular among a certain subset of students. Professor Lucienne Sanchez-Obrador had taught the course for over a decade, but this fall she would be starting a year-long sabbatical, and the plan had been to have an adjunct take it over.

Peter was stunned. This had to be a mistake. Not only did he know next to nothing about the subject, but he was terrified by the idea of teaching a class which would be filled with feminists, social justice warriors, out-of-the-closet lesbians and lesbians-in-waiting, all of whom would be on high alert for the slightest insult or the faintest suggestion of a patriarchal snub. And given his proneness for the off-the-cuff remark when his mouth got ahead of his brain, this was not a territory Peter wished to enter. He would have to get out of this —and fast.

But how?

Claiming subject matter ignorance was not a viable option for a professor of Peter's stature. Plus, he suspected that he'd been targeted for this Mafia-style hit by Bliss and his mob and there was no way he'd be able to convince them to let him teach something else.  His only hope was to trade for something else, even though he knew his hand was weak. Grodin had a long tradition whereby professors could petition to exchange courses as long as the swap was regarded as academically-neutral. It was a long shot because Peter's problem was that only a few profs would be interested in taking his unless they had something equally horrible. Still, for him, almost anything would be better. He skimmed through the list of other offerings, hoping to find something, anything, for which he might make a deal. He found seminars in:

*Late 20th Century Literature: From Magical Realism to the False Consciousness of Post-Colonial Heteronormative Triumphalism.*

*Literature & Culture: An Introduction to the (Meta)Dataologies of Misogyny.*

*Adventures in the Skin Trade: Deconstructing the Hetero-Erotic Myth in 20th Century American Literature.*

He wondered, 'whatever happened to plain old vanilla courses like *An Introduction to Women's Literature?*' While he was sinking further into his personal gloom, there was a knock on the door. Pierce poked his head in and getting a go-ahead nod from Peter, came in and sat down.

Not wanting to immediately launch into a whiny diatribe about his *Third Wave* course, Peter asked, "how bad is yours?"

"Not too bad. I have *An Intro to Twentieth-Century Comparative Lit* as my survey. I actually taught it a couple of years ago and my seminar is *Post-Colonial Lit*, with, of course, the obligatory after the colon gobbledygook, '*Narratives from Bali to Barbados and Mali to Michoacán.*' I have no idea what that means or how it all fits together, but…welcome to Bliss's world. What's your seminar?"

Peter told him about his *Flowering of Feminist Literature* course and ended by saying, "I can't help but think that sticking me with this was intentional."

"That I do not doubt," said Pierce, "though I bet Bliss wouldn't mind seeing it go, but Lucienne made it so popular they were probably afraid to drop it."

"Did you see some of the other seminars?" said Peter, who leaned forward, peered intently at his computer screen and read, "*Ride the Wild Peony: Poesy and the Semiotics of Sexuality.*" He leaned back and looked up at Pierce, "it's not even *Poetry and Semiotics*, but '*Poesy.*'" Peter gestured, surrounding "*Poesy*" with air-quotes. "Pretension knows no bounds."

"One could ask how anyone could come up with these courses, but apparently we did," said Pierce.

"And now we're going to have to teach them," said Peter. He gestured towards the PDF on his computer and said, "I read somewhere in here that they came up with the course list by polling the students. As if asking students tells you anything." He paused, then continued, "I'm guessing that they massaged the numbers to get the outcome they wanted."

"Would you have expected anything else?"

"Since when have we had to listen to what students want?"

"That's Bliss's game plan exactly. Marketing. Give 'em what they want. Or what they think they want," said Pierce. "Higher ed is a buyer's market these days. Unless you're Harvard or Yale."

"Good god, we're the ones who are supposed to be in charge."

"Yeah, but as my dad used to say about the hardware business, 'the customer is not always right, but the customer is always the customer.'"

"So is Bliss leading or is he just riding the wave?"

"I think he just got his surfboard out and strapped it to his Woody. The world has changed, old chap, and if we don't figure out how, the third planet from the sun might just wobble off its axis and roll over on us."

"So, adapt or die; the basic evolutionary issue," said Peter. "Too bad the Neanderthals weren't able to figure it out."

"Do you ever feel like one? An evolutionary dead-end?"

"A Neanderthal? I'm more of a Cro-Magnon kind of guy. The Lascaux Caves and all that," said Peter.

"In the grand scheme of things, it didn't go too well for them either," said Pierce.

"I get your point," said Peter.

With their badinage having petered out, both men went uncharacteristically silent for a moment as they pondered where they stood in the great existential drama of life as experienced on the western shore of the Naugahassett River in the early part of the 21$^{st}$ Century.

Pierce finally broke the silence with a question, "what are you going to do about your *Semiotics of Sexuality* class?"

"It's actually *The Flowering of Third Wave Feminist Literature.*" He paused, then added, *"Entering the Labyrinth.* Too bad we don't have a waiver wire like they have in baseball. I'd do anything to get rid of it."

"You could take mine. At least you know something about *Post-Colonial Lit,*" said Pierce.

Something in Pierce's tone caused Peter to look at him quizzically before asking, "you'd want to trade for this? You must be nuts?"

"We could petition to swap seminars. I'm pretty sure we could manage it."

"Why on Earth would you want to teach mine? You don't know any more about *Feminist Literature* than I do."

"Actually," said Pierce, "I'm going to take the buyout, though we need to keep it on the QT for now. We could make the swap now and I'll give my notice right before classes start. Too late for them to switch you back."

"You're not serious about this, are you?" asked Peter. This was the last thing he needed—the loss of his best friend and ally.

Pierce continued, "I see the writing on the wall and it says 'time to get the hell out of Dodge.' Besides, Sarah has been after me to retire for some time now, but Old Man Inertia has kept me in place. This financial thing was the tipping point. Or the cherry on top, if you'd prefer that metaphor."

"Will you be okay? I looked at the buyout numbers and it's not exactly like we won the lottery."

"I still have the Apple stock Sarah made me buy after Jobs came back, so we're pretty well set. And she's going to stay with the trust department for a few more years. She still likes her work."

"I liked my work when it wasn't work," said Peter.

"I know what you mean," said Pierce. "I hate leaving you in the lurch, old chap, but the time has come. 'Ask not for whom the bell tolls' and all that rot."

Pierce stood up to leave and added, "and if you would keep it under your *chapeau* for a while, I'd appreciate it."

After a few seconds of staring at each other with the possibility of real emotion breaking out, Pierce leaned over and offered out his fist for a farewell bump. Peter obliged and said, "I'll miss you, man."

After Pierce left, Peter slumped back into his chair and sighed deeply. He thought about his own retirement portfolio and was all too aware that it was thinner than a Swedish pancake.

# Chapter Thirty-Nine
## Spilt Milk

*D*espite the widespread and Botox-enhanced lip-service paid to the notion that everything done in an institution of higher learning was done for the students, the reality was something quite different. Were one to 'unpack' that old chestnut of conventional wisdom, to use the colloquial academic shorthand for the type of scholarly analysis which—surprise—ends up supporting one's previously-held positions, the dirty little secret was that for decades colleges and universities had organized themselves around the principle that what was good for the faculty was, *ipso facto,* good for everyone. And if the idea of 'everyone' included the students…well, that was simply a nice bonus.

Operating within the confines of what were the generally-accepted best practices of higher education management, Grodin adhered to these principles and thus was run by the faculty and for the faculty. When a nearly equal amount of money rolled in as rolled out, all was good, but the emergence of *The Situation* brought to the fore a more frightening reality—the vast gap between dollars coming in and dollars going out. The bottom line was that there was not enough money to pay the 'Bills,' not to mention the other Toms, Dicks and Harriets on the Grodin payroll.

For the faculty, day-to-day, hand-to-mouth existence had never been even a remote possibility.

And once again, it wasn't fair.

However, the professoriat's 'General Standard of Fairness' did not extend to those living and working outside beyond the royal realm of the faculty lounge. To the lords and ladies of the manor, whatever happened to the little people was sad and unfortunate, but with the coffers nearly bare, something had to give.

A certain number of the little people had to go. And they went.

On a sunny morning in mid-August, Miles' army of grim-faced, dark-suited young men and women descended on the offices of the various departments. One by one, staff members were summoned, read their severance contract, escorted back to their desks to gather a box of personal effects, then perp-walked out of the building.

Tenured profs had been advised to hunker down at home. On this matter, Peter was relieved that he was no longer Chair. In previous years, he would have been the one called upon not only to make the decision, but also be the one to drop the axe on The Unfortunates.

The mantra for the Day of Doom seemed to be that the firings would continue until morale improved.

Morale didn't, so the firings did.

The first casualty Peter heard from was Betsy. She called Peter, but he didn't pick up. He waited and listened to her sobbing message on voice mail. Although he felt like a coward, what could one do except avert one's eyes from the carnage? The time for solace and comfort would come later, although such support would most likely be offered by someone else, as Peter's shoulder was not one ready-made for tears.

Both Meg and Henrietta had avoided the axe. Initially, Peter had been miffed that he and his fellow Department Chairs had been ignored in the restructuring process, but when crunch time arrived and actual dismissals were the order of the day, he was glad to have had no part in it. However, had he been asked to weigh in on the firings, Henrietta would have been the one to go, with the inevitable result being the final, spectacular detonation of the 'Ticking Time Bomb.' He was sure that someone had warned Miles and his Minions to tread carefully before entering Henrietta's Danger Zone.

The various adjuncts, lecturers and part-timers were dismissed via email. Peter fielded calls from them throughout the day, tsk-tsked in commiseration about the callousness and unfairness of it all, wished them well in their future endeavors and promised to weigh in with hearty and fulsome recommendations to future employers should they find that necessary. Undoubtedly there would be some form of legal blowback for the abruptness of the layoffs, but Peter felt certain that he would not be someone who would be targeted. Still, seeing nearly half the staff laid off in a single day was a reality check of the sort which few people, and certainly not the faculty, had ever experienced.

He also felt little sympathy for Grodin as an institution should it eventually have to pay settlements of some sort. So be it.

Let justice be served.

Hot or cold.

With spoon. Fork. Or spork.

Whatever worked.

# Chapter Forty
## Time to Cram

$A$fter the firings, the faculty continued their effort to meet the challenge of *The Situation*, but to their surprise, they found themselves failing to find even a scintilla of support for their plight. The basic problem, which few on the faculty had foreseen, was that they had no constituency for their cause other than themselves.

They thought they could rally alums, students and parents to stand behind them, but once again, reality stepped up and took a serious bite out of their assumptions. Most alums were unsympathetic to their peddled narrative that the professoriat was a downtrodden, oppressed class whose working conditions were equivalent to those of migrant farm laborers or Appalachian coal miners. As for the student/parent contingent, the idea of paying for and being taught by full professors instead of lecturers, adjuncts and part-timers was, unsurprisingly, very appealing.

To the public at large, they argued the moral imperative: that the cutbacks at Grodin and the imposition of near-slave labor conditions posed a grave threat to academic freedom everywhere. The faculty argued that any infringement by the plantation overseers on their right to chart their own course was ill-informed, immoral and ignorant. The faculty's view was that simply by virtue of their obvious intellectual superiority, they should be the sole and ultimate arbiters of what should be taught, how it should be taught and who should be the grateful recipients of their collective knowledge and wisdom. When that plea was met with figurative shrugs of indifference by the Yahoos who made up the public-at-large, those shrugs went unnoticed, as one thing the professoriat had extensive experience in was that of ignoring the wishes of their audience.

Some members of the faculty suggested that when classes started, they should stage a slowdown strike, although it occurred to some of the less zealous among them to wonder, 'how would anyone be able to tell?'

In addition to the slowdown option, considerable intellectual firepower went into theorizing as to whether it was better to excel in teaching an undesirable course with the possible outcome being that one would then be forever condemned to teach only such courses in the future, or whether one should strive for mediocrity—admittedly not a high bar—with the hope that by thus throwing one's fate to the winds, randomness might yield a better result.

This complicated line of thought quickly found its way into the trashcan when word came down from Bad News Bliss about how future teaching assignments would be made. The bottom line was that performance evaluations would determine future assignments. These evaluations would take the form of 'pop-ins,' wherein teams of Miles' Minions would randomly drop in on classes and record data on their IPads. What the new criteria were quickly became a matter of intense speculation.

And, perhaps for the first time in any college's history, student evaluations would be taken seriously. Traditionally, they were essentially meaningless exercises to which no one paid attention, but now the faculty would have to perform up to the students' expectations or be downgraded, or perhaps even worse, marked down and set out for consignment.

While a few of the self-appointed leaders of the resistance continued to plot and release manifestos, the grunts on the front lines realized that the start of fall term was now only two weeks away. With many now having been assigned to teach unfamiliar courses, they needed to master new material and draw up lesson plans, factors that would actually require a fresh application of brainpower. And as much as they would have liked to avoid it, if they wished to be paid, the faculty would have to apply themselves to teaching the new curricula—and be graded.

They could hardly have imagined a worse fate.

They?

Graded?

Evaluated?

This was not the profession they had signed up for—one where results mattered.

## Chapter Forty-One
### Fresh Meat for the Grinder


$A$t Grodin, the arrival of the new freshman class signaled summer's end. Also long gone were the days of a lonely student, battered suitcase in hand, getting off at the train station and taking a bus to campus.

Instead, having been nursed, coddled and protected by their parents not only from the slings and arrows of outrageous fortune, but also from the dreadful dangers faced by walking fifty feet down the driveway to pick up the mail or encountering people whose ideas might differ from the received wisdom of twelve years of educated groupthink, the Modern Grodinites arrived like pampered princesses and princelings with their hyper-vigilant parents playing the part of the Praetorian Guard. They came in overstuffed SUV's filled with the modern necessities of college life—personal computers, laptops, cell phones, mini-refrigerators, wardrobes full of clothes, and wall hangings and posters which would stake out each one's claim to individuality and signify an identity which would shape-shift many times in the coming months. They also came with a bike or perhaps two, one for scooting around campus and one for long-distance treks in the surrounding hills. And there were skis and ice skates for the winter and rock-climbing gear for the fall and spring.

With dads doing the heavy-lifting and moms supervising the move-ins, the new students engaged in meet-and-greet rituals with their fellow fledglings, all ready to leave one nest for the next. One-upmanship was rampant and pecking orders were reshuffled on a minute-to-minute basis. Preppies took the early lead out of the gate, having 'been there, dun' that' before.


Behind the scenes, Orientation Day began well before dawn for the unsung heroes and heroines of any organization—those who did both the literal and figurative heavy-lifting of getting registration tables in place and the signage into the ground which directed the newcomers to the appropriate destinations for parking, unloading, etc., etc.—all of the varying kinds of advance work that went into getting everything ready before the fancy folks arrived.

A swarm of older students and still-thankfully employed admins wore *I Am Grodin—Ask Me Anything* T-shirts and directed the horde of incoming parents and students to their various destinations. They manned and womanned the myriad of registration tables for dorms, interest groups and most importantly, the table that sat in front of the administration office where every student needed not only to check in but to write one.

Bliss was more than on-hand for Orientation Day, he was hands-on and all over the place. With one of Miles' Minions whispering personal data to him via a wireless earpiece, Bliss was able to seamlessly connect names to faces as he greeted the arriving newbies like a presidential hopeful campaigning in Podunk City. Bliss gave the impression that he was completely familiar with the backgrounds and personal interests of every student he met.

Nothing escaped his notice. He was at the curb to greet students and parents as they unloaded. He was at the mid-day picnic to hand out box lunches after which he gave an inspiring speech on the Greatness of Grodin while parents and students picked through chicken-salad sandwiches, sipped organic juices from recyclable containers and munched away on chocolate-chip cookies. And when the parents finally drove off late in the afternoon, he was there to wave goodbye as they left their pride and joys in his hands.

The Charm Offensive worked. The newbies were giddy with excitement. People were nice and the food was great. In all, Orientation was like a day-long party, and when the parents finally left, there was beer.

What was not to like?

The faculty took a dimmer view of Bliss's approach. Bliss had encouraged, but not ordered them to come out to meet and greet the new students, but, with only a couple of red-hot defections, they declined, *en masse*.

However, they were at odds amongst themselves as to how they should express their dissatisfaction with Bliss and *The Situation*. Some wanted to hand out flyers with a Manifesto listing their grievances while others wanted to set up a picket line. A few wanted to stage a walk-out on the first day of class. Or go on strike. Another group advocated waiting until classes began, after which they would slow-walk their cooperation, thus wearing their discontent on the sleeves of their leather-patched tweed jackets. But, as usual, talk superseded action and nothing happened. Since staying away from campus when they didn't have to be there was their norm, no one missed them nor did anyone acknowledge their absence with so much as a 'never-mind.'

Because he hadn't had any real teaching responsibilities for years, Peter had always looked forward to freshman orientation. For him, everything was sweetness and light. New students, new parents, all hopeful—the kids ready to get out of the house, and the parents…also ready for the kids to get out of the house.

This year was different, what with Pierce, his best friend and ally having retired and The Resistance having faded to the point of being just a fleeting shadow on the wall. And now, with only a couple of days to go before classes started and with Grodin facing an uncertain future, reality had arrived. With a thud.

Not feeling up to mingling, Peter spent the morning puttering around his third-floor office, and when he looked down at the scene below, he imagined the swarm of students milling about below to be rebellious peasants preparing to storm the castle with the clear intention of moving in and taking over.

His old Ivory Tower now seemed more like a prison than a castle in the sky, and he was not sure that either he or The Tower would survive.

# Chapter Forty-Two
## The New Normal


$T$wo days after Orientation, the upper-class students returned, now battle-scarred veterans of the summer campaign, having endured skirmishes on the consumer front at fast-food places like Wendy's and Burger King, or perhaps having received better postings at Chipotle or the Olive Garden. If better-connected or simply luckier, they'd landed internships with Antelope Rights, the Baby Seal Conservancy or at Protest-Everything Nation. Or if luckier still, they'd spent the summer sojourning in exotic vacation locales. Those without jobs or those not so lucky as to have been the offspring of wealthy parents spent their summer cooling-off in their family's rec room, sucking down brews, watching the Red Sox on TV and embellishing their social networking profiles.

On this the first day of fall classes, Peter squeezed into the BMW and turned to Sirius XM for some old-time rock-and-roll, hoping that would cheer him up. But today, even Chuck Berry wasn't enough. Since the onset of *The Situation*, he had been too depressed to bike to campus and as a result, he'd had to slide the driver's seat back a couple of notches to accommodate his expanding waistline.

With his first class starting at ten and running late, Peter didn't have enough time to make even a thirty-second pit stop at the Tipsy Spoon, so he ended up fixing himself a cup of instant in the department lounge. But with the New Austerity having created a shortage of admins, there was no one to stock the refrigerator with half-and-half or milk, and heaven forfend that a full professor should have to attend to such a menial task. Even though he was reasonably alert at this early hour, his fingers were still half-asleep and he struggled to open a package of Coffee-Mate. With all the technological advances that had been made in the world, Peter wondered why it was still so difficult to open cellophane food packets?

After finally getting his coffee together, he headed towards his office and glanced in at one of the small lecture halls. He was momentarily-buoyed to see Margaret unleashing her wrath on the unsuspecting students who had signed up for her eight o'clock. Peter didn't know what course she was teaching, but just knowing that she had been assigned an eight o'clock moved the needle on his mood-meter from total despair to straightforward, standard issue depression. He did wonder for a moment what had happened to Lars, the billionaire shipping magnate, but was well-aware of the fact that everyone involved with Margaret eventually came to their senses.

After checking his email and gathering his notes for the first class, Peter headed across Squirrelle to the Max and Judith Ertz-Holman Learning Center, which had been built exclusively for large lecture classes. He hadn't given a lecture for a while but, like riding a bike, he was sure it would all come back to him. After all, he was dealing with nineteen and twenty-year-olds who knew nothing about anything outside of social media. He put on a wireless lavaliere mike, tapped it to make sure it was working, then turned it off.

After writing his name on the blackboard, he stood at the lectern and waited for the second hand on the clock to hit twelve before he began. He started with a "good morning," but most of the students ignored him and continued to talk and text. He repeated his "good morning" and added a "let's get started" for good measure. This got the attention of a few students, but most ignored him and continued to chat away with each other or text on their phones. Peter attempted a third launch but again was ignored. Finally, he thumped on his lavalier microphone until the noise from the P.A. system drowned out the students' chatter. Some of the students were clearly annoyed at having their conversations interrupted, but Peter plowed ahead.

"Okay, vacation's over. Time to get to work."

He introduced himself and started his lecture with a recitation of the course's subject matter, his expectations, blah-blah-blah. By now the room was quiet, but only a few had their eyes on him. The rest continued to tap-tap-tap away at their laptops or stare intently at their giant iPhones. Peter had no idea whether or not they were paying attention, so after about ten minutes or so of lecturing, he paused and asked if anyone had any questions.

They had none.

He hadn't taught a large lecture class for years, but he knew from colleagues that things had changed, and not for the better. Students wanted... no, demanded that they be entertained and made it clear that they were not there to be challenged intellectually. Even though this was a literature class, recent dispatches from the front had informed him that assigning any readings over fifty pages wouldn't cut it with this crowd. Knowing this, Peter had synopsized everything, but insisted as a point of principle that over the course of the semester they read at least one complete novel and write a paper on it. That this barely reached even the minimal threshold for what might be considered college-level work, such was the new reality.

He managed to get through the lecture, covering Cooper and Hawthorne, but he sensed the students' indifference. Why were they even there, he wondered, if they were so uninterested in the subject? The course, *Foundations of Modern American Literature,* was an elective, not even a requirement. Peter realized that it was a Brave New World out there and that it was going to be a long slog to the finish line.

Back in his office and killing time before his afternoon 'Retards' class, he prepped for his next *Foundations* lecture by re-reading Melville's *Moby Dick,* the next literary classic waiting in the on-deck circle. He skimmed through it for the first time in forty years, but after a few chapters, he dreaded having to talk about it to his students. It was boring. Horrible. Too long. Even for him, a seasoned literature veteran.

He soon found himself rooting for the whales.

## Chapter Forty-Three
### Young Holden


*B*ecause Bliss Had So Decreed, all first and second-year students were to take an introductory writing class and every Humanities profs had been drafted to teach one of them. In some societal circles, there existed the general notion that writing was *passé*. What with spell-check, grammar-check and the abbreviated forms of communication in text and Twitter, who needed to learn the rules of the road, writin'-wise?

Bliss disagreed, not on high-minded grounds based on the idea that there was a minimal standard of literacy that defined an educated person, but rather because there was a market for those who possessed, if not literary ability, at least a modicum of basic writing skills.

Of course, the faculty viewed having to teach basic composition as an effrontery of the first magnitude. In the past, introductory courses like this had been farmed out to lecturers and adjuncts, but now it was either teach or hit the road. So they taught.

By the luck of the draw, Peter's section was of the all-frosh variety, so he speculated that he could pretty much wing it, as the freshmen, still a bit dazed and confused by their first days at college, were most likely to be, if not intimidated by their profs, at least respectful of them.

But, when he walked into the classroom after lunch, like their peers that morning, the twenty or so students didn't come to attention right away when he called the class to order. They continued to whisper, giggle and text for well-beyond the socially-acceptable time that it would usually take to get down to business. Peter had to raise his voice and talk over them until they shut up. He let this pass, but it definitely irritated him.

After finally getting their attention, he introduced himself and talked about the objectives of the course. He then employed the tried-and-true academic time-killing tactic of going around the room and having the students introduce themselves, occasionally asking a question here and there along the way with the hope of loosening things up.

He then asked them to spend the rest of the hour writing five hundred words on *What I Didn't Do This Summer*, mainly so he could assess their skill level and their talent, had they any.

The writing didn't start right away because Peter hadn't factored in that the students wouldn't be bringing pens and paper to the class. A few had pens, but none had paper. The students came up with the solution of using their laptops and phones and emailing their five hundred word essays to him.

While waiting for them to finish their *oeuvres,* Peter spent the rest of the class hoping to set a good example by reading an actual book.

One student, a lanky young man, finished early and when he got up to leave, Peter heard his phone beep and saw that the young man's email had arrived. Peter opened the attachment and began reading.

*What I Didn't Do This Summer*
By Jason Feldman

One thing I didn't do was save the world—I didn't even save any fucking whales. Not a single one. And I certainly didn't help any old ladies cross the street. Jesus Christ, if they need help crossing the street, they should stay home. Or hire someone. There are plenty of worthless, unemployed people out there.

My parents, well, actually my Dad, made me get a job at Starbucks, so what I didn't do there was learn how to make a double mocha latte with soy milk. I was the low dude on the totem pole so all I did was bus-boy stuff—take out garbage, clean crap up off the tables and then wipe them down. Boy, did I do a lot of table-wiping. My Dad must have had to pull some serious rope to get me that crappy job (sarcasm alert) when he could have, had he wanted to, gotten me on writing code for Google or let me make some serious coin working the trading floor at Goldman, but noooo…I was to be punished for getting into a bit of a scrape in my last month at St. Paul's. (And yeah, I'm a fucking Paulie.) So what am I doing here at Grodin instead of Harvard, Yale or even Brown, you might ask? Well, apparently the morons running the college admissions offices consider me to be Trouble with a capital T. It seems that borrowing a golf cart for a moonlight spin around the old Country Club is considered a dingable offense. (So what if I drove it into a lake? It was eleven at night and the cart paths weren't lit so how was I supposed to know there was a lake in the way? No one died like at Chappaquiddick.)

Anyway, what I learned at Starbucks was that the Average American is a fucking loser/moron who thinks that because he has five bucks to blow on overpriced burnt coffee, he can lord it over you if you're wearing an *I (Heart) Starbucks* T-shirt, which you have to pay for, by the way. Plus, you learn that your fellow coworkers/peons are also imbeciles. It was horrible, but I toughed it out for five days. Then my 'manager,' the barista-in-chief who had all of three months experience, fired me because I was apparently not a team player even though I'd figured out how to do things better and more efficiently than the so-called 'Starbucks Way.' No biggie. I was only going to work there for two or three weeks anyway.

Then my brother and I were shipped out to the ranch in Montana which I also hated because we're expected to 'man up' out there by doing chores and crap. Thank god we were there too early for hay-bailing season because that is a real back-breaker. However, with lots of animals around, there was still plenty of cow and horse shit to shovel, which we did, dawn to dusk. (Good prep for college, BTW.) All we were really doing was providing cheap manual labor in the name of getting a so-called 'valuable life experience,' to quote my Mom, who talks like that.

But finally we escaped the prairie prison and it was off to the Cape for August where life is actually worth living, though the downside was that both my parents were there. Still, they do throw a lot of parties and aren't too careful about keeping track of the booze.

Then here.

Ugh.

Most of my fellow students need help tying their shoelaces. (You might have noticed that I like to write using stream-of-consciousness *ala* Holden Caulfield in *Catcher*. No need to overthink this lame assignment when you can knock it out in twenty minutes or less.) If you're interested in creativity, you've got it Big Time with me, but if you're interested in imparting the rules of grammar and all that crap, go fuck yourself. I learned all that shit in grammar school ('grammar school,' get it). No need to re-live that pathetic period in my life.

I see my five hundred words, give or take, are up. I'm done.

Reading the essay gave Peter the first laugh he'd had in weeks, but he immediately realized that he didn't want to spend the rest of the quarter dealing with Young Holden. Under normal circumstances, he would have relished taking the kid down a bit before building him back up, but given *The Situation*, he simply didn't feel up to the challenge.

Cowardly?

Yes.

Realistic?

Also yes.

Better to just deal with the below-average, slack-jawed dunderheads than Mr. Loose Cannon.

Before the next class, he arranged to have Young Holden transferred to Maggie Williamson, a newish literature prof who was still enthusiastic about teaching and was always busy espousing 'the life of the creative,' whatever that meant. Peter also convinced Young Holden that he'd arranged the transfer to a more advanced class because even reading his essay in class might discourage the other students. Of course, this explanation pleased the Young Holden immensely. When he called Ms. Williamson, Peter went on, perhaps a bit too much, about Young Holden's talent and promise and about how the other students in Peter's class would be 'Holden' him back. This was her chance to mold some real talent. Let them have at each other.

As he feared, the other students were exactly the pathetic drudges Young Holden had described, who, should they be forced to define it, would take a wild guess that 'gerund' was another option in their generation's ongoing gender identification roulette.

## Chapter Forty-Four
Cookie Wars


$O$f his three teaching assignments, the only one he was even remotely looking forward to was the upper-class seminar, *Post-Colonial Literature,* which he'd picked up in his trade with Pierce. Unlike *Entering the Labyrinth: The Flowering of Third Wave Feminist Literature,* at least he knew something about the subject and maybe the students would be interested.

But once again the students disappointed him, although not in their usual way. Of the sixteen who had signed up, only five showed. After vamping for fifteen minutes, thinking that perhaps the missing signups had simply gotten lost, Peter told the five that it was pointless to start the seminar as it would probably be canceled, thus bowing to the wisdom of The Great Yogi, 'if they won't come, you can't stop 'em.' He wasn't thrilled about possibly having to give up the *Post-Colonial* seminar, because he feared that he would be assigned to teach another about which he would most likely know even less. (Fortunately, he didn't have to worry about being forced to pick up the *Entering the Labyrinth* seminar which Pierce had abandoned when he retired, as one of the feminist profs had quickly snapped it up.)

It was only Day Three and he was beat.

Days Three through Twelve featured more of the same.

But for once, his luck, such as it was, held. He was not assigned a new seminar, instead, he became a 'rover,' filling in as a substitute for the 'Riting for Retards' program. Although it was humiliating to be a sub at his age, it had some benefits—all he had to do was show up, assign a writing topic, collect the 'papers' when class was over and email them to the absentee prof to grade.

As the days drifted towards the end of September, the faculty's mood had shifted radically from 'to the barricades' to one of sullen and grudging acceptance of *The Situation.*

Faced with this new reality, it was now paycheck over principle, or if you will, principal over principle. At any rate, with support from outside parties never having risen above zero, the faculty had little choice but to return to work, a circumstance with which many were unfamiliar.

There was also dissension in the ranks. Not everyone on the faculty was of the same mind regarding *The You-Know-What.* A rump group of computer geeks from Science and Technology let it be known that they had changed their behavior not a single whit and were not backing the rebels' actions. As one of them said while taking a Coke and pizza break, 'we like teaching a full load, and when we're not teaching, we're working with students 24/7. Why wouldn't we? That's who we are. We love it.' To say that the humanities profs considered the CS guys to be beyond weird was an unmeasurable understatement, not only metaphorically, but literally as well, since some on the humanities faculty would have trouble figuring how to measure out twelve inches using a twelve-inch ruler.

With Bliss now getting the job performance he wanted, albeit grudgingly given, most of the faculty was having difficulty dealing with the new reality. Their main problem was with the students. Raised as narcissists by indulgent parents, the students asked nothing of themselves but expected everything from others. They believed they already knew everything worth knowing, having been told for years that they were the best, the brightest, the smartest, most talented generation in the history of the world—and they were dim enough to believe it.

But, dim as they were, even they were very aware that *The You-Know-What* had turned the traditional student-teacher relationship upside-down. Knowing now that their faculty performance reviews were no longer just *pro forma* exercises, the students began to flex their muscles. However, they were still 'Da Yout' and behaved accordingly, which would be to say 'inappropriately.' They became even less attentive than normal, were snarky and demanding, and definitively failed to check their newly-discovered privilege at the classroom door.

In the end, the faculty caved.

Like jesters playing to the royal court, the faculty courted the students with flattery and obsequious toadying, constantly reminding them of how wonderful and brilliant they were. But the most humiliating form of groveling came during what would later be called *The Great Cookie Wars*.

It began when a couple of younger eager-beaver profs started bringing home-made cookies to their classes and seminars. Soon, in an unseemly effort to curry favor, everyone began bringing them, thus fostering a mushrooming competition among the professoriat to bring fancier and more exotic cookies to class.

No baker he, Peter realized that to remain competitive, he would have to buy his, especially after his attempts to enlist Glynnyth's help failed utterly. At first, he brought packages of supermarket vanilla wafers and Oreos, but after the students reacted negatively to his offerings, he ended up leaving a standing order at Carmella's Cookies 'n Cupcakes for several dozen organic, artisanal, non-GMO chocolate chip and oatmeal raisin cookies. Peter neither knew nor cared what all the foodie adjectives meant, but they seemed to be important to the Young Insufferables in his classes.

The net effect of all this was a noticeable weight gain by the student body, and since all the professors were doing it, it soon became a zero-sum game. A few profs from the science side of campus cautioned that too much sugar was not ideal for maintaining the students' alertness in the classroom, but that argument deterred no one—not while the battle for ratings was raging.

The final escalation in the Food Wars occurred when a couple of professors had pizzas delivered to their noon-time classes, after which they petitioned Bliss, asking to be reimbursed for their expenses.

Pizzagate was the final straw. Bliss put an immediate stop to the nonsense by decreeing that there would food in class no more than twice a quarter and that any purchases would be 'on your own dime.' The faculty members were then faced with the market reality that they would have to compete for ratings rather than trying to buy them.

In the end, it was probably the only one of Bliss's policy decisions with which everyone agreed.

## Chapter Forty-Five
### Autumn Leaves

$O$ne early October morning on his way out of the house, Peter ran into Harry Atwater, who was raking leaves in his yard.

"Morning, Peter. I hear there've been some big changes going on over at the commune."

"It's been a bit rough, but we're muddling through," said Peter.

"I'm not surprised. From my point of view, 'muddling through' is what you do," said Harry. "'Bidness' as usual."

"That would be the way you'd see it."

"I hear you're having to put in, what, fifteen, twenty hours a week teaching?"

"Fifteen's more like it," said Peter sheepishly. The truth was that for him it was twelve at the max, but Peter couldn't help lying, although he regretted it immediately.

"Man, you must be all tuckered out," said Atwater.

Peter lied again, "I'm actually enjoying being back in the classroom, and the students seem to be getting more out of it."

"Why shouldn't they? They're getting more for less."

Peter looked at him quizzically.

"Actually, they're getting more for the same, but you get my point," said Harry. "Better quality teaching for the same amount of money. Theoretically."

That this was the same argument Bliss had made didn't please him, but Peter couldn't fault the logic.

"Still, why anyone would spend forty to fifty-thousand dollars a year to miseducate their kid is beyond me."

Knowing that the figure was now closer to sixty-thousand, Peter resisted his professorial urge to correct and continued, "I see you're still repeating the same old anti-intellectual talking points. You're in a rut, Harry."

"Well, when I went to college, and I hate to seem like one of those old farts yammering about the good old days when…"

"Well, you just proved you are one,' Peter interrupted.

Atwater ignored him and rolled on, "…every school had a couple of 'gut courses' as we called them, mostly for jocks, but now you have a whole college devoted to them. I'll stick with my opinion."

"As you are so fond of pointing out, 'it's a free country,' and everyone's entitled to his or her opinion, regardless of how stupid it is."

"What time is it? Eleven-thirty in the morning? And you're just going to work?"

"See you later," said Peter grimly as he pedaled off.

Usually their conversations were not so sharp-edged, but Peter was still feeling raw about *The Situation*.

# Chapter Forty-Six
## A New Tack

*B*y mid-October, the revolutionary fervor of The Resistance had faded completely. Subsumed in a pall of gloom, the faculty had settled into a dreary daily routine—get up, trudge to class, teach, trudge home, go to bed…rinse and repeat. They no longer met in the hallways to discuss their latest trip to Europe or gossip the goings-on about their inferiors in D.C. and New York. Under Bliss's new regime, they were forced to put in more hours teaching than they had ever thought was humanly-possible, at least by their standards. Words like 'gulag' and 'Guantanamo' crossed their minds, but even they were wise enough not to voice that level of hyperbole in public. The Average Joes of the world who routinely put in forty or more hours per week would not overly-sympathetic to those who had been simply asked to do their jobs and were complaining about it.

As for Peter, here he was, nearly sixty-years-old, having to appeal to adolescents just to keep his job. With new rules in place, Peter realized he would have to dig deep to find ways to engage these spoiled children, but for the moment, the hole he was digging was winning.

One day when Pierce called about lunch, he answered.

The faculty club was not even a quarter full. The profs sat in small groups and spoke in whispers. In stark contrast to his former peers, Pierce came in looking well-tanned and happy. He waved at Peter, who had already been through the buffet line once.

"Bored with retirement yet?" asked Peter when Pierce sat down to join him.

"Life's never been better," he said, "especially given what I hear about the alternative. Rumor has it that life on the old plantation is not all it's cracked up to be."

Peter unloaded with a litany of all that had gone wrong and ended with a diatribe about the narcissistic brats whom he was forced to teach.

"Smug, self-satisfied little twerps. They already know everything and have nothing left to learn"

"Yes, but they've always been that way," said Pierce,

"But this time it's different. Now they're 'empowered,' and if you upset them in any way, they'll accuse you of a microaggression," said Peter. "I have half a mind to give them a micro butt-kicking."

"Far be it from me to be the one to advise caution," said Pierce, "but given the times we live in, I'd holster my sarcasm for a while—at least until normalcy returns."

"I'm afraid the 'good old days' are gone for good," said Peter.

"But not forgotten," said Pierce as he dove into his full plate. "Not yet, anyway."

Incongruously wearing sunglasses in the already-darkened faculty lounge, Mark Kohl sidled over to their table. He held his food tray in front of him as though it were part of his disguise.

With his back turned to Pierce and Peter, he whispered out of the corner of his mouth, "I don't want to arouse suspicion, so I won't sit down."

"Suspicion about what?" Asked Pierce.

"It's on," said Kohl.

"What's on?" asked Peter.

"We've got the goods on Bliss and we're ready to put a heavy move on him," said Kohl.

"I don't remember signing up for a 'heavy move,' whatever that is," said Pierce, who then asked Peter, "is it what I think it is?"

"You're out, Pierce,' said Kohl, "I'm talking to him, not you, but I trust you'll keep your lip buttoned." He glared down at Pierce and said, "if you know what's good for you." Then after more glaring, he added, "if you know what I mean."

"Oh, I think I know what you mean, but is it 'keep your lip buttoned,' or 'lips buttoned?'" asked Pierce.

"I think it depends on how "street" you want to be," answered Peter.

Kohl ignored their asides and continued, "we're having a sit-down on Friday…at Denny's…six a.m."

"Oh, wow! A sit-down at Denny's," said Pierce. "Don't you think the menu at Denny's might be a little light on the cannoli."

Kohl looked at him quizzically.

"Never mind," said Pierce.

"Be there?" asked Kohl of Peter, ignoring Pierce.

"Could we make it seven?" asked Peter. "Six is a little early for me."

"Just be there," Kohl commanded.

"I'll think about it," said Peter.

"You do that," he said disdainfully, "and if you come, make sure you're not tailed."

Kohl looked around to make sure no one had overheard their conversation. He then left, furtively trying to make himself invisible—a daunting task for someone dressed like an FBI spook from the 1950's.

"I think someone's taking this private dick thing a little too seriously," said Pierce as he watched Kohl leave. "I take that back, he's a very public dick."

"I think he's watched *The Godfather* one too many times," said Peter, who then asked, "do you think he might actually be on to something?"

"Who knows? Though it looks like you'll have to 'take the meeting' to find out."

"You know I'm not a morning person," said Peter, "but when you're dying a slow death, a lot of things start to look attractive."

"Just be careful out there," said Pierce. "Denny's is notorious for its mob hits. Especially at six in the morning."

## Chapter Forty-Seven
### Beantown Beatdown

$P$eter was late for the Breakfast At Denny's, but it hardly mattered—Kohl was the only one who'd showed up on time. That put him in a bad mood, but even he realized that it was useless to expect military-style punctuality from people for whom being late was a feature, not a bug.

The one advantage in picking Denny's for the meeting was, that unlike *Cheers*, Denny's was a place where no one knew their names. Or cared. It never occurred to Kohl that they could have met anywhere outside West Beresford because the working stiffs who were up for breakfast at six in the morning could have cared less what a half-dozen old-faculty codgers were up to.

When they finally got down to business after ordering breakfast, what surprised them all was that Kohl's private detective had come up with some useful dirt. Now they had to figure out how to use it.

After considerable discussion, they decided to take it to the Board of Trustees and they picked Thayer Bradford Endicott, a Boston lawyer, as their go-to. Endicott was a long-standing and well-respected trustee whose opinion would carry some weight with the rest of the board. Of course, 'well-respected' was a relative term, depending on where one sat. Most of the faculty held members of the Board of Trustees with the same contempt they had for members of the Elks, Lions or the Rotary Club. Bobos all.

They also wanted to keep their face-to-face on the QT and Endicott was safely-distant in Boston, yet only a couple of hours away from Grodin via the Massachusetts Turnpike.

As for the envoys, Kohl was an obvious choice, especially since this was his baby and he would have insisted. In unspoken agreement, the others understood that an unrestrained Kohl would most likely fuck things up and that steadier hands were needed to keep him from going off the rails.

Of course, no one wanted to go and all trotted out excuses, but duty called. With no straws to draw, they picked those to go with Kohl by the tried-and-true playground method of rock-paper-scissors. Having never been very good at rock-paper-scissors, Peter ended up as one of the three emissaries to accompany Kohl.

Late the following Friday morning, they left their cars in the same Denny's parking lot, piled into Kohl's Buick LeSabre and drove to Boston for a one o'clock meeting. The old Buick was a true road warrior and the drive in to Boston was smooth and comfortable.

When they arrived, Endicott was in another meeting, but they were ushered into his office which overlooked Boston Harbor, although the gray mist that hovered over the water muddled the view. A secretary brought in the fixings for coffee and a tray of cookies. Peter was grateful for the cookies as he was hungry after the long drive. Except for bottled water, Kohl had allowed no food or drink in the old LeSabre. No Kleenex either. 'You've never noticed all the crap that floats around in the air when you pull one out of the box? It's like a blizzard.' Needless to say, small talk on the way to Boston was small to the point of non-existent.

Endicott arrived and after the introductions, Kohl cleared his throat and began his well-rehearsed spiel, saying, "we have discovered some very serious issues regarding Bliss Moynihan's financial dealings and his academic background that we thought necessary to bring to the board's attention." He nervously proceeded to detail evidence that Bliss had purchased a house on Cape Cod with funds from the college and that he had never officially finished his Ph.D. thesis at UCLA.

While Kohl was detailing the facts the private eye had uncovered, Endicott stood up from his desk, walked over to the window and looked out at the harbor as though he were giving serious consideration to the issues Kohl was presenting.

For a brief moment, Peter thought that they might be getting somewhere, when Endicott suddenly turned around and interrupted Kohl, "I'm sorry you boys had to drive all the way in to Boston to tell me this, but…hell, we loaned him the money for the Cape Cod place. Do you think for a minute that we'd let him walk away from Grodin with his thirty-five million dollars?"

"And as for him not completing his Ph.D., we didn't pick him to be president based on whether or not he finished a goddamn degree—who the hell cares about that other than a bunch of college professors? Bill Gates, Steve Jobs, the Zucker…whatever the hell his name is…they didn't even finish college and it didn't seem to hold them back. What the board cares about now are results, not pieces of paper."

The Gang of Four could hardly believe what they were hearing—a member of a college Board of Trustees not caring about their president's academic background?

Heresy!

Endicott concluded by letting them know that the board had already decided that after his 'interim' contract ran out at the end of the year, Bliss would be appointed president.

The two-hour drive back to West Beresford was carried out in total silence.

Plan B had failed.

## Chapter Forty-Eight
Alone At Last


*L*ate that afternoon, after he had driven home from Denny's, Peter found an envelope propped up on a table in the foyer. Typical of Glynnyth, it was short and to the point.

She had left him.

For someone else.

Peter nearly dropped the note and looked around, as if hoping to discover that she might magically appear and put the lie to what he'd just read.

He called her immediately and while the phone was ringing, he wondered how long the note had been there. For a moment he thought of hanging up to give himself time to remember the last time he'd seen her, but before he could hang up, she answered.

"Hello, Peter."

"Glynnyth, I can't believe this," said Peter.

"So you found the note. I thought about not leaving one, just to see how long it would take before you realized that I wasn't around."

Peter made no reply to that, as anything he said would have been misconstrued as either a weak justification for ignoring her or an admission of the obvious—that he wouldn't have noticed that she had gone.

"Who is he?" said Peter.

"No one you know. He's in real estate. We share some common interests, including an interest in each other."

"But I'm interested...in you...in what you do," said Peter.

"Don't make up things now out of desperation," she said. "That train has left the station."

"Where are you? How can I get in touch with you?"

"We're in South Beresford. You can always call. Or email. I've taken the pets, by the way, so you don't have to deal with them."

"You...we can't just end a thirty-year marriage like this. We need to talk," said Peter.

Glynnyth laughed. "So, *now* you want to talk? Seriously? And it's thirty-five by the way, but who's counting."

"Of course I want to talk. I've always wanted to talk," said Peter.

"Oh, please, Peter. You only want to talk when your back's against the wall."

"We could get some counseling. Therapy," he said.

Glynnyth laughed. "Goodbye, Peter. Enjoy the rest of your life."

The phone clicked.

Peter was stunned. He and Glynnyth had had their problems over the years but he never expected her to leave. He'd always managed to stave off crises with the promise to 'do better,' spend more time together...etc., etc. He was an expert in the marital tactics of stalling, feigning thoughtfulness and fake listening. But after every tremor in the marriage, time would slowly erode his promises and he and Glynnyth would drift back into their familiar routines.

Now it was over.

Finito.

He felt the urge to toss back a couple of shots of Jack Daniels, but he knew that would render him non-functional for the rest of the evening. He also resisted the urge to call Janet, who would not even bother to feign commiseration and would mock him for what he had done to deserve what he was getting—ignoring his wife for more than three decades. Calling her could wait until he was in better command of himself.

He spent a restless evening trying to deal with his feelings, something he was not used to doing. He thought about driving around South Beresford to see if he could spot Glynnyth's car, then realized what a disaster that would be were he caught doing it. He then felt somewhat proud of himself when he realized he could use the 'Find My Cellphone' program on his Mac to locate Glynnyth's iPhone. He spent an hour trying to figure out how to do that before giving up. His technical skills were not at the level needed to figure that one out.

He went to bed with his mind still swirling.

Peter spent the weekend struggling to distract himself from the feelings which kept bubbling up about Glynnyth's leaving. For years he had rarely given much thought to her except when she was around, but now that she was gone, he was confused and anguished about what it meant for his future.

What was going to happen with the house?

With his pension?

With everything?

Uncertainty abounded.

The one thing he didn't think about was their goddamn cat, Meow. Good riddance.

He was surprised to find that it was a relief to get back to teaching on Monday. Although he'd hated nearly every minute of it since the start of the fall term, it was now a useful diversion. He carried on through the rest of the week in a dull fog, which was a definite improvement over the emotional anguish he'd experienced over the weekend.

## Chapter Forty-Nine
Open Mouth, Insert Foot

*N*ovember arrived on a gloomy Monday. Gone were the bright, crisp sunshiny days of October. The colorful leaves of fall had dropped to the ground, turned to a dirty grey-brown and waited for the first dusting of snow that would transform the terrain. Now-barren tree branches stood out starkly against the leaden skies.

It had been ten days since Glynnyth had left and the dreary landscape matched Peter's mood. Fall quarter was now well past its halfway point, leaving only a month of classes before final exams.

It was too cold to ride his bike, so Peter drove to campus only to find that his usual parking place had been commandeered by a paving crew that appeared to be in no rush to finish before the end of the century. He finally found a spot behind Jenkins and walked briskly over to the Holman Learning Center, realizing that he would not be late if he rushed, but would be sweaty and out of breath when he got there.

'What we don't do for the little snots,' he thought as he scurried across Squirelle.

He arrived at his classroom just in time, only to discover that his lavaliere mike needed a battery. He poked around the lectern but he couldn't find a spare.

Meanwhile, the students were filing in, chatting away and goofing off as usual. If he contacted tech support for a battery, it would be at least another ten minutes before someone could get one to him, so Peter tried to call the class to order the old-fashioned way.

"Good morning!" he bellowed.

But his voice barely registered over the din created by the students, many of whom were discussing the previous night's episode of *Werewolves of London*, a new gothic TV show which featured attractive teenagers. *Werewolves* was based on the song of the same name by Warren Zevon, whose estate, after a long dry spell, would finally be making some real dough off his 1978 hit song.

Peter tried again, this time speaking even louder.

Still nothing.

The chattering continued.

Finally, he boomed out, "let's get started here," with an edge to his voice that caused a few of the students to quiet down. But the students in the back of the hall continued to laugh and chat with each other, paying zero attention to Peter's plea. One of the students brayed loudly, "Aaa-hooooo...ooh...," imitating Zevon's werewolf call.

Finally, Peter had had enough. "You people in the back...time to get to work!"

They all quieted down and took their seats, but one of them said in a stage-whisper, "sounds like someone forgot to take his chill pill this morning."

"Can we please show a little respect for the process? Your parents are shelling out thousands of dollars for this, so the least you could do is shut up so that the few of you who are actually interested can listen to what's being said."

There was one more very quiet "Aaa-hoooo…ooh," followed by some muffled snickering.

Peter heard it and exploded.

"I will have some quiet now, thank you very much. I am so sick of this. You all think you're special," said Peter, using the air quotes around 'special,' "but you're not 'special.' You're average, at best. In fact, for some of you, 'average' would be a giant step up!" He raged on, admonishing them about how they were wasting his time and their parents' money, and learning nothing that would prepare them for the future.

While he spoke, several students packed up and walked out, with one of them sobbing uncontrollably. The rest sat and stared up at him in stunned silence. No one had ever talked to them like this.

Peter knew immediately that he had gone too far. He regretted what he'd said, but there was no taking it back now. Pausing, he took a deep breath, looked out over the audience and said, "okay, enough of the histrionics, let's get to work here." He began his lecture and to his surprise, the students opened their laptops and sat attentively as he spoke straight through for forty-five minutes on the two Williams—Faulkner and Styron. He didn't dare stop to ask a question because he was sure they would clam up and say nothing. The last thing he wanted to do was to try to drag an answer out of them.

During the course of the lecture, he noticed several of the students discreetly holding up their iPhones to record him.

He usually ended his classes with a self-deprecating story or a joke, but this time he just told them that the assignment for their next class would be to read excerpts from John Irving and Thomas Pynchon.

After the students had left, he packed up his notes and hoped that he had dodged a full magazine's worth of bullets, but then he heard a long werewolf howl echo in the hallway outside.

With a couple of hours to kill before his afternoon writing class, he thought about grabbing something to eat at the Faculty Club, but as he walked across Squirrelle Square, he heard a couple of 'Howls of the Werewolf' from some students after they had walked past him. He resisted the impulse to pick up his pace lest he be thought to be reacting to their mocking gibes.

He felt something was up but ever the optimist, he thought, 'no worries, I'll apologize to them at the next class.' Still, he decided he'd better have lunch in his office rather than possibly have to explain what had happened in class to his fellow profs at the faculty club, so he bought a package of Cheez-

Its, a chocolate chip cookie and a Coke from the vending machine in Jenkins. Hardly nutritious, but it would get him through the day.

Back in his office, he logged onto his computer and began checking his email. After a few minutes, he opened one from a student who suggested he check out the Twitter hashtag #GrandeRant. He barely knew how, but he managed to get on Twitter and discovered he was the center of a world-class Tweet Storm.

He was trending.

Fast and furiously.

The #GrandRant feed included a video fragment that repeated his line that "average would be a huge step up in class," over and over. Unflattering videos showed him exploding, melting into a puddle and morphing into an overweight, crying baby in diapers who was thrashing on the floor.

And there were tweets. Dozens of tweets. None were positive.

He was amazed at how all this could happen in just a few minutes.

His office phone rang and he picked it up. Meg was on the line. "Have you seen what's happening out front?"

He hadn't.

"You need to take a look out your window," she said. "I'll come up."

Peter looked out the window and saw a group of students with placards marching in front of Jenkins. Others raced across Squirrelle to get in on the action. He cracked the window open and heard them chanting, "Hey, hey, ho, ho…Old Man Grande has got to go."

Over and over. And over.

The Revolution had come to Grodin.

Meg came in, stood beside him and said, "I think you'd better go home. You don't want to get trapped in your office."

"But that would be the coward's way out," said Peter. "I'll go down and talk to them."

Meg grabbed him by the arms and forced him to look at her. She narrowed her eyes and slowly shook her head at his folly. "Talk…is what got you into this."

"I have my writing class at two," he replied weakly.

"I'll get a sub," said Meg.

Peter looked out the window again and heard in the din the cries of outrage coming from the swelling crowd below.

"Out the back way," said Meg. "Now."

Peter obliged.

## Chapter Fifty
### How Quiet Was It?

*W*ith no classes to teach on Tuesday, Peter decided it was best not to go in. Instead, he hunkered down at home. He checked online and found no indication that students were marching outside Jenkins shouting 'Hey, hey… ho, ho…the fat old white guy's got to go.'

However, Twitter was still a font of activity, although it appeared that the outrage level had subsided and had been replaced by a form of sophomoric one-upmanship where the participants competed with each other to see who could come up with the most outrageous mash-up videos, jokes and Photoshopped images.

Late in the afternoon, he called Meg to get the Lay of the Land. As far as she could tell, things had calmed down. It was quiet out there.

Perhaps too quiet, he thought.

What were his options? Other than grovel, ask for forgiveness at his next class, and hope that this, too, would pass—he couldn't think of any.

## Chapter Fifty-One
### Man on the Run

$O$n Wednesday morning, determined to take the abject apology route, Peter put on his favorite coat and tie and drove to campus in the Beemer. He had written out a *mea culpa*, and, depending on how he felt it was going, he planned on ending it with a self-deprecating comment about never being too old to learn from a mistake. It wouldn't be a complete grovel, but it would be close.

Not wanting to have to interact with anyone, he parked directly behind Holman Hall and crept down a back hallway that led to a side entrance near the stage. Standing in the darkened doorway, he watched the students file in. They were chatty, casual and seemed to be relaxed. Two male students rough-housed a bit, showing off for the ladies as they were wont to do. Nothing out of the ordinary.

He waited until it was a minute after ten, by which time most of the students were at least somewhat near their seats, though of course they had yet to sit down.

Taking a deep breath, Peter entered the auditorium and strode across the stage to the podium.

But, at the very sight of him, all hell broke loose.

The students rose as one and began shouting and shaking their fists in the air. As if out of nowhere, they hoisted *Fire Grande* placards. Cries of "fascist," "racist" and "elitist," rang through the lecture hall, along with the combination cries of "racist-fascist," "fascist-racist," and the Holy Trinity of "fascist-racist-elitist," along with a few "bastard's" thrown in for good measure.

Peter got the microphone working and yelled into it, pleading with the students to please let him speak. But it was a no-go. Every attempt on his part to be heard just enraged them further. Just being in the same room with Peter seemed to be enough to spark a paroxysm of furious, unrelenting hate. Several students began clapping and chanted the old familiar "Hey, hey…ho-ho…Old Man Grande has got to go," until they all took it up and began marching in unison up and down the aisles, pumping their placards in the air.

One black-clad, beret-wearing female student began shrieking and babbling incoherently. A second woman fainted and fell to the floor. A third began hyperventilating. It was unfortunate that Peter's ability to so quickly induce such a generalized panic could not be bottled and sold to the Department of Defense.

Several students rushed over to help the woman on the floor and one yelled, "Medic! Medic! Someone call a medic!" As a crowd gathered around the 'victims,' one student pointed at Peter and yelled, "it's his fault! He did it!"

When this was followed by cries of "get him!" and "kill the motherfucker!" Peter realized might be time to get out of Dodge and skedaddled off the stage without uttering even so much as a "class dismissed."

Unfortunately for Peter, when a prey animal turns its back on a predator and runs, it simply stimulates the predator's instinct to pursue.

And so they did.

Now running for his life, Peter raced down the hallway and left the building with the mob close behind. Fortunately for him, one of the pack leaders had trouble getting his oversized *Fire Grande* placard through the doorway, thus slowing the horde down just enough to give Peter time to hit his remote, unlock his Beemer and jump inside. Despite his usual clumsiness in all matters physical, this time, when seconds mattered, he managed to squeeze behind the wheel and lock the doors before the throng descended on him and his hapless BMW. Screaming and shouting, the students leaned over the front window and spit at him—all while chanting and banging their placards on the car. A couple of students literally kicked the tires, but seeing that they were doing more damage to their shoes than to the rubber, they joined those who were already pounding on the hood and the roof. For the first time since he'd bought it, Peter was glad he hadn't sprung for a convertible.

His mind flashed back to when he was in college and he'd laughed while watching old newsreels of a hapless Richard Nixon, trapped in his limo by a mob of angry Venezuelans.

It was not so funny now.

With no Secret Service agents around to wrestle his attackers to the ground and clear a path for his escape, Peter was forced to back out slowly so as not to run over anyone. He hoped no one would go crazy and use his or her body to start a human logjam, but fortunately, even in this over-amped mob, there was no one foolish enough to do that. After finally backing out far enough to put the Beemer into drive, he began to inch forward, slowly at first but then was able to gather enough speed to force the screaming students into a trot and then into a sprint. When he was finally clear of the last one, he put the pedal to the metal and left them standing behind, furiously shaking their placards at him.

He left campus and drove up into the hills until he came to a small county park high above Great Beresford. At mid-morning on an early November Wednesday, no one was there. Peter got out and walked to the edge of the overlook. The only sound was that of his footsteps crunching the gravel.

He stood at the cliff's edge and realized that the life he had known, was over.

## Chapter Fifty-Two
### Hang 'em High? Hang 'em Low? Oh, What the Hell...Just Hang 'em

*M*eanwhile, back at the ranch, the Mob was not yet ready to call it a day. Infused with youthful enthusiasm and hoping for more victories, the students turned their sights on the President's Office. Chanting variations on the familiar "hey, hey, ho, ho...racist profs have got to go," they marched towards their new target, although the 'march' was more of a disorganized ramble than a Panzer-like blitz of Poland.

As the motley crew rolled across Squirrelle, other students saw them and realized that this was the moment they'd been waiting for. They poured out of their classrooms *en masse* to hook up with the ragtag army. With this action, the Grodinites had officially joined the nationwide Snowflake Rebellion and thus had succeeded in achieving their generational mission—that of thumbing their collective noses at adult authority from the lofty heights of their perceived moral superiority.

Now numbering several hundred, the Mob arrived at the Henry Phillip Cates House, the ornate two-story Queen Anne which served as the president's office. They milled about in front of its wide veranda, shouting for Bliss to come out and immediately acquiesce to their demands, although the fact that they had not yet come up with a list of demands was lost on them. Bliss let them wait long enough to let them know that he was not at their beck and call, but not long enough to provoke them into storming the building.

When he finally stepped out to speak with them, he chose not to stand, emperor-like, above them on the veranda. Instead, he calmly strode out and sat down languidly on the wide stone balustrade at the bottom of the steps as if posing for a fashion shoot. Although the day was gloomy, his favorite sunglasses rested in their normal perch atop the mass of his sculpted hair, ever-at-the-ready in case a random ray of sunshine were to poke its way through the grey skies. Wearing perfectly-creased pants, a classically-tailored shirt and a maroon Hermès tie, he looked more like a hunky movie star than a college president, which caused a bit of be-still-my-heart palpitating on the part of those Grodin coeds who had yet to decide whether or not they were lesbians.

Bliss invited the students to speak and patiently listened as their chants turned into rants, ranging from the faculty's insensitivity and professional shortcomings to their concerns about global warming, income inequality and the underlying fear they all felt about eventually having to leave the nest and deal with Real Life.

For his part, Bliss listened intently, asked a question here and there, and occasionally summarized or clarified a point that had been made. He made no obvious effort to persuade them of anything or guide them towards a particular point of view.

During the speechifying, a steady stream of self-appointed spokes-dudes and dudettes took turns at Rabble-Rousing 101, but quickly discovered that effective demagoguery was more difficult than it looked like on TV. Nonetheless, they did their best to infuse their protestations with profundity and significance. And, after taking turns at strutting and fretting upon the stage, each one exited to salutations from their fellow Rabble-Rousers in the form of high-fives and mini fist-bumps.

Off to the side, several faculty members from the School of Critical Social Theory listened to the students' lamentations and whenever a rare salient point was made, murmured words of approval to each other and engaged in sage head-nodding and chin-tugging at their proteges' hand-me-down rhetoric. Engrossed as they were in their anti-establishment mentoring, it never occurred to these modern-day Marats, Dantons and Robespierres that in the future, they might meet a similar fate at the clumsy hands of the fledgling Frankensteins they had created. Mobs can be unforgiving, and mobs bursting with a youthful exuberance fueled by early harvest winter-wheat ales and the latest crop of Colorado *cannabis,* could easily make serious errors in target selection.

For the students, this was a day to be celebrated. With their actions, they had proved their mettle on the field of battle and thus had joined their fellow firebrands nationwide in their collective struggle against the scourge of microaggressions, unsafe spaces and professorial insensitivity that blighted the collective collegiate landscape. In the end, Bliss assured them that after going through the appropriate channels and following all the proper procedures, their grievances would be heard, after which justice would be served and the guilty party—i.e., one Dr. Peter Grande—would be taken out and...well, not shot, but would receive an appropriate punishment, whatever that meant. Bliss was clever enough to let the students know that although he supported their cause, he was powerless to act without dotting every 'i' and crossing every 't.'

Now satisfied with the knowledge that they had thoroughly-routed a charter member of the Oppressor Class and had pressured the president of the college into validating their demands, they broke for lunch. Nothing, it seemed, not even The Revolution, would ever come between them and their smoothies, pizzas, and kale and cranberry salads.

In taking their leave, they vowed never to forget the humiliation and suffering they had endured under the Reign of Terror instigated by the despised and now-disgraced Dr. Peter Grande.

They had struck back against the Empire—and won.

## Chapter Fifty-Three
Banished


$W$hen he got home late that afternoon, Peter picked up a phone message from Miles Plummer informing him that for the 'Good Of All Concerned,' he should 'stand down' and stay at home until 'things settled down.' His two classes would be taken over by a tag team of professors to be named later. Miles gave no indication as to how long he thought it would take for 'things to settle down.'

Miles also said that everyone in the President's Office was trying to work something out with the student leaders with the hope of avoiding a full-blown crisis.

'Isn't that what we have now?' thought Peter. He hated to think that Bliss's people could imagine something worse.

Later that night Pierce called and asked, "what the hell is going on up there?"

"Where are you?"

"Saint Lucia," said Pierce.

Peter didn't answer.

"In the Lesser Antilles."

"I know where it is," said Peter.

"Then I won't depress you further by describing what Paradise looks like." Pierce then continued on to the topic *du jour*, "I was on Twitter and it looks like you've run into a major shit-storm. What happened?"

"I popped off a bit in class. Said a few things about our student body, which, though true, I should have kept to myself. And, not to add it on as a footnote, but Glynnyth's moved out."

"Good god," said Pierce. After a few seconds of silence, he added, "sorry, Old Chap."

"As you know, it's been rocky for years."

"So, is it salvageable?"

"At this point, I'm not sure I want it to be. We've been at odds for so long...and now, she's moved on and I don't blame her."

Pierce sighed, "what's your next step?"

"We haven't talked about it. I've tried to call a few times, but...then this other thing popped up."

"I saw some of the videos. It looked like the Storming of the Bastille in 1789, though of course they didn't have videotape back then."

"Hopefully it'll blow over."

"I wouldn't count on it," said Pierce. "Not given the current mood. I'd say the snowflakes are just getting warmed up, to mix metaphors."

"I may have over-stepped, but I certainly don't believe I deserve this kind of blowback for just telling them to sit down, shut up and listen."

"What can I say? Life ain't fair. I think you'd best do a major grovel, take a slap on the wrist and move on. Just put a bandaid on it and get it behind you. The last thing you want is to let this escalate into some kind of misconduct charge that would land you in a Kangaroo Court."

"It may be too late for that," said Peter.

On that point, Peter was prescient. Having achieved victory in their first skirmish, the students set out to win the war. Their next move was to file a complaint charging Peter with faculty misconduct.

On Friday morning, two days after being chased from class, a large man in a cheap suit rang his doorbell and after Peter acknowledged that he was indeed Dr. Peter Grande, the man handed him a hefty envelope containing the official complaint. Peter had to sign for it, so he no longer had to go out looking for trouble, it had officially come to him.

Cloaked as it was in dense legalese, Peter managed to find his way down to the actual charge: that he had engaged in "conduct which impeded the orderly process of teaching and learning," and that he had violated "professional standards of respect for all students, faculty and staff, regardless of…" blah…blah…blah.

The complaint was exhaustive in detailing the process by which justice would be prepped, marinated, cooked and served. First, there would be an investigation, and if the investigation warranted, there would be a formal hearing. And if the hearing judges found him guilty, they would recommend a punishment ranging from a mild verbal reprimand to outright dismissal. Should Peter be found guilty, Bliss Moynihan, as Grodin's acting president, would decide on the level of punishment. In order of severity, the punishments were:

- Oral reprimand
- Written reprimand
- Suspension with pay (it would hard for anyone to see how this was a punishment)
- Suspension without pay (okay, that we understand)
- Dismissal
- Dismissal with loss of benefits

Unless the misconduct involved some form of sexual harassment, the offending faculty member normally would get one of the reprimands—a figurative slap on the wrist, accompanied by an admonition to never do it again. But, with the peasants revolting on campuses all across the country, college administrators, desperate to appease and hold onto their positions if not their power, didn't want or need justice, the just needed someone to hang.

Shortly after receiving the complaint, one of Miles' Minions called to inform Peter that, pending the outcome of the investigation, he was suspended until the complaint was resolved and that he was not to appear on campus unless he was required to be there for something related to the hearing process.

Like Napoleon, he had been banished to his own private island.

# Chapter Fifty-Four
## Please Allow Me to Introduce Myself

$T$he following week saw a storm of activity, legal and otherwise. On Monday morning, Peter got an email from Associate Dean of Students Haines Rutherford Burwell, who had been appointed to be the official grievance investigator. Burwell wanted to interview Peter at Peter's convenience, but made it clear that sooner would be better. Peter had no objection because his informal sentence of home confinement had already worn thin after just a few days.

Peter got the sense that Bliss and his people were fast-tracking the complaint, hoping that by giving the impression that they were moving quickly, it might lower the heat that they were getting from The Mob.

However, the students weren't letting up. Urged on by two Critical Studies profs, John "Jack" Russo and Robert S. Pierre, they confronted the administration with a list of non-negotiable demands, which included:

- Written and verbal apologies from Peter followed by his immediate termination
- Mandatory faculty sensitivity training
- Veto power over all future faculty hires
- Elimination of exams and grades
- Establishment of the Right To Not Be Offended.
- Safe spaces stocked with pillows, Teddy bears and video game consoles
- A pledge to support world peace and wage war against climate change
- No eight o'clock classes
- Free pizza and beer on Fridays

It would have surprised no one to hear them call for the hourly execution of a faculty member until their demands were met. As Yippee leader Jerry Rubin said in the 60s, 'Satisfy our demands and we've got more. The more demands you satisfy, the more we've got.' To use a bit of outdated phraseology, they were proud to be 'Sticking It To The Man,' even though they were getting huge doses of advice from faculty members who, given their age and position in life, were fairly accurate representations of 'The Man' themselves.

Hoping to keep it light and perhaps create some goodwill, Peter admitted to Burwell that his schedule was fairly open. Burwell replied that he could come over that afternoon and Peter agreed.

Peter didn't know Burwell, who had been one of a half-dozen associate deans under the dean of deans, Chet Duchin, whom Peter did know and believed to be a Compleat Idiot, an opinion shared by nearly everyone else on the faculty. And, believing that the Idiot Virus was contagious, they naturally thought that it had been contracted by everyone else in the dean's office, all of whom the faculty viewed as paper-pushing hacks and toadies. In turn, those in the Dean's Office held a similar opinion of the faculty, whom they saw as lazy, under-worked and arrogant underachievers. The fact that a revolving door existed between the faculty and administrators went unrecognized as each new teammate donned not only the uniform but also adopted the new team's utter disdain for the other side. Think Yankees/Red Sox.

Burwell himself was a former cultural anthropology prof, though not at Grodin, where he had been an associate dean for only a couple of years. As was common in academia, he had moved into administration for the bump in pay and with the hope that Grodin would be nothing more than a brief stop at a dreary, provincial way station on the road to the presidency of a more prestigious college somewhere else. But with the decline in the perceived value of a small-college liberal arts education and the subsequent shrinking of the job market, Burwell now found himself stranded at Grodin. With Manchester's sudden departure, he had thought briefly about angling for the presidency, but quickly realized that he had not been in residence long enough to develop the allies needed to mount a successful campaign. He now found himself struggling just to hang onto his current job. This did not bode well for Peter, since Burwell's personal interest was thus closely aligned with that of the administration, to wit—keep the creaky old USS Grodin afloat for as long as possible. And if it meant that Peter was to walk the plank, well, that would be seen by those in the administration as a smallish price to pay.

Burwell arrived a little after two—too late for lunch and too early for a glass of wine, except in France and Italy, of course. Peter offered him coffee or tea, but Burwell declined both. Tall, thin and angular to the point of gauntness, Burwell carried himself like a praying mantis, all legs and angles. Bent at the waist and permanently leaning forward, he appeared to be in constant danger of toppling over.

Burwell suggested that he set up in the dining room which was okay with Peter. He then said that he would be recording the interview, which wasn't. Although he was pretty sure that recording the interview wasn't a good idea, Peter didn't object, not wanting to color it before it had started.

While Burwell was setting up the recorder and getting his notes in order, Peter mentioned that he didn't know too many people in the Dean of Students Office, but that he regularly played tennis with Burwell's former boss, Chet Duchin and his wife, Lois. This attempt at small-talk flew completely unimpeded right over Burwell's head and, had it been open, would have flown right out the window.

When he was ready, Burwell motioned for Peter to sit down and told him that he had already interviewed several students and was here to get Peter's side of the story.

He had scarcely looked directly at Peter since he arrived, but now he finally looked at him and asked, "shall we start?"

"Fine with me, the sooner the better," said Peter, a little too eagerly.

"This is the official grievance hearing interview with the Dean of Students Office, Grodin College, on November 10$^{th}$ about events occurring in Dr. Peter Grande's class, *Foundations of Modern American Literature* at ten o'clock on the morning of November 3$^{rd}$ in the Max and Judith Etz-Holman Learning Center."

By the time he finished his scene-setting, Peter determined that he didn't like the vibe he was getting from Burwell and decided he shouldn't volunteer too much.

Finally turning his attention to Peter, Burwell started the interview with a question. "So, can you give me your version of what happened in class last Monday?"

Peter wanted to say that the little bastards wouldn't shut up so he had to yell at them to be quiet, but instead, he blandly stated that he'd had to raise his voice and ask them to please pay attention so the class could start.

He was getting no clues from Burwell as to how his remarks were going down.

Burwell then asked, "could you tell me exactly what you said?"

Peter remembered what he said, but he also remembered the advice he'd heard on a legal TV show about not volunteering, and he also remembered that saying "I don't recall" was better than re-enacting. This, of course, went against his natural inclination to over-explain. After all, he was a college professor.

"I may have raised my voice to call the class to order, but I don't remember exactly what I said."

"Did you say anything that may have offended them?"

"I might have chastised them for not coming to order. It was a Monday, and Monday mornings are always tough. They're just back from the weekend and aren't always quite ready to get down to business."

"So, what did you say to them?" asked Burwell again.

"Well, I don't remember the exact words, but I knew they were upset and I tried to apologize to them at the next class," said Peter.

"So you don't recall what you said?"

"No, not exactly."

"Did you call them idiots?"

"I don't remember," said Peter.

"Did you call them lazy?"

"I don't recall saying that."

"So, do you recall much of anything?"

Peter didn't like the 'so' line of questioning, so he decided he had best shut up.

"Did you know that there's a video recording of what you said?" said

Burwell.

Peter could definitively say that he did not know that. He tried not to look terrified.

"Is there anything else you can tell me about the incident?" asked Burwell.

"Not that I can think of," said Peter.

Burwell turned off the recorder and said, "since you don't seem to remember much about the incident, there's no point in continuing." He began packing up and advised Peter that he would submit his findings to the Panel on Student-Faculty Misconduct and if they found enough evidence to warrant it, they would schedule a formal hearing.

Peter had been holding out hope that he might get off with a reprimand after an apology, but after the Burwell interview, which seemed more like a cross-examination than a search for the truth, he realized he was in deeper water than he thought, although 'deep water' was not the first metaphor that occurred to him.

After Burwell left, Peter decided he'd better get some professional advice and called Per Johannsen, an econ prof who represented Grodin's faculty in salary negotiations. After expressing surprise at how quickly things were happening, Johannsen arranged for Peter to call a New York attorney who specialized in advising academics charged with misconduct.

Peter called and got a recorded greeting featuring a voice with a heavy Brooklyn accent. "You have reached Sam Abernathy, attorney for the Faculty Misconduct Hotline. For Sexual Harassment, press one. For Accusations of Racial or Gender Insensitivity, press two. For Microaggressions, Violation of Safe-Spaces and General Insensitivity, press three. For all other offenses, press four.

"If you wanna speak with an operator, fergedaboudit. Leave your name and number, then hang up as no operators are standing by. Either I or one of my associates will get back to you."

True to his word, Abernathy called back late in the afternoon.

"So the crybabies got your number. What's the misconduct?"

"There's been no misconduct," Peter informed him.

"Yeah, yeah, I know. Everybody says that, but misconduct is an 'eye of the beholder' kind of thing, and I say that with no intention of suggesting any kind of religious connotation," said Abernathy. "I'm agnostic."

'Agnostic' also had a religious connotation, thought Peter, but he kept that notion to himself.

Peter explained what happened. After he finished, Abernathy was silent, apparently letting it all sink in.

"So, what do you suggest?"

Abernathy began. "Look, this is what we call in the legal biz a *pro forma* process and the complainant holds all the cards. The little snowflakes got their feelings hurt and these days that's a punishable offense. You're the adult in the room; you're supposed to know better."

"If the system were rational, you'd get the proverbial slap on the wrist and be told not to do it again, but the mob wants its pound of blood or whatever the fuck the metaphor is. The only question is whether the punishment is a slap on the wrist or the guillotine. And the people in charge know that they could be next, so you're going down. Your peers are too scared to fight back. Watch for it, because in the end they'll all cave. It will all be very orderly and civilized, but, what you gotta understand is that the system is rigged. This ain't a search for the truth."

"You're a big help, I thought you might give me some advice as to how to get out of this."

"I am."

It doesn't sound like it.

"It's what's going on at colleges these days. Now all the delicate flowers are playing the game of 'Let's Get The Professor' and it's gone national. But in order to play, they need a target. You happened to pop up at the wrong time in the wrong place."

"Then what should I do?" asked Peter.

"Look, my advice is keep your mouth shut and throw yourself on the mercy of the court. There's no due process. There are no attorneys present. The panel members will ask all the questions. You can't cross-examine, in fact, you'll be lucky if you even get to listen to the testimony. You guys' teaching job is to explain things, and you think if you yak long enough everyone will come around and understand. What you don't understand is that somewhere, sometime, you'll make a mistake, contradict yourself, get angry...something. One little mistake and it'll be all over, and if you're fired for cause, you could lose a lot of your benefits. You can sue, of course, but there's not a *pro bono* attorney in the world foolish enough to take your case. Going that route will cost you big-time dough and there are no guarantees. "

"But you're a lawyer, can't you help?"

"Maybe, after this process plays itself out and you get punished. Then you can get out of the Kangaroo Court and into a real one—if you can afford it."

"But by then it's probably too late," said Peter.

"Bingo. Look, there's nothing to do right now but go through the charade. Remember, there's no due process here, you have no rights."

"Can't the faculty union help?"

"Are you kidding? They're scared to death. You have to realize what's going on. It's a witch-hunt and gender differences aside, you're the witch. Call me when it's over. Then maybe you'll have a case against Grodin, depending on how bad the punishment is."

"You've been very encouraging," Peter said sarcastically.

"I'm just telling you how the cow ate the cabbage."

"I've heard that before, what does it mean?"

"It's just something I heard when I was growing up. Look, I'm seventy-eight years old. I grew up in the Bronx and I have no idea what goes on on

farms. What it means? I have no fucking idea other than cows like cabbage."
With that, he hung up.

## Chapter Fifty-Five
### The Snowflake Rebellion

$M$eanwhile, back on campus, the students were revolting—and causing trouble as well. In keeping with the long-standing Massachusetts tradition of mass hysteria that began with the Salem witch hunts, the students were on high alert for any new transgressions. The slightest something that made them feel uncomfortable or unappreciated became grist for the grinder. Hurt feelings became the measure of truth. It didn't matter that feeling discomfort in certain situations might simply be a part of growing up because even the slightest perturbation was now something that 'just shouldn't be.'

On-campus awareness and sensitivity workshops educated them as to how grievously they had been victimized and enlightened them about who should be held responsible. Counselors from the Health Center worked overtime to console students suffering from the newly-discovered maladies of 'classroomophobia' (fear of classrooms), 'testophobia' (fear of exams), and 'anxietyophobia,' (the fear of fear itself).

The members of the faculty, now suffering from 'studentophobia,' were terrified of committing even the smallest offense, knowing that anything that upset their charges' delicate psyches could land them in the dock alongside Peter.

For the students, they finally had 'A Cause,' something that established that they were hip, happening and fully 'Down with the Struggle,' generation-wise.

They did their best imitation of Occupy Wall Street by setting up a tent city on Squirrelle Square where they vowed to stay until their demands were met. As it turned out, not one of them actually spent a single night in Tent City, not with heated dorm rooms and comfy beds just a few steps away. It was November, after all, and they weren't in Venice Beach. However, during the day it did provide a novel meeting space for the social media-inclined to actually meet face-to-face, although it didn't prevent them from assiduously staring at their devices while texting the person sitting right next to them.

They also built a 'Wailing Wall,' on which they created a giant Collage Of Injustice where they posted 'narratives' under their photos detailing the atrocities they had suffered.

One night, after learning about the 'Wailing Wall,' a gang of computer science nerds, wearing yellow rain-slickers and carrying harpoons, marched down to Squirrelle Square. They feigned surprise when The Occupiers indignantly informed that it was not a 'Whaling Wall,' and since whales were a revered and endangered species, even their symbolic harpooning was something to be frowned upon. All parties reached a compromise and agreed to jointly tear down the wall when the evil Peter, 'Cap'n Ahab,' Grande was terminated.

But the truce between the Occupiers and the Nerds remained shaky because on another night they lit torches and marched zombie-like through Squirrelle chanting 'Rich Pay Fair Share' while carrying signs proclaiming *Math is Racist*, *Yout Lives Matter* and the old standby, *Free Pizza on Fridays*, with the last being the singular point of agreement between The Occupiers and The Nerds.

Bliss tried to keep things calm, or at a minimum, keep them from spinning out of control. He met with the leaders and attempted to assure them that justice would be done through the hearing process. One night he even sent several dozen pizzas over to the Tent City, an action which sparked a lengthy discussion as to whether offering pizza to students was a food-stereotyping micro-aggression.

Nevertheless, while that discussion raged, no pizza went unconsumed.

## Chapter Fifty-Six
Hunkered in the Bunker


$M$eanwhile, back at home and banned from campus, Peter was cut off from his world. He rarely left the house and even stopped going for coffee at the Tipsy Spoon. For a few days, he held out the hope that Burwell would discover there was no need for a formal hearing, but that faint glimmer was snuffed out when he received formal notice that the hearing would be held at ten a.m. on the Monday before Thanksgiving.

Peter had twelve days to get ready.

He spent the rest of the day reading through the rules that would govern the hearing, which was formally called the *Panel of Inquiry Into Student-Faculty Conduct*. (Previously, the hearing had been called the *Panel of Inquiry into Student-Faculty Misconduct*, but the '*Mis*' in '*Misconduct*' was judged by some to be a gender-based micro-aggression. A few thought that interpretation was a '*Mis-take*,' but wisely kept that opinion to themselves.

The process was straightforward: a panel of five would hear the complaints, interview the various parties and come to a decision about guilt or innocence.

The panel would consist of three faculty members, one administrator and one at-large selection. For the three faculty judges, the Dean of the School of Humanities would pick one, Bliss, as President, would pick another, and the third would be someone of Peter's choosing. He could either submit the names of three profs willing to serve and Bliss would pick one, or he could have his choice selected in a random drawing. For the remaining two panel members, one would be an administrator appointed by Dean of Students and the fifth would be someone appointed by the Board of Trustees. The trustees could pick anyone—student, faculty, staff or alum—as long as the said person had some connection to Grodin.

After being sworn in, the panel's chair would read the charge and the complainants would then make their statements. Because the 'aggrieved class' in this case was so large, the students were to select three of their members to sit through the hearing and 'bear witness' for the rest. The five judges would listen to witnesses as they read their statements and then ask questions. Peter could listen, but not cross-examine. He could submit written questions to ask of the witnesses, but it was up to the panel to decide whether or not to ask them.

After the complainants completed their testimony, Peter would take the stand and the judges would then ask him questions, after which they would retire to make a decision, which could come immediately or at any time within two weeks after the hearing. Should they find for the students and against Peter, they would submit a recommendation to Bliss, who would make the final decision about the extent of the punishment.

Peter began calling around to a few potential friendlies on the faculty to see if any would serve on as his pick on the panel, but no one volunteered. Suddenly there was an outbreak of life-threatening illnesses among mothers, fathers, mothers-in-law, wives, husbands, sisters, brothers, grandparents, dogs, cats…you name it. No one stooped to the level of 'my goldfish died,' but some came close.

Peter soon realized that he was asking them to volunteer for a potentially career-ending suicide mission.

## Chapter Fifty-Seven
### Strategery


*T*he next day, Peter arranged to meet with Pierce to discuss the new situation. Not wanting to be seen at one of their usual hangouts, they met for lunch in downtown Beresford at The Oasis, a beer 'n burger place rarely frequented by Grodinites.

Just back from his Caribbean vacation, Pierce was tanned and relaxed, unlike Peter, whose haggard face was the pallor of oatmeal. "Should I have worn my trench coat and sunglasses?" Pierce asked as he slid into one of the wooden booths.

"Only if you wanted to be taken for the local pervert," answered Peter, "which might not be a very good idea around here," he said, gesturing towards the non-Pajama Boy clientele who patronized the Oasis. For Peter, it felt good to be able to joke around again with someone as that kind of chummy badinage had been in short supply of late.

"Quite a pickle you've gotten yourself into, Ollie," said Pierce, who was always one to favor the frivolous over the serious. "At least they can't throw you in jail."

"No, but I might end up having to teach at a community college somewhere. Maybe even in Kansas, god forbid," said Peter.

"Well, in case you haven't exceeded your daily dose of bad news, 'wait… there's more,' as they say in the infomercials." Pierce paused for a moment to let Peter know it was truly news of the not-very-good variety. "Bliss has been appointed president. As of today."

"Oh, god, I knew it was coming, but…why is it that good things always happen to bad people?"

"I think you've got that backwards, but I get your drift," said Pierce. "What's happening on the hearing front?"

In between bites of a juicy burger and fries, Peter got it all out—the charges, the judges, the process. For the first time in weeks, he was able to vent to someone, especially since Bark had gone off to live with Glynnyth.

He then asked if Pierce would be willing to serve as his choice to sit on the Panel. Pierce said he would, but since he was no longer on the faculty, he was pretty sure it wouldn't be allowed. Plus, he was certain that Bliss wouldn't pick him even if Peter could find two others. He suggested that Peter take the random drawing route. That Unfortunate could then make it known far and wide that he or she was in no way the endorsed the actions of the soon-to-be guilty party, but was merely doing his or her civic duty.

After they'd finished the burgers and a pitcher of beer, Pierce said, "By the way, right after this happened, someone from the president's office called. They wanted me to come back and take over your two courses. I declined, of course."

"Clueless bastards," said Peter.

"I hear they've bringing in an adjunct to handle the writing class and Brossard is taking over your lecture. Not sure whom they've designated as the floater. As we know, any idiot can teach that." He paused, then added, "no offense."

"None taken. We both know that anyone halfway-literate could teach these morons."

"Now, now. Enough of that. That's precisely the kind of talk that got you into trouble in the first place."

With that, they parted.

"Good luck, old chum. I know it's going to be rough. Call if you need anything," said Pierce.

Under a gray overcast sky, the mid-November afternoon was already turning dark.

## Chapter Fifty-Eight
Prep for the Perp

*W*hen he arrived home, Peter found a notice that a registered letter was waiting for him at the West Beresford Post Office. It annoyed him that he would have to drive back into town to collect it. Hadn't the sender heard of email? Or even just a voicemail to let him know that the letter was on its way?

At the Post Office, he opened the letter and found that the date of the hearing had been changed to the Friday before Thanksgiving Week, which was now just a week away. Peter knew instantly exactly why this had happened—by scheduling the hearing on the Monday of Thanksgiving Week, Bliss had created a furor on campus.

Now, for the average person living and working in the real world, such a decision would have passed unnoticed because, depending on what one did for a living, again for the average person, the Monday before Thanksgiving was either a work day or a school day.

In higher education, however, there had been slippage.

In the prior century, when things were sensible, the Mondays, Tuesdays and Wednesdays before Thanksgiving were regular class days at most colleges and universities. But seeing they could get a jump-start on travel home, some students began sneaking away early on Wednesdays or began skipping Wednesday's classes altogether. Then others started leaving on Tuesdays to avoid the inevitable Wednesday airport crush. With Mondays now the last official class-day standing, many schools raised the white flag of surrender and declared all of Thanksgiving Week to be...ta-da...class-free. But, human nature being what it is, Mission Creep occurred and colleges then saw a decrease in attendance on the Friday before Thanksgiving Week as both students and faculty began to regard it as the new Getaway Day for a week-and-a-half vacation.    If one believed in trends, the trend was definitely pointing towards a class-free November.

But for once Grodin had stood tall against the crowd, having not yet totally succumbed to the class-free concept, it still held classes on Mondays and Tuesdays, although more and more profs were finding reasons to postpone them and schedule make-up days which rarely occurred. However, there were dissenters to the notion of a class-free Thanksgiving Week—the geeks from Computer Science. They complained that the extra vacation days meant they'd have to spend more time at home, thus being forced to interact over turkey with their non-techie relatives instead of being able to spend that valuable time with their beloved devices, especially if the parental units insisted they turn them off during dinner.

So, with many students already thinking about skipping classes during Thanksgiving Week, they rebelled, as being 'forced' to attend or protest the

Monday hearing would now cut into their unspoken plan for taking a ten-day vacation. Of course, Bliss had counted on some students leaving as a way to reduce the potential for trouble, but with the students now if full revolt mode and feeling righteously indignant, Bliss decided that this was not the field of battle upon which he wished to make a stand.

With the change, Peter now had only a week to get ready; however, the truth was there wasn't much for him to do. He reviewed the list of students who would be testifying against him and was sad to discover that he had difficulty putting faces with names, even after checking out their photos in the students' class book. He then read the hearing protocol to make sure he understood precisely how he was going to be screwed.

Following that, he watched a lot of TV and ate a lot of the dinners named after that activity.

## Chapter Fifty-Nine
A Blissful Encounter?

*O*n the weekend before the hearing and needing some light bulbs, sponges and a few other household odds and ends, Peter left his hideout and headed off to the True Value hardware store in Great Beresford.

After the first real snowfall of the year, gloomy grey skies portended the start of a serious New England winter. Driving to the store, Peter carefully navigated the slick, icy streets. It was just one more reason he was not looking forward to the future. The present was bad enough.

As he was going into the hardware store, he saw Bliss coming out. There was no avoiding this chance encounter. They nodded stiffly and almost passed each other without comment when Bliss turned and dove straight into it.

"Look, Peter, even though I'd like to resolve your situation for the sake of the school, things have gone too far. The students have thrown the bit and are running wild. I think you and I both know that the Panel is not going to absolve you, and I seriously doubt that you'll be teaching at Grodin again. As president, my job is to save the college if I can, and even though you probably don't believe it, 'it's not personal, it's just business.'"

They stared at each other for a few seconds, then Bliss added, "I'd suggest you polish up your résumé."

As he walked away, Bliss turned and said, "by the way, this conversation never happened."

With that he got in his car and drove off.

Peter wished he'd learned how to make a video recording on his iPhone, but, like many things he'd meant to do but never got around to, this was just one more example of why—were there such a thing—he would be a member of the Procrastinators' Club of America. Not a charter member, of course, as that would have been an oxymoron.

## Chapter Sixty
### Glynnyth Phones Home

*G*lynnyth called a few days before the hearing. He thought about letting her call go to voicemail but then decided to pick up. She was in sunny South Florida. The gist of what she had to say was that divorce papers were on their way and that she wanted to put the house on the market in the spring.

"We need to tell the kids," said Peter.

"They've been told."

Peter was reluctant to ask how they'd taken it. Undoubtedly Cybelle would have sided with her Mom and as for Glynn, Peter realized he hadn't talked with him for months. Nor had he thought much about him and he was sure it was also true for Glynn. After all, like father, like son, the 'out of sight, out of mind' syndrome was probably genetic.

"You aren't going to give me any trouble over this?" asked Glynnyth.

"Not about the divorce, but I'll have to think about the house."

"You do that. There's plenty of time."

After a long pause which was typical of their conversations when neither could think of anything to say that didn't lead directly into a danger zone, Glynnth broke the silence.

"Well, good luck with your hearing."

He resisted the urge to say his hearing was fine, and simply said "thanks."

With that, she hung up.

Peter realized that in the last month, and even before the blowup, he hadn't given much thought to Glynnyth, other than the fact that he missed her cooking.

He also realized that he missed Bark far more than he did her.

Late in the afternoon before the hearing, Peter called Abernathy for some last-minute advice, which could be summarized as follows:

- Answer questions as simply as possible.
- Don't volunteer nothing.
- Don't lose your temper.
- And remember, the deck is stacked against you.

Abernathy ended the call by saying, "I shouldn't have to tell you to 'dress appropriately,' but you are a college professor, so who the fuck knows."

## Chapter Sixty-One
### Calling All Kangaroos! Court Is Now in Session!

$O$n Hearing Friday, a fitful night's sleep and a skimpy breakfast were all Peter could manage, although he took Abernathy's advice and put on his best Chair-wear for the big day.

Hoping to avoid the anticipated mob of students, he made sure he arrived early, but after driving to the rear of the Wheeler Center where the hearing was to be held, he saw that a large crowd had already gathered in front of the building. The Mob had propped their placards up against the wall and were casually chatting up each other, but were ready to spring into Full Outrage Mode the moment The Great Satan arrived.

What a surprise, thought Peter. Chet Duchin, who had been called back to duty to coordinate the hearing, had left a message the night before to let him know where the hearing would be held, having kept the location secret until the last minute with the hope of avoiding a confrontation. Peter wondered how he could have thought that the student witnesses, though sworn to secrecy, wouldn't share that information with their comrades, stupidly believing that they would respect the ancient and creaky Grodin Honor Code.

But then he remembered that Chet was an idiot.

He called Chet, who said he'd send Officer Jim over to escort Peter inside, to which Peter replied, "I think we need a bigger boat."

To which Chet replied, "what do you mean, 'a bigger boat?'" As though he were talking to a small and rather dense child, Peter exasperatedly explained what he'd meant by needing 'a bigger boat.'

Grodin had two security guards, Officer Jim and Officer Jannelle. Their basic responsibility was to make sure the buildings were locked at night and opened in the morning. If there was anything that required actual police work, they called the men and women in blue at the West Beresford station.

A half-hour later a team of West Beresford's Finest arrived in two squad cars and escorted Peter through the now-screaming mob, the members of which, at the sight of Peter, had been roused from torpor to hysteria in a New York nanosecond. The students waved their placards and shouted the now-familiar "hey, hey, ho, ho...racist Grande has got to go" as the cops surrounded Peter and phalanxed their way through the crowd. After an intense minute of frenzied activity, everyone got what they wanted: the students their photo-ops, the cops their good deed, and Peter...well, he had arrived safely in one piece.

Once inside, an admin quickly locked the door behind Peter and then discussed with the cops whether or not they should stay. After a flurry of phone calls, the cops were asked to wait until Officers Jim and Janelle arrived to take over. Peter thanked West Beresford's Finest and they returned to their regular duties of patrolling the high crime areas of their fair city and conducting quality control tests at Dunkin' Donuts.

Officer Jim stayed behind to guard the door while Officer Janelle and one of the admins escorted Peter down the hall to a windowless seminar room where he sat and waited.

And waited.

With the only sound inside the room coming from the hum of the fluorescent lights, it was quiet enough that Peter could hear the crowd continue to chant outside. After a while, he imagined them constructing a makeshift gallows in Squirrelle, Spaghetti Western-style, but then realized that such an endeavor was most likely beyond their capabilities, not to mention that its construction would require actual planning and effort. Much easier to run in circles and scream and shout about the falling sky.

After waiting alone long enough for Peter to think that everyone might have forgotten about him, the admin reappeared and led him to a small lecture hall where a single chair stood in the center of the well, surrounded by semicircular rows of seats. The admin motioned for Peter to take a seat in the front row, after which Officer Janelle opened a door at the back of the auditorium and led a stream of twenty or so somber-looking students down to their seats across the well from Peter. They sat down and stink-eyed him with their best Death Stares.

The hearing was supposed to start at ten, but in keeping with the Grodin tradition of nothing ever starting on time, four of the five judges entered at ten past the hour. They filed in and sat down in the center row across from the witness chair which had been situated so it could face them. It was now empty, but would soon be filled by a steady stream of complainants.

To avoid being harassed by The Mob, the judges' identities had been kept secret. Peter recognized only two of the four and was puzzled by the absence of the fifth. Of the two he knew, one was 'Mad Max' Thomasson, an officious, on-the-make administrator from the Dean of Students' Office. The second was Armando Alphonso Arroyo, a full professor from Critical Social Theory. Like the first listing in the Yellow Pages, Arroyo was known around campus as Triple-A, due to his penchant for being one of the first to jostle his way to the front of any anti-establishment controversy. His 1,216-page tome, *Uprising! Race, Gender & Class: The Paradigm for a New 21st Century Dialectic*, was hailed in progressive circles as a ground-breaker in the world of radical intersectionality, but of course no one had actually read it.

Right out of the box, Peter counted these as two negativos.

As the senior faculty member, Triple-A had been designated to chair the panel. He first introduced himself and then the other judges. Bliss's pick for the panel was Amanda Wright-Spangler, a young associate prof in Environmental Studies from the School of Human and Natural Sciences. Peter didn't know her, but he hoped that with her science background, she might bring some measure of objectivity to the proceedings. However, he was aware of the natural inclination   which younger faculty members had to create opportunities for themselves to move up in the pecking order. And because they had been long-suffering eyewitnesses to the penchant of the imperious older profs to soak up the cream of the academic spoils, thus blocking the harder-working and more deserving up-and-comers from taking their rightful place at the trough, such long-simmering resentments might causing them to to decide against one of their elders, thus removing one more obstacle in their climb up the ladder.

The Board of Trustees had appointed Bradley Friedman, a retired businessman and board member who had generously donated both time and money to Grodin. Peter hoped he might at least be a neutral voice in the jury room.

While Triple-A was introducing Associate Dean Thomasson, there was a commotion at the back of the auditorium. Like a flaming comet exploding out of the darkness of deep space, the fifth judge burst into the room. Paying no attention to the fact that Arroyo was speaking, the late arriver loudly announced how sorry she was to be tardy, but if they only knew how difficult her morning had been…well, they would understand.

It was Margaret.

With her arms full of books and an oversized bag hanging from her shoulder, she bustled down the aisle, squeezed in behind the other judges and settled into her chair. Only after sitting down with a thud did she stop speaking. She then tossed her hair, crossed her arms across her chest and glared at Peter.

Margaret had won the lottery to become the fifth judge, or at least that would probably become the official mantra. Peter wouldn't have put it past Bliss to have stacked the deck and dealt him its worst possible card. With it now clear that a solid majority was already dead-set against him, Peter thought about standing up and declaring, 'I'm outta here.' But of course he didn't, as there was always the remote chance of divine intervention in the form of a meteor strike.

After finishing the introductions, Triple-A described the hearing process at length and then, finally, read the charges against Peter. By this time, nearly everyone had dozed off.

When he finished, he asked the students and Peter to stand up and be sworn in, asking them to "swear to tell the truth, the whole truth and nothing but the truth, upon your personal honor?" (Years ago, the Powers That Were at Grodin had removed the phrase 'so help me God' and replace it with the thin gruel of 'upon my personal honor.')

Triple-A then ordered the room darkened. He nodded and an AV tech started running a grainy cellphone video of Peter's now-infamous rant. Peter's words were garbled and hard to make out, but his anger came through clearly.

Triple-A then asked if this partial recording of the event was accurate and the students all responded with a loud and clear "yes." He then asked Peter the same question. Peter nodded, but Triple-A insisted, "please answer orally with a yes or no."

"Yes," Peter said reluctantly.

With that, Triple-A asked all the aggrieved students, but for the three who would 'bear witness,' to leave the room. As they went out the door, several dropped their solemnity masks and 'high-fived' each other.

After they'd filed out, Triple-A turned and addressed Peter. "Before we begin hearing from the witnesses, the students have indicated that they feel your presence in the hearing room would be intimidating and would cause them such discomfort that they would not be able to express themselves fully. Consequently, they have asked that you leave the room and observe the proceedings via closed-circuit TV."

"The Panel has concluded that their request is reasonable and agree that it will lead to more openness and transparency. You will be allowed to pass questions of the witnesses to the Panel, which, at our discretion, we may or may not ask."

Of course, Peter thought this was utter bullshit—a weak and cowardly cave to the students' demands. He was about to stand up and declare that this was a mockery of justice, fairness and The American Way, etc., etc., but remembered Abernathy's advice against losing his temper. All he needed was to demonstrate to the Panel that he had a pattern of losing control and thus validating the students' complaints against him.

Instead, he just gathered up his notes and left.

For the rest of the morning, the Panel listened to student after student recount the feelings of inadequacy, the loss of self-esteem and the anguish they had felt as a result of Peter's harangue. They told stories of visits to counselors and therapists and cries for help to family and friends. They begged the Panel to understand their pain. Were this to ever become a reality TV show, it could be framed as a contest for the title of 'Most Distraught.' In essence, the students validated all the generalizations about their generation as weak-willed, soft-minded simpering whiners who, if called upon to defend their country or even themselves, would immediately drop to their knees and beg for mercy.

Some of the students spoke with anger about how they had been 'disrespected' and that a person in Dr. Grande's position should have realized that they were not be spoken to as if they were...well...children, even though they routinely behaved like children. After all, some argued, because they were paying for their education, they should have the right to determine whether they were getting fair value for their money. And if they thought they weren't, they had the right to behave as they damn well pleased. And if a particular professor wasn't able to capture and keep their attention, that wasn't their problem; it only proved that the professor in question was a lousy teacher. In short, the teacher-student relationship had been turned upside-down, a fact with which the judges on the Panel were quite aware.

The judges' questions were of the gentle, soothing variety which they asked with a 'tsk-tsking' undercurrent of sympathy for the emotional hardship the students had endured. They occasionally tossed in self-serving anecdotes of how they had extended aid and comfort to those students whose wounded psyches barely allowed them to function in a world filled with cruelty and hate.

Peter had no questions for them. How could one challenge their right to their feelings without coming off an uncaring, overbearing member of an out-of-touch elite?

After more than two hours of cringe-worthy testimony, the Panel broke for lunch and dined sumptuously, buffet-style, in Bliss's conference room. Seemingly forgotten in his windowless seminar room, Peter could hear them chatting and laughing down the hall. An admin finally brought him a cucumber sandwich, a plate of *crudités* and a can of Diet Coke. It wasn't exactly bread and water, but it felt close.

When the hearing resumed, the final witnesses were called and the Panel heard their lamentations with as much interest as they could muster while their bodies were busy digesting their lunch.

It was then Peter's turn.

He returned to the 'courtroom,' whereupon Triple-A asked whether the short video clip was a fair and accurate representation of what he had said to the class. Since it was a recording of exactly what he had said, Peter had to concur, but he did argue that because the tape didn't show what the students had been doing or show his attempts to bring the class to order, his outburst was justified.

"Well, we may disagree about that," said Triple-A. "Do any of the other members of the panel have questions?" he asked.

"I have questions," Margaret interjected quickly, "and I am very much interested to know if Dr. Grande has answers."

She pulled out a thick yellow legal pad from one of her many bags, opened a notebook and began her interrogation, "Dr. Grande, are you familiar with *Controlling The Classroom: A Methodology of Instructional Aids for Teachers,* by Dr. Ambrose D. Turnbull, of the Murphy State Teachers' College?"

It was easy for Peter to answer "no" to that question.

Margaret then asked, "and are you familiar with the work of Peter J. Schwartz on *Effective Instruction: From Seminars to Large Group Lectures*?"

Peter answered "no" to that as well. And, given the uncomfortable, wide-eyed looks he saw in the eyes of the other judges, he was certain that they had never heard of these works either.

Margaret continued her cross-examination with several more 'Gotcha' questions about other obscure tomes on teaching techniques, to which Peter had to answer 'no' as well.

She then asked, "Dr. Grande, have you ever taken any formal courses on large group instruction?"

Peter truthfully answered "no," and wished he could ask that question of any of the other panelists, including Margaret. It was well-understood by everyone in the room that few college professors had ever taken any classes or read any books about teaching. Their job was to present material and the students' job was to deal with it as best they could. Over time, of course, the professors did pick up on techniques that worked for them and their personalities, and they blatantly poached and plagiarized from their colleagues. However, once they had passed their final, final exam and been granted tenure, what they did in class and how they did it was no longer anyone else's business. Certainly, there were a few who made an effort to make themselves popular with students, but if they weren't or didn't want to, so be it. Let the students pound sand.

"So, Dr. Grande," Margaret said in summation, "it appears to me that in more than thirty years as a college professor, you never made an effort to formally improve your teaching either through research or by taking self-improvement classes."

"I believe I've always tried to improve my teaching skills," said Peter.

"I asked you if you had ever formally made an effort to improve your teaching by taking education classes," she said.

Peter wished for a moment that he could ask Margaret if she ever had, but instead, he said, "I believe my student evaluations show that I have been an effective teacher, should you be interested in reviewing them."

"May the record reflect that the witness is being non-responsive," said Margaret.

Triple-A answered hesitantly, "Margaret, um, Professor Dreighton, I don't believe we have a formal record."

Margaret glared at him and then turned back to Peter.

"Then it is my sincere hope that we can all remember what has been said here," said Margaret. With that, she slammed her notebook shut and added, "As to my question about whether you have ever made an effort to improve your teaching, I believe your answers clearly show that you have not."

Margaret leaned back and folded her arms triumphantly, daring anyone to challenge her or even to speak.

No one did.

Triple-A broke the silence by asking if there were any more questions. As no one dared follow Margaret, there were none.

"Then this hearing is officially closed. The Panel will take the evidence presented here under advisement and will now retire to deliberate. We will then submit our written decision to President Moynihan within two weeks, as prescribed by the rules governing hearings into faculty misconduct." He looked around for a gavel, but seeing there wasn't one, he awkwardly slammed his palm onto the table.

"All rise," said one of the admins.

With that, the Panel members rose and solemnly marched out of the room.

Peter, after gathered his things and his thoughts, left as well.

Peter needed no escort to his car. Now nearly dark and with the late November cold making its presence felt, the members of The Mob had dispersed and had long since departed for their Thanksgiving break. Their quest for truth and justice had been superseded by the more immediate lure of a ten-day vacation.

## Chapter Sixty-Two
A Thanksgiving Invite

$P$eter spent a desultory weekend recovering from the hearing. He did manage to drag himself to the couch on Sunday afternoon to watch the Patriots steamroll the Bills, but even that trouncing failed to invigorate him the way it usually did.

On Monday afternoon, he got a formal notice from the Dean's Office that because of the Thanksgiving break, the start of the two-week deadline for the Panel's decision would begin on the following Monday. Bliss would now have their decision on his desk near the end of Final Exams, which was three-and-a-half weeks away.

Conveniently for Bliss, it meant that he could announce his decision during the Christmas-Hanukkah-Kwanzaa and the Festivus-For-The-Rest-Of-Us holiday break—a time when the students would be at home and presumably preoccupied with other activities.

Realizing that Bliss had planned this, Peter had to give him props for making sure his decision came at a time when the student body's already-limited attention span would be even more limited than normal.

While taking the recycling bins out to the curb on the day before Thanksgiving, Peter ran into Harry Atwater, who was raking leaves. This was practically his first human interaction since the hearing.

"Hey, Peter," said Atwater, "wanna come over for dinner tomorrow? Watch some football?"

"Thanks, but I'll be going to dinner with some friends over in Springfield," he lied.

"Doris knows how to cook a mean bird," said Harry.

"That's tempting, Harry, but I'm already committed." Peter wasn't in the mood to socialize, especially with a Neanderthal like Atwater.

"Well, if you change your mind or your car breaks down…"

"It's a BMW," said Peter. "It was made for crappy weather."

"That's why I'm out here. I wanna get these leaves cleared up before it snows and becomes a real mess."

"You're a trooper," said Peter.

"I like to keep on top of things. Not let 'em get out of hand."

"I wish I could do that."

"I heard about the hearing. How'd it go?"

"Tough."

"Well, don't let them make it your Waterloo," said Atwater.

"Despite my last name, I'm more English than French."

"Okay. Then don't let it be your Dunkirk. Make it your D-Day. Think Omaha Beach." Harry stopped raking and leaned on the handle. "You do know what I'm talking about, don't you?"

"Yeah, I do, although most of my colleagues don't."

"Well, screw 'em. Were any of those rat-bastards in the foxhole with you or have they run up the white flag?"

"This is getting a little too militaristic for me," said Peter, "but thanks for your support."

Ending the conversation, Peter again began pushing the recycling bin towards the street.

"Good luck, Peter. Anything I can do….let me know," said Atwater.

"Thanks," said Peter.

## Chapter Sixty-Three
A Turkey Day for Turkeys


*T*hanksgiving Day arrived sunny and cold. Peter and Glynnyth usually spent every other Thanksgiving with Pierce and his wife, but this was the year the Harringtons spent it with Pierce's wife's family in Boston. So, Peter had nothing to look forward to in the way of celebrating Turkey Day.

Given how he was feeling, socializing with anyone was more than he wanted to deal with, but he still felt the need to get out of the house. By late morning, provoked by percolations emanating from his stomach region, visions of turkey, gravy and pumpkin pie were beginning to dance in his head. Because he didn't want to be seen dining alone by anyone he knew, he drove to Great Beresford in the afternoon and ended up at the Golden Corral, where the likelihood of running into someone he knew was close to zero.

Inside the Corral at this hour of the day, the mood was quiet, almost funereal. There was the occasional couple, but most of the customers were singles who had scattered themselves around the room as though their primary objective was to sit as far away from the nearest person as possible.

Peter paid and loaded up his tray with heapings of turkey, stuffing, mashed potatoes and gravy and a spoonful of Brussel sprouts which he added as a garnish—all of which were surprisingly good. Peter went back through the buffet line for a second helping of everything, which he then followed up with two slices of pumpkin pie topped with whipped cream. Then coffee.

Heartburn would likely follow in a couple of hours.

He enjoyed the meal more than he'd expected, but as he looked around the room, he saw a future filled with holidays which, were his circumstances to remain the same, he would likely share with other social losers—not that there was necessarily anything wrong with that.


When he got home, he turned on the TV to check out the late game between the Cowboys and the Redskins, but promptly fell asleep on the couch. He woke up somewhere in the second half to a Southwest Airlines' *Wanna Get Away?* commercial which featured the sun, piña coladas and girls in bikinis dancing on the beach.

What about that was there not to like?

After nearly a week of total inactivity and a future filled with more of the same, Peter felt a desperate need to 'get away.' But, however enticing it might seem, hitting a beach somewhere in the Caribbean was not it—where watching others having fun would only depress him further.

He then remembered a conference invitation that he'd declined in the spring. He'd dismissed it at the time, mostly because it was to be held in Portland in early December. But now? What did he have to lose? He might even run into someone he knew and perhaps get a lead on a deanship somewhere. He had no illusions that a ready-made job offer would fall into his lap, given that there was now a paucity of openings for even the most junior-level profs, not to mention positions for someone with Peter's seniority. Still, going to the conference would be a change and the thought of hanging around the house for the next few weeks waiting for the axe to fall was not all that attractive. The main thing was that it would be an adventure, even it was just a Comp Lit conference in Portland.

Conferences attracted academics in the same way that cow-patties attracted flies. To a normal person, everything about them was crappy, but professors found them irresistible. It was, an opportunity to get dirty, roll around in the mud and hang out with like-minded people on someone else's dime.

Peter looked up the details online and discovered it was taking place the next weekend. If he wanted to go, he'd have to act fast. The next morning he'd have to call Clive deBreville, the conference organizer, and wangle an invitation.

DeBreville, a Comp-Lit prof a couple of years older than Peter, hosted a symposium every other year at Mt. Hood College in Portland. The symposium existed mainly as a means for early and mid-career profs to establish their academic street cred by publishing in *Fissures: A Journal of Synoptic Disambiguation,* a journal deBreville had established decades ago. But if you wanted to be published in *Fissures*, you couldn't just mail it in, you had to show up at the conference and present your paper. So what if this kind of forced appearance smacked of blackmail, as no one would willingly travel to Portland in December? But, if you needed to publish or perish, you went.

In his early years, Peter had presented papers several times at deBreville's conference, but after getting tenure, he only went occasionally—once just for fun and a few times when he had acted as a 'respondent,' a senior prof who offered soft-pedaled 'constructive criticism' of the papers being presented. Few of the heavy hitters in the Comp Lit world attended the conference—they didn't need to and Portland in winter wasn't at all enticing. DeBreville would publish papers from these more established, big-name profs without forcing them to come, but they sometimes showed up anyway just to stay in deBreville's good graces. Even though they were high-ranking members in one of the most secure professions ever created by humans, one never knew, as Peter had discovered.

The title of this year's conference was *Palimpsest and/or Plagiarism? Modalities of the Mashup: 'Remixing' in the Digital Terrain Where Literary Forms Collide.* The fact that the titles of conferences and scholarly papers were, in essence, little more than gibberish never stopped those in the professoriat from creating them. Until recently, deBreville's journal had been titled *Fissures: A Journal of Culture, Aesthetics and Literature*, but change came when even that title was deemed too straightforward, as the over-riding principle in academic nomenclature was to use words in combinations that rendered their meaning incomprehensible to anyone outside the in-group. The overriding principle was that simple language and plain-speaking were to be avoided at all cost, lest the King's 'Royal Smart Person' be shown to have little or nothing to say.

The conference website invited one to "spend a weekend exploring the synchronicity of the tautological in cyberspace." (Who could resist that?)

Clive deBreville was usually ahead of the curve. Peter had to congratulate him for having the foresight to pick a symposium topic so complex and confusing that it could be a career-enhancer and thus entice a younger prof into spending the time needed to write a paper on it. And if the younger prof had an actual understanding of the issue at hand…well, that wasn't necessary, but would be a nice bonus.

## Chapter Sixty-Four
Making the Call

*T*he next day, Peter waited until shortly after noon to call deBreville on the West Coast. He didn't want to appear to be too eager, but he also needed to get a move on. Naturally, at nine in the morning on a quasi-holiday, deBreville wasn't there, so Peter left a message and several hours later, D.B., as he was known, called back.

Peter opened the conversation with a bluff, telling deBreville that he would be on the West Coast visiting one of his kids and, if it wasn't too late, he'd like to drop in on the conference.

But deBreville was having none of it. "Don't try to slick me, Peter. I've heard."

Peter caved quickly. "Look, I'll sub on a panel, do a critique. Anything. There's always someone who doesn't show up," he said. "Just put me on standby." After a pause, he added, "I just need to get away."

DeBreville sighed, "okay, I'll slot you into something if someone bails, and I'll waive the conference fee, but you'll have to get yourself out here on your own dime. These days I can only cover expenses for the Keynoters."

"Times are tough in Liberal-Artsville," said Peter.

"Don't we know it. See you next weekend." With that, de Belleville hung up.

Despite the minor humiliation of not having access to departmental travel money and having to pay his own way, Peter was energized by the fact that finally something was about to happen, even if it should prove to be pointless and futile. He spent the rest of the day making travel plans.

The conference would start on Friday afternoon and run through to the end of the day on Saturday and was to take place at Mt. Hood College, located near downtown in Southeast Portland. DeBreville had reserved rooms for attendees at a nearby DoubleTree Hotel. Although it was not exactly the Four Seasons, the DoubleTree was acceptable, especially because at some conferences, accommodations often involved stays in college dorms.

He checked the room rates on deBreville's site and was surprised to find that one could share a room with another attendee. DeBreville had even added a form to help match people up as roommates. Peter could hardly believe that some attendees were so desperate to save money that they would be willing to share a room with a total stranger. At this stage in his life, the last thing he needed was to exchange deep thoughts with someone he didn't know at eleven-thirty at night about Visser's response to Plantanget's *Theory of Cultural Misappropriation and Trans-Cultural Diffusion*. Despite the expense, it was a no-brainer for a nearly sixty-year-old Dr. Peter Grande to spring for a single. Hopefully, one with a view.

He then began to check flight schedules and realized how much he'd leaned on Meg and Betsy to take care of that kind of stuff. After struggling with airline websites, he finally figured out that since there were no non-stops that would get him to Portland by Friday noon, he'd have to leave on Thursday and fly home on Sunday.

That meant he would miss the Patriots game on Sunday, but so be it, he was now A Man on a Mission, although the Mission's goal was To Be Determined.

## Chapter Sixty-Five
### A West Coast Weekend

*F*or Peter, Getaway Day could not come soon enough. After Thanksgiving weekend, he had yet to receive any updates from Grodin about the hearing and no one had called to see how he was doing. The news and compassion vacuums further convinced Peter that leaving town was the right thing to do.

On Thursday morning he drove to Boston through a fitful, bitter and windy snowstorm. He worried all the way that the flight might be delayed, but luck was with him. It took off without a problem.

He relaxed, bought an onboard lunch and a glass of wine. Even though neither the lunch nor the wine were worth what he'd paid for them, the further away from Grodin he got, the better he felt.

It was drizzly and nearly dark when Peter arrived in Portland. With traffic on the freeway going nowhere, the Supershuttle driver detoured and took his passengers on a Magical Mystery Tour through the grungy, east end of Portland which featured a *mélange* of tattoo parlors and coffee cafes. On the streets, young men with backpacks and beards looked like they'd just come from a lumberjack camp while the young women could have been working as product testers for neon lipsticks and skin-piercing needles. On one corner, a homeless man with a puppy begged for spare change, ostensibly to buy the pup some Purina Dog Chow. Peter wondered if there was a local business where one could rent dogs by the hour.

He was struck by how young everyone looked. He realized he'd been seeing things for way too long through the professorial monocle. Also, in the back of his mind, he'd already begun to believe that he would never again be standing in front of a class at Grodin delivering a lecture to bored-out-of-their-minds students.

But, what would his new life be, should there be one?

# Chapter Sixty-Six
## Portlandia

$A$fter checking in and settling into his room at the DoubleTree, Peter began to think about getting something to eat. There was a restaurant downstairs, but he was afraid he might run into someone from the conference and get shanghaied into sharing a dinner. He was tired and not in the mood for shop talk and inside-baseball stories. There would be plenty of that over the next two days. He felt like Italian and used the in-room guide to find a restaurant in downtown Portland.

Glynnyth had long ago loaded an Uber app onto his iPhone, but Peter had never used it.

Because he was in a 'what the hell' mood, he decided to give Uber a try. He was beginning to feel like a new man.

His Uber driver represented his city well by wearing the Full Portland: porkpie hat, plaid lumberjack shirt and a full load of earrings, nose-rings and eyelid rings. Garish tattoos covered every visible part of his anatomy. He quickly scoped out Peter as an Uber newbie.

"Your first time?" he asked.

Peter answered in the affirmative and the Uberista spun out his personal history. Long story short, he was as a struggling film major looking for his big break and driving for Uber had allowed him to quit his other part-time gigs and pursue his dream of becoming a screenwriter. Naturally, he had a script or two he was working on.

Peter wondered if the guy wasn't living in the wrong city for this, but he kept that thought to himself and asked Mr. Uber what he was writing.

The Uberista glanced in the mirror at Peter and smiled wryly, "you wouldn't be trying to steal my idea, would you?"

"Hardly," said Peter. "I'm a college professor. Even if I knew what it was about, I wouldn't know what to do with it."

"Okay," he said, taking a deep breath as though he were about to reveal state secrets. "It's about an Uber driver who picks up rides at night in the city, takes them out to the woods and dismembers them with a rusty hacksaw."

Not caring much for this turn in the conversation, Peter furtively looked around to see if he could jump out at the next light.

The Uberista grinned as he watched Peter's reaction in the mirror. "I'm just messing with ya," he said. "It is about an Uber driver, but about one who has long conversations with a bunch of weird people and ends up writing a movie about it and winning an Oscar."

"Sounds like it has a happy ending," said Peter.

I'm getting a lot of great material with this Uber gig. What are you in town for?

Peter briefly explained who he was and why he was in the city.

"So what do you think of our fair city so far?"

"A lot of strange people seem to live here," said Peter.

"You can say that again. Ever see *Portlandia*?"

Peter said he was vaguely aware that it was an offbeat TV show, but he hadn't seen it.

"Well, the bastards stole my idea. And then they fucked it up. I got screwed and now I'm driving for Uber. It sucks."

Hoping that they were getting close to the restaurant, Peter changed the subject. "Do you mind if I ask how much you make a week?"

"If the weather doesn't get in the way..." and then, waving his hand as if to say that the weather only got in the way for about fifty-one of the fifty-two weeks in the year, he added, "...about two grand."

"Not bad," said Peter, figuring that he was lying by half.

"But I gotta work on my people skills because rating-wise, I'm not doing too well."

"It might help if you didn't bring up that business about being a serial killer," said Peter.

Mr. Uberista laughed as they stopped at D'Angelo's. "I'll keep that in mind."

After dinner, Peter decided he'd go the traditional route and took a taxi back to the DoubleTree. His Nigerian cabbie was likely not a serial killer, but his driving was probably just as life-threatening, as he drove back to the hotel at a speed almost equal to how fast he was jabbering away on his cellphone.

Still, all in all, it had been a good day. He felt good about having safely gotten himself three thousand miles across the country and into the hotel without a major screw-up, but mostly he felt good about having used Uber successfully. Following this admittedly-modest victory in dealing with the New Economy, he no longer felt like a complete dinosaur.

Back in his room, he realized it was nearly one in the morning East Coast time. He quickly got into bed and, for the first time in weeks, he looked forward to what the next day might bring.

# Chapter Sixty-Seven
## Mt. Hood


$P$eter slept through his alarm and missed the breakfast buffet. After showering, he made sure he had his phone and laptop and headed down to the lobby to wait for the shuttle. A half-dozen other academics were lounging nearby, easy to spot in their conference-wear: khakis and tweedy jackets for the men and more formal suits for the women, who were identifiable as non-business types by their frizzy hairstyles and flat, comfortable shoes. He nodded politely but didn't recognize anyone. He then busied himself with a copy of the NY Times which he'd picked up from a stack of complimentary papers the DoubleTree had provided, at least he assumed they were 'complementary.' He slipped one into his briefcase to take to the conference in case he needed to look engrossed in something.

After they were dropped off in front of Mt. Hood College, the conferees formed a ragged caravan and dutifully followed a series of signs which led them to the Johann Fritz Mayer Conference Center. Several admins stood at decision points along the way to make sure no one got lost. Arriving at Mayer, they all checked in at a long table which was piled high with presentation papers and hefty packets which contained the agenda and glowing descriptions of the conference participants. Peter signed in, hung a personalized lanyard around his neck and picked up one of the packets.

Box lunches waited expectantly on a nearby table. Most contained the standard-issue conference fare of roast beef, turkey and veggie sandwiches, but off to the side were a few of the vegan, gluten-free and halal varieties. Peter wondered what would be the next niche market item to go mainstream and become a 'must carry.' Having missed breakfast, Peter picked up both the roast beef and turkey boxes, a can of Pepsi, and, in an homage to healthy living, a large plastic bottle of glacier-fed spring water, which, packaged as it was in a plastic bottle, struck Peter as the physical manifestation of an oxymoron.

Now, with two box lunches tucked under one arm, a briefcase, a conference packet, a bottle of spring water and a can of Pepsi in his hands, he looked like a well-dressed looter making off with organic swag following a riot at Whole Foods—except for the Pepsi, of course.

Because it was too damp and cold to eat outside on the patio, Peter decided to take his lunch inside the lecture hall where many of the other attendees were already chomping away. But as he was going in he almost knocked over Clive deBreville, who was coming out. Seeing that Peter had both hands full and a box lunches under an arm, deBreville raised a satirical eyebrow. "Glad to see your appetite's still good…considering your circumstances."

"I just flew in this morning," said Peter, "and as I'm sure you know, there's never anything decent to eat on the plane."

DeBreville cast a cynical eye at Peter's remark but didn't challenge it. Instead, he said, "amazingly, so far everyone has shown up. But stay ready, my man. If someone oversleeps or doesn't show up, I'll give you a call."

They were interrupted by a harried admin who seemed to have an important problem that demanded deBreville's immediate attention. She pulled him aside and started an intense conversation.

Peter immediately regretted his impulsive lie and worried that deBreville might somehow catch him in it. He felt his new-found swagger begin to sag.

Inside the hall, he looked around to see who was there. Most of the crowd were early to mid-career academics, although there were a few around Peter's age who clustered together near the front and chattered away. Given their age, he assumed they were either major presenters or respondents and he was surprised he didn't recognize any of them, but in his haste to just get to the conference, he hadn't looked into who would be attending. He'd try to introduce himself to them later, but for now, he sat in the back and kept to himself, pretending to be intensely interested in the conference agenda while he worked his way through the first of the box lunches.

Later, when most of the participants had finally assembled for the plenary session, deBreville took to the podium and welcomed the president of Mt. Hood who, in turn, welcomed the conferees to his campus. After a few minutes of laudatory remarks about how honored Mt. Hood was to host them, he departed, not to be seen again.

DeBreville then went through his list of house-keeping remarks before turning the stage over to the first panel's moderator. His final house-keeping comment was to state vigorously that the moderators would be in enforcing strict time limits for speakers and respondents, implying that violators would be taken out and, if not shot, would be given a severe and bruising tongue-lashing.

From his long experience as an academic and conference attendee, Peter was well aware of his fellow professors' tendency to filibuster endlessly on their academic specialities, failing to understand that the general public's interest in subject areas such as *The Semiotics of Split-Infinitives and Their Effect on Societal and Cultural Decay* in no way matched that of the speaker. Trying to pry a microphone from a professor's cold, dead hands was like attempting to separate a Second Amendment supporter from his favorite firearm. As McCluhan suggested in *The Medium is the Message*, the purpose of a filibuster was not necessarily to make a point, but to hold the floor as long as possible.

While the first set of speakers were making their presentations, Peter realized once again how PowerPoint had ruined public speaking. The mind-numbing effect of listening to a speaker read nearly word-for-word what was displayed on the screen lulled the audience into believing there was little need to pay attention to what was being said, so they didn't. What they did was what their students did, surf the web on laptops or smart-phones.

After the first two panels lasted nearly three hours, the conference mercifully broke for afternoon refreshments. As a seasoned conference veteran, Peter believed that in the past few years there had been a distressing trend in the World of Nosh towards bottled juices, fresh fruits and packets of trail mix instead of the traditional trays of high-calorie cookies ready to be washed down with coffee and sodas. Peter picked out several packages of trail mix which contained some M & M's, which he would separate out from the healthy stuff during the afternoon's final panel.

One thing he hadn't thought through was whether or not the other participants had heard about his personal situation. He had the feeling that he was being avoided. He thought he noticed people glance at his name tag, then lower their voices and politely move on, but he couldn't tell if he was just being paranoid or had everyone heard. Naturally, he couldn't ask and find out.

He was also feeling out of place among so many younger people. As one who had often been the leading man at conferences like this, he was now not even a supporting actor, but an extra with no speaking lines.

But there was one person who didn't avoid him. Halfway through the break, he was cornered by a Boring Guy. After a couple of minutes of one-way conversation, Peter tried to shake him, but, like serial killers and vampires, Boring Guys possessed an innate sense of who, like the old or wounded herd animal ripe for culling, could be run down, cornered and talked to death.

When the break ended and everyone shuffled back into the lecture hall, the Boring Guy glommed on to Peter as though they'd been life-long buds.

Two hours later, the first day's final session mercifully ended, going over its allotted time by only fifteen minutes, after which the conferees gathered up their gear and made the five-minute trek to the faulty club for a reception which was to be followed by a formal dinner.

At the reception, Peter tried to distance himself from the Boring Guy, but the Boring Guy was determined and proved to be as hard to shake as one's own shadow. And, like stupid people who don't know that they are stupid, boring guys  are also completely unaware of how uninteresting they are. Because they are clueless about picking up on normal social cues, their success hinges upon the inability of their victims to escape the Boring Guys' unrelenting intrusions into their personal space. Leaving the scene entirely would obviously work, but for most people, that would not be a viable option. Better to come from a culture where 'fuck off, buddy' was an acceptable way to end an unwanted social situation. Peter thought about going ballistic, but feared that such an outburst would only serve to remind everyone of his newly-acquired reputation as A Loose Cannon.

When the time came to go in for dinner, Peter finally shook the Boring

Guy by excusing himself and making an extended stop in the restroom. When he emerged, he was determined to find another table to sit at, but when he stepped into the dining hall, he recognized an old nemesis, Harrison Lodge, laughing and chatting away with deBreville and several other Pooh-Bahs near the main table at the front of the room. Peter immediately realized that Lodge was to be the Keynote Speaker.

Lodge was a Man For All Seasons. In addition to being one of the leading professors in his discipline, he had authored a series of novels about a Comp Lit professor who moonlighted as a master detective. Lodge's fictional hero, Lamont Wainwright, lived in a small New England college town whose inhabitants murdered each other at a rate which, if left unchecked, would have reduced the population to near zero within a generation.

For many years, the only line item missing on his sterling CV was a TV miniseries based on his scribblings. The standard Hollywood criticism of his novels was that they were 'entirely too British,' to which Lodge would reply, 'that's entirely the point.' Lodge finally hit the big time when Netflix bought the rights to *Murders on the Quad: The Lamont Wainwright Mysteries*, and produced a series which ran for several years until its star ran into the usual Hollywood problems of drugs, domestic violence and divorce—not exactly the image in keeping with that of a thoughtful, sensitive scholar-detective. Still, Lodge ended up with a nice residual check and had plenty of Inside Hollywood gossip to spread around. He was always ready to drop a name, particularly if the celebrity name being dropped belonged to someone who was 'not one of my favorite people,' he would say with a sad smile and a rueful shake of the head, indicating that the great one in question had been a bitter, personal disappointment to him.

More than twenty-five years ago, when they were younger, Peter and Lodge had a public dustup at a semiotics conference where they had argued on-stage about whether non-verbal communications could convey subtlety, nuance and intellectual depth. They ended up emphatically giving each other the finger, the ultimate in non-verbal communication, thus proving that non-verbal forms of communication could convey strong emotions, though perhaps not with subtlety, nuance or intellectual depth. Given his position as one of Comp Lit's emerging princelings, Lodge was unused to such overt public challenges and since that time had nursed a serious grudge against Peter.

Peter hated his guts as well.

Had he examined the conference agenda more carefully, Peter probably would not even have bothered to come to Portland and, had he noticed earlier in the day that Lodge was to be the keynote speaker, he certainly would have skipped the dinner. But now he was stuck and he hoped to just stay under the radar and get back to the Doubletree without running into Lodge.

Naturally, there were spots available at the Boring Guy's table and Peter quickly took the one which let him keep his back to the stage. During the meal, he began to ask questions of the Boring Guy, who was momentarily stunned and suspicious of Peter's sudden attentiveness, used to as he was of being completely ignored. However, he quickly recovered and began a long disquisition on intertextual analysis of non-literary forms, a monologue which he continued through the appetizer, salad and entree courses. Peter nodded occasionally to keep him going, which was not difficult. For a Boring Guy, having an attentive audience of even just one was like winning the lottery.

The dinner was the usual conference fare—a choice of appetizer, a salad, a beef, chicken or fish entrée followed by coffee and dessert. All were items which were made to be served quickly to a hundred a fifty diners without having anything getting cold—or warm, as the case might be. With dessert and coffee would come the keynote speech, undoubtedly preceded by a deBreville's lengthy and fawning introduction of the Keynoter, Harrison Lodge.

When dessert finally did roll around, Lodge stepped up to deliver his keynote address and even the Boring Guy stopped talking.

He began with a self-deprecating anecdote about being nominated, but failing to win an Emmy for *Murders On The Quad*, but since no one else in the audience had ever come within miles of such a non-academic cultural achievement, his story definitely qualified as a world-class humblebrag.

After dropping a few names in describing the Hollywood after-parties, he finally launched the meat of his speech which he accompanied with a fast-paced PowerPoint featuring a mash-up of clips from movies, tv shows, news feeds, Twitter, Facebook and Snapchat—all of which were combined in what Lodge described as the next great form of literary expression.

He went on about how all significant expressions of culture were conveyed through words and symbols and that interpreting their meanings was the key to understanding the synchrony and intersectionality of every civilization—past, present and future. The fact that what he was saying was gobbledegook was ignored by all.

And who was best equipped to understand and explain all this? Well, that would be none other than the audience of distinguished Comparative Literature professors assembled in the room before him.

He rambled on about his vision for creating this exciting, new academic discipline that would inspire universities and colleges to form new departments replete with tenured professors and newly-commissioned Ph.D.'s, all locked, loaded and ready to write a proposal for *beaucoup* bucks at the drop of an R.F.P.

No one objected to Lodge's job-creating vision. There was nothing that could excite an audience of academics more than the prospect of a new area of study that cried out for funding, and Lodge's suggestion that profit-rich companies like Facebook and Google might be inveigled to drop, for them, a pittance into the pockets of worthy scholars was as energizing as the sudden appearance of a bevy of strippers at a political convention. Many in the audience entertained visions of themselves sitting, figuratively of course, in the Priscilla and Mark E. Zuckerberg Endowed Chair for the Study of

Symbiotic Interdisciplinary Literature, or whatever the new academic field would end up being called.

For all the enthusiasm Lodge was engendering in the audience, his Keynote Address had no effect on Peter. With his back to the stage and having downed several substantial glasses of red wine to accompany the roast beef entrée, he began to doze.

It had been a long day.

And soon he was sound asleep.

He awoke to the sound a voice in his head singing the paraphrased lyrics from David Bowie's *Space Oddity:*

"Ground Control to Doctor Grande…"
"Ground Control to Doctor Grande…"
"Dr. Grande there's clearly something wrong…"
"Can you hear me…can you hear me, Doctor Grande?"

But the words weren't in his head. When Peter looked around, he saw that everyone in the audience was staring at him and the voice in his head was actually that of the real-life Harrison Lodge.

Seeing that Peter had finally woken up, Lodge stopped singing and said, "welcome back, Peter. Welcome back, if not to the land of the living, at least to the place where someone's had waaaaaay too much to drink."

The audience laughed and Lodge continued "I'm sorry if my words put a spell on you, but you'll be glad to know that your snoring at least served one purpose…it kept everyone else awake." Lodge smiled triumphantly and everyone laughed again. "And, to paraphrase late, great Karl Marx, 'to each according to his needs, and from each according to his abilities…however modest.'"

The crowd laughed and Lodge gave Peter a hearty 'thumbs up' gesture with both hands. Peter managed a forced, uncomfortable smile and feebly waved back.

All he wanted to do was to crawl under the table.

And die.

Lodge went back to his talk and continued on for what seemed Peter to be an eternity. Finally, it ended, the crowd applauded and everyone milled about for a while before filing out to take the shuttles back to the hotel. Peter was determined to avoid riding with the Boring Guy, but he needn't have worried —even the Boring Guy avoided him.

While Peter was shuffling along in the line to board the shuttle, a limo pulled up and Lodge, deBreville and a few others piled in, laughing with each other and clearly having a great time. Peter imagined that they were on their way to a party at the Four Seasons with hookers and booze—one to which he and the rest of the little people were definitely not invited.

## Chapter Sixty-Eight
### When One Door Closes…Another Opens

*R*iding back to the hotel after what had been perhaps the second-worst day of his life, Peter felt that going to the conference had been a huge mistake, one capped off by Lodge's humiliating him in front of everyone. He thought about not showing up and flying home tomorrow, or maybe calling in sick, even though either option would be seen as an obvious cop-out.

He also thought about going down to the bar for a nightcap, but not wanting to risk further humiliation by running into anyone from the conference, he raided the minibar in his room, expense be damned.

While he was nursing a whiskey on the rocks, he opened his laptop and found that deBreville had sent him an email. A sudden storm in the East had grounded one of his panelists and deBreville needed someone to fill in as the chief respondent on one of the afternoon sessions. So, was Peter interested?

Still feeling the sting of the falling asleep incident, Peter wasn't sure he wanted to put himself out front so publicly, but he realized that backing out on his promise to fill-in would be a tacit admission that Lodge's put-down had had an effect. He also realized he now had the perfect excuse to skip the morning sessions, as he would need to 'bone up' on the paper's details.

So he promptly emailed deBreville and said 'yes' to an offer he realistically could not refuse.

He then opened the PDF of the paper which deBreville had attached. Its title was *Mashup/Smashup: Contextualizing the Non-Contextual—From Twitterdee to Twitterdom*. He almost wished he hadn't agreed to critique it.

After reading two pages, his head hurt and it wasn't from the whiskey. The usual academic tripe. The paper did pick up on Lodge's keynote theme—something about social networks and cyberspace offering the possibility of new forms of expression which ultimately might be deemed worthy of being described as 'literature.' However, the writing was so turgid and dense that it was impossible to make sense of the author's argument.

Still, Peter's main reason for appearing tomorrow was not to point out any of the paper's many failings, but to use the occasion to rehabilitate himself. He would voice some mild criticism, offer tidbits of not-too-effusive praise, and make a few suggestions for improvement, thus hopefully proving to everyone that he was an all-around good guy.

Then exit stage left.

Or right.

Whichever.

He didn't care.

He was determined to show that he was not cowed by the humiliation he had endured at the dinner.

## Chapter Sixty-Nine
### The Mea Culpa

$P$eter slept in, but this time not late enough to miss the breakfast buffet downstairs. He then re-read the paper and made some notes about what he would say in his critique. Having been a professor for more than thirty years, handling his response to the paper would be a piece of cake. The harder part was figuring out how to deal with last night's debacle. The main problem with his plan was that he didn't have one. He had some ideas, but nothing that he felt would be a sure winner.

When faced with uncertainty in the past, he could usually count on his intuition to kick in at some point and come up with something. He knew that this was not the wisest approach, but for the most part it had served him well before, and hopefully, would again.

Peter took an Uber to Mt. Hood shortly after noon and arrived just in time to pick up another box lunch. This time he limited himself to just one. He nodded to a few people as he made his way into the main conference room, found a quiet spot at the back of the room and pretended to be absorbed in his lunch and his laptop.

The first panel of the afternoon was slow out of the gate. Some of the conferees had already left and of those who remained, many were less than diligent about returning to the auditorium for a second afternoon of inspiring intellectual discourse. It was the weekend, after all, and it was axiomatic that the last sessions of a two-day conference would be sparsely-attended, especially if the final day was a Saturday. Had the conference been held in a more desirable location than Portland in December, some of the participants would have drifted away early to shop, play *tourista* or get together for a nice dinner with old friends. And if one lived reasonably close to the conference's location, one could head for home and avoid having to spring for an extra night's lodging.

DeBreville kept these early departures to a minimum by making sure that, should anyone decide to play hooky, he or she would have to pay their own way back to the hotel or the airport because the first free shuttle would not leave until the final speaker had finished. He also sweetened the deal with the lure of a reception with an open bar and a spread of better-quality *hors d'ouevres* than had been served before. Box lunch season would be over. His enticing 'carrot' was something no self-respecting academic would ever pass up without good cause. Time to party.

Following the break after the first afternoon panel, Peter found himself feeling somewhat anxious as he waited for his session to start. He hadn't been nervous about speaking in public for years, but as he sat through the first afternoon panel, he'd felt a knot grow in his stomach. He reminded himself that he was a professional and that a few jitters and nerves were part of the process. The only positive he'd gleaned from having to sit through the first panel was that his intuition had finally kicked in. He now had a plan.

While what was left of the crowd filed back in, Peter came down to the well and introduced himself to Dr. Schweibel Wently, the paper's young author and the last session's presenter.

"Go easy on me, Dr. Grande," said Wently nervously.

"Oh, you don't have to worry about that. If there's one thing I've learned in the last few weeks it's that 'too much criticism can bite critic in butt.' Big time," said Peter. "Old Chinese proverb proved true for a certain Comp Lit professor."

Wently laughed as deBreville came over. "We're going to get started now. Make sure you leave time for questions." With that, deBreville stepped to the podium and called the group what remained of the conference participants to order, even though many were still sucking up refreshments outside in the hallway.

Wently meandered through his presentation and, showing his inexperience, went over his allotted time by only a couple of minutes. A seasoned pro would have pushed it until the moderator was forced to intervene. He then ceded the floor to deBreville, who offered a brief description of the *bona fides* of Peter and the other two panelists without going into any of the gory details about Peter's recent trouble, a topic about which the audience would naturally have been more interested.

For his part, Peter began by going through a *pro forma* thanking of deBreville and congratulated those in the audience for staying to the bitter end, though, catching a glimpse of a stern deBreville, added that it was not that 'bitter, 'as there would be certain amenities offered at the reception, compliments of their generous host, Clive deBreville. Peter then suggested they all give their host a hand and they did.

With that out of the way, Peter said that since it was the last panel of the last day, "just by being here, you all deserve an award, and if you manage to stay awake during my critique, you'll get a gold star for extra credit." He paused and looked around at the audience before adding, "but, if you don't, I promise I won't break into song to wake you up—unlike what happened to me at last night's dinner."

Everyone laughed and he continued, "hopefully I can make this interesting enough to keep you all awake, including me. And on a personal note, far be it from me to be overly-critical of anyone since the repercussions of excessive criticism can be extremely unfortunate, as I am personally quite aware. In fact, I've even gone so far as to stop criticizing Republicans and I'm sure everyone here can appreciate how difficult that would be."

"And, I also hope I can give my remarks here inside the..." Peter paused and made the air quotes gesture, "...'safe space' of constructive criticism—the kind of criticism my wife all too frequently feels free to give to me, but which I dare not give to her."

It was not a blockbuster of a *mea culpa*, but the audience laughed politely. Peter then eased into his intentionally mildly-critical analysis of Wently's paper.

The panel proceeded apace with no fireworks, and as far as Peter could tell, no one fell asleep. And at five-fifteen, a quarter of an hour over schedule, the session ended and the panelists received the customary polite applause from the audience. DeBreville then gave, for him, a brief summary of the conference and invited everyone to the reception.

Peter, Wently and the other two panelists stayed in the well for a few minutes as audience members approached them with questions and congratulations about how well they all had done and then lied about how interesting and provocative the panel's presentation had been for everyone. And the fact that he had survived and that people were not avoiding him was enough for Peter.

Definitely an improvement.

## Chapter Seventy
Night Moves


$O$n the shuttle back to the hotel, Peter watched the lights shimmer on the wet streets. The standard-issue Portland drizzle had turned into a cold, wintry rain. It matched his mood.

By all rights he should have felt better after clawing his way back to respectability by virtue of his self-deprecating remarks, but he didn't. The best that could be said for the entire West Coast adventure was that he'd gotten away for a few days. But the thought of going home was like coming back from a fantastic vacation only to have to take out the garbage and shovel the snow off the sidewalk.

At the Doubletree, the shuttle emptied and its passengers shook hands, hugged and said their goodbyes. Peter hung back and waited until the crowd had dispersed before going up to his room.

He took a short nap which he followed up with a long shower. His plane was to leave at ten in the morning and he didn't feel like going out. After watching some college football and checking his emails, he decided to head down to the bar. He wasn't particularly hungry as he had loaded up at the reception, but he was tired of hanging around his room.

A Doubletree lounge on a Saturday night would never be mistaken for a hot night spot and this one, this night, was no exception. The bar was inhabited by a dozen or so people who, like Peter, had gotten tired of sitting in their rooms and staring at the TV, so instead, they sat at the bar, nursed a drink and stared at the TV.

Peter ordered a Manhattan and watched Western Washington wallop Eastern Oregon on the tube. Or maybe it was Eastern Washington who was walloping Western Oregon—he wasn't sure. He thought about asking the woman bartender if there was anything else on when one of his fellow conferees came over and sat down next to him.

"Mind if I join you?" he asked.

Peter minded, but didn't say so. He figured he would finish his drink, honestly claim fatigue and retreat to his room.

The guy introduced himself as James Benson from Gaither State in Kentucky. They exchanged the standard background info and then chatted away about how great the conference had been. It was clear after a few minutes that somehow Benson hadn't heard about Peter's personal troubles and Peter certainly wasn't going to bring it up.

"How's Bliss doing?" Benson asked. "Is Grodin going to survive?"

"Right now I'd say it's too close to call. Financially, things are tight. I even had to pay my own way out here, if you can believe that," said Peter.

"Ouch. So times really are tough," said Benson.

"Yeah. We're going to have to figure out how to increase enrollment, keep costs down and still provide for a quality education. It's not going to be easy." Peter could scarcely believe he was parroting such pap, but all he wanted to do was to politely get through this and leave.

"Well, if anyone can figure it out, Moynihan can. I knew about him a bit during our college days at Santa Barbara. He was a senior and I was a sophomore. And even though he was studying drama, I always thought he would end up in show biz or politics, not academia."

Peter's interest was piqued and he nodded that he'd like to hear more.

"He was kind of a big man on campus, always organizing conferences, outside speakers, the occasional protest, that kind of stuff."

"Bliss? Was a radical?" asked Peter.

"Hardly," said Benson. "He was a huge conservative. Into Objectivism, Ayn Rand and all that crap. That's why he stood out. There weren't too many of them on campus in those days. Or now, for that matter."

Benson stirred his drink, then continued, " but he did have charisma though. Very entrepreneurial. Still does, I suppose. I've heard about what he's done at Grodin."

Benson then rambled on about his own work at Gaither State, but Peter had stopped listening. The news that Bliss might have been in the Ayn Rand Society was mind-boggling. There was nothing about that in Kohl's opposition research and he was pretty sure this was not something Bliss had ever, ever highlighted in his CV. What Peter was sure about was that Bliss would definitely not want to see this go public.

Peter finished his drink and then begged off, citing his early flight the next morning.

Mind racing, he headed up to his room.

Peter thought about how he would use this information, Go to the board? Deliver it anonymously? He was already in enough trouble, did he need more? Do a Deep Throat and find a willing Woodward/Bernstein?

Whatever.

What he did know, given the state of political realities in the Faculty Lounge, he knew that if this were true and it came out, Bliss would be toast.

Burnt toast.

As usual, his imagination leapt far ahead of the facts as he knew them, but before he could speculate on what to do with this information, he needed to make absolutely certain that what Benson had told him was true.

Peter fired up his laptop and got down to business. He spent a solid hour searching UCSB and Santa Barbara newspapers for information.

He found nothing in the local papers, and unfortunately, the student paper's on-line archives didn't go back far enough to cover Bliss's years as a Gaucho undergrad. When another hour of internet sleuthing failed to turn up anything, Peter decided that he would have to head down to UCSB and do some old-fashioned research in the library.

Although he wasn't sure what his next move would be, he knew he couldn't 'press charges' against Bliss without some solid, corroborative evidence. Whether he would go to the board, the newspapers or confront Bliss directly, he needed more than Benson's hearsay to go forward.

With nothing to look forward to in West Beresford other than an empty house, and even though this spur-of-the-moment side trip to Santa Barbara would put a serious dent in his bank account, Peter was willing to gamble that it would be worth it.

He spent the next hour arranging a flight to LAX and a car rental. He then went to bed where he slept well for the first time in months.

# Chapter Seventy-One
## Gaucho Land

The flight to LA was nothing but pleasant. Five minutes into the air, the plane broke above the clouds to cerulean skies and sunshine. Soon, even the clouds below disappeared and the azure waters of the Pacific shimmered beneath the plane's wings.

Peter treated himself to a glass of champagne which put him in a good mood as he landed in LA. A quick stop at Budget put him into a new sedan and he headed up the coast, taking the scenic route through Malibu. He had plenty of time. The sun was setting over the ocean when he arrived at the Santa Barbara La Quinta. No Motel 6 for him on this trip—he needed to keep his mojo working.

On Monday morning, he drove the ten miles up the 101 to UCSB, eventually found the library and asked one of the student workers at the information desk where he could find the microfiche collection.

"Microfiche? Is that some kind of French computer?"

"It's a device for reading data on rolls of film," Peter explained carefully.

"Well, it sounds French," the student said sullenly.

Peter wanted to tell him to ask someone over fifty who knew something, but realizing he might need to stay in the Young Knucklehead's good graces, he simply said, "it's old technology. For dudes my age."

He then opened the campus guide he'd picked up and said, "it's supposed to be in the Special Collections Room."

With a look that implied, 'why didn't you say that in the first place?' the Young Knucklehead pointed towards the elevator and said, "third-floor."

Peter spent some time looking through the newspaper index and then checked out several rolls of microfilms to scroll through. It appeared that the library's microfilm readers hadn't been used in years. He took the dusty plastic cover off one and turned it on.

He'd forgotten how tedious and inefficient the microfilm readers were; it was like searching Google with a hand-crank. One could spend hours scrolling through a year's worth of *The Daily Nexus*, UCSB's student newspaper, come up with nothing and wonder what one had missed. And given his usual lack of focus, it was easy for Peter to become distracted by the issues of the day from nearly three decades ago. But finally, after several hours of scrolling, he stumbled upon the Mother Lode.

He found several stories which indicated that in his junior year Bliss had indeed been the founder of the UCSB Ayn Rand Society Chapter. It also became clear that the UCSB Ann Rand Society had been a very small, very dedicated and not very popular student group. Over the course of that year, its members sponsored a couple of speakers and held some recruitment meetings, but apparently Ayn Rand's philosophy of individualism, personal effort and self-reliance did not resonate with a student culture dedicated to suntans, surfing and weed.

Peter found only a few mentions of the Society in Bliss's senior year. After becoming frustrated with his classmates' lack of interest, Bliss decided to close down the ARS Chapter and wrote a Nixonian 'you won't have me to kick around anymore' letter to The Daily Nexus, in which he ranted on about the stupidity and mindless hedonism of his fellow Gauchos. That, too, apparently fell on deaf ears, or on the ears of those who instead were listening to the sound of the waves cresting on the beach, as there were no letters or stories after that.

Peter Xeroxed the pertinent pages and left. He hadn't spent such a fruitful day in the library since that time as an undergrad when he and Helen Morrison had smoked a joint in the stacks.

# Chapter Seventy-Two
Satori

*N*ot knowing how long his sleuthing in Santa Barbara would take, Peter had planned to fly home on Thursday. Changing his return ticket a second time would just mean more piling-on to an already budget-busting adventure. Plus, he was in no particular hurry to get back to West Beresford because he had yet to figure out how to deliver his message to Bliss without the messenger possibly suffering significant personal damage. In truth, he was not even certain about exactly what message he wanted to deliver.

So, with no clear next step, he hoped a road trip might sharpen the mind. He thought about going back to LA, spending some time at the Getty, the Huntington or maybe another museum, but having just left there with the still-fresh memory of having to deal with eight-lane freeways, LA was a no-go. Michael Jackson's Neverland Ranch was close by, but did he really want to deal with the weirdness? His third option was to drive up the coast to the Hearst Castle.

He decided to visit San Simeon before he died.

The next morning he drove up the 101 towards Cambria. The autumn rains had turned California's coastal hills from their dry summer coat of burnt umber into a lush, Technicolor green. Here, in what was once Reagan Country, there were no pale pastels, just brilliant blue skies and a Pacific Ocean that shimmered silver in the December sun. Unlike the grayscale monotone of the western Massachusetts he'd left behind, there was no snow, no slush, and no bitter, angry people forced to hunker down in outsized overcoats. In the words of that local former president, 'if the Pilgrims had landed in California, the East Coast would still be a wilderness.'

While driving, he began to run over the options about what he might do with his new-found dirt on Bliss. He was sure that divulging it would make life very uncomfortable for Bliss with the faculty, who, for the most part, already hated him. But although the faculty could hate him like crazy, they couldn't get rid of him—all they could do was run in circles, scream and shout.  Only the Board of Trustees could get rid of Bliss, but what if they didn't care? They'd already made it clear they didn't care about loaning him money for his Cape Cod house.  Or the fact that he hadn't finished his Ph.D.. For the Board, performance mattered and there was no doubt that Bliss was performing. This long-past peccadillo would most likely be viewed as a minor embarrassment, easily explained away as a youthful indulgence, one which in no way represented of his current thinking. And whether it represented 'his current thinking' or not, it might not matter to them, which was also something about which Peter couldn't be certain.

So, after closer analysis, what he had initially thought of as a huge win, might, in the end, turn out to be…not so much.

That was the big-picture issue. However, another important consideration was, how would disclosing this affect him? He could leak it discreetly and most likely remain anonymous and suffer no repercussions. But if it went nowhere, what was the point? The fact remained that however things turned out for Bliss, he was most likely still going to get the axe.

There had to be a better way, though not 'better' in an ethical sense, but 'better' in the way of ensuring a good outcome. For himself.

Over the course of the next few days, he hoped he would figure out that 'better way.'

Peter spent the night in a bed and breakfast in Cambria and the next morning drove north in the fog to San Simeon and took the shuttle up the hill to the Hearst Castle.

Remembering *Citizen Kane*, Peter realized that the black and white scenes from the movie did not do justice to the magnificence he saw before him. Well, yes, some of the rooms were a bit gaudy, but the grace and elegance of Julia Morgan's Mediterranean Renaissance architecture easily overcame those minor quibbles.

As he walked around the gardens, he thought about the contrast between a day spent at Hearst Castle and his last weekend at the DoubleTree. With no offense to those associated with 'The Tree,' it was not even diamonds to rhinestones, but rather diamonds to lumps of coal.

As the shuttle rolled back down the hill to the parking lot, Peter came to a realization: he really didn't give a shit about his life back home—teaching, academia, Comp Lit—the whole shebang. Oh, there once was a time when he cared, but he realized that what he enjoyed was hanging out with Pierce, Meg, Betsy and the rest of the gang. He loved the day-to-day interactions, the give and take of joking and jiving with his peeps. He even enjoyed the minor dust-ups with his so-called 'enemies,' the academic kerfuffles over nothing. Or at least over nothing of importance. And, back in the day when he was new to the game, he even enjoyed teaching and hanging out with his students. But now he was too old, and could one say, too wise? Well, even Peter might have to admit that would be a bit of a stretch.

He wanted out, but not the 'out' which he was likely to be offered.

The next day he drove down to LA and flew home to a freezing and very gloomy Massachusetts.

## Chapter Seventy-Three
### The Pitch


*O*n the flight back to Boston, Peter again thought through his options. He could go to the board and let them take action discreetly, but what if they didn't? They had already chosen to look the other way at Bliss's other indiscretions. And once this news was out, his leverage would be gone as well.

The press? Same deal. What if no one cared? (Except for the members of the faculty who, of course, would go batshit.)

And what would he get out of it? There would be no guarantee that he, as 'The Whistleblower,' would be taken care of. The students wouldn't stand for having him back, at least not until the current crop had graduated and moved on.

The basic choice was between letting everyone know or letting no one know—except for Bliss, who had to know. Although he didn't think of it in those terms, he realized that his best move, his only move, was to make Bliss an offer he couldn't refuse.

When he got home he sent Bliss an email, typing in the subject line, 'Who is John Galt?'

His message was:

> Bliss,
> Don't "shrug" this off. Give me a call.
> Peter

He was fairly certain that Bliss would respond quickly. And he did.

## Chapter Seventy-Four
### Under the Tuscan Sun

$O$n an early summer evening as the sun was setting over the Tuscan hills, Peter sat on the terrace of the Villa San Michele which overlooked Florence and nursed a second glass of a 2008 Tenuta San Guido Sassicaia. He had just finished a meal of pappardelle with wild boar ragu and a side of rapini and roasted shallots and was waiting for a dessert of apple crostata, hazelnut gelato and thymed caramel sauce.

All in all, it was a dining experience that befitted the status of Grodin's newly-appointed Dean of Overseas Studies. The only negative was that for tonight, he was dining alone, but after all, he was on a business trip.

As of yet, the new Dean had no Overseas Studies campuses to administer, and given Grodin's ongoing financial difficulties, he was not likely to have any in the near or even the distant future. Still, there was always hope, and should the money to create new overseas outposts magically appear as a result of the new President Bliss Moynihan's fundraising efforts, Grodin College would be in a prime position to send its students overseas to enrich and enhance their academic experience. The job demands on the Dean of Overseas Studies were onerous, requiring the person holding that position travel year-round to evaluate potential locations for foreign study, and despite enduring the rigors of first-class travel, dining in world-class restaurants and staying at five-star hotels, someone had to do it.

And that someone was Peter.

After realizing his *satori* moment in California, Peter and Bliss struck a deal regarding Peter's situation. In taking his new position and thus being forced to endure the hardship of near-constant travel, Peter agreed to leave teaching at Grodin behind—forever. He also agreed to never-ever-ever even offhandedly mention to anyone that, as a much younger and less-sensible person, Bliss had once supported a philosophy which differed radically from the vision of a progressive Utopia that was the shared dream of his peers—the wise, all-seeing, all-knowing denizens of the modern, tolerant faculty lounge.

Bliss and Peter agreed that he would serve a four-year term as the Dean of Overseas Studies, after which he would transition to semi-emeritus status by assuming a less-rigorous schedule of three-months on, three-months off for an additional two years. By that time he would have reached the age of retirement and, should he choose to, he could.

Or not.

Where had the money for this boondoggle come from? Peter didn't know, didn't want to know, and didn't care.

If you're living the dream, keep dreaming.

After all, life was good.
In fact, life was better than good.

Life was great.